SCHEHERAZADE'S ONE THOUSAND AND SECOND NIGHT

(AND THE NIGHTS THAT CAME AFTER)

A Novel, in Four Scrolls

BY

S.R. DAUGHERTY

Also by S.R. Daugherty:

Ballad of the Rails and other Stories (2022)

CONTENTS

SCROLL ONE:

THE SPELL OF BLIND
AND HOPELESS LOVE

1. Prologue

A ROYAL PROCLAMATION

His Majesty, Shahryar, first of his name, King of the Age,
defender of the faith, ruler of Persia and all tributary lands,
hereby orders the public beheading of his Queen Consort,
to take place on this spot tomorrow. The King's subjects
are invited to attend, bear witness, and take instruction.

Slavemaster Bourzou read to me from the weather-stained parchment that was nailed to the west gate of the Baghdad market. The people streaming past took no notice of us or the Proclamation.

"But Master, I saw the Queen Consort myself before we left the palace today." I was quite confused. "Everyone bowed as she passed."

"Scheherazade? I bet no one met her eyes. This announcement has been up for a month. The execution was delayed. No one knows why, or dares ask."

Bourzou showed the gatekeeper his pass.

"Don't you usually come by yourself?" The gatekeeper's brow narrowed.

"This is Ariana." Bourzou pulled me forward by the elbow for inspection. "She lives in the Pavilion of Slaves. I'm showing her around the market. I'm going to turn over my buying responsibilities to her."

The gatekeeper eyed me with clear disdain.

"A slave? Are you joking? Can she read? Does she even know her numbers?"

"Try to cheat her. You'll find out how smart she is."

The compliment pleased me. It was not like Bourzou to hand out praise. But then, it was praise for himself. Of all the slave children, I had been the one he had chosen to mentor and teach (except for my letters, which was absolutely forbidden, of course).

The gate opened, and we passed into the market, which occupied the arena floor and tiered seats of the old Baghdad amphitheater. I hurried to keep up with Bourzou down the stone steps.

I had never seen so many people gathered in one place. Traders, vendors, buyers, scribes, craftsmen, children, slaves. Candy makers, glass blowers, entertainers. Horses snorting and rearing in their rope pens. Hammering and sawing as new stands went up. Asses, parrots, monkeys, chickens, and turtles for sale. Endless tables of sandals, tunics, tools, pots, lamps, jewelry. Skeins of silk, muslin, cotton; I remember their bright colors in the morning light. Pots of daffodils, lilacs, roses, orchids, lilies, peach saplings. The flash of the fishmongers' knives in the sunlight. The birds that swooped overhead and perched on awnings.

"Ariana, do you know what marital infidelity is?" Bourzou asked as we stopped to inspect a collection of copper cook pans.

"I'm not innocent, Master. I also know it is a grave sin against Heaven."

"And, in this case, against the King. This was Scheherazade's crime, or so people said—"

I thought back.

"That slave, what was his name, uh, Zan—"

Bourzou put a finger to his lips and shook his head.

"Best not even say it."

The slave whose name I was not to say was a well-known braggart. He had constantly boasted about his romantic conquests. I remembered him telling us he had even bedded the new Queen Consort. Well, the women in the Pavilion of Slaves knew him for a liar. We disregarded anything he said. But come to think of it, I hadn't seen him since he had made his boast about Scheherazade.

The Slavemaster guessed what I was thinking.

"Don't ask what happened to him, either. I suspect he would have preferred beheading."

"Master, are you saying anyone actually believed what Zan—that slave—said?"

We came to a stall where bone-handled knives were laid out on red velvet. The vendor recited his prices while Bourzou picked up a knife and tested its weight. The Slavemaster lowered his voice.

"Gossip doesn't take long to spread from the palace out into the city. Politically, the King was in a bad position. He felt humiliated. He made a public vow to have his bride beheaded. Well, he's always been impulsive."

The Slavemaster looked at me meaningfully. "Naturally you shouldn't repeat any of this."

"Yes, Master. But why did the King change his mind?"

"I didn't say he did. He—but let us drop the subject. Too much talk like this could cost us our own heads."

*

How wide-eyed I was that day. The crowds, the smells, the noise—everything was overwhelming. And to think, that was three years ago. The traders at the Baghdad market certainly came to know the palace slave in her veil and headscarf. A few of them indeed tried to cheat her—none succeeded.

Bourzou steadily added to my duties. I attended in the kitchen, gardens, laundry, and nursery. I learned midwifery and delivered babies. I delivered messages to one party or another in endless palace intrigues.

Along the way, I learned a lot of secrets.

One of them was why Scheherazade's head was still on her shoulders.

2. The Slave, the Poet, and the Storyteller

"Ariana—?"

The morning light slanted through the vaulted window of the palace library. I didn't have to look up from my work to know who was addressing me. The voice was high, for a man, and slurred. The court poet composed his verses (and pursued his other adventures) by night, goblet in hand.

Our holy book forbids alcohol, and King Shahryar stoutly defends our faith—but Ali-Haram carried out certain delicate missions for the King, and in return the Holy Ones were under instructions to look the other way whenever the poet sinned (which was frequently).

I carefully laid my flower-knife and basket of irises next to the crystal vase. I got down on all fours and touched my forehead to the woven carpet.

"Good morning, Master. What does Ali-Haram need from his lowly slave?"

I had just sprinkled the carpets with lavender and soda, and the smell was dizzying.

"To get up," he said. "And stop being ridiculous. In that order. You're not my slave. And as for lowly, nothing of importance happens in this palace without your hand in it. Can King Shahryar himself say the same?"

I didn't take the poet's bait but climbed to my feet with a smile for an answer. I went back to arranging the flowers.

Ali-Haram's eyes were black and bloodshot. His dark hair was cut close to the scalp, while a bushy beard fell to his chest. He wore a robe of red velvet, wide-sleeved and wine-stained, with yellow leggings and yellow satin slippers—also wine-stained.

"I need to find Scheherazade," he said. "I think she's avoiding me."

"I'm not surprised, Master. Her dealings with you usually leave her lighter in the purse."

"You wound me, Ariana. I pay her back, sometimes."

I studied my irises and reminded myself to take my flower-knife to the South Garden later. The lupines were in bloom and would go well in the arrangement.

Ali-Haram had always been kind to me. He took an interest in my opinions. He read his new poems to me before he recited them at court feasts. He made me laugh. In his way, he brought light to my world.

"If you want to see Scheherazade, just wait. She comes to the library every morning to smell the fresh-cut flowers."

He raised his goblet, as though toasting me. I watched him consider his next words carefully.

"Listen, Ariana. There's something I don't understand, and no one else at court seems to know either. Scheherazade was unfaithful to the King. He ordered her executed. But here it is years later, and she still has her head on her shoulders. I think you know what's really going on. Everyone knows the two of you are close."

The conversation had suddenly turned dangerous.

"We do have things in common," I admitted. "She doesn't have any other friends. No one at court will even look her in the eye. A slave knows well what that feels like."

"You're dodging my question. Why hasn't her sentence been carried out, or the Queen Consort at the very least given a nice dark dungeon to stay in?"

"Master, I remember a verse from a poem you once recited for me:

'The rose a-bloom in dark of night
Upon her lover shines pure light.'"

"I wrote that? I blame the fruit of the vine."

"The rose a-bloom at night is our Scheherazade," I said. "And it's not a thorn that guards her, but rather her own—"

I stopped myself.

"Her own what? You're speaking in riddles, Ariana."

I shook my head and stopped talking; it was Scheherazade's secret to tell, not mine. I had a feeling he would know soon enough.

There was a delicate cough. We both looked toward the arched opening of the library. I quickly returned my knees and nose to the carpet.

In another poem, Ali-Haram had written that Scheherazade's hair was the color of the raven, that her eyes were like almonds, her teeth like pearls. But that morning, peeking over my hands, what I saw was a bleary-eyed girl of barely nineteen, wrapped in a silk robe, wearing mismatched slippers and a single earring.

"Ah, the court poet." She brushed back a curl that had slipped free of her orange headscarf. "You're up early."

"I am, in fact, up late. As are you, your Highness."

Scheherazade leaned over to smell the flowers in the crystal vase. Then:

"I suppose you need another loan. What is it this time? No, let me guess. One of the ladies at court has found herself with a surprise growing in her belly?"

Ali-Haram shuffled his slippered feet.

"I am a victim of political and economic forces, Highness. The Holy Ones are cracking down on wine again. They have scared off my usual sources. It is driving up prices."

She turned from the poet to me.

"Get off that smelly carpet, Ariana, and return to your duties."

"Yes, Highness."

I kept a stick with a clump of lambswool propped against the library shelves. I got up and applied the duster to the stacks of scrolls, which were already spotless.

"How low you've fallen." Scheherazade said to the poet. "Begging for money so you can buy your wine."

"Sadly true, Highness. Although in my defense, the King never paid me for my last poem."

"I'm not surprised. It was drivel. Ali-Haram, by helping you sin, I sin myself."

"Sometimes one must sin in order to sleep at night."

They eyed each other while I watched from the shelves. At last Scheherazade gave a sigh.

"I hope fifty darics will do; it is all I can spare right now. I'll send a purse to you by Ariana this morning."

"May Heaven bless and protect you, Highness." He bowed. "I'll write a poem in praise of your beauty and generosity."

"Don't bother with the poem," she said. "Repaying me would be nice, though."

The deal was set. But she was chewing her lip. She had something else on her mind. Finally:

"Ali-Haram, do your talents run only to poems—or can you write stories too?"

"Stories, Highness?"

"You know, made-up narratives with a beginning, middle, and end, told for entertainment. Dialogue, action, love. Tales to excite the mind. Adventures to rouse the blood. The lines would not even have to rhyme. Write me a story. If it's good, I'll forgive this latest loan."

"Lines that don't rhyme," he said, musing. "A novel concept. A different kind of wordsmithing. My poetry's poor enough. Who knows how bad I might be at writing stories."

I couldn't stay silent any longer. Only in me, the lowly palace slave, had Scheherazade confided her darkest worry. Only I knew how desperate she was.

"You have to tell him, your Highness," I said. "Please. He needs to know what is at stake."

She looked at the ceiling, the carpets, the tapestries on the walls, everywhere but at the poet. At last, she half-smiled. She had come to a decision.

"Ali-Haram, once I was accused of a sin. It was ordered that I pay the ultimate price. The night before the payment was due, I begged the

King's leave to tell him a story. I knelt on the carpet next to the bed where he lay and began a tale I had learned from my old aunty, the magical adventure of a sailor named Sindbad. All through the long night I told this story. The moon rose, the moon set. I left off on a point of such suspense that the King could barely wait for me to pick the story back up the next night. Night after night we continued. And by this means I became his storyteller. Sindbad was followed by Aladdin, and Sindbad by Ali Baba, and so on for a thousand and one nights."

Ali-Haram raised his goblet again, this time to the Queen Consort.

"Ah. I understand now." He grinned. "The rose is guarded by her own words. A brilliant strategy, Highness. I approve."

"Yes, well. The thing is this. I'm not a writer—I'm a collector. Not only my aunty's stories, but tales from scrolls my tutors gave me to read as a child. But I have run out of material. Last night I used the last story I know. You might say the King's storyteller has reached the end of her own scroll. So you see, Ali-Haram, I need your help. Not to put too fine a point on it, but I suppose I could say my life is in your hands."

The poet pulled his beard.

"Story-writing and life-saving, you say? I lack experience, of course—"

"He'll do it!" I burst in. Ali-Haram turned to look at me. He scratched his head.

"I will?"

"Yes," I said. "And I'll help you."

He still looked doubtful.

"Ariana—do you even know how to read or write?"

"Master, you know very well I don't. Those aren't skills permitted to slaves. But you can read me what you write, and I'll listen—the way you practice your new poems on me. And I'll pour your goblet and refill your inkhorn. You must help the Queen Consort. Honestly, you owe her nothing less."

What I didn't say was that I had experience of my own in this area. When I was on duty in the nursery, I often created stories to tell the children. I had the idea to use one of my own tales to get him started, and let his natural talents take care of the rest.

Ali-Haram had the grace (not to mention the promise of the fifty darics) to surrender. As he and Scheherazade worked out the details of the deal, I gathered up my basket and flower-knife.

And I thought: when it comes to storytelling, could the King of Persia be any more difficult to please than the children in the nursery?

*

"Ariana—it's me." A whisper from the kitchen doorway. I looked up and saw Scheherazade.

It was late afternoon. I had spent most of the day with Ali-Haram, working on our story for the King. As a result, I was behind on my usual duties. There were still oranges and pomegranates to peel for the evening platters. I had to mend Bourzou's torn tunic and lay out flints and irons for the next day's cook fires. Blessed sleep lay far away.

"Highness?"

A dozen flatbreads lay cooling on a counter. The rice was cooked, and the fire under the pot banked. The cook had gone to the garden to cut sumac for the stew; the other slaves were sitting outside, polishing the silver and gossiping. The kitchen was empty save for the Queen Consort and me.

I did not kneel. Scheherazade had instructed me to do so only when others were present.

"Do you have the story with you?"

I pulled the scroll from a fold of my apron. She untied the ribbon and let the parchment unspool to the floor. I watched her eyes move; her hand flew to her lips.

"Ariana—you have saved me. This is so much better than our poet's usual work. The King will love it." Her eyes went farther down the scroll. "How do I pronounce these names? Let's see: Khashar, Ghazi, Naseem—"

Scheherazade was transformed from the morning. Her eyes were skillfully painted. Emerald rings dangled from both ears; her green satin slippers matched. Her dark hair was down, and lustrous from brushing.

At first, Ali-Haram's main contribution to the scroll had been taking dictation. He inked the lines on parchment while I created the story. Then he began to make suggestions of his own. Soon we were producing characters and scenes as fast as he could write them down. We worked well together, which gave me the greatest of pleasure—

Scheherazade rolled up the scroll and retied the ribbon.

"Tonight, the King's new story begins. All right, I have till then to memorize this. But listen, I need you to join me in the King's bedchamber."

"Join you, Highness?"

"Shahryar will be weary and sore after a hard day of hunting and gaming and feasting and whatever else the man does. I presume you have experience in the art of massage—? I'll bring a jar of scented oil."

I was shocked.

"You want me to touch the sacred body of the King? What if my hands are too forceful? Not forceful enough? What if my massage displeases him?"

"What if this new story displeases him?" She shrugged. "We must all do our best and trust in Heaven. Come at moonrise, by the east staircase. Knock like this."

She tapped the kitchen wall twice, paused, and tapped three times more.

"Yes, Highness."

"And Ariana—"

"Highness?"

"You know the alcove at the top of the staircase? The one behind the purple velvet drapery? There's a wicker bench in the alcove. Leave tomorrow's chapter behind the bench. It wouldn't do for my lord husband to know I'm paying for the stories I tell him."

"Yes, Highness."

Massage? Tomorrow's chapter? My heart sank. Farewell, blessed sleep—

3. A Turban, a Sunbeam, and a Tin Drainpipe

He only looks asleep.

Scheherazade mouthed the words and handed me the jar. The oil smelled of almonds and geraniums. His Majesty lay sprawled atop a heap of blankets, on his side, eyes closed. My hands trembled—this was the sacred body, the defender of the faith, the beloved of Heaven.

Scores of candles lit the royal bedchamber. The air was dense with the smells of amber and cedar from incense sticks burning in a clay bowl. The soft splash of water came from a marble fountain in the corner. A tapestry on the wall opposite the bed depicted a lion with a crown and mantle, a soldier pinned beneath a bloody claw.

Go on—he's only a man. More mouthed words. I took a deep breath and put my fingers on the mounds of flesh overlaying the ribs. I began to knead. The beloved of Heaven grunted and rolled onto his belly.

Scheherazade joined us on the bed. She reclined on her side and propped her elbow on a pillow.

"Lord husband," she said, "For a thousand and one nights I have spun stories for you. I've told you about sorcerers, Djinns, princes, mariners, giant rooks, magic eggs, and scheming viziers. Tonight, I begin a new adventure. It is the tale of a poor child who lived in the time of your own ancestor, King Alcimedes—"

*

This story begins (Scheherazade said, while I massaged) with a boy who shouted and played and ran barefoot through the alleys with his companions. He was a bundle of dust and noise and motion, like any boy.

In age, Khashar was ten years and one. He had pleasingly high cheekbones and a ready smile. His dark flashing eyes hid nothing of his character; one knew right away this was a friendly and intelligent child. But Khashar had a secret, which—but lord husband, you must be content to learn this secret later, in the story's own time.

Khashar lived in the Ragged Quarter of Baghdad, where the people (may Heaven protect them) were so poor they had no word for riches. The shanties and hovels and tumbledowns of this district withstood time and the elements purely out of habit. They had forgotten how to do otherwise.

Khashar and his parents lived on the ground floor of an old building that had been patched and chinked with rubble, straw, and plaster of lime. The roof was slate and thatch and moss, a place where crows gathered to roost and quarrel. One often heard footfall and creaking beams above—the residents who lived on the next floor reached their rooms by rickety steps attached to the back wall by rotting wooden pegs. Bulbuls and tits made nests on the stairs.

The Persian name Khashar means inventive and imaginative, and to be sure, the boy was both. The name also means fun-loving, but Khashar's father, who repaired sandals and boots, and his mother, who interpreted dreams, did not make having fun easy for their only child. In fact, they did not allow Khashar to venture outside the home unaccompanied. Only when the Cobbler and Dream Interpreter dozed during the middle of the hot Baghdad day was Khashar able to slip away and join the games of the boys in the streets.

On one such day, certain familiar miaows and barks came from the street. Khashar ran to check that the Cobbler and Dream Interpreter were still asleep. Then he quickly changed clothes, for what he had to wear at home hardly suited outdoor play. Once outside, he carefully streaked dirt on his face. The miaower and barker came out of the shadows.

"Ghazi! Naseem!" Khashar spoke in a whisper, so as not to wake the dozing. "Is there work for us?"

From time to time the boys of the Ragged Quarter found themselves drafted to labor—hauling stone and timber to building sites, cleaning animal droppings from the streets, hawking goods for merchants. Sometimes the boys were paid in food, sometimes in promises, and, once in a great while, in real darics.

"Greetings, Khashar," Ghazi whispered back. Ghazi had a wide face and hazel eyes. He wore a yellow skull cap. "No, not today. We are free to do as we will."

"Ghazi and I are going to play a game of Sunbeams," Naseem said. Naseem was a tall, hawk-faced boy. He wore a red skull cap and had hard dark eyes. "I think you are too little to play, but Ghazi said to give you a chance."

"Sunbeams?" Khashar said. "How is this game played?"

"First you climb up to the rooftops," Ghazi answered, glancing uncertainly at Naseem as he did so. "That is where the rays from the sun are at their most brilliant. When you find the perfect sunbeam, you leap upon it and ride it all the way to the ground."

"It takes skill and bravery," Naseem said, "and so I doubt you will be very good at it."

Khashar was dubious that one could ride a sunbeam like an ass or camel, but the Cobbler and Dream Interpreter had taught him nothing if not politeness.

"The Sunbeams game sounds fun," he said. "I will join you."

"Say, I have always wondered," Naseem said, "why you cover your head in such a strange manner."

Khashar did not wear the usual skull cap found on boys in the Ragged Quarter, but rather a tall wrap of wound green wool.

"My uncle gave me this turban. He was persecuted as a Sufi scholar, and beheaded."

Khashar's uncle had often entertained him with tales of travels in Arabia and Nubia and Constantinople, and brought gifts such as a vial of sand from the banks of the White Nile, the entwined jawbones of serpents that had swallowed each other, and the green Sufi turban. The story of the beheading was only a partial invention: the uncle's execution had in fact been for camel thievery.

Although Khashar loved and revered his ancestor, he had another reason to wear the turban—but as with his secret, let us pass over this reason for now.

In their threadbare tunics and bast sandals and leggings of homespun wool—clothing handed down from their fathers and grandfathers—the three boys raced through the Ragged Quarter: down shadowed alleys, over vine-covered fences, through the crowded markets. A muezzin called the faithful from a makeshift minaret on an upended wooden crate, old men played backgammon on chalked flagstones, children took turns riding a barely moving ox, dogs snarled and fought in a whirlwind of noise and violence—none of these bothered to glance up at Naseem and Ghazi and Khashar running past.

In time the three reached a certain sweetmeats shop. The shop was built from wood planks and discolored stone blocks. The second story of the shop was a roofed pavilion, enclosed by a railing of worked iron. Crotons and rubber plants grew in pots along the railing. From the pavilion came the clinking of cups and the buzz of conversation.

The sweetmeats shop shared a wall with a tulip-grower's nursery, which in turn shared a wall with a potter's shop, which—well, in short, all the buildings were joined, and their roofs went on forever, and when you looked into the distance you could not tell where the roofs ended and the sky began.

A drainpipe hung by a hook to the roof of the sweetmeats shop. Naseem gave the drainpipe a tug, testing it. He put his arms and then his feet around the pipe.

"This is how we will get up to the rooftops," he said.

"Wait," Ghazi said. "I am changing my mind. What we are doing may be wrong."

Naseem hauled himself up. The pipe rattled and shook under his weight. When he reached the pavilion roof, he knelt along the edge and looked down at Ghazi and Khashar.

"Go home if you are scared," Naseem said.

Ghazi hesitated, but at last shimmied up and swung himself onto the roof. Naseem shook and yanked the pipe till it broke free from its hook. The pipe clattered to the ground; Khashar jumped out of the way.

"Hurry!" Naseem called down. "Lug the pipe behind the shop and hide it in the weeds. We will come back tonight and get it. There is a dealer who will give us a half-daric for the tin. We will split the take with you."

A diner looked down from the pavilion railing.

"Hey, you with the turban! What do you think you are up to?"

Khashar heard racing footsteps drum across the roof. He realized his companions had left him to his fate. He thought rapidly (in keeping with his name).

"Two would-be thieves!" he shouted back. "They tried to steal this drainpipe, but I foiled them in the attempt."

"Good boy!" A second diner joined the first. "Where are the wretches? We will chase them down and give them a proper punishment."

"Take me to the roof," Khashar said.

The sweetmeats shop did not permit children to enter, lest they witness sinful customers straying from the teachings of our holy book concerning the consumption of alcohol. Mounted on the pavilion floor, however, was a hoist used to lift platters of fruit and joints of meat. The diners lowered the hoist-rope over the railing and brought up the boy Khashar. Then they pulled the handle of the trap door in the ceiling; a rope-ladder swung down. Khashar flew up the ladder, with several diners (including sinners with their sloshing goblets) right behind.

Khashar glanced down the endless row of rooftops. Four legs dove behind a triangular facade. He spun and, shading his eyes, looked in the opposite direction, studying the streets below.

"There they go, the dogs!" He pointed toward a pair of faraway figures silhouetted by the sun. "The thieves are escaping. Look at them, pretending to look like honest bystanders."

"May Heaven reward you!" the diners said. They turned and clambered back down to the pavilion. A moment later, they spilled onto the street, where they gave chase to the randomly chosen figures. Khashar turned and headed down the plain of rooftops. When he reached the facade, he stood on tiptoe and looked down at his companions hiding there.

Ghazi looked abashed, Naseem less so. Khashar summoned the courage to speak his heart.

"My friends, you have done wrong. You said we were going to play a game of Sunbeams, but what you really planned was to steal the drainpipe for its tin."

"I am ashamed." Ghazi rose and stared at his feet. "I ask your forgiveness, and—"

Naseem broke in.

"Khashar, you were a fool to think anyone can ride a sunbeam. We only brought you along so we would have someone to blame if we were caught with the tin pipe. Come on, Ghazi."

With that, Naseem took to his feet and strode away across the plain of rooftops. Ghazi gave Khashar a sorrowful look before turning to follow. Khashar watched the receding backs of the two till they were gone from sight. How painful friendships could be, he reflected—

The brilliant midday sun sent glints off the domes and weathervanes and heads of eagles soaring overhead. A single cloud wandered through the sky. As Khashar watched, a hole developed in the cloud, a ragged opening of blue in a fluff of white. The hole grew and grew until a shaft of light burst through. The brilliant column lowered toward the earth, like a pillar holding up Heaven.

The end of the pillar lay squarely across the triangular facade. The light connected the roof to the cloud.

Khashar tentatively moved a hand toward the pillar, touched it, felt its heat, watched the motes of dust dancing in it. The light was not diffuse, but had a solidity, a firmness, a density. He took a deep breath and permitted himself to believe. As Naseem and Ghazi had done with the drainpipe, he wrapped his arms and legs around the sunbeam.

Beneath him, the sunbeam moved.

The rooftops fell dizzyingly away.

*

"He's asleep at last," Scheherazade murmured. She slid off the bed. "He will not wake until midday. Come with me."

I followed her out of the bedchamber, stretching my tired thumbs. We made our way down the carpeted hall to the alcove behind the purple velvet curtain. Scheherazade drew the curtain closed behind us. There was no window in the alcove; we had not brought a candle. We sat in the dark on the wicker bench, our elbows touching, palace slave and Queen Consort.

I felt beneath the bench and found the scroll I had left there earlier in the day. I put it in her lap.

"The next chapter, Highness," I told her.

"I thank you with all my heart," she said. "May Heaven preserve you and Ali-Haram both."

"It is our pleasure. And I know the poet can use the fifty darics."

"Ariana, you're my friend. You know my secrets and fears. But what do I know about you? Next to nothing. We have time now—tell me your story. Not the one about Khashar, but about you. How were you raised? How did you end up here, in this place?"

Scheherazade was, in a way, the most powerful woman in all of Persia, for her lord husband held every subject's life in his hand. And yet, because of the sentence hanging over her, she was all but friendless. So she had chosen me to confide in. In some ways we behaved like sisters— at least when others were not there to see and judge. I treasured our relationship, and did not take it lightly.

"Highness, I come from Maqazza, in the north."

"Maqazza," she repeated. Then: "One of our tributary states, constantly in rebellion against the King."

"I was born into slavery. I don't remember Papa; after Mama was sold, I never saw her again. I belonged to a wealthy carpet dealer. He was openly in league with the occupiers. He gave the Persian officers discounts to win their favor, and paid bribes and tribute on top of that. As for me, I was only one of a dozen slaves. The carpet dealer barely knew I existed.

"Emre was a boy who lived in the streets. We were both fifteen. His father had died fighting on the rebel side, and his mother had been taken as a slave by a Persian general. When the carpet dealer was away, Emre would come around the house. The slave women would feed him while he told us stories about the rebels and their bravery. He said we would overthrow the Persians would one day. We slaves would be liberated. His words drew a picture of freedom for me."

Scheherazade found my hand in the dark. I went on:

"Our master often threw feasts for the Persians. Of course, the slaves had to do all the planning, cooking, serving, and cleaning, in addition to our other duties. There were cruelties and outrages at these affairs—honestly, I can't bear to describe them to you. At last we could take no more. We conspired to do a terrible thing.

"As slaves, we had no experience with weapons—but Emre did. By a ruse, he and I managed to get our owner alone. Emre wrested the man's dagger from him and drove it into his heart. I will never forget the blood and dying curses. By the time the alarm was sounded, Emre had hidden in the stock house. The plan was for him to make his escape when the Holy Ones arrived to read the rites over the body. I had fallen in love with Emre and begged him to take me with him. When the funeral began, we slipped away together.

"We traveled on foot for many leagues, skirting Persian encampments and watchtowers. Finally, we reached the rebel camp in the hills. The rebels took Emre in as a fighter; I joined the camp followers as a cleaning girl. I scrubbed the rebels' clothes and drinking cups and night pots. I was free, and at night Emre and I were together.

"I had never been happier.

"The rebels planned a raid to take back a certain village. Everything was in place. Our men had javelins and bows and firebrands. The villagers had agreed to rise and join the fight. But the Persians had a well-placed spy. They were warned and ready. When they counterattacked, the rebels broke and ran. The Persians chased them down and killed them, to a man."

"You lost your Emre," Scheherazade said quietly.

"The Persians enslaved all the women in the camp. I ended up here, in the royal palace. Others were less fortunate. I gave birth to Little Emre in the Pavilion of Slaves. I was still squatting over the birthing blankets when the child was taken away from me. He would be ten now. I don't know where he lives. I don't know what became of him. Only one man does."

"Ali-Haram?" Scheherazade guessed.

"He was sent to take the baby to the Ragged Quarter and find a wetnurse to become foster mother."

"Of course. It is the kind of mission he undertakes, when sober. King Shahryar doesn't keep him at court for his uninspired poetry. But wait—wouldn't the child have been born into slavery?"

"Slavemaster Bourzou had a tablet of freedom engraved and sealed for him. This was to pay off a favor he owed Ali-Haram. It is a kindness the poet has done for me."

"I suppose you begged Ali-Haram to tell you where the child is now."

"The foster mother made him swear never to reveal who she was, for fear I would one day come to claim the boy. O Highness, is there anything worse than not knowing?"

I started to cry and could not stop. For all the years that had passed, the hurt was still fresh and deep. Scheherazade cried too. Finally—

"We better say our good-nights, Ariana. Dawn is not far away. You and I are women who must get what sleep we can."

4. A Palace, a Princess, and an Alliance

"Tell the slave to massage our feet." King Shahryar lay on his back, hands behind his head. Scheherazade pulled the silk coverlet up to his knees. "And tell her to make it a better job than last night, or we'll send her out to massage the chickens."

I perched on the bed next to the defender of the faith and looked with distaste at the royal toes. I could not stop yawning. Maybe I could sleep in the morning, while Ali-Haram worked on our next chapter—

"Now," the King continued, "is this Khashar truly going to ride a sunbeam? What a wonder. You never run out of ideas; where do they all come from? No, don't tell us. It doesn't matter. Just start tonight's adventure. Go on, we're waiting."

"I obey, lord husband." Scheherazade reclined on a stack of pillows. She had committed every word of the story to memory and spoke without the scroll. "As our last chapter ended, Khashar wrapped his arms and legs around the pillar of light—"

*

—and felt its heat spread through him. He squeezed his eyes shut, and when he looked again, he had risen high above the city.

Buildings flew past below. Diners in the sweetmeats shop looked up and pointed. A swoop of swifts cruised alongside him. A muezzin in a minaret saw the boy in luminous flight and fell to his knees singing praises to Heaven.

Khashar had no control over the sunbeam. He could only hold on and let it go where it would. He had somehow entered a magical adventure; what use to question?

The sunbeam dipped. The streets rose up. On the looming plain of rooftops, two figures gaped. Passing close, Khashar clutched the sunbeam with one hand and waved with the other.

"Look, Ghazi, I am riding a sunbeam, after all! See how easy it is, Naseem!"

If the two made any answer, Khashar could not hear it. The column of light rose again, drawing him higher, till the people in the streets were the size of ants. Shops, gardens, and mosques passed far below.

Gone was the Ragged Quarter. Khashar had come to an unfamiliar part of the city. A complex of domes, towers, spires, pavilions, and cupolas rose before him. The towers were built of blue-enameled bricks; atop one of these towers was a tall vaulted opening called a windcatcher. It drew in air to cool the levels below.

The sunbeam hovered above an open balcony that projected from the windcatcher tower. The sunbeam set Khashar down gently, gently, gently on the balcony, and then, while he watched, drew back up into the cloud whence it had come. The hole in the cloud closed over; the sunbeam was gone.

A railing of wrought iron scrollwork enclosed the balcony. Far below, a line of date palms stretched away. Colorful mounds of flowers dotted a vast sward. A rectangular pool of motionless water reflected the clouds and crossing hawks. Gleaming white tiles lined the sides of the pool. At the far end of the courtyard, a dark grove of walnut trees was alive with the noise of songbirds.

But then the world grew still. A single sound came from above, despairing and bitter. Even the songbirds in the walnut grove fell quiet before such a sound of sadness. Khashar looked up. There, not far away, leaning over the iron railing of another balcony, was a girl.

The sound was the girl's weeping.

The girl wore a green gown and green veil. The jewels in her silver headdress cast sparkles with each heaving sob. (Oddly, an orange turkey feather stuck up behind the headdress.) Moved by the weeping, Khashar called up.

"O sad girl on the balcony! What terrible thing has happened that causes you to—"

"Who are you?" the girl demanded. The weeping ended. "What is your name? How did you get past the guards of the royal palace?"

"I am Khashar, from the Ragged Quarter. I came here upon a sunbeam."

"A sunbeam, you say? So that is what I saw cross the sky. Was that you? If you can command magic like that, then perhaps Heaven has truly answered my prayers. Khashar of the Ragged Quarter, you see before you a girl in her hour of need. I am Princess Sorayah. The evil court sorcerer Vahid has imprisoned me in this tower. Where has your sunbeam gone, by the way? If you can ride it, I am sure I could, too. Help me escape from this tower. I will reward you with great riches."

Khashar's head spun. Magic was something that only happened in stories and dreams; his parents had often said so. Yet how else could he have come here to the royal palace, save by magic? But the magical sunbeam had vanished. Nor could he say he had truly commanded or controlled the light. It had acted with a will of its own, flying him through Baghdad, dropping him on this balcony, and then leaving, going wherever sunbeams went.

The Princess had more to say.

"Khashar, boy wizard of the Ragged Quarter, I will tell you my story. Then you will understand why my life is soon to become a well of sorrow."

"I am listening, O Princess Sorayah." He decided to add words that his mother, the Dream Interpreter, often used with her customers. (Once she knew their problems and concerns, she was able to find dream-meanings that pleased them and made them more likely to pay her fee.) "To tell another your worries is to gain a greater self-understanding."

"Well, I doubt that very much." The Princess sniffed. "But here is why you must help me. My father, King Alcimedes, has proposed a scheme that depends on my future unhappiness. He plans to sign a treaty with Charles Magnus by which Persia will ally with the distant kingdom of the Franks. Father says that, as allies, he and Charles Magnus will be able to counter the schemes of their common enemies. Besides, by agreeing not to engage each other in war, both sides will save on military expenses."

"So the alliance is designed to bring peace," Khashar said. "Our Holy Ones teach that peace is something we should strive for. Why does it bring you unhappiness?"

"Because Father and Charles Magnus plan to seal the alliance with their marriageable children. Sadly, this is the way of diplomacy."

Sorayah went on to explain that a delegation from the Frankish court, after a lengthy journey across sea and land, had recently arrived in Baghdad with marriage documents, gifts, seals, and Sorayah's betrothed, whose name was Maria Irena.

"But wait," Khashar said, "is Maria Irena not a girl's name?"

For a moment Sorayah was quiet, as though thinking. Then:

"The Franks speak a gobbledygook tongue. No doubt their interpreter makes mistakes in his translating. Anyway, I have not yet viewed my betrothed. It is Frankish custom to seclude the bride until the rites take place. But the interpreter described her blue eyes, long yellow hair, and skin the color of milk. Can you imagine it! This Maria Irena is a monster out of a storybook."

Learning that she was to be joined in holy union to the monster, Princess Sorayah had thrown a tantrum in front of the court. She stamped her feet, flailed her arms, howled in defiance. The entire Frankish delegation witnessed her disgrace. The King ordered her restricted to her tower bedchamber as punishment.

"And when is the wedding?" Khashar asked.

"My sorrows begin—" Sorayah stopped to issue another heartfelt sob. "—at midday tomorrow."

Khashar could hardly imagine a more pleasant existence than being a child of the King of Persia and living in a windcatcher tower, with the added prospect of traveling to exotic lands such as the kingdom of the Franks.

"Heaven has decreed your fate," he said in counsel. "My advice is to take comfort that your union with Maria Irena will bring peace to the world."

Princess Sorayah was having none of it.

"That is easy for you to say. I have not told you the worst part. To ensure the happiness of this Frankish monster, Father has ordered his sorcerer Vahid to impose the Spell of Blind and Hopeless Love on me. This is a terrible magic by which I will fall in love with the first person I see in a mirror at the wedding—who by our Persian traditions will naturally be my new bride. I will be condemned to love Maria Irena forever. O Khashar, boy wizard and new friend, if I cannot escape, I shall leap from this balcony and end my life!"

Another tantrum, Khashar thought. But it was not for him to judge. No doubt royal children experienced more intense emotions than boys from the Ragged Quarter. At any rate, Khashar felt sorry for Sorayah, and wanted to help her. Besides, with the riches she had promised he would be able to build a new home for the Cobbler and Dream Interpreter.

(Moreover, he happened to know a certain someone who might indeed be able to help him rescue the Princess—)

"Be brave, O Highness!" he called up to her. "I shall return before you and Maria Irena are wedded. I vow to save you!"

"Do you mean it? A vow is serious business," Sorayah said. "Anyway, if your sunbeam does not return, how are you going to get down from that balcony?"

Khashar looked down doubtfully. The balcony was the height of several men above the ground. To leap down was out of the question. The sunbeam was nowhere to be seen. Before him a door of oaken planks was set into the tower wall. Broad plates of iron crossed the planks, and above the iron plates, a massive lock of bronze.

Back in the Ragged Quarter, no dwelling places had door locks of bronze (or any other metal), since no dweller could afford a door. By custom, one called one's name and business from without and waited for admittance. Khashar addressed the oaken planks loudly:

"I, Khashar of the Ragged Quarter, request to be let into this great tower, so that I can—"

The door creaked, groaned, slowly swung open.

"Aha, I thought I heard someone out here." A figure came onto the balcony. He wore a tin helmet with a golden spike, a blue doublet, and boots of polished black leather. He drew a scimitar from the curved scabbard behind his back. He looked at Khashar with hatred and suspicion. "You are obviously a criminal. Prepare to bid your filthy head farewell."

The brilliant sunlight threw glints off the edge of the raised scimitar. Khashar backed up on the balcony till his back pressed against the iron railing. There was no room left to retreat. When times were most desperate, the Cobbler and Dream Interpreter had taught him, truth was often one's best course.

"I have vowed to rescue Princess Sorayah."

In a rush of words, he recounted all the Princess had told him—how an evil sorcerer had imprisoned her in the tower, how she had been threatened with the terrible Spell of Blind and Hopeless Love, how she had resolved to perish before joining the Frankish monster in holy union.

The guard's eyes narrowed.

"The King's wayward child is indeed locked in this tower." He laid the curved blade against Khashar's neck. "However, the one who is being punished is not Princess Sorayah, but rather Prince Feroze. I see what you are about, sir young criminal. Your game is to deceive me and gain access to the tower, thence making your way to the palace, where you doubtless plan to steal everything you can carry. Well, we have a place reserved for heads like yours—an iron stake in front of the palace. There could even be a promotion in it for me."

From behind the guard came a familiar voice.

"Lower your weapon, worm, or I will have you impaled! See if I won't!"

*

I woke up on the carpet, with Ali-Haram's stained tunic in one hand and a sponge in the other. I had only meant to close my eyes for a moment—

"Well, Ariana, I finished the chapter." The poet sprawled in his bed, the scroll of parchment unrolled past his knees, the inkpot perched perilously on a pillow by his elbow. "All this writing is making me thirsty. Pass that wineskin over, will you?"

I pulled myself back up. I dipped the sponge in my paste of soda and vinegar and returned to the wine stain.

"Master, think of how much better you could write with a clear head. Imagine your life without a hangover every morning."

He rolled over and downed what was left in his goblet; I watched the inkpot nervously.

"You work me like an ox in the field. A whole chapter in a single day. And now no wine?"

"I'll pour you a quarter-goblet after we go through this chapter one more time. Although come to think of it, aren't you supposed to recite a new poem at the King's feast this evening? I think I'll keep this skin stoppered for now, Master."

"And you call yourself a lowly slave. I forbid you to call me Master anymore. But before we get back to work, may I recite that new poem for you? I want your honest opinion."

"I'll give you an opinion, Master, but don't make me promise honesty."

"In other words, if you hate it, you'll lie. Fair enough." He rolled over and leafed through a stack of parchments on his bed table. "Ah, here we go:

> "A leaf hangs from a banyan tree.
> The tree sways in the wind.
> Heaven creates the wind,
> Allah blows the wind to earth.
> We are all but leaves on the tree.
> But in Heaven waits an empty seat
> For our virtuous King, at Allah's feet."

"It's beautiful, Master," I murmured.

"I agree; utter tripe. But it flatters Shahryar. Maybe he'll pay me a bonus above the usual ten darics I get for verse. Heaven knows I can use it. But all right, back to our story." He dipped his pen and poised it over the unspooled scroll. "You know, my favorite part of the last chapter was the Spell of Blind and Hopeless Love. I laugh every time I think about it. Where did you get that idea?"

O Ali-Haram (I thought, but didn't say), the King asked Scheherazade where her ideas came from, too. Like her, I dare not answer. I've seen how you look at me sometimes, in the way a man looks at a woman, when you think I'm not watching you. I know your reputation for conquests. But do you joke and laugh with those court ladies the way you do with me? Do you talk with them as if what they think matters? Do you spend your days writing stories with them?

I've fallen under a spell myself. The spell is Blind because I cannot command my heart. The spell is Hopeless because you're a free man, and I am a woman enslaved. You are a noble of the King's court, and I am the lowest of the low. Every day I warn myself to stop yearning for you.

The poet was looking at me curiously, still waiting for an answer to his question. I felt heat rise to my face. I held his tunic by the sleeves in front of me, and said:

"Look, I got the stain out for you!"

5. The Child Who Vanished, By Parts

Scheherazade settled herself on the edge of the bed.

"O lord husband, last night my story left off with Khashar on the balcony of the windcatcher tower at the royal palace. A guard brandished a scimitar at him and backed him against the railing."

"Yes, but then somebody suddenly came and ordered the guard to stand down. We wonder who this newcomer could have been."

The Queen Consort pulled the silk blanket up over the King, but he pushed it off with a gesture of irritation. The night was too warm for bed cover. At the height of Baghdad summer, the heat of day forgets where its night hiding-place is.

His Majesty said: "The newcomer threatened to have the guard impaled, so we think he must be someone of high rank, who means to protect Princess Sorayah. But then Khashar thought the voice sounded familiar—"

"Tonight, Majesty, all will be made clear."

I waved the fan, a palm leaf fixed to a bamboo stick, in long slow circles. I had been excused from massage duties—and given an even more boring job. The velvet curtains were drawn back from the windows of the

King's bedchamber, and the scents of jasmine and roses drifted in from the gardens below.

*

The guard spun on his heel. There, in the doorway, in her green gown, green veil, and silver headdress (with the orange turkey feather), stood Princess Sorayah.

"Your Highness—" The guard looked confused. "What are you doing here?"

"I came to visit my brother Feroze, of course. Why are you not kneeling? Shall I tell Father you do not pay me the proper respects?"

The guard lowered his scimitar and, with a seeming reluctance, went to one knee.

"I used all my arguments on the Prince," Sorayah continued, with a sniff. "But he is quite willful. He still refuses to wed the Frankish Princess. He always finds ways to defy poor Father. What can we do with him? Anyway, I order you to unlock the door at the base of the tower. I wish to walk in the garden before returning to my own chambers in the palace."

The guard looked up doubtfully.

"Your Highness—forgive me—your voice sounds unlike you—"

"A summer cold. Do not make me tell my brother how uncooperative you have been. When he comes into his royal powers, it will be your own head on the stake in front of the palace. As for this urchin here, I find him interesting. He and I will walk in the garden together. You may have his head after I am done with him."

Khashar was confused. Why had Sorayah told the guard that it was her brother Feroze, and not herself, who was betrothed to the monstrous Maria Irena? Why had the guard said it was Feroze, and not Sorayah, who was restricted to the room in the windcatcher tower?

The guard rose and sheathed his blade. He led the way to the interior of the tower, repeatedly casting doubtful looks over his shoulder at the Princess (and pursed-lip scowls at Khashar). Wooden steps corkscrewed around the dank interior. Mushrooms and lichens grew where the planks had split. Swallows and bats circled. Thin streams of light issued from chinks in the stonework. For a moment, Khashar imagined being the size of a lizard and riding one of the miniature sunbeams—

No matter what she had told the guard, the Princess surely did not plan for him to lose his head. The business of walking in the garden was doubtless a ruse for him to escape the palace grounds, so he could get on with the business of rescuing her.

The steps ended at a ground-level door of iron and timbers. The guard keyed the heavy lock.

"Very good." The Princess dismissed the guard with a wave. "You may leave us now."

"Highness."

The door groaned open, and with dignified steps Sorayah passed into the courtyard. Khashar hurried to catch up.

Sunlight reflected off the tiles beside the pool. Frogs sat their lily pad thrones in the still water, regally ignoring the dragonflies that flitted past. The Princess knelt to sniff a patch of chrysanthemums.

"Stay five paces behind me while we walk," she said without looking up. "It will be good practice for you in learning court ways. Khashar, I have given this matter a lot of thought, and I have come to a decision. When my brother ascends to his royal powers, you are going to serve as his vizier. That means you will be chief officer and advisor. Also, you will organize and command the Imperial Fleet of Sunbeams. Say, why is your belly making so much noise?"

Khashar tried to will his insides to silence. He had not eaten since the previous day's grilled lizard.

"Forgive me, Highness."

Sorayah pulled a cloth bag from a silk purse tied to her gown and tossed it to Khashar. In the bag were almonds and sugared dates. The two resumed their walk. Khashar carefully kept his respectful distance as he munched. He chanced a look back; the guard was still standing in the open doorway of the tower, watching them, open hand shading his eyes.

Sorayah and Khashar arrived at the walnut grove. The trees rose in long, perfect rows, equally spaced. The floor of the grove was a spongy carpet of leaves and moldering nutshells. Mottled light passed through the canopy.

"You said you were locked in your bedchamber," Khashar said. "How did you get out?"

"Father gave my sister Sorayah permission to visit. She brought me her clothes for me to wear and left the door unlocked when she left." Her sister Sorayah? Khashar stared at the Princess in confusion. She drew back her veil. "You are vizier-in-waiting, Khashar, and therefore it is time for you to know."

She removed the silver headdress and turkey feather, and shrugged off the green gown, which slid in a silken heap to the floor of the grove. Khashar gaped.

The gown had concealed a tunic and boy's leggings. The headdress had covered short hair, cut like a boy's. And without the veil, the first wisps of chin-whiskers were visible. The voice was lower pitched, too.

"I no longer need my disguise. Now to win my freedom. Father's sorcerer is never going to make me fall in love with the yellow-haired monster. I am coming to live with you, Khashar, in the Ragged Quarter, where none know me. Father will send his guards and troops, of course, but they will never find us. We will live in hiding, as I prepare to rule. You will serve as my bodyguard, cook my meals, set out my clothes, and so forth."

"My family is very poor, Highness," Khashar said hurriedly. "I am not permitted to bring guests home. The Cobbler and Dream Interpreter are quite strict about such things. In fact, I will be in great trouble today when they wake from their nap and find me gone."

"Khashar, when will you understand that personal matters pale before matters of state? Very well, you will have to run away from home. Believe me, your parents will forgive you when they move into the grand home you are going to build for them with your reward. It will be the finest palace in all the Ragged Quarter. They will sing your praises as a good son. But first, you and I will live secretly for a few years. We will make a camp in the woods, or maybe in the desert. No one can know where we are. I will bide my time till I come of age. Then the people will rise up. They will demand that Father step down in my favor. My first act of office will be to order the beheading of the sorcerer Vahid. In fact, you will have several beheadings to carry out, because—"

"Prince Feroze!"

The guard with the tin helmet and scimitar appeared from behind a walnut tree, this time followed by several more similarly uniformed guards. The guards were dragging a large net weighted with stones. Khashar and the Prince were quickly surrounded.

"Do not fear." Feroze tucked the turkey feather behind his ear. "You will get to behead these worms as well."

"Highness," said the guard with the scimitar, "I am disappointed in you. Dressing as your sister, for shame. Your deceit could have cost me my rank, or even my life. But if you come agreeably back to the tower, we will keep it our little secret."

"I will never return." Feroze drew himself to his full height. "My vizier Khashar will not permit it. I have spoken."

In short order, the guards had the Prince ensnared in the net. He howled and flailed, in vain. Khashar did not wait but turned and dashed further into the walnut grove.

No one pursued him.

*

Khashar's sunbeam did not return to carry him back home. He made his way through the narrow streets, running, walking, and from time to time hopping on the back of an ox-drawn carriage.

Learning the Prince's real identity did not alter Khashar's resolve to come to his rescue. Did Heaven not forbid the breaking of vows? Besides, Sorayah—Feroze, that is—had promised a reward of riches and a palace in the Ragged Quarter for his parents.

Khashar had an ally in mind for his rescue mission. But to enlist this ally, he would have to travel beyond Baghdad, to a certain wood. He had been there years earlier—could he find the way again? In any event, there was no time to lose in the trying.

What would he tell the Cobbler and Dream Interpreter? He considered inventing a story, but his imagination paled before the actual events of the afternoon—after all, he had ridden a sunbeam, come face-to-blade with a scimitar, and been appointed vizier to the heir to the Persian throne—and anyway, lies did not spring easily to Khashar's lips.

Upon reaching the Ragged Quarter, he turned into a certain alleyway and right away came upon two familiar figures.

"Ghazi! Naseem! What a day I have had. Did you see me on the sunbeam?"

"You owe us for the tin in that pipe," Naseem said. "You—"

Ghazi unexpectedly interrupted.

"No, Naseem. Let us apologize instead. Stealing the tin would have been wrong. It would have brought disgrace upon our families. Khashar with his honesty prevented this. O Khashar, what may we do to make up for our shameful behavior?"

At this point, a pair of ostriches trotted past.

The ostriches were black, with white tails. Khashar smiled at this sign from Heaven; now he knew how he would find the wood—

"Ghazi, behind my home is a courtyard. You will know it from the weeds and lizards and cracked stones. The families of our block gather there for dinner after waking from their midday naps. Look for a woman in a blue headscarf, and a white-haired man with her. Both have long terrible scars across their faces. Say to the two: 'Your child has gone to collect ostrich eggs for breakfast tomorrow.' The white-haired man will threaten to beat me for leaving home without permission, but do not concern yourself with that; it is an idle threat."

"It is as good as done," Ghazi said. And he went off at once to find the cracked courtyard. Naseem grumbled and followed without enthusiasm. Meanwhile Khashar turned and dashed away after the black ostriches—

*

My arms were heavy, my hands sore from waving the fan. I caught Scheherazade's eye and made a show of letting my wrist and shoulder go limp. She understood right away: she unfastened her bracelet and let it slip to the carpet. The King did not open his eyes.

"Ariana!" The Queen Consort's voice carried a convincing note of alarm. "I've lost the bracelet the King gave me for a wedding present, the one with the three opals. Check the floor and every corner."

"Yes, Highness." I set the fan down and leaned against the wall for a moment's blessed rest.

"We have some observations to make about your story," the King said, eyes still closed. He was attentive to Scheherazade's tale, if not her bracelet.

"Majesty?"

"We find much merit in this idea of an alliance with the Frankish king, Charles Magnus. Alcimedes, our ancestor, was a shrewd statesman. Of course, the Franks are unbelievers, but we understand they are at least people of a Book."

"Your Majesty is wise," Scheherazade murmured.

"As for the behavior of this Prince Feroze, we find it most unseemly. By disguising himself he looks to escape the punishment decided on by his father, who knows best, as fathers always do. In fact, the Prince sins twice, once in the act of deception, and again in dressing as a girl. Because of these sins, the people will not respect him, and so will not rise to support him."

Feeling had returned to my thumbs.

"Highness, I found the bracelet!" I knelt to pick it up where she had dropped it.

"Ariana," she said, "like my bracelet, you are beyond price."

My break was over. I picked up the fan and returned to moving the warm and heavy scented air.

*

Khashar chased the ostriches through Baghdad. The flat-topped buildings, the spires of the minarets, the leaves of the palms and ironwoods—all these cast their short midday shadows across the rapid passage of birds and boy.

(Of course, Khashar knew no one could outrun an ostrich. The trick was to chase at a speed one can keep up. An ostrich would always slow down to stay just out of reach.)

When the pursuit reached the Tigris, that Angel of Rivers, the ostriches stopped in their tracks. Ahead was a long bridge of rafts, joined by hemp lines. The rafts rose and fell on the swell; they rocked and bumped against each other. The distrustful ostriches hissed at the bridge. Khashar shouted and waved his arms behind the birds until they overcame their doubts. With hoots and whistles, they hopped onto the first raft, and then the second—on went the chase.

On the other side of the Tigris lay the fields that supplied the city's grain, where peasants bent over the stalks with rakes, pitchforks, and bells (these last, to scare away the blackbirds). Past the fields were the homes of the rich, with their pavilions and pleasure-gardens. At last, the trail split.

The ostriches turned onto the fork, which led to a scape of rocks and scrub brush. Khashar did not follow (although he still planned to relieve them of their eggs).

Had the ostriches looked back, they no doubt would have been amazed to see the boy vanish by parts: first his nose, then his hands, his striding legs, and finally his green turban.

*

"O my wise and all-powerful husband," Scheherazade said, "often a smaller bowl may fit inside a larger. In such a way a storyteller may nest one tale within another, to show how something came to be. And that's why tomorrow night I will tell you a story about someone Khashar met when he was much younger."

"Much younger—" the King repeated sleepily. He issued a snore. O blessed sound!

6. A Demi-Goddess, a Tree-Cavity, and the Bottom of the Heart

I thought I might slip back quietly into the Pavilion of Slaves and make it to my sleeping rug without running into Bourzou, but he was waiting for me at the threshold. Did the man ever sleep?

"Ariana, I need you to supervise the egg gathering in the morning."

The women's chamber was very dark. The curtains were drawn back from both windows, but the moon had set, and what slave had darics to buy candles? One of the children cried softly while a sleepy mother tried to hush him. The chamber smelled of burnt vanilla beans. An emissary from Madagascar had brought the sticks of vanilla incense as gifts to the court, but they caused the King to sneeze. And so Scheherazade had given them to me.

"The eggs? O Master, please let me sleep past sunup just this once." I didn't look him in the eyes. The Slavemaster did not allow such familiarity from his charges, even one he had taught and mentored for years. "You already have someone for that job."

"Of course I do. But she's a thief. I've noticed the counts are low. My guess is, she's selling eggs outside the palace. Ariana, you are the only one of my slaves I can trust."

It was no use to explain that the roosters were growing old and could not keep up with their henhouse duties the way they once had. In the view of Bourzou, every problem resulted from the dishonesty of slaves.

"Fine," I said. "I'll take care of it."

The palace kitchen buyer kept a larder stocked with eggs and other items brought in by our suppliers. The buyer owed me a favor. If he would loan me enough eggs to make the count. I could return the eggs later and keep the game going every morning till Bourzou turned his attention to some other imagined thievery.

"Also, the Queen Consort wants you to report to the royal physician tomorrow. He's going to give you a certain potion, which you are to leave under a certain bench in a certain alcove. I was told you would know what all that means—?"

A potion to leave in the alcove? That meant the King was not to know about it. I nodded, curious. Bourzou was annoyed.

"Ariana," he grumbled, "everyone knows you have high-placed friends. But when they presume to assign you work, your fellow slaves mock my lack of authority. They are already worthless and lack motivation."

The remark made me angry. Lack of sleep made my tongue sharper than usual.

"You know what would motivate the slaves, Bourzou?" I said. "The prospect of freedom. You should try it."

His eyes narrowed, but for once he held his tongue. I pushed past him and went to my sleeping rug.

Sometimes having high-placed friends was useful.

*

Majesty, I promised you a story within a story (Scheherazade began, while I slowly waved the heavy palm-leaf fan). This one takes place four years earlier than last night's tale—a long enough time to us, Highness, and an eternity to a child. In this chapter, then, Khashar is not ten years and one, but five years and two. And yet this tale begins the way the other one ended, with Khashar chasing the same black ostriches with the same white tails.

He was determined to bring their tasty eggs back for the Cobbler and Dream Interpreter's breakfast. He left the Ragged Quarter, crossed the Tigris on the bridge of rafts, passed the grain fields, skirted the vast homes of the rich, and found the narrow trail.

But when the trail split, Khashar stopped in his tracks—the birds dashed away to safety—for he had come face-to-face with an owl that was neither flying nor perching. The owl's wings were folded behind its shoulders. The talons curled as though grasping the invisible limb of some invisible tree.

"O wandering boy." (A woman's voice was somehow quite clear in the owl's hoots.) "From your threadbare clothes and the way you follow those ostriches, whose eggs are said to be delicious and nutritious, I can tell that you are poor. You no doubt come from the Ragged Quarter of Baghdad."

Khashar was astounded to be addressed by an owl, but remembered his upbringing. He answered with politeness.

"I am Khashar. How do you do?"

"Well enough, well enough, I thank you. You may call me—let me see, what name am I going by now?—Abi. I am almost sure that is it. I am the demi-goddess of the Ever Dark Wood and may assume the form of any that live in it. Say, would you like to visit?"

Khashar shook his head sadly.

"I cannot, demi-goddess Abi. I must get food for the Cobbler and Dream Interpreter."

"Devotion to one's parents is most praiseworthy." Hoot hoot. "But yours will receive all that they need, in time. Now blink, blink, and then blink again. A film will drop away from your eyes."

A dark forest took shape. The boy saw oak, yew, alder, and many other trees he could not name. Abi was, in fact, perched on a long leafy branch that was now quite visible. With a single wing-flap, the owl launched and landed on Khashar's shoulder. Talons gripped firmly but not painfully. Ahead lay a narrow path which wound between the trees. Khashar took a tentative step, and then another.

He looked back once—the trail whence he had come was gone. The Ever Dark Wood had closed him in. The trees grew densely, embracing each other with their arm-like branches. Knotted roots rose from the earth like giant subterranean knuckles. As Khashar's eyes adapted to the dark, he noticed eerie green glows lighting up the path.

"The light arises from mushrooms that take root on the branches," Abi remarked. The Wood absorbed her voice and returned it distant and muffled. "The canopy is woven so tightly that daylight only penetrates at dawn and dusk, when the sun is low. The mushrooms glow to attract insects."

"O demi-goddess Abi," he asked, "why did you have to clear the film from my eyes before I could see?"

"The Ever Dark Wood has not always been dark, nor has it always been uninhabited by your kind. In ages past, many a wayfarer traveled through. I even let the odd hermit or two live here. Back then Baghdad was known for its bountiful harvests. No one went hungry, and Persia used its surpluses to trade for goods with cities along the Silk Road. The land was fertile and made all prosperous.

"But certain merchants in Baghdad wanted to multiply their own personal riches. They wanted more grain to sell. They hatched a scheme to slash and burn my Wood to sow new fields. This provoked me. To protect the Wood, I cast a spell called the Curtain of Blessed Invisibility over it."

The trail ended at a narrow brook, where a row of stepping stones, polished smooth by aeons of flowing water, led across.

"When the workers came to start the slashing and burning, they scratched their heads in confusion. The Wood they sought had vanished. Their eyes could see only the ancient plain of stones that lay beneath the forest floor. Everyone knew grain would not grow in such a place. That is how my Wood survived.

"But now that it was invisible, man or beast could no longer enter. Every denizen of the Ever Dark Wood descends from the ones who inhabited it in those long-gone days. You are our first guest since then."

"I followed the ostriches," Khashar said. "That is how I found your Wood."

"Ah, the ostriches. Yes, they have begun to wander ever farther afield. You see, those greedy merchants, disbelieving the tales of the slashers and burners, came to inspect the site themselves. In a fit of anger, I turned them all to ostriches—black with white tails, so I would always know them. They keep making their way to Baghdad because in their dim minds they remember having once lived there."

The stones continued in a row up the bank, leading to a circle of alders. The dark round scales on the alder bark watched the passage of boy and owl in brooding silence. Bluebirds in the branches watched too; but if they sang in greeting, the Wood swallowed up the sound.

"Why did you choose me to be a guest in the Ever Dark Wood after all this time?" Khashar asked.

"Because you are young and have not yet learned to disbelieve in magic. Besides, as a demi-goddess I have future-sight. I have foreseen that one day a descendant of mine will enable you to do a kindness for someone you love, in his hour of need."

Past the circle of alders came row upon row of enormous, twisted oaks. Light began to seep into the Wood, not from overhead, but from behind the trunks of the oaks. Long bars of shadow crossed the forest floor. In the world beyond the Ever Dark Wood, sundown was at hand.

Abi released her hold on Khashar's shoulder and after a short flight landed on the forest floor, before one of the oaks. The giant trunk had split, leaving a cavity like a vaulted window. Khashar followed and stooped to peer behind the owl.

The cavity smelled of earth and heartwood. A heap of leaves, bark, and brush rose and fell regularly. With each shift odd bits of blue and pink showed through the heap. Abi hooted:

"Idrosun dear, time to wake up. We have a visitor." The owl's head spun round to face Khashar. "When I invoked the Curtain of Blessed Invisibility, she got bored and decided to hibernate till the next traveler came by."

The leaves and detritus and other tree-stuff fell away as a blue head rose. The creature wore a vest and trousers of pink silk. Blue hands groped along the floor of the cavity and found a pink scrap—a veil, fumblingly pinned into place. Atop the head was a top knot, from which a long unruly fall of pink hair descended. The bare feet were padded, furred, and clawed.

"O traveler," the blue creature said, "you have summoned—no, summoned is not exactly the right word. Commanded? Sorry, I am still a little groggy. How long have I slept? My top knot has grown to my knees. Anyway, I am Idrosun, Djinn of the Ever Dark Wood."

"Greetings, Idrosun," Abi called. "This is Khashar. He comes from the Ragged Quarter."

"Greetings, Khashar," Idrosun said. She stretched her blue arms and yawned hugely through the veil. "It is my duty and privilege to grant you a single wish. The only rule about this wish is that it must come from the bottom of the heart."

Khashar gaped. Djinns were magical characters in stories; no one expected to come upon one in the blue flesh. Still, what child had never privately thought about what to wish for, should he or she meet a real Djinn one day?

The thing to wish for was money. One could use money to satisfy every desire. He drew a deep breath and spoke solemnly.

"O Idrosun, Djinn of the Ever Dark Wood, I am tired of being poor, and for this reason I wish for a chest filled with gold darics."

Idrosun shook her head.

"No, no. A chest of coins? You can do better. A wish like that comes not from your heart at all, but from your misguided mind. Look into your heart, where your truest desires lie."

Khashar thought this over.

"I wish for trousers of white silk, and a matching jacket of white rabbit fur."

"Nor can I grant this wish. It does not come from the bottom of your heart, but somewhere in the top or middle."

He asked in turn for a pony, a talking parrot, and eyes that could see into people's hearts. Idrosun rejected each of these wishes, on the grounds that they came from the wrong location of the heart.

Khashar's belly growled. He remembered the ostriches he had been chasing before he came to the Ever Dark Wood. He thought about the time the Dream Interpreter had scrambled ostrich eggs with pepper and coriander. The Cobbler had loved the meal and praised the flavor as rich and buttery.

Khashar knew what to wish for.

"O Idrosun, my real wish is to find the nests of the ostriches who live just beyond the Ever Dark Wood. I want to take two of their eggs to my parents for dinner."

"Did I not tell you he was a nice boy?" Abi hooted. "So devoted to his parents."

"I can tell this wish truly comes from the bottom of your heart," Idrosun said. "And therefore, I am happy to grant it. Ah, Khashar from the Ragged Quarter, now I remember how good it is to be a Djinn, how satisfying it is to grant the wishes of passers-by. I have decided that you deserve a special bonus—the Ancient Blue Ones, who raised me and gave me my training back in the Blue Land so long ago, might disapprove— but if you ever pass this way again, I will grant you a second wish."

And with that the Djinn Idrosun and the demi-goddess Abi were gone. The oak tree with the cavity, the glowing mushrooms, the Ever

Dark Wood: all gone. Khashar found himself in a field of scrub brush. Black ostriches with white tails were scrambling about. They pecked in the ground, they strutted, their heads bobbed on long swaying necks. They paid no mind to the turbaned boy who had appeared in their midst.

In a sandy hollow lay a clutch of large, speckled eggs. Khashar chose one egg for the crook of each arm, and another to lay atop the first two, and headed for home.

The moon was up when he finally reached the Ragged Quarter. The Cobbler was angry that his son had stayed out and worried the Dream Interpreter so. But when he saw the ostrich eggs he smiled and gave Khashar a kiss on the head.

*

"And so, lord husband, tomorrow night you'll find out why I told you this story of the younger Khashar, and then at last I'll reveal his secret."

The King answered with a snore.

Follow me, Scheherazade mouthed. She lit a candle in a brass candle holder, and we left the King's bedchamber. The hallway was empty; we slipped into our curtained alcove. She reached behind the wicker bench for the cloth pouch I had left there hours earlier.

"What would I do without you, Ariana?" she said, unwrapping the cloth.

"The royal physician said to rub it in every night," I told her. "Belly and loins. It is a paste of fish liver, sesame seed oil, and lentils gone to sprout. Don't smell it. Dreadful is too kind a word."

I didn't ask what the ointment was for. She told me anyway.

"That won't be a problem. The ambassador from Nubia brought all the court ladies a quite strong perfume. Believe me, there's no odor it can't mask. Besides, if I conceive it won't matter how my belly smells."

She smiled and put a finger across my lips. We each went our way then, Scheherazade to bedsheets of satin scented with cedar, and I to a ragged sleeping rug in the Pavilion of Slaves. Fortune walked with me—when I got there Bourzou was nowhere to be seen.

Heaven, where all our needs are known, blessed me with dreamless slumber.

7. Idrosun in Love, Khashar Unmasked, and the Sunbeam Chilled

"Thief!" "—stealing food out of my children's mouths!" "—greedy devil!" "I'll give your name to the Holy Ones, and then you'll be sorry!"

The quarrel was coming from the great room of Ali-Haram's chambers. I was in the kitchen, showing the wine merchant's slave which pegs to hang the new skins on. Red-checked cloths cased the skins. Even stoppered, the wineskins filled the kitchen with their sweet and powerful aroma.

"I thought you were buying a dozen—?" I said to the poet after the irate merchant and his slave left.

"I reduced my order. The merchant wasn't pleased about it."

"Can he really ruin you, Master?"

"I doubt it. If he exposes me, he'll expose his own business. Then he'd be lucky if the Holy Ones let him off with a bastinado. And he's too fond of his feet for that."

"But you only have enough wine for—" I did the reckoning in my head. "—another six days."

"Really? I make it closer to three weeks." He smiled; I suppose I looked confused. "You see, Ariana, you were right. It seems the less I consume, the clearer my mind is. My work is better. I sold two more poems. Your quarter-goblet-after-this-chapter is working. Thank you."

I laughed with delight. How unusual for anyone to show me gratitude. How pleased I was.

"Think of the money you're going to save, Master."

"Speaking of money—" He pulled a pair of coins from his tunic and laid them carefully on the counter. "Let's call this your fair share. Please accept."

I stared in astonishment at the gleaming golden coins. The stamped images of Darius, with his spear and bow, stared back at me. I pushed the money back toward Ali-Haram.

"Master, surely you know that no slave may possess money. It would be worth my life. But now—if you really want to reward me—" I felt my heart racing. He pursed his lips and watched me measure my next words. I suppose he knew what was coming. We had had this conversation before. "It's about the boy—no, please, Ali-Haram, listen—if I could see him, just once. If I could only see him once. I could only know what he looks like—"

"No. Absolutely not. I made an agreement with his foster mother; you know that."

"But it's been ten years! Think of it. I'm his mother, and I don't know anything about him. Does he have his father's eyes? What does he like to do? What is his voice like? Who are his friends? Does he—"

Hot tears stung my eyes. I couldn't speak. The poet was silent too, looking away. Finally:

"She calls him Merdad. As for the rest—please don't ask. I can't go back on the agreement."

Merdad? I tried to imagine his friends calling him. Merdad, come outside! Merdad, let's play games! No, the name felt false. He could only be Emre. Emre, son of my Emre.

How I yearned for a single glance. I longed to see his face and fix it in my mind forever, to drive away and replace another image: the wrinkled dark face, the clenched fists, the startled eyes as the midwife used her tiny clamps and knife to unjoin us. The baby issuing a wall-shaking squall. The midwife handing him to another, who took him from the birthing chamber and out of my life forever.

Only a single glance—

*

O mighty King (Scheherazade related), last night I told you about the visit Khashar had made years earlier to the Ever Dark Wood. How he met Abi, a demi-goddess who had taken the form of an owl. How the Djinn Idrosun had granted him a wish and promised him another should he ever return to the Wood.

But now let us return to that older Khashar. At age ten years and one he has vowed to prevent the joining of Prince Feroze and Princess Maria Irena in holy union—and to that end he has left the Ragged Quarter in pursuit of some white-tailed black ostriches.

It might have seemed to the ostriches, had it occurred to them to look back, that their turbaned pursuer simply disappeared. But what Khashar himself saw (he remembered to blink three times) was quite different: a vast, dark, silent place. The green glows of mushrooms, the enormous protruding roots, the slender watching alders.

He had returned to the Ever Dark Wood.

"O two-legged creature, what are you doing in my Wood?"

Khashar looked all around. Who was speaking to him? And why did the words sound like croaks?

The answer presented itself. A frog perched on the broad leaf of a fern. The frog had wide-set red eyes and bright red toe pads.

"O Abi, do you not remember Khashar from the Ragged Quarter? You taught me how to drop the film from my eyes. That was back when you were an owl."

"I am feeling my aeons." Croak, croak. "My mind keeps betraying me. I cannot remember my true form. The owl was not right. I have also eliminated mole, vole, deer, fox, kestrel, beetle, and walking stick. Well, I hope to find myself in time. But you, dear—why, look at how you have grown. One forgets how time passes in the world beyond."

"Please, demi-goddess. Take me to the tree hollow where Idrosun lives. I need to ask her to grant another wish. It is very urgent."

"She will be happy to see you too. Too much so, perhaps—but you can be the judge. Come closer, then. No, closer still. Crouch down."

The frog leapt through the air, plopping wetly on Khashar's shoulder. As he and the demi-goddess made their way through the Wood, he considered how best to win the Djinn's help. He would begin with a few wishes from the top of his heart: a top carved from mahogany, a pair of viper-skin boots, hot funnel cakes soaked in saffron—that sort of thing. He would play to her Djinn's pride by making wishes she could easily deny. Then he would spring on her the wish he really wanted.

At last, he and Abi came to the oak with the cavity in the shape of a vaulted window. A neatly braided pink top knot popped out, followed by a blue head.

"I am Idrosun, Djinn of the Ever Dark Wood. I will grant you one wish, which must come from the bottom of—but Khashar, my turbaned one, is it truly you! My own wish is fulfilled."

"Peace be upon you," Khashar said politely.

"You promised to grant him a second wish," Abi croaked.

"Yes, but before we take up that matter, I have something very important to discuss with you, Khashar." Idrosun wound the braid around her wrist. "It is so important that I begged Abi to send a sunbeam to find you and bring you to me. But while passing over the palace in Baghdad the sunbeam heard a weeping boy, who for some reason was pretending to be a girl, and decided to take you there instead, to help him. Sunbeams can be impulsive and disobedient. As punishment, Abi made it go to the moon, sit in the cold, and think about its disobedience."

"That is why I sent ostriches for you to follow," Abi added. "Idrosun remembered how fond your father is of their eggs."

"The sunbeam came for me," Khashar said, "And the ostriches too. They have all been part of the strange adventure I have had today. And that is why my new wish, which comes from the bottom of my heart, is to use the sunb—" He remembered his strategy in time. "—ah, that is, my wish is to have silver hair."

"Granted. But Khashar, here is the thing. Ever since Abi cast the Curtain of Blessed Invisibility over our Wood, I have had such a lonely time. No visitors, no wish-granting. How gratifying it was those years ago to hear your heartfelt wish for ostrich eggs for your parents' breakfast. It got me thinking. What if I granted myself a wish? The Ancient Blue Ones never said it was against the rules. Not in so many words anyway. You see, what I want, above all things, is to experience lo—"

His one wish (Khashar thought), wasted! His clever plan, ruined. Idrosun had gone against her own rules and granted a wish that did not come from the bottom of the heart. If Khashar did not help Prince Feroze escape, he would break his vow, and not win his promised reward. His parents would never get their palace in the Ragged Quarter.

But what was Idrosun saying now?

"—can live here, in the tree hollow. I know there are bats and bird droppings, but I will tidy things up, you will see. You can go out during the day and collect mushrooms and moss and whatever else your kind eats, and then when you come home to me, we—"

Khashar stared at the Djinn in astonishment.

"I do not understand. I came today because I made a vow to the Prince that I would—"

"O Khashar, will you make me say it aloud? Very well, I cannot afford pride. You see, the wish I granted myself—it came from the bottom of my heart— was to experience the glories and pleasures of love. Specifically, I wished to fall in love with the next person to pass by my tree. And having so wished, I asked the demi-goddess to send for you right away, Khashar. True, we are different creatures, Djinn and boy, but the power of love—"

"Idrosun, love has muddled your mind," Abi hooted from her perch on a wobbling fern frond in front of the tree. "Think about the age difference. The boy is ten years and one; you have been around for centuries."

"It is all in how you look at it. I am only a little older than Khashar, if you reckon my age in Djinn-years."

Abi countered: "It would not be fair to him to live with you in your tree, in this invisible Wood where no one comes. He has his own friends, and his parents to take care of."

"Fine. Khashar, the rule against multiple wishes is not hard and fast. One must use judgment. Why not just wish for me to be human? You and I will leave the Ever Dark Wood. I will live only a mortal's span and lose my Djinn powers, but what do I care? I will have you, and you me."

Khashar was dumbfounded.

"But I am a child," he said. "I am not old enough to wed."

"I have learned patience in my time, if nothing else. We can wait till you become a man. Then we will wed. How happy I will make you then!"

He tried a different approach.

"O Idrosun, I come from the Ragged Quarter. I am poor. I cannot support you as a man should support a wife."

"This too is simply solved," the Djinn said. "The last time you were here, you wished for a chest of gold darics. Well, wish for it again, while I am still in my tree and can grant wishes. It comes from the bottom of my heart, if not yours. Wish for ten such chests, or a hundred. Be as rich as you want. But why should we concern ourselves with such things? What do we care for money? We will be rich in love."

Khashar had reached wit's end. One argument alone remained. He flung off his turban and revealed the secret that he kept from the world.

Hair (now startlingly bright silver) tumbled down.

"O Idrosun, I am no boy." Khashar's voice rose to its natural higher pitch. "Here is the truth. I am a girl, and I have always been a girl. I only pretend to be a boy. My real name is Dilara. I wear this disguise so I can go out and play. Why should girls not have fun too? Why should I waste my childhood sitting at home, waiting to grow old enough to wed one of the Ragged Quarter boys? They use you to steal tin drainpipes, and then when you finally marry one you must cook his meals and bear his children, and then grow old while—"

"O my Dilara!" Idrosun cried. "As I listen to you speak from your heart, and see you without your turban, in your true girl form, I realize that I love you more than ever. Love will fulfill us in ways a man and woman can never hope for. Why, we can—"

"Foolish Djinn!" Abi said. "You know nothing of the world beyond the Ever Dark Wood. No woman may love a woman in Persia, nor a man love a man."

"Fine, then." Idrosun crossed her blue arms. "Dilara, use your wish to transform me into a man."

Abi had another argument.

"If you go into the outer world, you will have to find work, you know."

"I could be a professional wish-granter. Dilara will be my manager and tell customers my rates: one daric for little wishes, five darics for big."

"And how will you grant wishes if you are no longer Djinn? Only by the sweat of your brow and the labor of your muscles will you support her."

"Perfect. One daric for little muscles, five for big."

Dilara felt her situation growing ever more tangled. She was already daughter to the Cobbler and Dream Interpreter, and playmate of Ghazi and Naseem and the other Ragged Quarter boys. She was to be Prince Feroze's vizier when he came into his royal powers. And now she was to be wife to a Djinn as well?

Light seeped sideways across the floor of the Ever Dark Wood. In the outer world, the well-rested sun had crept across the horizon. The Prince's wedding day had arrived.

"O Djinn of the Wood," Dilara said formally, "forgive the poor sunbeam and let it return from the moon. I have made a solemn vow to rescue poor Prince Feroze from the Frankish monster, Maria Irena. My wish, which truly comes from the bottom of my heart, is for the sunbeam to take me back to the royal palace and help me fulfill my vow."

"Feroze, you say?" Idrosun rubbed her blue chin thoughtfully. "That must be the boy the sunbeam heard weeping. The very thought of him fills me with jealousy. Demi-goddess, the sunbeam deserves more punishment for taking my Dilara to him."

"Now, now," Abi answered. "Matters of great diplomatic importance are taking place in the world beyond the Ever Dark Wood. Dilara made her vow before Heaven, and now she has made a wish to you from the bottom of her heart."

Idrosun threw up her blue arms.

"Very well, then. Your wish for the sunbeam is granted. But I am taking back your silver hair. No double wishes. I understand all too late. Just because I wished to fall in love with you did not mean you would fall in love with me in return. How hard are the lessons one must learn in this life. Go to your Prince, then. Leave me to my loneliness and suffering."

In the next instant Dilara found herself balancing on a raft of lashed planks, turban still in her hand. Beneath her, the Angel of Rivers stretched forever, and the bobbing bridge of rafts stretched from bank to bank. The wind blew chill off the water. In the distance, fishing boats rose on white crests. Godwits raced along the shore, and grebes wheeled above. At the far end of the bridge of rafts, picking their way toward her, a stream of peasants with rakes and shovels and hoes trudged toward another day of labor in the King's grain fields.

Gray clouds piled on the horizon; a bright orange crescent peeked over them. From a single gap in the pile, a beam of light shot out. The light skimmed across the water and set the crests and foam and diving river birds aglow. The startled peasants pointed at the light and buzzed among each other.

The pillar of light ended at Dilara's feet. The pale morning moon (possibly sulking over the loss of its sunbeam) watched from the far side of the sky. Dilara confidently wrapped arms and legs around the sunbeam. It was not as warm as she remembered.

"How chilled you got on the moon," she murmured, rising into the sky. "Well, we have a long trip to make and an important mission to fulfill. You will warm up soon."

8. *Dilara's Inventions and Parsi's Clumsiness*

I tapped twice, and then three more times. Scheherazade opened the door.

"Come in, Ariana. He's still in the bath."

She kissed me on the cheek. Palace slave and Queen Consort, best friends, practically sisters—away from the eyes of others, anyway.

"The Holy Ones teach that only the clean may enter Paradise," I said with a smile.

"If so, Shahryar will be running the place when he gets there. The man bathes constantly."

She walked through the royal bedchamber and lit each candle. I took one of the candles and lighted the sticks of sandalwood incense.

Scheherazade went on: "When I was in my own bath today, he stuck his head and said: 'I have an observation about your story.'" I laughed at how she imitated the King's gruff, self-important voice. "'Abi may be a demi-goddess and Dilara only a girl, but they have something in common. They are both trying to rescue something—Abi the Wood, and Dilara the Prince.'

"That got me thinking. I gave him an observation of my own. I said that Abi keeps the greedy merchants from destroying the Wood for their profit. And Dilara vows to stop the King from trading his son's happiness for a political alliance. The women in the story are trying to stop the men from doing wrong."

"And what did he say to that?" She rolled her eyes. I thought for a moment. "All right, here is one for you. The Persian name Dilara means beauty and ornament. In our world, a woman's destiny is often to become an ornament in some man's home, but Dilara wants more than that. And so she wears a boy's disguise to pursue adventures of her own."

"His Majesty might not appreciate that observation either."

The inner door to the bedchamber opened. King Shahryar came in, dripping, in his purple linen robe. An earthy-woody odor I was coming to know well entered with him: the ambergris his slaves applied to him after his bath. I went to the corner where the palm-leaf fan patiently awaited me.

The King settled himself on the bed, arranging his pillows and coverlets. Scheherazade drew the robe off his shoulders and gave it several neat folds. He said:

"Wife, when this story began, you told us that Khashar had a secret. His secret turned out to be that he was Dilara in disguise. And meanwhile Princess Sorayah was Prince Feroze in disguise." More observations. The King held out his empty goblet. "You fooled us both times. But we commend you for that. A good story will have its surprises. But now we find ourselves wondering—how many other characters might be in disguise?"

"If there are others, O Majesty, they will be revealed in their time." A pitcher of water and a plate of fruits sat on the table next to bed. Scheherazade filled the goblet and added melon, crushing the slices with her fingers. "After all, lord husband, do we not all have disguises to wear?"

His eyes narrowed at that. He spoke sharply.

"We are the King of Persia. We would never conceal who we are. And neither would you, we hope. To disguise oneself is a sin."

Scheherazade bowed her head and said nothing. Shahryar switched topics.

"Wouldn't you say the poet's verse is getting better? We found that new poem he recited at our feast very moving. Remember? The one about leaves on the banyan tree?"

The verse that Ali-Haram wrote to flatter the King—I tried not to smile. The King added:

"If only he could write stories too, the way you do."

"Yes, if only," Scheherazade murmured.

O King, I said to myself, not every disguise is as simple as covering one's hair with a turban. Ali-Haram himself wears a disguise, and you gave it to him when you named him your court poet. Who is he beneath his disguise? He is the man who was sent to find a mother for the son I never knew. And he is the man who helps me write the story that keeps your wife alive.

*

Imagine it, your Majesty (Scheherazade said, beginning the next chapter). The early risers of Baghdad, in their courtyards, sitting at breakfast. They glance up from their flatbreads and pots of quince jam. And what should they see, but a column of light crossing the sky—

This light is no comet or falling star. Nor is it some lost wanderer from a lighthouse along the Tigris. It is like one of those glowing columns that will sometimes pierce a cloud off in the distance and descend in solitary majesty to the earth. But this shaft of light lies aslant the world. It comes to a terminal point—a point which is moving swiftly across the city. And astride the light, arms and legs wrapped about it, like one on a galloping pony, is a silhouetted figure with hair streaming behind.

Now picture these same breakfasters later. The dishes have been cleared, and goblets of hot pomegranate syrup served. The breakfasters are sitting at their leisure. They are talking with one another about the astonishing sunbeam they had seen earlier. They happen to look up again, and—wonder of wonders!—a second shaft of light, with its own rider, making its way through the pale morning sky, in the same direction as the first.

But let us return to this second sunbeam later—

For Dilara, hurtling across Baghdad on the first sunbeam, the royal palace soon hove into view, with its domes, spires, pavilions, terraces, gates, towers, columns. Fountains, gardens, courtyards. The cypress walls, carved with bas-reliefs of those conquerors of ancient times: Cyrus, Darius, Xerxes.

A moment later Dilara found herself leaning on shaky legs against a scrolled ironwork railing. Before her loomed an expanse of whitewashed stone set aglow by the sunbeam. Once more she had been deposited on the balcony of a tower.

She looked down at the courtyard, the date palms, the rectangular pool with its still water and gleaming tiles, the sward with its mounds of colorful flowers, the dark walnut grove. On the other side of the pool rose the windcatcher tower, where the day before she had stood on a different balcony and listened to the Prince's weeping.

Having done its duty, the sunbeam retreated across the courtyard. It set the sward and walnut grove alight.

"Wicked girl! Why is your head uncovered?"

Dilara whirled—a hand struck, seizing her ear and yanking her across the balcony and through an open doorway. Her turban, which she had been carrying, slipped out of her hand.

Inside the tower was a fever of activity and noise. Shouts boomed and echoed off the stone walls. A multitude of figures hurried past, baskets of flowers strapped to their backs, or clothes heaped in their arms, or rolled-up rugs laid across their shoulders. Barefoot slaves came and went in pairs, sagging under the weight of mirrors, tables, and stools. Arches, screens, cutlery, wooden stands, glass goblets: all were making their way from somewhere to somewhere else. Trays wheeled through, loaded with cakes, breads, fruits, and sizzling joints of meat.

Dilara's ear was released. She found herself facing a stern-faced woman in a white gown, white veil and headscarf, and orange velvet slippers. Long frown-lines enclosed the woman's narrowed eyes and clenched lips.

"Why are you away from the post assigned to you?" the woman demanded.

Lies did not spring easily to Dilara's tongue. Still, the Cobbler and Dream Interpreter had always taught her that to tell less than the truth was not necessarily a sin—for example, if a truthful account was not likely to be believed or risked unjust punishment. Besides, she had her vow to fulfill. The situation called for an invention.

"I am attending the Prince himself, Mistress, may Heaven protect him. The barbers sent me to test the breezes before they applied beeswax to his hair. I bared my head to feel the air for myself, and a stray wind grabbed my headscarf out of my fingers and took it away."

"Humph. I, Ko-kab-a, have the charge of this wedding, and I do not remember assigning anybody to the barbers." She reached into a purse that hung from her gown and produced a worn headscarf and veil. "Very well, then. Put these on and get back to your work at once."

But where was her work?

"I obey. But O Ko-kab-a, there are so many places in this tower. It is very confusing. I have already forgotten where—"

"Use the stair shaft to go to the next floor up. Count chamber doors. The barbers and tailors are attending the Prince behind the fifth. I will be there myself soon. Hurry, there is no time to lose."

The stone steps ascended in a steep spiral. When Dilara finally stepped out of the shaft onto the next floor—

"Look out!"

The warning came too late. A cold spray caught her in the face. She put hands to her temples above the veil; her fingers came away smeared with a substance like white mud. Before her stood a figure, barefooted and clad only in a white breechclout, holding an open bladder. The stopper had popped free. White muck oozed out.

The figure bowed his head abjectly.

"I, Parsi, faithful slave of the fearsome sorcerer Vahid, beg you not to tell my Master what I have done this time. He will turn me into a sheep again."

The smell of the muck left Dilara queasy.

Parsi hurriedly explained: "He sent me to the south garden to find a white lily of peace to chop up in the ointment. Now I am bringing the ointment so my master can apply it to the Prince."

"I will not tell him, Parsi." Dilara picked up the cork stopper and reclosed the bladder. "But what if your master is angry at finding some of his ointment on me? I think I would make a poor sheep."

The first door in the corridor swung open and closed as if on its own. Dilara had a moment's glimpse of massed alembics, retorts, and coiled tubes. Then, following Parsi's eyes, she looked down and saw an extraordinarily small figure coming out of the chamber. The figure was in a tiny blue robe and tiny conical turban. The top of the turban was on a level with Dilara's knee.

"O fearsome sorcerer Vahid, I have prepared and brought the ointment, as instructed." Parsi displayed the bladder.

"Did you chop the lily into equal quarters, as I specified?" One might have expected a squeak from such a tiny figure, but the sorcerer's voice carried and boomed off the tower walls. "Was the spadix intact? Did you use the exact proportions? The spell has certain instabilities. Everything must be precise."

"Yes, yes, and yes, O fearsome one."

The door of the stair shaft opened, and Ko-kab-a came onto the floor. She stopped and loomed over Vahid, hands on hips.

"I trust you are ready to cast your spell on the Prince."

The sorcerer bowed.

"My somewhat competent slave Parsi has brought the ointment, as you can see." Vahid waved grandly toward the stoppered bladder.

"The Prince should be out of the bath soon, and then it will be time. I am on my way to explain today's rites to him."

"I wish you fortune in that endeavor."

As Ko-kab-a hurried down the corridor, Vahid seemed to take notice of Dilara for the first time.

"You. Who are you? And what is that above your veil? I find it ill-smelling and unsightly."

Dilara saw her opportunity. Thinking rapidly, she compounded the invention already given Ko-kab-a.

"It is a special dressing for the hair, your fearsomeness. I am Dilara of the Ragged Quarter. The barbers assigned me the task of applying the pomade to the royal hair. But as I did so, the Prince thrashed about, and pomade splashed on me."

Vahid looked up at her thoughtfully.

"Hmm—you say you have experience applying substances to willful Princes? I can tell you are a girl of intelligence. The barbers are inartistic oafs. They do not deserve you. I hereby confiscate you from them. I have something else for you to administer to the Prince's royal person. Henceforth you will serve as my Apprentice. You will manage my laboratorium while you begin your training. Parsi will acquaint you with the schedule of deliveries and transformations and so on. This is a great opportunity for you. You may trust that my judgment in such matters is unerring. I have spoken. Come, you two."

"We obey," Dilara and Parsi said together. They followed the sorcerer until a harried-looking figure with a tailor's tape hanging from his neck came from the third door. As the tailor knelt to confer with Vahid, Parsi set down the bladder. Dilara scratched her face; she felt the cold muck again.

"Best not to spread it any further," Parsi advised.

"What is it made of?" Dilara asked.

"Let me see, horny goat weed, of course. Saffron. Iron filings, for magnetic attraction. A binding agent. Certain other secret ingredients; to reveal them would be worth my life."

"I have never seen a sorcerer before. Are they all so tiny?"

"Vahid was the size of any other man when I started in his service. But one day a sorcerer from Egypt came to pay a visit. I understand the two had been best friends at the college of magic in Babylon. Vahid threw a feast for his visitor, and then they started drinking moon aura fizzes.

Between us, our Master has never been able to hold his moon aura fizzes. He grew boastful. He claimed he could ride sunbeams. His visitor bet him he could not. Vahid summoned a sunbeam and even managed to mount it. But regrettably he was unable to stay on. Not only did he break his arm and leg, but he became shorter, as the terms of the wager obliged the loser to forfeit five feet of height."

The conference ended. The harried tailor led the way to the fifth door, which opened onto a chamber that was at once crowded, noisy, hot, and misty. At the center was a wooden barrel with brass hoops, gilt rim, and engraved royal seal. Poking above the rim were the wet bare shoulders and wet sulking face of Prince Feroze.

Slaves poured water from ewers into the barrel while they swarmed over the Prince with soapy sponges. Squeezing between the slaves, the barbers attacked the royal hair: combing, teasing, fussing, despairing. The tailors worked at a nearby table, adjusting Feroze's wedding tunic and other garments. They snipped threads with their teeth and used their notched strings to measure and re-measure seams, arguing all the while. Slaves came in with pots of crushed nutmeg (to sweeten the groom's scent) and olive oil (to soften his hair).

And there was Ko-kab-a again. She had taken up a position next to the barrel, her green gown soaked. She attempted to address the Prince above the hubbub.

"—will be on the prayer rug beside you, but you will not see her face until she lifts her veil. Your first view of her will be in the mirror. This rite symbolizes your future, in which—"

"The yellow hair and white skin will shatter your mirror!" Feroze shouted and splashed bath water. "You are wasting my time. I will be rescued before the rite, you will see. My faithful new vizier Khashar is going to—"

It was the Prince's usual tantrum. For an instant, his eyes met Dilara's—his gaze moved on. He did not recognize her. She was no longer Khashar.

"Do not speak ill of your bride, O Prince." Ko-kab-a patiently interrupted the tantrum. "To do so is to invite bad fortune. But now, barbers, bathers, tailors, all of you step aside. Hurry, now. It is time to dress the groom."

Slaves rushed forward to screen the barrel with muslin sheets that hung from wooden rods. Two more slaves—one carrying a stack of embroidered bath towels and the other a fringed cushion on which lay blue silk pantaloons figured with geometric designs—pushed the sheets aside and past the screen.

Parsi handed Dilara a mitten.

"Dip the sponge," he said, unstopping the bladder. The ointment in the bladder stank. "Then rub it on the Prince. Be careful not to get any on yourself. Or more than you already have, anyway."

"Your Highness," Vahid called, "it is time for the spell I promised. Do try to be cooperative. The ointment will make a good husband out of you, and thus contribute to peace among the nations."

Ko-kab-a looked down at the sorcerer with clear disapproval.

"The King himself assigned this job to you. You are turning it over to the barber's Apprentice?"

"She is my Apprentice now. And she happens to have a great deal of experience in this area. As for the Spell of Blind and Hopeless Love, it is my personal invention. To apply the ointment myself would introduce certain incongruities to the ether; these might endanger my own person. Besides, there is the difference in our present heights to consider."

"But your Apprentice will view the Prince's sacred nakedness!"

"The child is a guttersnipe. Male or female, I hardly know myself. I am sure it will be entirely beneath the notice of his Highness."

Ko-kab-a's frown-lines hardened, but she threw up her hands and surrendered.

"If his Highness finds fault, it will be with you."

Parsi gave Dilara a helpful shove, and she found herself within the screen of sheets. The air swam with the mist that steamed from the bath barrel. One slave was fastening the drawstring of the pantaloons. The Prince's lip curled. He fastened Dilara with a look of royal disdain.

"And who are you? Where is Khashar, my vizier-to-be? Did you bring my undertunic?"

9. *The Light Angels See*

Ali-Haram held up a parchment of writing for me to admire. Except—it was whiter, thinner, smoother, and shinier than any parchment I had ever seen. The Farsi letters were lovely, of course, but they held no meaning for me. A slave may not learn to read, since writing may contain dangerous ideas, such as freedom. Nothing can be allowed to turn the slave's mind away from her duties.

"It's called Paper," he said. "A trader from Cathay brought it to court. It is made from mulberry tree bark. It takes ink better than parchment. How fortunate we are to live in this modern age, Ariana, and be witness to such progress."

"The way I progressed from freedom to slavery when I was brought to Baghdad?"

My remark was inappropriate, irrelevant, and disrespectful. Only in the company of Ali-Haram did I dare say such things. At any rate, his Paper engrossed him.

"One day, when Paper is cheaper, we will use it for all our writings. Our scrolls will become curiosities of history."

"What if the writing is something long, like our story? It wouldn't fit on a single Paper."

"We could continue the story on a second Paper, and a third, as many as we need, and then join the edges of all the Papers with glue or thread. And then we could—"

He was warming to his topic. But I wanted to talk about something else.

"Master, have you ever noticed how some of our story lines reflect one another, like mirrors?"

He looked at me quizzically. I shared the observations of Scheherazade, the King, and myself.

"Interesting." He looked thoughtful. "All right, here's another one for you. Guards encircled Prince Feroze in the walnut grove. Then, on his wedding day, he was encircled again, this time by barbers and bathers and tailors. Both times he was a prisoner, in a way. This may be a feeling everybody experiences from time to time."

"Especially if they are not free to begin with."

Another remark he chose to ignore.

"By the way, Ariana, what you see on this Paper is a new poem I have written." I already knew the writing was his own. He always signed his work with a sketched eye at the bottom. "It is about—someone. May I read it to you?"

"Who is this someone?"

"Hmm—listen. See if you can figure it out.

> "I walked in the garden at end of day.
> My feet knew every step and way.
> Familiar beauties called and waved:
> Lotus, Jasmine, Hyacinth,
> Lily, Tulip, Saffron.
> When the weary sun lowered,
> They turned away their faces.
> But in a corner, unknown till then,
> Tiny golden petals spread,
> And there to me, in twilight, shown
> A Primrose, for my eyes alone."

I pretended to have a fit of coughing. I ran from his chambers before he could see me cry.

I understood this poem only too well. The garden was the King's court. The familiar beauties were all the ladies there. The Primrose was some new lady, freshly arrived at court. She was fascinating, beautiful, and already under the poet's watch.

O Ariana, I said to myself, who are you to enjoy the luxury of jealousy? Best to bury your feelings for Ali-Haram. Only pain will ever come from them. Accept that you and he live in different worlds.

Is anything under Heaven crueler than Blind and Hopeless Love?

*

(Your Majesty—Scheherazade said, beginning the next chapter—last night I left Dilara awkwardly face to face with the soon-to-be-wedded Prince. One slave toweled his arms and legs, while the other fastened the drawstring of the royal pantaloons.)

"And who are you?" Feroze demanded of Dilara. "Are you here to dry and dress me too?"

"O Prince—" Dilara awkwardly held the coated mitten away from him, and from herself. "Do you not recognize me? I listened to you weep yesterday. I vowed to rescue you, and now I am here."

"Whoever you are, you are most assuredly not here to rescue me. My rescuer—I expect him any moment now—is a boy named Khashar. He comes from a magical land known as the Ragged Quarter. He can command sunbeams. When I come into my royal powers, he will serve as my faithful vizier. But—I only ask this out of curiosity—why are you wearing a mitten, and what is that white muck all over it?"

The slave pair concluded their duties and left Dilara and Feroze alone, shielded from sight by the screen of muslin sheets.

"Have you applied the ointment yet, Apprentice?" Vahid called.

"Hurry; we need to get the Prince dressed." This, from Ko-kab-a. "There is no time to lose."

"O Prince Feroze, look at me!" Dilara yanked off the borrowed veil and headscarf. She held her hair up behind her.

The Prince's mouth flew open.

"Khashar! Is it you, then? You sin by wearing a girl's clothes."

She chose not to remind him that, only the day before, he had worn the clothes of his own sister, Princess Sorayah. Was it fair to hold royal blood to ordinary standards?

"Directly to the manhood is best," Vahid boomed. "Otherwise, the spell might fade after a few years."

"Do your duty, guttersnipe," Ko-kab-a echoed. "Hurry, we are ready to queue up the procession."

Feroze looked again at the mitten, and back at Dilara.

"It is all clear," he said sadly. "I understand now. In this ointment is the Spell of Blind and Hopeless Love. Even my faithful vizier and rescuer has turned on me."

"No, Prince." She pitched her voice Khashar-low. "You see, I came to find you. Along the way, Vahid made me his Apprentice. But I brought a sunb—"

"I am not hearing any shrieks from the Prince in there," Vahid called.

"Here is my plan," Dilara said urgently. "Shout and protest, as though you are resisting me, and a moment later say loudly, so Vahid and Ko-Kab-a can both hear, 'Very well then. Go on, do your worst.' Then go out with your head bowed and shoulders slumped. Let the tailors dress you. Before the procession starts, ask for a moment to be alone with your thoughts. Go into the stair shaft, walk down to the next floor, and then onto the balcony. I will join you there. We will fly to freedom on the sunbeam, and discuss my reward later."

"Khashar," Feroze said, "clearly you are a great magician. Yet now I find myself torn by doubts. My father and mother, Vahid, Ko-kab-a, the Holy Ones, the people of Persia, even Charles Magnus—all these want me to wed the Frankish monster. You alone advise me to flee, although only yesterday you said I should take pride in being an instrument of peace between two empires. Perhaps to wed Maria Irena is my true destiny, and to father the next King of the Persians and Franks my duty. Heaven has called me to suffer. Well, if I can face my destiny with courage, so can you. You may apply the ointment. I have spoken."

He pulled the drawstring, and the pantaloons fell to the floor. Dilara blushed and squeezed her eyes shut.

"What a strange boy you are," Feroze said. "Here, give me the mitten. I will do the job myself."

The slaves carried away the screen. The tailors put the Prince into his blue wedding tunic with gold sashes and brocade. White silk leggings and boots of polished ox leather followed. Bands of pearls were strung over his shoulders. The barbers gave the royal hair a final fuss, and laid a circlet of gold on his head. Feroze still had the orange turkey feather, and this he stuck inside the circlet.

Ko-kab-a took note of Dilara.

"Wicked girl! Where did your veil go this time?"

She tried to give Dilara a cuff, but the Prince would have none of it.

"Do not touch him. Khashar is my vizier-in-waiting. You will treat him with all deference. He is to stay at my side in the procession. Barbers! Come give Khashar's hair a quick trim. You, tailors! Throw away his girl's disguise. Find him a tunic with a sash and brocade, and proper boots. A silk cap with a ruby on it would be nice too."

The Prince took his place at the head of the procession, with Dilara behind him. Barefoot slaves in white shifts came next. The first of these carried an infant's wooden stool, on which the sorcerer Vahid was placed.

The other slaves bore, in turn, a basket of painted eggs (symbolizing fertility), a bowl of silver coins (wealth), and a platter of grapes, apples, and pomegranates (the fruits of Heaven).

Dilara glanced down at her worn hand-me-down tunic. She put her hands to her hair, still unbound and uncovered. (In their confusion and despair, the barbers and tailors had already forgotten the Prince's orders.) She wondered: what role she was to play in the wedding? Who was she to obey first—the sorcerer, the bridegroom, or Ko-kab-a (who continued to give her disapproving and suspicious looks)?

Having changed his mind about fleeing, would the Prince still give her the promised reward of a palace in the Ragged Quarter? What would it be like to serve as his vizier? Once she had watched weeping as Naseem picked the wings off a fly—how could she ever bring herself to carry out a proper beheading?

Parsi appeared before her with the green turban.

"O Mistress, while carrying out my duties, which never end, I found this on the balcony."

"Keep it," she said. "I will not need it any longer."

"What if you turn back into a boy?"

She stuffed the turban inside her tunic. Parsi also returned her borrowed veil and head covering, which still had smears of white muck—these she put on. On Ko-kab-a's signal, the procession filed out into the corridor, and from there to the stair shaft. A slick patch of lichens on a wooden step caused Dilara to lose her footing and stumble into the Prince, who reproached her.

"Dignity above all, Khashar. People will remember our behavior today. It is important for us to show courage. We must not recoil in horror when we view my bride."

The procession reached the bottom and entered the courtyard, where two rows of barefoot children had formed. The children, whose filthy faces contrasted with their clean new tunics of bright green and red, reached into sacks for flower petals, which they tossed into the air. The startled recognized two of these petal-tossers.

"O my friends!" she cried. "How far from home the three of us have come!"

"Who are you?" Ghazi stared at her uncomprehendingly.

"Whoever you are," Naseem said, "better stick to your duties while we stick to ours."

Ghazi added: "We are earning one eighth of a quarter-daric each to shower the bridal couple with flowers. And we get to keep these new tunics."

Dilara remembered that her veil and headscarf concealed her. She tried a different approach.

"Do you know a boy in the Ragged Quarter named Khashar?"

"Yes, once we saw him ride a sunbeam," Ghazi said.

"He stole a tin drainpipe and then accused us," Naseem said.

"No, Khashar is a true friend," Ghazi said. "I told his worried parents that he was out looking for ostrich eggs. This pleased his father very much. But speaking of sunbeams—"

Dilara followed Ghazi's glance to the glowing walnut grove, where the shaft of light shone, obediently awaiting the Prince's getaway. Oddly, a second sunbeam had appeared above the courtyard.

"Do not interact with the rabble," Vahid instructed his Apprentice from the infant's stool behind her. "You are in my employ now, and it does not become your new station."

The procession moved on toward the tiled poolside, which had been prepared for the rites. A trio of Holy Ones stood beside a tall arch; they wore black hooded cloaks and heavy gold chains. Lotus flowers and white silk draperies covered the arch. Beneath the arch lay a prayer rug and a brass-framed mirror on a wooden stand. Along the poolside slaves wearily chased flies from the pots, tureens, and platters—these last heaped with baklava, cookies, cheeses, and other foods known to bring good fortune to newlyweds. High atop wooden poles, candles burned in bronze sconces.

King Alcimedes, proud father of the groom, waited next to the Holy Ones in his general's uniform, red with brass buttons, gold piping, and blue epaulets with gold stripes. He wore a diadem with emeralds. Flanking him was his chief wife, who wore a gown of silver satin and a headdress with emeralds to match the King's diadem. Other dignitaries and guests had taken their places—including a knot of attendees standing apart and whispering among themselves. A number of these had yellow hair, blue eyes, and skin the color of milk.

"The Frankish delegation," Vahid explained behind Dilara. "Plenipotentiary, scribe, interpreter, honor guard, the bride's aunties, and so on."

Dilara felt emboldened to observe: "Their clothes are very strange."

"Their furs, cloaks, and mantles are most impressive," Vahid said in answer, "but they will suffer under our Persian sun. But now let us hush, for Princess Maria Irena is entering. By custom she has been secluded till this moment. Only now will she be viewed in her new homeland."

The bride approached the arch atop a slow-moving gray ass, led on a short line by the slave Parsi. The ass wore his own circlet of yellow roses. A veil of white lace concealed the bride's entire face. Her white gown was embroidered with gold. The gown's satin train was so long it dragged the tiles, concealing the ass's tail and hind legs.

The bride's unbound yellow hair lay neatly atop the train and was nearly as long. The sharp fragrance of roses filled the courtyard, and Dilara realized, to her utter astonishment, that Maria Irena's hair was not the color of roses, after all.

The Princess did not, in fact, have hair.

Rather, large yellow roses appeared to grow directly out of her head. They twined into a thick, golden mane. Atop the roses, the Princess wore a circlet identical to the Prince's, save that it lacked a matching turkey feather.

The assembled, privileged to witness such a miracle of hair, emitted sighs of pleasure. But then the daylight itself underwent a change, and gasps and cries replaced the sighs. Silver sparks shot through the already brilliant blue of Persian noon.

"Such is the light Angels must see," Vahid observed. "Heaven itself is casting a blessing on this union of two empires."

With unease, Dilara watched as the second sunbeam hovered above the courtyard. The brilliant newcomer lowered to earth and joined Dilara's sunbeam in the walnut grove. The two sunbeams glowed as the world itself must have on the fourth day of creation.

Dilara tried to peer into the dazzling light. A silhouette? A figure with a top knot? But the light resisted her; her eyes filled with black spots. The spots swam and circled and merged.

She tore her stare away. The Holy Ones were unspooling their scrolls to begin the rites—

10. A Reunion, of Sorts

The carriage bumped over endless rocks and ruts and cracks. Ali-Haram pulled aside the curtain so I could look out. Houses, tenements, shops, sheds, market stands, warehouses, mosques—all were mudbrick and rickety timbers and jumbled, mismatched stone, black-streaked from past fires. The buildings huddled together, they rose from each other's rubble, they leaned over dizzyingly, they overhung the road. Men diced on corners, dogs and rats and monkeys roamed at will, beggars and thieves plied their trades.

How I had looked forward to this day. Such happiness I had anticipated. But now the day had come, and I could enjoy nothing. Worry and dread were eating at me. A conversation overheard that morning—Slavemaster Bourzou and a man I had never seen before, arguing over money.

I wanted to beg the poet to find out what he could about the argument. But even if he confirmed my most desperate fears, what was there for me to do?

It was a matter in which I was powerless.

"Your first time to travel in the Ragged Quarter," Ali-Haram remarked.

I was determined to keep my voice steady.

"Or wear a jeweled headdress." Scheherazade had insisted I accept her satin gown and headdress on loan for the important trip. Beads clinked with every move of my head. How did women endure these things? "Or ride in a horse-drawn carriage."

"There are many who, with the right clothes and jewels, can become beauties. And then there are the few who need neither to be the most beautiful of all."

"Of course. The Primrose, in your poem."

Bitterness and jealousy—my new constant companions. I turned my face away from the carriage window.

"Ariana, that Primrose—"

He broke off as the carriage stopped. A filthy face poked through the curtain. Scarred hands displayed a cloth pouch.

"Tears of the Poppy, your honor." A hoarse, unhealthy voice. "Source of all bliss. Bringer of dreams from Heaven. Dessert of Angels. Only five darics."

The hand pulled a dark grain from the pouch and held it out between thumb and finger. Frightened and curious, I tried to lean forward to examine the grain. Ali-Haram pulled me back. He rapped his fist on the ceiling—the carriage resumed its progress. The curtain fell closed; the scarred hand disappeared.

"People like you and I don't dare take Tears of the Poppy," he said. "If you're not used to that kind of happiness, it can be very difficult to bear."

O Ali-Haram, I thought, who could be less used to happiness than I? If Heaven answered my prayers, and set your heart to love me—would I be able to bear that?

But why waste breath asking such questions? Ali-Haram would always be out chasing some new Primrose. We rode on in silence.

My dread returned in force. I turned over in my mind again a single phrase I had clearly overheard Bourzou say to the other man: "—worth more than all the other slaves put together—"

"How did you become the King's poet, master?" Talk to me, Ali-Haram. Distract me. "You have never told me about your childhood. What is your story?"

He raised an eyebrow and grinned.

"Very well, you asked for it. I suppose my earliest memory is playing with tin warriors, with the other boys, in the Foundlings Home. We—"

That startled me.

"Wait, the Foundlings Home? You lost your parents?"

"Not exactly. I met Mother for the first time on my eighth name day. A carriage from the palace arrived to fetch me. I was instructed not to ask after my father or try to learn who he was. Beyond that, I was told nothing. I had no idea what to expect. Mother turned out to be a court lady, unwed when I was born. My existence had been inconvenient for her—or perhaps for my mysterious father—thus my life in the foundlings' home.

"Anyway, I was escorted to a large chamber, where I was formally introduced to Mother. Several other ladies were there. Court officials, eunuchs, minstrels, and slaves, too. I remember the amusement on the faces. I recognized my own chin and nose on one of the lyre players. I was about to ask him in front of everybody if I was his son, but at that moment the King—this was Shahryar's father—came in. The slaves prostrated themselves. Everyone else bowed or knelt. Everyone except me, that is, who knew no better.

"The ignorant foundling walked right up to the King, pretty as you please, and introduced himself. I was full of myself. I told him I was a poet. I suppose I said this because the head lady at the Foundlings Home always gave us children poems to memorize and recite. Laughing, the King told me to compose a poem on the spot about Mother. I produced a few childish lines, who knows what they were, but I vividly remember the King stamping his foot in approval. He announced to everyone that I was to receive an education. My tutors would come to the Foundlings' Home, at his expense. If I did well at my lessons, he added, I might be his court poet one day.

"And that is when I began to learn mathematics, history, astrology. I learned about Gilgamesh, Ptolemy, and the Song of Solomon. I studied our holy book. My tutors started me writing poetry in earnest. It didn't take me long to realize my verses got the best marks when they contained flowers and ended with clever rhyming couplets."

There to me, in twilight, shown—a Primrose, for my eyes alone. Flowers and couplets.

"After that I was brought to the court once a year. When I turned sixteen, the King informed me that I was to accompany his negotiators on a mission. He said this would benefit my education. The city of Antioch had demanded a reduction in its tribute payments. The Bey of Antioch was my age. He fancied himself a scholar and artist—his own nobles called him Poet Boy.

"How excited I was. We journeyed for days to reach Antioch. Upon meeting our delegation, Poet Boy challenged me to a poetry contest. He said a group of learned men would serve as judges. If they rated his verse the better, Antioch would be clear of the owed tribute. If I won, the entire amount would be paid over. The Persian diplomats I had traveled with were horrified. They pleaded with me to back out, but I was young and quite sure of myself. In any event, Poet Boy was the Bey of Antioch, and his word there was law.

"Hourglasses were set out, and the two of us began composing. I dashed off my usual lines about lotus and tulips and roses. Then I tacked on the inevitable couplet. Inexplicably, the learned judges declared my poem the winner. I must say Poet Boy kept to his bargain. Our delegation returned to Baghdad with a chest of gold darics. Our mission was a success. The King praised me in front of the entire court and even gave me a cash award out of the tribute.

"When I turned eighteen—this would have been the year before you came to the palace, Ariana—a plague swept through Baghdad. It took Mother and the King's top diplomat and many others. The court poet took ill. At the same time the King needed someone to oversee a prisoner exchange with Maqazza; I found myself appointed. Well, by the time I got back to Baghdad, the court poet had died. Sure enough, the King appointed me to replace him. I moved from the Foundlings Home to my own chambers in the palace, where I have lived ever since. Meanwhile the King kept sending me on more missions."

Like taking my newborn away in search of a foster mother—

"Now his son Shahryar is my King," he continued, "and I am still court poet. True, I'll never make anyone forget Homer or Sappho, but—"

We jolted to a halt again. The driver called back to us.

"Lord, you said to tell you when we came to the alley with the fallen fence—?"

Ali-Haram answered: "Ah. Now look for a courtyard with broken stones and boys with shovels. When you reach that courtyard, stop."

"I obey, Lord."

We jolted along the alley. I could not contain myself any longer. My worries tumbled out.

"O Master, a man I've never seen before was in the Pavilion of Slaves this morning. I saw him arguing with Bourzou the Slavemaster."

He pursed his lips and was quiet. Then:

"Argue, you say? About what?"

I can't read a scroll, but I can read a face that conceals the truth. At that moment I knew beyond all doubt what Bourzou and the unknown man had been arguing over.

It was my head-price.

"Tell me, Master. What have I done wrong? Why am I being sold away? Surely you know."

He covered my hand with his. He seemed to struggle for words.

"Ariana, Bourzou would never sell you away from the palace. This I can promise. Believe me."

It was no answer. How could I trust his promise? I pulled my hand away and said nothing. He reached into his bag of writing supplies and pulled out a square of Paper.

"Do you remember the last poem I recited for you?"

The hated Primrose! Did he think I could forget?

"Is that what's written on your Paper?"

"Yes, plus everything I know about the woman in the poem—her history, how she came to Baghdad, all the facts of her life."

He waited for me to say something. But I closed my heart. As with happiness, there is only so much pain a woman can bear.

The carriage stopped. Ali-Haram drew back the curtain. The air smelled of fire and smoke and rock dust, and the sudden light of midday made me blink.

"Take a look, Ariana."

I wiped my eyes and leaned forward. Out the carriage window lay a long open yard, where barefoot boys worked in threadbare tunics and torn skull caps. Some were sweeping with straw brooms; others were picking up brush and trash, which they hauled to a fire pit. An adult—the boys' supervisor, no doubt—lay snoring, his head on a heap of straw.

"I know the merchant who bought this yard," Ali-Haram said. "He's going to put up a new building here, to rent out to lawyers and scribes and such. These boys earn a quarter-daric each for a long day's work."

One of the boys stopped his sweeping. He leaned on his broom and turned to stare at the carriage. I studied the boy: the curly brown hair, the swooping nose, the full lips. A thrill raced through me. My heart pounded.

"That's him!" I whispered. Ali-Haram peered over my shoulder. "I know it is. Emre, son of Emre!"

"And so he is. But his name now is Merdad, which means gift of the sun, for he was a gift to a certain woman who had lost her own newborn, and now he is all her light in life."

"Can we ask him to come near? May I talk to him?"

"No. Remember our deal—you asked for one look. Be content to view him from here. You must understand. It's only natural for his foster mother to fear your presence in his life."

I buried my face in my hands. Why had I asked for a single glance? O Emre, it would have been better to know you only in imagination and dreams, than to be this close and not speak. If only I could touch your perfect face and hands. If only I sit next to you and tell you stories about your papa—

"Here's a gift for him." Ali-Haram produced a gold daric. "You can toss it out of the carriage."

Anger seized me. Again Ali-Haram was trying to prove his unselfishness by giving away money. I slapped the coin from his fingers; it fell ringing to the floor of the carriage.

"If I were Emre—Merdad—I would hate the stranger in the carriage for giving me what it would take me many days to earn."

"I only wanted—"

To do a kindness, for the child he had taken from me those years ago—yes, I knew it was so. I had overstepped my bounds again. But my heart was still hard. Ali-Haram chewed his lip. Then, producing his inkhorn and pen, he carefully inked another line on the Paper.

The boy was still staring intently in our direction.

"I have an idea," he said. "Forget money. Let's give the boy this Paper instead."

With quick pen strokes he drew the eye that served as his signature and blew on the ink to dry it. He dropped the Paper from the carriage window. It drifted to the rocky yard. Emre took a tentative step toward us. My heart leapt. But then Ali-Haram yanked the curtain closed. He rapped on the ceiling.

The carriage lurched back into motion. For a while we sat in silence. Then:

"Why did you give him your Paper? I thought you said children in the Ragged Quarter aren't taught to read."

"If he's as smart as his mother, he'll find someone who can read it to him."

"Why would he want to know anything about your Primrose?"

"What son wouldn't want to know about the mother he's never known?"

What was Ali-Haram trying to tell me? I did not understand. I dared not understand.

He took both my hands then. He looked into my eyes.

"Ariana, I have something important to say to you, although I'd planned to wait till tomorrow. I wanted you to see your son first. He's the reason we made this trip. When you think about today, I wanted you to remember him, not me. But I see that I better say my piece—now.

"The man you did not recognize was my agent. He and Bourzou weren't arguing. They were bargaining. You weren't supposed to see. But of course, nothing in the palace escapes you. Bourzou named a head-price which I found acceptable, especially since Scheherazade agreed to front the cash for me. And so, Ariana—" He took a very deep breath. He held my hands tightly. "—I bought you. In the morning, I will file a legal tablet to free you."

I was dizzy. The world was spinning beneath me.

"But Master—*why?*"

"You are going to be free, Ariana. Don't call me Master anymore. Why did Scheherazade pay your head-price? Because we are nearing the end of Scroll One of our story, and I pledged her three more."

"I meant, why would you buy me, only to set me free?"

"Because you have taught me something. Freedom is the state Heaven intends for all. I don't have the means to free every slave in Persia. But with Scheherazade's money, I can at least free you."

I found myself wondering who would oversee the next day's egg count for Bourzou—the idea of freedom was still too large for me.

But hadn't I been free once before, in that brief time of loving Emre and cleaning the rebels' night pots?

"What did you write on the Paper before you threw it out the window?"

"These words: *Merdad, son of Emre, today you saw your mother Ariana, the woman whom Ali-Haram loves. May Heaven be praised.*"

He let go of my hands and pulled a velvet cloth from his tunic. He unwrapped the cloth.

I could not breathe. The band was gold; the stone was an emerald.

He said: "The Primrose is not some rich, idle court lady—she is you, Ariana. You see, I love you. Now, I am about to ask you an important question. You'll be free tomorrow no matter what your answer is, but—"

He said more, but I couldn't make out the words for the roaring in my ears.

11. A Royal Transport of Love and a Greedy Spell

King Shahryar was restless. He usually went straight from his bath to the royal bed, but this night he climbed up onto his elephant instead.

As elephants go, this one was small, but still large enough that the bedroom furniture had to be moved to make room for it. The noble beast, made of alabaster and teak, was a gift for the King of the Age from the King of Assam.

"Tonight, before you go on with your story, tell us more about this Maria Irena." The King adjusted the velvet cushion between his back and the tall gilt saddle horn. "You spoke of her riding the ass to the wedding arch. We find her a pitiful figure. She is alone, even among her own people. A child, so far from home. What is her story, we wonder?"

Scheherazade gave me a quick, imploring look. The King had caught us unprepared. I kept the palm-leaf fan in motion and gave an ever-so-slight nod.

"My lord husband," she said, "I have been teaching each chapter of my story to this slave, in the event I should ever take ill, or be called away. May she be the one to tell your Majesty the story of Maria Irena? I wish to judge her progress."

It was a hasty invention on her part. I would have to think rapidly: Ali-Haram and I had dreamed up the Princess, but we hadn't yet thought a great deal about her as a character. What would being the daughter of Charles Magnus have been like? Why did she have a mane of yellow roses?

Shahryar looked at me with distaste, and then at Scheherazade with disapproval.

"You waste your time teaching these creatures. Holding them in bondage is our duty to Heaven. We thereby give them a happy and simpler life, free from the difficulties and uncertainties of life—money, decisions, and so forth. Besides, learning can lead to dissatisfaction and unhappiness. What if the slaves were to rise against us one day?"

Scheherazade didn't inform the King that this particular slave was about to be freed herself. Or that an enslaved person faces the same difficulties and uncertainties as one who is free—but does so without any personal control or power.

Instead, the Queen Consort played for time:

"Majesty, even the ancients often had slaves who could read and write. There was Cicero's slave Tiro, who wrote down his master's speeches to the Roman Senate exactly as dictated, so we can read them today. And didn't Plato himself teach that the more someone read, the less he remembered? I am testing this principle with Ariana. She can't read a word, but her memory is superior. I will demonstrate. Ariana, what are the opening lines of Dilara's story?"

I didn't pretend to hesitate.

> "This story begins with a boy who shouted and played
> and ran barefoot through the alleys with his companions.
> He was a bundle of dust and noise and motion, like any
> boy—"

"Fine, fine." The King waved. "Wife, it is our weakness to deny you nothing. Go ahead, then. Let her tell us about the Frankish Princess."

Courage, I told myself.

"Majesty, Maria Irena was the youngest daughter of the tenth wife of Charles Magnus." I invented rapidly. "She arrived in this world with a single hair on her head. Her mother prayed and offered sacrifices, but when the day arrived for her naming rite, the girl was still all but bald. During the rite, the Frankish Holy One plucked out the single hair and dedicated it to Heaven. At once, a yellow rose grew directly from the girl's head. A second appeared next to the first, and then a third. The fragrance filled the air. The astounded Holy One said the roses were a sign of Heaven's favor, and they must never be cut or bound. By the time Maria Irena was five years of age, the mane of roses reached to her shoulders.

"Now, Charles Magnus held to the novel child-raising philosophy that his sons and daughters should receive the same education— arithmetic, reading, poetry-writing, principles of governance, military tactics, and astrology. In fact, his daughters were taught to ride and even use the dagger and short-sword.

"On the other hand, Charles would not allow his daughters to wed, for fear their husbands or children might one day challenge his own power. But he made an exception in the case of Maria Irena, for he planned to use her to seal his alliance with King Alcimedes of Persia. She was promised to the King's heir, Prince Feroze.

"Naturally, Maria Irena knew she must do her duty, but how she suffered at the thought of traveling so far to wed a man she had never met. The people of Persia (her mother told her) did not look like her. They spoke in a gibberish tongue. The climate was oppressive. Charles Magnus promised the girl that once the union had served its proper diplomatic ends, he would order the Pontifex—this is the highest ranking Holy One of the Frankish religion—to issue an annulment."

"An annulment!" The King was incredulous. "But they had an alliance. That would have been an act of war. Ah, but of course. That means clashes of armies and ships are to ensue in this story. What makes a tale more exciting than a good battle!"

I dared to answer: "O Majesty, armies and battles there may yet be—and annulments—but I think what takes place in this particular union will surprise you much more."

The King climbed down from the elephant and made his way to bed. Scheherazade drew the silk coverlets over him. He rolled onto his side and looked my way, as though seeing me for the first time.

"We are amazed. To think, a slave who can commit whole stories to memory. Very well—what did you say this one's name is? Ariana? Her voice is not that displeasing. She may continue our story, if she keeps the fan moving."

*

At last, the wedding was set to begin (I said, as the King closed his eyes, and Scheherazade settled herself on the bed beside him). Parsi went to all fours so Princess Maria Irena could use him for a step; she descended gracefully, her train of yellow roses following. She went to kneel next to Prince Feroze on the prayer rug by the arch and mirror. The bride and groom bowed their heads and avoided looking at each other, or into the mirror.

While the Holy Ones intoned the rites of union, the Frankish interpreter kept up a running translation. The Frankish delegation gathered around him to hear. Vahid, still perched on his wooden stool, was set near the arch. Dilara, his new Apprentice, waited beside him. Gathered on the other side of the arch were the Ragged Quarter children, holding their sacks of flower petals. They prepared to toss their flowers in the air at the sacred moment the Prince and Princess viewed each other in the mirror.

Dilara carefully kept her own gaze from the mirror. If she accidentally saw someone's reflection there, she too would suffer a life of love.

She looked over her shoulder at the walnut grove. Her eyes watered from the brilliance of the light of the two sunbeams. The trees glowed like the forest of Heaven. But was the crouching top knotted figure in silhouette in front of the sunbeams preparing to spring—?

The rites were ending. The Holy Ones, speaking in High Persian, recited as one:

"—and now, Maria Irena, Princess of the Franks, lift thy veil." (The instruction was translated, and the Princess uncovered her milky-white face. She blinked against the Persian sunlight.) "And thou, Feroze, Prince of Persia, look into the glass for thy first view of thy beloved bride." (He raised his noble head, eyes squeezed shut for several heartbeats before resigning himself, with a sigh, to his fate.) Ghazi and Naseem and the other children emptied their sacks, and a cloudburst of flower petals rained on the newlyweds and their guests.

At that moment something completely unexpected took place.

Feroze leaped to his feet. He sang and twirled and spun on his toes. He shouted and danced. He was a Prince transformed. He broke all rules of royal decorum. The assembled watched in open-mouthed wonder.

Then the Prince took his unveiled bride by the hands. He raised her to her feet.

"O Maria Irena," he said (loudly, so all could hear), "before today, I knew only crushes and puppy loves. Now, as I gaze upon your blue eyes and yellow roses, my heart pounds and races. My throat is drier than the desert, and my breath quickens like the wind. I am light-headed. My fingers tingle. What can this be but true love, of which I have heard so much but never experienced."

He paused while the interpreter translated. Hearing, the Franks tittered. The Princess blushed, and the yellow roses (heaped with countless flower petals) rippled and floated above her waist.

"Your beauty shames the moon itself." The Prince was inspired. "I love you blindly and hopelessly, and I vow before man and Heaven that henceforth I shall devote my entire existence to bringing you happiness, so that we—"

At the edge of the walnut grove, the silhouetted figure let loose an ear-curling cry.

"Do you hear that, Apprentice?" Vahid said thoughtfully. "I would wager it is the love cry of the Lesser Tree Djinn, had scholars not proven that race to be extinct."

"Master, those scholars may have a film over their eyes," Dilara said. "You see, I once met a demi-goddess who—"

She broke off. The blue top knotted figure—who, of course, was the Djinn Idrosun from the Ever Dark Wood—came bounding across the sward toward the courtyard. She trampled mounds of flowers and sent platters of food flying. The wedding-goers cried out and scattered.

"My beloved!" Idrosun cried, locating Dilara in the confusion. "I have arrived to take you away! By leaving my tree, I have lost my powers as a Djinn, but what does it matter when we can live happily as woman and wife?"

The sorcerer hopped down from his stool. He walked several circles about Idrosun, examining her critically, exercising his professional curiosity.

"I understood your kind stayed inside the cavities of trees. How do you come to be here, in the palace courtyard?"

Idrosun twirled her long pink braid.

"I left my assigned tree of my own will. I know I may no longer grant wishes from the bottom of human hearts, or any other places. But this is a sacrifice I am prepared to make. You see, I granted myself a wish, which was for love, and the fair Dilara, formerly known as the boy Khashar, arrived and won my heart."

Feroze had broken off his own love-speech to attend this exchange.

"You are misinformed, Djinn," he said coldly. "This Dilara of whom you speak is a made-up person. She is a disguise that Khashar wears for his own mysterious purposes. I forbid you to take him with you. When I ascend to my royal powers, he will be my vizier. He must begin his training straightaway. I am going to be busier than ever, now that Heaven has made me responsible for the sacred happiness of the Princess."

Vahid continued to interrogate the Djinn.

"Am I correct that you rode here on one of those shafts of light? I would like to interview you for a scholarly scroll I am preparing on magic-based modes of conveyance."

Idrosun crouched to address the sorcerer (although she still loomed over him).

"Sunbeams are as easy to ride as camels, my tiny wise one. With practice, anyone can do it. The trick is to find a cloud willing to accept a hole for the light to shine through. Many clouds in Persia owe favors to the demi-goddess Abi. When I asked for a sunbeam so I could help my beloved rescue the Prince from the Frankish monster, Abi—"

"What!" The Prince reached an extremity of emotion. His transport of love transformed into righteous fury. "A monster, you say? You have insulted one for whom the very word beautiful is inadequate. Khashar, take this blue-skinned beast into custody. Requisition a sword from the palace armorer and prepare to perform your first beheading."

"Dilara cannot be your vizier, Prince," Vahid said. "Nor may you take her with you, Idrosun. I have appointed her my new Apprentice. She is to begin her training as soon as today's rites conclude."

Everyone looked on: King Alcimedes and his family, the Frankish delegation, the Holy Ones, and the flower-tossing children. The King put a thoughtful finger to his chin—he waited to see what action his son would take in this moment, and judge the boy's wisdom accordingly.

The interpreter stood next to the bridal couple. The Princess's trains—one of satin, and another of yellow roses—swirled about her. Prince Feroze faced the assembled with raised arms.

"I have discovered a solution by following the methods of the prophet Solomon, who we find in the sacred scrolls of Franks and Persians alike. Sorcerer, cut Khashar into three parts, one for each of us."

The observing King frowned. In a growing panic, Dilara looked toward the walnut grove, where the two sunbeams waited. The grove glowed intensely. Her plan to rescue the Prince had come to a disastrous turn. Nothing remained but to make a dash for freedom. Taking a deep breath, she planted a foot—at that moment Idrosun whirled and seized her arm.

"No, I must have all of her!" the Djinn cried. "Or at least the part with her perfect face."

Blue fingers reached, reached; Dilara tried to draw back.

"O Idrosun, do not touch—"

The silk veil tore free. The Djinn, who was standing in front of the mirror, had a new smear of white muck on her wrist. She gazed into the glass.

"What a lovely blue creature I am," she said. "But wait—who is that handsome figure behind me? I have just now fallen blindly and hopelessly in love with him. O my fearsome and miniature darling, come to me!"

She scooped up the sorcerer in her arms and applied her blue lips to him. Vahid squirmed and kicked his tiny limbs, to no avail.

"Do not fall in love with me, Djinn!" he shouted. "We of the wizarding profession cannot afford to lovr. Our careers must receive all our devotion."

"Heaven is smiling on you, Vahid," Prince Feroze said with satisfaction. "The Spell of Blind and Hopeless Love was your invention, and now you are receiving the proper reward for your labors."

"Apprentice!" cried the squirming Vahid. "Run to my laboratorium in the tower. Prepare a paste of chamomile, cloves, and dandelions, in the ratio two to five to six. Better toss in a chip of number-two tourmaline. Hurry, there may still be time to reverse the ointment."

"Beloved, do not fight the spell," Idrosun said between kisses. "Dilara, I countermand his order. You see, you have been fully driven from my heart. I wished for love in the Ever Dark Wood, but only now, when I saw the sorcerer in the blessed mirror, have I discovered what true love is."

Feroze had forgotten the plan to divide and share Khashar. Inspired, he made a grand announcement.

"In honor of my father's alliance with Charles Magnus, let us proclaim an annual day of love throughout the empire! Let enough barrels of Vahid's ointment be prepared so that the sacred bond of every husband and wife in Persia and our tributary lands may be renewed and sealed."

The King nodded in approval at the unexpected outbreak of wisdom from his son. Meanwhile, Idrosun tenderly positioned Vahid on his infant's stool. She beckoned to the Holy Ones.

"Come, you three. Wed me to my little dear one at once. Interpreter, ask the Princess if she will loan me her veil for the rite."

The Holy Ones gathered their black robes about them and cowered.

"These are Heaven's emissaries," Vahid pointed out. "They are not permitted to join such as us, a Djinn and sorcerer, in holy union."

"No? Very well, I shall return to the Ever Dark Wood and fetch the demi-goddess Abi. She is several aeons in age and therefore outranks mere Holy Ones. She naturally will consent to perform the rites."

And so saying, Idrosun bounded away across the sward toward the walnut grove. A moment later, the two sunbeams merged. The single shaft of light—with its rider in silhouette—moved off in the direction of Baghdad's eastern gate.

The brilliance of the light left Dilara momentarily blinded. Bright darkness swam in her eyes. When she could see again, she found herself before the brass-framed wedding mirror. Do not look in the mirror! she sternly reminded herself—as she looked in it. A face appeared behind her and over her shoulder. The face was beaming and blissful. And above it lay a gold circlet and orange turkey feather—

Poor Dilara! The greedy Spell of Blind and Hopeless Love, which had an appetite of its own, had its third victim of the day.

12. A Suitable Reward

"And so, Majesty," I said, "the first part of the Queen Consort's story draws to an end."

"We are satisfied. Feroze finally fell in love with the Frankish Princess even if it took magic." His Highness's eyes were closed, but of course he was awake and paying attention. Next to him, atop the silk coverlets, Scheherazade slept soundly. "A son's duty is to love the one his father chooses for him. Thus the realm will be assured of descendants of appropriate blood, and the father's sacred line will be extended."

A candle in the corner of the royal bedchamber guttered. Shadows slid across the bed and elephant; the shadows broke and re-formed. The moon, making its nightly slow fall to earth, stood bright in the open window.

"But tell me," his Highness continued, "who ended up with Dilara? Was it Vahid or Feroze or Idrosun?"

More rapid inventions.

"None of them, O King. You see, at a feast that very night to honor the newlyweds, King Alcimedes quizzed Dilara at length on the details of her attempt to rescue his son from the wedding. At first, he was angry at her presumption, but he was a great believer in love. When he considered that the failed rescue had led the Djinn to fall in love with the royal sorcerer, he gave Dilara his wholehearted forgiveness. In fact, he instructed both Vahid and Feroze to formally release the girl from service, and further, that she receive an official Parchment of Appreciation, with royal seal, suitable for framing.

"'O Khashar,' Feroze told Dilara before she took her leave from the palace, 'I will never forget your faithfulness and devotion. Although you are returning now to your magical realm in the Ragged Quarter, remember that your release lasts only until Father passes to the next world and I come into my royal powers. Be waiting for the day when you receive word from me. Then you will return to the palace and begin your training as my vizier.'

"Because of the ointment and the unfortunate glance in the wedding mirror, Dilara had fallen blindly and hopelessly in love with the Prince. She knew a commoner from the Ragged Quarter could never hope for love from the heir to the Persian throne, yet how painful it was to have to leave him—

"And so, spilling tears on her Official Parchment of Appreciation, she rode home in a carriage with furnishings of brass and silver, and seats lined with satin and velvet. The King's prized white Arabian mares pulled the carriage, and a uniformed driver in boots and gloves of white mouse skin drove the mares. (Once the carriage reached the Ragged Quarter, of course, Dilara had to walk the rest of the way, since the poverty and smells would have offended the Arabians.)

"Having lost his Apprentice, Vahid had to be satisfied with the continued services of long-suffering Parsi. But of more immediate concern was his imminent matrimony. After Idrosun left, the sorcerer spent endless hours in his laboratorium searching for counter-spells to Blind and Hopeless Love, his own creation. Perhaps a paste of ground-up marjoram leaves and oil of camphor—?

"As she had promised, Idrosun returned to the palace, accompanied by a talking owl which she introduced as a great Holy One of the woods, fully authorized to perform the rites of union for Djinns and sorcerers. Vahid coated his face with the marjoram-camphor paste and allowed the Djinn to plant a multitude of kisses on him. The counter-spell proved malodorous and useless.

"Idrosun proudly displayed her wedding veil for the royal family; she had woven it herself, from ferns, ivy, and oak leaves. King Alcimedes ordered a great banquet prepared in honor of the happy couple-to-be. Even Vahid's friend from the college of magic in Babylon flew in from Alexandria on his magic carpet to attend. Songs were sung, and toasts drunk.

"At last, the joyful day arrived. The Holy Ones, charged with administering the holy rites, waited by the wedding arch in their hooded black cloaks and glittering gold chains.

"But where was the prospective groom? Slaves went to fetch him from his laboratorium or scrollarium or wherever he had hidden, but they returned empty-handed. Parties of guards went to check every corner of the palace, but these also came back without the tiny royal sorcerer.

"Indeed, it was as though Vahid had disappeared from the very face of the—"

King Shahryar interrupted. (This was fortunate, as my inventions were running out.)

"The Djinn's father must have already passed to the next world. Had he been alive, he surely would have made a more proper match for her. Well, we have a feeling Vahid will turn up again before this story is over. We will learn his fate in time. For now, we have one further observation to offer.

"An official Parchment of Appreciation is a fine gift to bestow on a commoner, but in this case, King Alcimedes surely owed Dilara an even greater reward. She rendered invaluable service to all on the day of the wedding. And by offering Prince Feroze a way to escape marrying Princess Maria Irena, she gave him the opportunity to prove his nobility by refusing."

I found myself unexpectedly charmed by the suggestion.

"But Majesty, how would he reward her?" I asked. "What sort of gift would be suitable?"

"A bag of ostrich eggs, of course," he said. "After all, her father loved them so."

A moment later the King of the Age issued a snore, praise Heaven. I slipped out of the royal bedchamber very quietly.

SCROLL TWO:

THE SORCERER
WHO BECAME AN ANGEL

13. *The Prospect, a Summons, and the Will of Heaven*

Scheherazade picked up the sweating pitcher and refilled my goblet.

"This must be what the Angels drink." I sipped contentedly. From the courtyard beyond the window came shouting, arguing, and braying.

"They would, if they had to endure a summer in Baghdad," she answered. "But it's only water with honey and slices of cucumber and lemon."

"But these clear floating chunks—how cold and delicious they are."

"I bought them from a Turkish trader. He was in the Zagros mountains looking for copper and instead discovered water in solid form. He mined the chunks and brought them here to court to sell for the unholy price of ten darics the bag. Copper would have been cheaper. Shall I have him bring a few bags to your chambers? He—but Ariana, what's the matter?"

I tried to blink away my sudden tears. But I couldn't hide anything from Scheherazade.

"I can't afford luxuries like that." My worries spilled out. "Ali-Haram cut my allowance for food and expenses. I rarely see him in our chambers anymore, and when I do, he's in a foul mood. And whenever he thinks I'm not looking, he's studying a certain parchment. He groans and holds his head in his hands."

"This is very alarming to hear, Ariana."

"Do you think he's seeing another woman? Maybe he started drinking again. Scheherazade, what am I going to do?"

More noise came from the courtyard. She got up from the divan and went to the window. Two sealed tablets (with royal seal) sat on brass pedestals there: one documented that Ali-Haram and I were joined in holy union, and the other certified my legal status as a free woman. Scheherazade pulled aside the thin silk curtain—a regiment of flies invaded as she did so—and looked out.

"The men are racing asses." She took the fan from the corner and swept circles through the still air. The flies, loyal subjects who respected the Queen Consort's authority, retreated back into the heat. "It's all they care about this summer. They look ridiculous. If only they could be content themselves to race horses, or even camels. The royal physician said he has run out of plaster to splint the broken bones."

She came back to the divan and sat beside me.

"Ariana, my advice is to be loving and watchful, for now. Let me snoop around before you start asking questions." She patted my hand. "But listen, Shahryar returned to Baghdad today. He's been away inspecting his troops in Damascus. That means I'm back to storytelling tonight. Do you have the next chapter ready?"

"I finished it this morning—alone, I'm sorry to say. Ali-Haram did not write a word. But to my shame, I am the only free woman at court who can't read or write. I have the chapter memorized, though. Are you ready to copy? Ali-Haram's inkhorn and parchment are around here somewhere—"

"I'm not going to write anything down either. You tell the story to me, and I'll commit it to memory. Do begin."

Scheherazade refilled our goblets with the Water of Angels.

"Dilara was rushing through—"

*

Dilara was rushing through her weaving, as usual.

She was making a bed hat, or possibly a washing-up cloth. Cross the warp, go through the loop, pull up—the Dream Interpreter insisted that weaving was a necessary skill for a girl. But Dilara had little patience for warps and wefts. She wanted to be outdoors. She wanted to run and shout and play games. Every day, as soon as the Cobbler and Dream Interpreter retired for their midday doze, Dilara would slip into a ragged tunic, put on her green turban, and smear her face with dirt. Then she would go out on the Ragged Quarter streets, disguised as the boy Khashar.

But today it was well past nap time, and her parents were still dashing about their dwelling place, straightening, dusting, tidying. (Being poor, they had little to tidy, and so tidied it repeatedly.) Dilara laid down her weaving.

"Dear mama and papa, why are you cleaning everything over and over? Is a guest coming?"

The Cobbler was a shrunken, white-haired man. A scar, faded to nut-brown, ran from temple to temple.

"Dilara, you are now ten years and five." His eyesight was poor; he squinted and gestured at the other side of the room while he spoke to her. "The time has come for you to be joined in holy union to a good boy."

"Your papa and I have met with the Matchmaker," the Dream Interpreter said. Silver spirals covered her thin blue headscarf. Like the Cobbler, she had a long scar across her face. Her eyes had no whites, but rather pools of dull red. "She will be here any moment, with the suitable candidate she promised."

"Other girls your age are already producing grandchildren for their parents to dandle on their knees," the Cobbler added.

Dilara did not know any girls her age, or any age, for they too had to stay at home to practice their weaving.

A call drifted in from the street:

"O Cobbler and Dream Interpreter! It is I, Baghdad's number one Matchmaker. I have brought a superior candidate for your inspection."

As with most dwelling places in the Ragged Quarter, a patched woolen rug hung over the vaulted opening that gave onto the street. A willow pole stood in the corner; one used it to draw back the rug-curtain. While the Cobbler fumbled about for the pole, the Dream Interpreter steered Dilara toward the dwelling's back chamber. Behind two sleeping mats lay a battered wooden chest, and inside the chest were the family's meager possessions.

"In here," the Dream Interpreter said, "you will find a gown of white silk, with matching veil. I wore that very gown when your father and I wed. Put it on now. To save time, I will brush your hair for you."

The gown was silk only in the Dream Interpreter's foggy memories. And if the wool had ever been white, time and wear had turned it to a dingy yellow. Dilara struggled to tug the gown over her hips; the sleeves pulled uncomfortably across her shoulders.

"What a lovely girl you are." The dim-sighted Dream Interpreter ran the hairbrush down her daughter's arm. "What a bride-price you will fetch. What wonderful grandchildren you will bear. Of course, there are things you should know. If you want to have a baby girl, find a rose bush over which a white-necked stork has flown, and dig under it one foot down. For a baby boy, the stork should have an orange neck, and you should do the digging two feet down, in a melon patch. Or wait, is it the other way round—?"

(This information did not strictly accord with what Dilara's Ragged Quarter playmates often talked about with knowing laughter.)

Dilara permitted herself a moment's daydream: the Matchmaker's candidate before her, on bended knee. (The white silk wedding gown fits her perfectly and flatteringly.) A golden circlet rests on the candidate's respectfully lowered head. The candidate rises. He bows to her with a noble flourish. His swirling robes are of the finest purple silk. His beauty dazzles like the sun. An orange turkey feather sticks up jauntily behind the circlet. The Cobbler and Dream Interpreter gasp to realize that their only daughter's intended is none other than Prince Feroze, eldest son of King Alcimedes and heir to the throne of all Persia—

"There, you are all ready." The Dream Interpreter sighed happily. "O my child, how wonderful true love is. How happy you will be."

Dilara's daydream faded.

Could four years have passed since the time she had ridden a sunbeam, had her wishes granted by a Djinn, and suffered under a spell that left her blindly and hopelessly in love with Prince Feroze?

"Mama, what if an ordinary girl fell in love with a Prince? Do you think he could ever love her back?"

"Do not be foolish. You are a poor girl from the Ragged Quarter. No Prince will ever know you are alive, much less fall in love with you."

"Come, Dilara!" the Cobbler called. "Meet the boy who is destined to father my many grandchildren."

"It is time," the Dream Interpreter said. "Lower your eyes respectfully."

Dilara studied the freshly swept earthen floor as she followed her mother.

"Ah, and here comes the prospective bride!" the Matchmaker chirped. "Quite a beauty beneath the veil, I understand. Excellent complexion, upturned nose, and so forth. And, I understand, quite skilled at weaving."

Dilara sneaked an upward glance—and nearly collapsed in shock.

Standing before her, tugging at his tunic collar, his hair brushed and pomaded, his face shiny from unaccustomed scrubbing, was one of her Ragged Quarter playmates—Naseem.

"Say, I know this place," candidate Naseem said, looking about. "The boy Khashar lives here."

"You are mistaken," the Cobbler said. "No Khashar lives here. Dilara is our only child."

"An understandable mistake," the Matchmaker said cheerfully. "Here in the Ragged Quarter one hovel looks quite like another."

Dilara realized that Naseem did not recognize her behind her veil. He knew only the turban-wearing, dirt-smeared boy with whom he and their friend Ghazi played during the long Baghdad afternoons. Nor, evidently, did Naseem remember her from Prince Feroze's wedding procession—of course, that meeting had been brief, and her head and face modestly covered.

In short, Naseem had no idea who his prospective bride was.

"And now you can all get acquainted." The Matchmaker prepared to make her departure. "Did I mention my daric-back guarantee that the candidate's family is largely free of criminals and unbelievers? Remember, refer a friend, and get a discount on your next match."

Naseem and Dilara's parents knelt on the prayer rug, facing each other while Dilara stood respectfully apart. The Cobbler put several questions to the candidate—what his financial prospects were, did he properly honor his parents, did he attend to his prayers. To each question the nervous Naseem gave barely a one-word answer. But then the Cobbler said:

"Tell me about your friends."

"I have many friends. In fact, I taught one of them how to ride sunbeams, although later he tried to steal a tin drainpipe, and wrongfully accused me of the crime."

Dilara held her tongue with great difficulty. She permitted herself another daydream: she is dashing past the door-curtain and into the street. No one can stop her; she is too fast. A sunbeam comes to lift her high above the Ragged Quarter. Arriving at the royal palace, she resumes her career as Apprentice to the fearsome and tiny sorcerer Vahid. There is a knock on the door of the sorcerer's laboratorium. The visitor is Prince Feroze, with his golden circlet and orange turkey feather. "The spell on me has worn off!" he cries. "I am no longer in love with the Frankish Princess Maria Irena. I am free to love you, my beloved Dilara—"

Her attentions were yanked back to her immediate situation. Negotiations for dowry and bride-price had begun. Naseem offered one eighth of a quarter-daric and once-a-month use of his new green tunic. (He had earned both prizes scattering flowers at the Prince's wedding to the Frankish Princess.) Naturally, this was only an initial proposal; no final agreement would be reached today. One did not rush such things. At last Naseem took his leave.

"Child," the Dream Interpreter said, "after you put the gown back in the chest, go out to the cracked courtyard. A sweet potato vine has come up on its own, behind the fallen column. See if it is bearing yet. If not, catch a lizard for our supper. Meanwhile your papa and I will discuss your handsome suitor."

The cracked courtyard lay behind the block where Dilara's family lived. Rocks, shards, and joints of busted flagstone formed a rough square enclosed by tumbledown walls. On one wall were words chalked years earlier by a passing scholar. Of course, no one in the Ragged Quarter could read the Farsi characters, but it was commonly accepted that the inscription was a prayer that blessed and protected the courtyard. For this reason, it was the custom of the families of the block to dine together there, in the cool evening hours.

Dilara found the sweet potato vine, and a pointed stone to dig with. No tubers were forthcoming.

What would married life be like? Would she still be able to put on her turban and boys' clothes and play outside? And (she added, with a little resentment) how could her parents wed her to a braggart and liar like Naseem?

"Are you Dilara? If so, I come bearing a message from the greatest sorcerer of our age."

Startled, Dilara jumped to her feet. She looked out over the cracked courtyard. No one was there—only a wandering ass with twitching ears and tail. The ass, gray all over save for a white muzzle, daintily stepped over weeds and trash and ant mounds, and cast large brown eyes at her.

"I have come to fetch you." The words were clear, within the ass's brays. "I, Omid, am under orders to bear you back to the royal palace. A mission of the utmost importance awaits you. This is a service for which I personally stand to earn a great reward."

A mission of the greatest importance? But that could only mean Prince Feroze was finally summoning her back to the palace to serve as his vizier—

"Then the Prince is ascending to his royal powers? King Alcimedes is near death?"

"The King die? By no means, mistress!" Hee haw. "His health is excellent; may Heaven protect him."

Dilara was relieved. At least she would not have to conduct any beheadings.

"What is this important mission, then?"

"The greatest sorcerer of our age did not share details with his lowly slave. He only said that world peace hangs in the balance."

Dilara groaned. She was a humble girl of the Ragged Quarter, but fate, which loved nothing more than a good laugh, kept inserting her into matters of state.

"This great sorcerer—you refer, of course, to Vahid?"

"Vahid?" Omid tilted her head to the side, as though deep in thought. "Where have I heard that name? It seems vaguely familiar. But no, I was sent by the sorcerer Thukamon, who hails from a distant land known as Egypt."

"There is a problem with Thukamon's plan, Omid. I am the only child of the Cobbler and Dream Interpreter. Their eyes are quite poor, and their daily lives would be difficult without me."

"Thukamon has foreseen all. After I bear you to the palace, he is going to transform me to a girl. I will, in fact, be you. That is, I am to be a girl identical to yourself in every respect. I will return here to your home, where I will take up my new life as your parents' beloved Dilara, at least until you return from your mission."

"The Cobbler and Dream Interpreter would never fall for such a deception."

But then Dilara thought about her parents' poor eyes. She remembered the Cobbler gesturing to the other side of the room while he spoke to her, and the Dream Interpreter brushing her arm instead of her hair.

And as for her soon-to-be husband Naseem, he had not even recognized her in her gown and veil. He knew only Khashar. One objection remained.

"I have not told you the worst of all, Omid. My parents have made a deal with a Matchmaker. If you become me, you will have to wed Naseem."

"Oh! Is he handsome? Rich?" The ass then lowered her head. "But of course that matters nothing. If Heaven wills that Naseem and I join in holy union, then I must submit."

14. The Happiness Seller

I set the dough on the window ledge. It was the sun's turn to work. My hands were white with flour, and my wrists ached from kneading. The sweet two-note song of a lark came from out in the corridor. The bird was Scheherazade. I returned the whistle—our private signal—so she would know that Ali-Haram was not at home, and we were free to talk.

"Ariana!" The Queen Consort stood before me, startled. "Is that a loaf rising? What will the other ladies of the palace say when they hear you do your own baking?"

"They'll say my husband has cut my household allowance again." I couldn't keep the bitterness out of my voice. "Or they will say it's another thing that sets me apart. Another reason I'm not worthy to be one of them. I may not be a slave anymore, but in their eyes, I will never be their equal. They were born to this life; I wasn't."

Scheherazade looked away. She was silent for a moment. Then: "On the matter of your allowance, I may have discovered something. Come with me."

We covered our heads and left Ali-Haram's chambers. We moved through the prayer chamber, the library, and the six-sided vestibule with its tapestries, carpets, and divans, the winding narrow passage behind the Pavilion of Slaves. This last passage opened onto an abandoned courtyard. The courtyard ended abruptly in front of a crumbling wall of mud bricks. From beyond the wall came a din of shouting and braying.

"Come on, Ariana!" There was a ragged gap halfway up the wall. A heap of rubble trailed down from the gap. Hiking her gown above her knees, Scheherazade picked her way up the rubble. "We can look out there."

The sun was playful and merciless. By the time I arrived beside her, my headscarf was dripping with sweat. I peered through the gap.

A clearing spread out, a long rutted chop of dust, sand, and earth. Everywhere men were arguing, conferring, and exchanging pieces of parchment—I recognized courtiers, palace visitors, ambassadors, royal officials. Ropes marked a pair of lines, and between these lines several donkeys were ambling, bucking, or stubbornly stopped. Their riders tugged reins and wielded switches, to little effect. A man with a silk flag waited at the end of the makeshift course.

"The ass has moved out of your story," Scheherazade said, "and into our lives."

"It doesn't make sense," I said. "What's the point of all this?"

"Money is the point, Ariana. The men are always looking for something new to wager on."

At that moment, another ass moved into view on the course. Atop this creature was a bearded man in a wide-sleeved red robe and yellow leggings.

Scheherazade was saying: "My lord husband says we women bear the blame. He says that men's minds are simple, and it is our duty to keep them occupied."

Without warning, the new ass's hind legs shot up. The bearded rider fell, landing heavily on the rutted chop. I held my breath and watched Ali-Haram struggle to a knee, then to his feet. He brushed sand from his robe, and then limped off with head bowed. The onlookers jeered.

My lord husband's mind was far from simple. I thought about our arguments over money, and the parchment he constantly pored over and frowned at. Our Holy Ones teach one may find sin and profit alike in gambling, but the sin is greater than the profit.

Ali-Haram, it was clear, was earning no profit from his sin.

*

(O Majesty, that the Matchmaker arrived at the dwelling place of the Cobbler and Dream Interpreter. She introduced her candidate, Naseem. Afterwards Dilara met the talking ass Omid, who had brought an urgent message: a sorcerer named Thukamon had summoned her for a mysterious mission, on which the fate of nations depended.)

The day after the Matchmaker's visit, as soon as the Cobbler and Dream Interpreter retired for their midday nap, Dilara dressed (this time as a girl) in her best ragged tunic, leggings, and sandals, and her least threadbare headscarf and veil. Stuffing her green turban in a pouch at her waist (just in case), she slipped out into the cracked courtyard. The ass Omid was waiting, grazing on the weeds that grew up between the stones. Dilara mounted Omid's back from a low crumbling wall, and soon girl and beast were making their slow dusty way through the Ragged Quarter.

"Bray me your story, Omid," Dilara said. "Leave out nothing. How did you gain the power of human speech? Are you a demi-goddess like my friend Abi of the Ever Dark Wood?"

"I am far from divine, I assure you, Mistress," Omid answered. "I was born on the usual bed of straw in the royal stables, to a jack and jennet, as is our way. Only yesterday I was in the pen with the other foals, learning my lessons. Advanced techniques of bucking, the seven levels of stubbornness, the philosophy of stoicism, that sort of thing. Then a grinning, bare-chested man with a blue stone in his forehead arrived at the stables. He inspected all of us closely."

Dilara swayed gently atop her mount and watched the slow passage of hovels and date palms and street vendors. Once, she caught sight of her friend Ghazi on the other side of the road. She waved—he stared back blankly. He knew Khashar, not Dilara.

"Under the visitor's arm was a shiny brass lamp, which he talked to as one might to an old friend. He said, 'Well, I suppose one ass is as good as the next. Would you not agree?' I did not hear the lamp answer. Then he looked at me and said: 'Heaven has chosen to bless you today. I am Thukamon, greatest sorcerer of our age, and henceforth, you are to be my trusted slave. Your name will be, let me see—Omid. Let me hear you say you understand.'"

"I hee-hawed in my usual way, but to my amazement, human words also issued from my mouth: 'I understand, Master. I am your slave Omid. Yours is to command, and mine to obey.'"

"'Now, Omid,' he asked, 'would you like to be a girl?'

"'What is a girl, Master?' I said.

"He grinned and said, 'Why, being a girl is far better than being an ass. You spend your life on two legs instead of four. You gather bouquets of irises and brush your beautiful hair, and handsome men fall in love with you.'"

"Omid, being a girl is so much more than these things," Dilara said. "Although in a way so much less—"

"You would not speak that way had you been born an ass. You would jump at the chance for girlhood. I especially liked the part about handsome men and falling in love. Anyway, my first mission for Thukamon is to bring you to him."

"Best be careful. To work for a sorcerer can be dangerous. I know a sorcerer who turned his own slave into a sheep as punishment for—wait, who is that?"

A man in a tattered brown robe and stained white cap was moving toward them. Every few strides the man leaped and clicked his heels. He whirled, danced, sang. The crowds on the street moved aside to let him pass. Everyone smiled at his happiness. Dilara, curious, signaled the man to stop.

"O happy man," she said, "tell me your name and where I can acquire such joy as yours."

"Why," said the man, "I am Masoud. As for joy, you need only turn on the next block. There you will see a stand with a striped blanket for an awning. At this stand is the blue-skinned merchant who sells happiness." He continued to beam and break into frequent jumps and spins.

His words left Dilara dumbfounded.

"Sir, my ears may have played a trick on me. Did you say 'blue-skinned?'"

"Why yes, I did. Strange, come to think of it." Another heel-click.

"Did this blue merchant happen to be bald, except for a long braided pink top knot?"

"Now that you mention it."

"O Masoud, what form did this happiness take, and what price did the merchant charge?"

"I will tell you, but first listen to my story. The name Masoud means fortunate and happy—was any man ever so misnamed? An excruciating growth has taken root in my belly. A wise woman examined me and said I had two years left to live. I am a very great sinner, and for this reason fear passing from this world.

"Thus you may guess that I desperately wanted to cheat the growth in me, and thus cling to sweet life. When I told this to the blue merchant, she offered to sell me the very greatest happiness, for ten darics. Ten darics—a life's fortune! I borrowed and mortgaged all I had to produce such an amount. After paying, I own nothing but the clothes on my back. But the happiness seller guaranteed that in exactly two years, less one day, the growth in me will miraculously dissolve. And then I, Masoud, will live out my time in the fullness of health. What a blessed world we live in, that has blue-skinned happiness sellers."

Masoud resumed his joyous progress down the street.

"Let us visit this mysterious merchant," Omid brayed. "Soon Thukamon will transform me into my Dilara-self. How wonderful it would be for a tall, dark, and handsome man to fall in love with me. We will ask the merchant what this would cost. Can you imagine a greater happiness, Mistress?"

"It is natural to want one's wishes fulfilled," Dilara said. "But who has ten darics to give to a swindler? Still, I agree. Let us pay a visit to the blue-skinned merchant."

Ass and girl continued on their way. They passed a stand where fish and goat skewers sizzled on charcoal braziers.

"How hungry I am," Dilara said with a sigh. "If only this Thukamon who sent you had remembered to send along money."

"The greatest sorcerer of our age predicted your needs. Look in the cloth bag that hangs across my right flank, mistress. You will not find any darics there, but there are dried carp, dried dates, and dried leeks."

"Is there anything that is not dried?" Dilara reached behind her for the bag.

"When I complete my mission and become you, I will taste the delights of dried leeks for myself. For now, I will take a handful of oat straw, which you will find packed in a layer beneath the dried carp."

When Dilara and her mount reached the next block, a familiar voice called out.

"Dilara, formerly known as Khashar!" Under a striped awning strung on four rickety poles, a merchant waved her braided pink top knot in greeting. "Greetings!"

"Greetings, Idrosun," Dilara said. For of course, the happiness seller was none other than the former Djinn of the Ever Dark Wood.

"Ah, Dilara," Idrosun said with a heartfelt sigh. "How I loved you, forever and with all my heart, until by chance I viewed the foot-tall sorcerer in the wedding mirror."

"A girl and Djinn alike may become victims of the Spell of Blind and Hopeless Love. To think, Vahid's spell proved even more powerful than the wish for love you granted yourself in the Ever Dark Wood."

"Ah, Vahid, Vahid! The very name is like honey on my lips." Idrosun heaved a sigh of longing. "When I think of all the ways I have tried to win his heart. I spoke words of love. I prepared special dishes, such as braised slugs in poplar leaves, and bat wings in pond water broth. But for some reason my lovely blue skin did not attract him. Truly, Dilara, to love is to suffer."

Dilara decided that stern words were in order.

"And so, spurned by your would-be lover, you turned to fraud? Taking ten darics from Masoud, that poor man with an incurable growth? Letting him think that magic will make him well? You know very well you have no powers outside the Ever Dark Wood. You should be ashamed."

Idrosun's eyes welled with tears.

"O Dilara, how can you scold me so? I gave Masoud the greatest bargain any man ever received. For the next two years, less one day, he will live in the joy that the painful growth will not kill him."

"But the next day after that, he will die. You sold him a false hope."

"I did not pretend to sell him a cure," Idrosun answered virtuously. "I sold him happiness, which is a bargain at any price. But let us not argue. Tell me about yourself. Is all well with your home and family?"

Dilara told of her imminent betrothal to Naseem.

"If only I could find in my heart the love I once had for you," Idrosun said sadly. "I would find this Naseem and give him a good thrashing with my top knot."

"Make it just a mild thrashing," Omid hee-hawed. "When Thukamon transforms me into an exact copy of Dilara, Naseem will be all mine. His handsome body must not be too bruised and battered."

"I will thrash no one," Idrosun said. "This is because I no longer love Dilara. The fearsome and adorable sorcerer Vahid has won my heart forever."

Dilara turned Omid toward the street.

"O Idrosun, I wish you fortune as you pursue your new career," she said in farewell. "But remember, it is wrong to sell false promises and call them happiness."

Idrosun said sadly, "Between those two, is there really such a difference?"

*

We sat on stools in Ali-Haram's library. Scheherazade picked up something from a wooden stand.

"Ariana, what is this? It is like parchment, but different. Thicker, and not as smooth."

"Ali-Haram calls it Paper. He says it's a marvel of our modern age."

"Hmm—the Paper has a poem on it. And here is the eye drawn at the bottom, so we know it's your husband's work. I'm glad to see him writing new verses."

"Read it to me?"

I watched Scheherazade's eyes move down the Paper. She frowned.

"Are you sure? I think it's about your household allowance, in a way." But I nodded, and so she read:

> "'My tunics and vests and sandals
> Have weight and cannot rise from the shelf.
> The lily and croton and rose
> Have weight and cannot rise from their ledge pots.
> The eggplant and bread and peaches
> Have weight and cannot rise from the table.
> The gold darics in my purse have weight,
> And yet, like birds, they rise on wings.
> Upon me lies some heavy curse;
> My money seeks another's purse.'"

O lord husband! Your money is seeking another's purse, and I am doing my own baking—

15. A Vow of Infant-Talk and the Sorcerers' Code of Ethics

(Highness, recall from last night that the sorcerer Thukamon summoned Dilara to the palace. Along the way there, borne by the talking ass Omid, Dilara met Idrosun, who was no longer Djinn of the Ever Dark Wood, but was earning remarkable profits selling happiness.)

Night drew its cloak over Baghdad. A necklace of stars hung from the black throat of sky. The spires, domes, and pavilions of the palace came into the travelers' view.

"The royal stables lie on the other side of the walnut grove," Omid brayed. "Let us go there straight away. O Mistress, how excited I am. My transformation is at hand. I will be an ass no more. I will be you, and your Naseem will be mine."

But Omid (Dilara thought) if you become me, who will I be? If two Dilaras walk the earth, which is the true one? Fate was laughing at her again.

(On the other hand, the prospect of someone standing in for her as Naseem's bride was not without its attractions—)

The two came to a low, rambling structure of cypress timbers and red stone blocks. The fenced-in yard stood empty, save for a barefoot slave who was applying a rake to the soft dirt and sifting out gravel that might offend the royal hooves. A pair of guards sat on wicker stools next to a gate of tin crossbars.

"Oho, the talking ass has returned," one of the guards said. "Hee haw, hee haw!"

"I advise you to show politeness," Omid said with a bray. "I will soon wed the strong and protective Naseem. I hate to think of what he would do if he found out you treated me with disrespect."

"Let them through," the other guard advised. "Best not risk Thukamon's displeasure. You saw what happened to Vahid."

Dilara started to ask the guards what had, in fact, happened to her former Master, but when the gate swung open, the impatient Omid bore her inside without delay. The stables smelled of hay, manure, and leather tack. The stalls, each beneath a mounted candle box, were built of polished oak, with brass fittings. Heads poked curiously over the stall doors: sorrels, chestnuts, and the King's prized white Arabians with their noble flaring nostrils.

Beyond these stalls was a filthy pen enclosed by a rusted iron gate. Here asses crowded before a filthy trough.

"To think, only yesterday I was one of them, lapping at that same brown water," Omid reflected. "As usual, horses get the best of everything. They are fed first, and the curry combs used on them have bone handles. This explains their arrogance. Horses have great status in the animal kingdom, higher than asses. But when I become a girl, my status will be greater. This is another reason I look forward to being you, Mistress. Use that bell rope to signal our arrival to Thukamon."

The rope hung from a ceiling beam. Dilara slid off Omid's back and gave the rope a tug. A bell sounded in the distance.

"Something puzzles me," Dilara said. "Why did your master choose me, of all girls in Persia, for his mission?"

"I only know that world peace depends on it."

"Gu Gu." A voice caused Dilara to turn. Before her stood a boy in a vest of purple silk, purple leggings, and leather sandals. His black hair fell to his shoulders in fancy ringlets. The boy stamped his foot. "Gu Gu!"

"Mind your manners, urchin." Omid stamped her hoof. "You happen to be Gu Gu-ing a great lady, who will soon be in the service of the greatest sorcerer of our age, namely Thukamon."

"Gu Gu." The boy gave another foot-stamp and an unimpressed shrug.

"Let us act properly toward all strangers, Omid," Dilara said in mild reproof. "Heaven is pleased by good manners."

Then, to the boy:

"I am Dilara, from the Ragged Quarter. The ass is Omid. We are pleased to meet you. What is your name?"

"Gu Gu. Gu Gu." The boy appeared incapable of saying anything else.

"I am aged ten and five years," Dilara said. "How old are you?"

The boy spread the fingers of one hand and added four fingers of the other. His lips worked, parting, closing, parting. He clearly had important things to say but could not remember how to move his tongue.

Then, unexpectedly, words spilled from him.

"O Dilara, I never mewled as an infant. I did not begin to speak or make words when expected. My family and tutors concluded that I was simple. They despised me as useless, irrelevant, a burden on the family. I sensed their loathing and loathed them back. Now all call me Gu Gu, because I took a vow to make only infant-talk until I met someone who addressed me with respect and solicitude. Today, I have met that one, and for you alone I hereby suspend my vow."

Dilara was amazed by this speech from a boy of only five years and four.

"But who are your parents, Gu Gu? What is your true name? Where do you live?"

"Why, my name is—but we can speak of all that another time." Gu Gu's voice was boyishly high, and yet he spoke with a natural-seeming authority. "For now, I wish to be of service to you. I overheard you refer to undertaking a mission for Thukamon. This mission doubtless has to do with the unfortunate events involving the late Maria Irena. Ah, I see surprise on your face. You have not heard the news. The Princess has departed our world of sorrows. A tragedy. Well, you can guess the diplomatic implications."

"Omid said that world peace depends on my mission."

Dilara thought about the Frankish Princess from Prince Feroze's wedding five years earlier—the blue eyes, the milky-white skin, the ankle-length mane of yellow roses. She remembered the impassioned declaration of love Feroze had made to his bride after viewing her in the wedding mirror.

The memory caused Dilara a most painful stab of jealousy, and she comforted herself with a moment's daydream: the handsome and dashing Prince, standing next to the wedding arch with its silk draperies. The turkey feather sticks up jauntily from his circlet. He grieves as Angels arrive to bear away poor Maria Irena. But then he looks anew into the wedding mirror. He views Dilara. The Spell of Blind and Hopeless Love still lies upon him. At once, she captures his heart. His father, his mother, the fearsome sorcerer Vahid, the Holy Ones, the Franks, and the Ragged Quarter children all watch as he begins a noble, impassioned love-speech to her—

Footsteps sounded from beyond the doorway of the stables. The blind and hopeless daydream vanished.

"The greatest sorcerer of our age is on his way." Omid kicked her hind legs excitedly. "O Mistress, soon I will see with your eyes and speak with your tongue. And it will not be long till I am kissing dear Naseem with your lips. I shall know the delights of love, with your heart."

"When it comes to making agreements with Thukamon, I would advise caution," Gu Gu said. "He is exceedingly cunning, and I have heard that—but here he comes now. I will speak no more, for I am Gu Gu."

And so saying, the boy plopped cross-legged onto the tiled floor and occupied himself with the construction of arabesques from the loose straw.

The approaching personage wore a white linen wrap from waist to knees. A stone of blue topaz was set into his forehead. His dark skin shone with oil. His headdress was in the shape of a serpent, and black gemstones studded the straps of his leather sandals. He carried a polished brass lamp under his arm. Grinning, he held the lamp to his ear and pretended to listen to it. Then he made the slightest of bows.

"You are Dilara, then. I am Thukamon. You were recommended to me for a mission on which world peace depends."

"Greetings, sir," Dilara answered politely. "Are you the one who won five feet from Vahid in a wager?"

This caused bubbly laughter to issue from the sorcerer.

"Yes, my old friend is quite unlucky when it comes to the science of betting. He would greet you himself, but he is, let us say, indisposed. As for his height, I gave it back to him in a gesture of goodwill, not that it is of much use to him anymore." More laughter.

Omid lowered her head and gave Thukamon's knee a nudge.

"Master," she brayed, "I have fulfilled my mission. I brought Dilara to you. Now fulfill your promise to transform me into a girl; specifically, her."

"Later; do not interrupt," Thukamon said sharply. He turned to Dilara, still grinning. He held his fingers in a diamond before his eyes, as though inspecting her through a glass. "Hmm—lighten the skin, blue the eyes, shorten the spine. Heavier in the belly. Minor shifts in the facial planes. The roses, of course. Not overly difficult. I could do it blindfolded, and perhaps will, for the challenge."

As Dilara listened, her alarm grew. In her (admittedly brief) experience, sorcerers were constantly performing transformations—Vahid's slave Parsi into a sheep, Omid into a girl—and now she herself was to have blue eyes and shifted facial planes?

"O Thukamon," she said, lowering her eyes respectfully, "first tell me the details of this important mission, so I may choose whether to accept it, and whether to submit to a transformation."

"No," Omid brayed stubbornly, "first transform me into Dilara, as you promised."

"I will turn you into a scorpion if you interrupt me again. The girl's transformation is more important than yours." Thukamon's voice flashed with anger, although his grin never wavered. His face seemed fixed in expression. He turned back to Dilara. "There is no question of your accepting or not accepting. The King himself authorized Vahid to execute the mission. I am acting as Vahid's proxy and have a seal to that effect. Do your duty, and you will receive a reward. We need say no more on the subject."

Gu Gu looked up with a scowl. He opened his mouth, as though about to make a retort on Dilara's behalf. But then, no doubt remembering his vow of infant-talk, he resolutely closed his lips and returned to his straw arabesques. Was the scowl meant for Thukamon or her—or both? Dilara found herself desiring the approval of the strange, strong-willed child.

The Cobbler had taught her that an act of courage often required one to first fill the lungs fully. She took a very deep breath and faced Thukamon squarely.

"O greatest sorcerer of our age, I must ask you again. Tell me the circumstances of my mission, and the nature of my reward. Leave nothing out. Then, if I refuse to take on the mission, you may do as you will with me, even if it is to take away several feet of my height."

She spoke more courageously than she felt. Her heart pounded; her mouth was dry. Thukamon gazed at her in grinning silence for a long moment. Then:

"I see why you come recommended for this mission. You own the trait of bravery, which might prove useful. Very well, I will explain.

"The Prince and his bride recently celebrated four years of holy union. Feroze announced that the Princess was at last with child. A great celebration was planned, with feasts and festivities. The Frankish delegation even returned to be part of the happiness. There was a reenactment and renewal of the wedding rites. It was the height of the Persian summer, and the day was hot and bright. Sun sickness struck down the Princess. The blood in her veins reached a fatal boil. In short, she passed from our world.

"The Franks requested the body, but the Holy Ones ruled against them. The Franks are unbelievers. The bride of a Persian noble may not be buried with the rites of infidels.

"Outraged, the delegation left Baghdad to make its long journey home. Once Charles Magnus learns what has taken place, he will doubtless end his alliance with Alcimedes. He may even declare war on Persia. His army has already conquered much of Europe.

"To complicate matters, the grief-stricken Feroze has left the city in the company of the Franks. He intends to offer his own head to Charles Magnus in place of his bride's body—well, everyone knows how impulsive and willful the Prince can be. But he is the King's heir. We must find him and bring him safely back.

"This, then, is the mission. You and I will leave at first light. When we overtake the delegation—my magic carpet is swift, and the journey will not take long—the Prince will be overjoyed to see you alive."

Dilara's heart fluttered at the thought of being with Prince Feroze—but she was confused. Why should the Prince be happy to see her?

But then she remembered Thukamon mentioning the "blue eyes" and "yellow roses" and "heavier belly." The answer was growing clear.

"Of course, not speaking a word of the Frankish tongue, you will only smile and act as Feroze's loving wife. I will do all the talking. You will say nothing whatsoever. I will explain that I cured you with my great powers, but the sun sickness mysteriously took away your ability to speak. Your miraculous recovery will keep the alliance between Alcimedes and Charles Magnus intact. We will preserve world peace. And as for your reward—well, what do you want?"

What did she want! Dilara remembered the wishes she had made in the Ever Dark Wood. She had asked the Djinn Idrosun for hot funnel cakes and a white pony and silver hair—of course, these wishes had come from the middle or top of her heart. Then she thought about the Dream Interpreter using a hairbrush on her arm, and the Cobbler looking at the other side of the room when he talked to her. A new wish welled up from the bottom of her heart.

"Many years ago, when Mama and Papa were courting, they both suffered terrible accidents to their sight. For my reward, I wish them to receive new eyes."

"Is that all? Nothing could be easier." Thukamon grinned and bowed. "Very well, your reward is settled, and therefore so is our bargain."

But deception was a sin. If only she could talk to the Cobbler and Dream Interpreter. Did the fate of nations outweigh violating the holy teachings?

But she had no more time to consider her dilemma, for Thukamon was already raising the lamp and tilting it, as though pouring invisible oil on her head. The blue topaz in his forehead glowed. The links in the lamp chain clinked, and the shiny brass sent sparkles into the light issuing from the mounted candle boxes.

Dilara's skin goose-pimpled from the cold of the invisible oil. Her heart and breath took on subtly different rhythms. There was an overwhelming fragrance of roses. Gu Gu watched with widened eyes. Omid twitched her tail excitedly.

Afterwards, Thukamon held the lamp before Dilara. A new girl gazed back at her from the polished brass surface: short, plump, with close-set blue eyes. A mane of yellow roses sprang from her head.

"I must say, you are some of my best work." Thukamon congratulated himself. "Now, as for you, my impatient ass—"

The topaz glowed again. Thukamon tilted the lamp above Omid's muzzle, forelock, and croup. The ass's ears shortened, the toes turned to hooves, the back rose and straightened. In short, Dilara stood before herself.

"Now go straight away to the Ragged Quarter," Thukamon directed. "Take up your new life as the daughter of the Cobbler and Dream Interpreter until the day Dilara returns, should that day happen to come."

Omid stroked her new hair, touched her new nose, kicked up her uncloven heels.

"I will soon be the handsome Naseem's blushing bride!" Hee haw.

"O mighty Thukamon," Dilara said (her tongue and lips felt quite different), "listen to Omid. She is still braying. You, the greatest sorcerer of our age, must give her a proper girl's voice."

"Yes, the larynx does sound unmodified. A small defect in the lamp." He cupped his chin in thought. "I will do the next best thing."

He touched the lamp spout to Omid's lips.

"Hee haw," Omid said. This hee-haw was the sound of a common ass; Dilara could detect no human speech whatsoever within it.

"But now what have you done to her?" Dilara cried. "How will she talk to my parents? What will she say to Naseem when she weds him?"

"Quite little, I think." More bubbly laughter. "I would advise her to silence, which doubtless will please her new husband."

Omid, still dancing and hee-hawing and skipping about, did not appear overly concerned with her larynx. Dilara imparted some final advice to her.

"The Cobbler will threaten to beat you for having been out so late, but do not worry about this. His eyesight is quite poor. But if you happen to come across some ostrich eggs, bring them for his breakfast."

With a last skip and bray, Omid disappeared into the night. The royal stables were alive with noise: whinnies, whickers, and snorts from the stalls of the horses, brays of all pitches from the ass pen, squeaks from the mice scurrying across the hay-strewn tiles—now a new sound made its appearance. This sound was best described as: baa baa.

Dilara looked at the sheep with its wide-set black eyes, ears a-flare, pink nose, and pink tongue sticking out. The brown fleece smelled of earth and grass. Human words intertwined with the bleats:

"Greetings, Dilara, otherwise known as Khashar. Well, we have both changed. You are pale and have gained weight. And what have you done to your hair? Still, I recognize your essence. Surely you remember your old friend Parsi, slave of the fearsome sorcerer Vahid?"

"Is it truly you!" Dilara said. "Why are you a sheep again? Did you annoy your Master?"

"I will relate my sad story," Parsi answered. "Vahid's latest project is the invention of wearable wings. He sent me to the Tigris to gather swan feathers, which are the airworthiest in the natural world, but the swans put up an unexpected fight. Exceedingly difficult and taxing work. When I finished, I took a well-earned snooze on the bank. But a sudden storm came up. I awoke to find the swan feathers fouled. They needed time to dry. Well, this set Vahid's experiments back, and he lost his temper. He threatened to transform me into a springtail or water strider, which I understand are common swan snacks. In the end, taking mercy, he sentenced me to two years as a sheep. It is not that bad a life, but now Vahid has disappeared. No one knows where he is. If we do not find him, I could remain a sheep to the end of my days."

"O Thukamon, turn Parsi back into a man," Dilara said. "This is my final condition for undertaking your mission."

The sorcerer grinned.

"Alas, only the sorcerer who performs a transformation can undo it. This is our code of ethics."

He gave Dilara her instructions: she was to proceed to the palace windcatcher tower and climb to the sixth floor, where she would find the unlocked private chambers of the mysteriously vanished Vahid. She was to spend the night on the divan there, being careful not to touch anything or enter his laboratorium. At first light, she was to go out on the balcony, where Thukamon would come for her on his magic carpet.

"Hmm—I think I could use those wearable wings you spoke of, Parsi." Gu Gu found his voice once Thukamon departed. (He could converse with Parsi, who was a ruminant.) "Let us search Vahid's chambers. With such a device I could follow the magic carpet at a discreet distance. We should not trust the grinning Thukamon. Our holy book teaches that to smile is to spread love, but when a man has no other expression, is it love he spreads, or distrust?"

16. The Usefulness of a Pure Heart

The first ass bucked. The rider fell sprawling in the dust. The second ass, seeing this, abruptly went down rump-first. Its rider, reaching too late to seize the floppy ears, tumbled off, tangled in the legs of the first rider. The third ass kicked in circles, chasing a horsefly on its flank. Its rider landed on the other two. Lined on both sides of the track, barefoot boys in patched tunics and worn skull caps hooted. They taunted and jeered their fallen comrades.

Meanwhile the fourth ass made a slow, steady progress toward the judge with his silk flag. I sat under a muslin awning and studied the rider.

The brown curls escaping the skull cap. The hawk-like eyes and full lips. The look of utter resolve as he headed for the finish line. The boy with whom I was forbidden to talk.

"What's all this foolishness, Ariana?" The veiled Queen Consort slid onto the wicker stool beside me. "Isn't it enough that the men have lost their heads? Now you're getting boys involved in this ass racing too?"

"Look, Scheherazade, my Emre's going to win."

"I thought his name was Merdad now. Hmm—I notice he's riding that brown jennet with the white dapple, who wins every race, no matter who is riding her."

"A coincidence," I lied. I handed her a coin. "Here is the prize. You make the presentation."

"And I suppose this came from your reduced household allowance? Didn't you lose your temper at your own husband for trying to give the boy money that day in the carriage?"

"These are all poor boys from the Ragged Quarter. I promised them cash awards. Besides, Ali-Haram restored my allowance."

Another lie. I saw the disbelief on Scheherazade's face, but she chose not to answer.

The jennet crossed the line. The judge waved his flag. The crowd of boys cheered. Emre slid off the ass's back and clasped his hands over his head. Then he approached the two veiled ladies who were presiding over the games—Scheherazade and me. He knelt before us while the Queen Consort improvised a speech.

"As swift as time itself rode thou yon steed. In the names of Sindbad, Aladdin, Idrosun, Dilara, Vahid, and the King of Persia, I award thee this prize of one daric."

Did Emre know who Scheherazade and I were? Did he suspect I was the same woman in the silver headdress who had observed him from the carriage? He looked directly at me—I felt my heart pound—but he made no sign of recognition. Then he turned and joined his companions as they filed noisily out of the courtyard.

Scheherazade's reproach had not been solely on account of the money. It was her way of reminding me that, under Ali-Haram's bargain with the foster mother, I was to have no contact with the boy.

O Scheherazade, how can I make you understand? The child was taken away from me in the hour of his birth. Ten years passed before I saw him again. I have never held him, never fed him, never watched over him while he slept. Not a single word has passed between us. Whose heart is strong enough to bear such pain?

*

I was on my way to the royal bedchamber when a new thought suddenly seized me. I grasped the cool brass rail of the staircase, trying to find my breath. The idea was enormous and terrifying.

It was a way to pay off my husband's debts.

I thought about the whirlwind—how it swoops up brush and leaves and dust, and even fish from the river. It throws everything before it violently into the air, to toss and spin for leagues before landing in some entirely new place.

I had a whirlwind of my own in mind. It would upend my life. It would upend Ali-Haram's life. But the guilt and shame might break him of his gambling disease.

I knew how to send that whirlwind.

But—did I have the courage?

*

(O Majesty—I began, as Scheherazade lay on a stack of cushions, having decided to keep showing off my memory for King Shahryar—last night I told you how the sorcerer Thukamon transformed the ass Omid into Dilara, and Dilara into Princess Maria Irena, in the service of preserving the alliance between the Persians and Franks. Now Dilara and Gu Gu stood in Vahid's chambers on the sixth floor of the windcatcher tower. The sorcerer's chambers were unlocked—not so the inner laboratorium.)

"Greetings, O most virtuous and well-oiled Locque, behind whom every secret is secure." Gu Gu and Dilara addressed the oblong of molded goose-bone that secured the laboratorium. "We the friends and allies of the noble and ensheeped Parsi beg admittance to the laboratorium which you are so cruelly made to guard day and night."

"Your compliments are accurate and demonstrate your worthiness." Locque's voice boomed and carried like that of Vahid, who had created and cultivated him in a vat. Vahid had modeled Locque's larynx on his own—hence the voice. "Still, when you leave, I plan to count the spoons."

The door creaked open. Dilara and Gu Gu passed inside. (Parsi was in the courtyard below, munching flowers, his cloven hooves quite useless on the tower steps.)

Made from the muscle and brain of a goose (that natural guard animal) and encased in a lock-shaped goose-bone shell, Locque took no key as such. Instead, one pressed a hand along his length—if the pressure and warmth precisely matched those of his designer and creator, the tumblers would fall. Otherwise, Locque would emit a foul odor and a bellow of alarm.

Unbeknownst to Vahid, however, Parsi (at that time still in his human form) had befriended his fellow oppressed creature. He discovered the weakness of his Master's security device, which was Locque's susceptibility to flattery.

Thus Parsi and Locque became fast friends, and Parsi gained access to the laboratorium. (This proved useful when deliveries of potions and other supplies arrived; his master could be ill-tempered when disturbed by such.)

The laboratorium was a vast clutter of retorts, alembics, and coiled tubes on iron stands. Scrolls lay scattered on shelves. The bleached skeleton of an ape hung by a string from the ceiling. Two cases sat glass-to-glass: a viper in one kept an eye on nervous rats in the other.

"O Master Vahid!" Dilara called. "Are you hiding somewhere in here, your fearsomeness?"

No answer came. (The sorcerer's whereabouts regrettably remained a mystery.)

"Aha, here is the plan for wearable wings." Gu Gu unrolled a scroll across the floor. "Let me see—well, I might have expected. The design is flawed. The wrist girth is too small for the weight of feathers."

"O Gu Gu," Dilara said sincerely, "how I envy your learning. If only we had schools in the Ragged Quarter."

"My father spares no expense in my education. I will order my tutors to teach you. You will learn the abacus, Latin verbs, and the campaigns of Alexander Magnus."

"Say, Gu Gu, look at these strange insects."

The silk curtain covering the laboratorium's vaulted window flapped on a passing breeze, and a stream of flying somethings invited themselves in. Gu Gu reached for one; it darted away from him.

"One does not find pupils or lobes in the insect family. Our visitors are eyes and ears. Thukamon's spies, no doubt. Well, what do we have to hide?"

"He did tell us to stay in the outer chamber."

An open scroll on a countertop caught Dilara's eye. A drawing in ink showed a sorcerer in full gown and turban, knees bent, arms spread wide, hair streaming behind, slippered feet on a carpet. The carpet tassels rippled as though in the wind. Beneath the drawing lay row upon row of crabbed Farsi characters.

"I think Vahid has been working on a carpet like that of Thukamon." She handed the scroll to Gu Gu. "But I confess, to my shame, that I cannot read."

"What! You will begin lessons as soon as we complete your mission. I shall have my tutors whipped daily until you have mastered Herodotus." He studied the scroll. She wondered if traveling by carpet was like riding a sunbeam.

"Could you use a magic carpet like that instead of the wearable wings to follow Thukamon and me?"

"The design merits some study, although one must question Vahid's competence in such matters. Hmm—I wonder if there is an armillary sphere in the laboratorium. I will also need an astrolabe, gum Arabic, regulus of antimony, a handful of straining gauze—"

Gu Gu rose and began to search the shelves. She considered asking him to look for the chamomile, tourmaline, and other ingredients Vahid had mentioned for a paste to reverse the Spell of Blind and Hopeless Love—but then, could her heart even sustain life if she no longer had Feroze to love? Instead, she said:

"Do your tutors teach you magic, then, as well as Latin?"

"No. Father forbids it, as he does all joys. But I managed to acquire a scroll of basic wizardry without my tutors finding out. I study it in secret. I wish I could grow up to be a sorcerer instead of—but never mind all that. My concern now is to help you, if you really are determined to go through with this plan to bring back Feroze."

"I made a solemn agreement with Thukamon. I am Maria Irena now, after all. I can only become myself again by doing my duty." Dilara had become used to speaking more bravely than she felt. "You, on the other hand, have nothing to gain by following me. Will your parents not expect you at home?"

"Father and Mother will be relieved to be rid of me. I embarrass them by saying only Gu Gu."

In the outer chamber, past the open door of the laboratorium, lay a long divan, taller on one end than the other, with a curved half-back worked with ornate scrolling. Mother-of-pearl inlaid the wood. The purple velvet cushions were embroidered with gold stitching.

Dilara yawned. What a long, exhausting day. She had ridden on a talking ass to the royal palace, met the happiness-seller and former Djinn Idrosun. She had been transformed into a Frankish Princess. The divan looked inviting.

"While you work on the magic carpet, perhaps I will take a little nap."

"Yes, yes—" Gu Gu was already intent on his project.

She snacked on dried carp. If she had been at home, the Dream Interpreter would have made her brush her hair ten strokes by ten times. But how did one brush roses? She swept the mane of flowers over her shoulder and curled up on the divan.

Slumber overtook her.

"—up, Mistress! Do wake up!" Gu Gu shook her.

He pulled the cloth curtain back from the outer chamber's single window, which overlooked the balcony. The brilliant morning light poured in. The mother-of-pearl inlay on the divan gave off rose glints. The eyes and ears circled excitedly before making for the open window.

"—found some rolled-up carpets to experiment on," he was saying. "But none of them would fly. On a hunch I took the liberty of sprinkling regulus on the divan while you slept. It is doubtless less elegant than a carpet, but in theory may be every bit as swift through the air. There is one difficulty, however. It seems that—"

Dilara swung her legs to the floor, sneezing as the perfume of roses filled her nose. There was a bleat, loud and piteous. A large, brown-fleeced form sailed through the window, legs pinwheeling. Alembics and retorts crashed in the beast's wake. The panicked Parsi skidded to a stop. Then—

"Greetings." The familiar voice called from the balcony. "I see the laboratorium door is ajar. You have disobeyed my instructions. Well, I brought Vahid's ensheeped slave in case I need to impress you with a demonstration."

Through the window the magic carpet came into view, gold and red, with rippling emerald tassels. The eyes and ears streamed through the window and assembled in formation above their master, who was kneeling on the carpet in his serpent headdress. Next to Thukamon was another sheep, yellow-fleeced and struggling to balance on wobbly legs. The sheep stared intently at Dilara, head a-tilt as though trying to understand something.

"We leave at once," Thukamon instructed Dilara. "Collect your things. We will overtake the Frankish delegation in Nineveh, where all stop to take the waters. Remember, you are now Maria Irena, the Prince's bride, newly recovered from sun sickness, which struck you dumb and all but killed you."

Gu Gu took hold of Dilara's elbow and pulled her aside, out of view of the window.

"Mistress, that one difficulty I mentioned—it has to do with our new flying divan—"

"Where did you go?" Thukamon called. "Come back at once. There is no time to lose."

"Vahid's scroll specified that the pilot must be pure of heart," Gu Gu went on with urgency. "This regrettably excludes me, for the truth is, I bear uncharitable thoughts toward my family, my tutors, and frankly everyone save you, Mistress."

Gu Gu's honesty gave Dilara pause. She reflected upon her own uncharitable attitudes. Even wishing Omid the good fortune of landing Naseem as a husband—had that not really been in her own selfish interest?

A solution presented itself.

"Jump up on the divan, Parsi," she said. "Would you like to go for a nice ride?"

"On that thing?" Parsi backed away. "I am not in the mood for jokes. I already had the shortest of trips on Thukamon's carpet up from the courtyard, and it was terrifying."

"Yes, do reconsider, Mistress," Gu Gu said. "The divan will be a tight fit with a full-grown sheep aboard. And then there is the odor to consider."

"Not to mention that a fall would damage my valuable fleece," Parsi bleated. "Best listen to him."

"O Parsi, do you not understand?" she said. "Of the three of us, only you are pure of heart."

At this point, Thukamon stepped through the window and into the chamber, the brass lamp under his arm.

"Why are you delaying?" he said. "I see I will have to give you a demonstration, after all. Come here, Parsi. You must be tired of being a sheep."

Thukamon raised the lamp. Parsi cowered.

"O sorcerer, wait!" Dilara moved between Parsi and the sorcerer. "Parsi's master Vahid turned him to a sheep. Did you not say that only the one who performs a transformation may undo it? It is your code of ethics."

"I will make an exception in the case of food." Thukamon grinned.

He stepped around Dilara and drizzled invisible oil over Parsi's muzzle, head, and neck. The blue topaz in the sorcerer's forehead glowed. Parsi's knees and hooves dissolved. His legs turned to thin pointed rods. His shoulders, loins, flanks, and all the rest of him vanished, replaced by sizzling chunks.

The chunks were nicely browned, spitted on the rods, and presented on rice, with garnish, on a white platter. The aroma of the kebabs made the mouth water.

The grinning Thukamon turned the lamp on Gu Gu.

"And you, I think, would make a nice chimpanzee—"

17. How Thukamon Got His Grin and His Lamp

"O Bourzou," I said, "how can you send these beauties to their doom? You know they won't survive our Persian summer here in the open."

Slaves, toiling under the midday sun, were digging a line of holes. Beside each hole rested a sapling with small, delicate leaves the color of copper, and an attached jute sack in which were the roots. Slavemaster Bourzou and I stood beneath a broad parasol (held for us by another slave).

"Shall I pass on your criticism to the King?" Bourzou asked. "He chose this location."

An implied threat. Well, I wasn't cowed. I knew too many of Bourzou's secrets.

"Didn't the trader from Nippon bring these maples? Like you and I, they need shade in the afternoon."

"Nippon wants an agreement with the King," Bourzou said. "If the trees die, the trader's gift will be worthless. He'll lose his leverage for bargaining. Don't underestimate the cleverness of King Shahryar, may Heaven protect him—you, Peki!"

One of the slaves, partway down the line, had stopped digging. He leaned on his spade, sweat pouring off him. Bourzou stepped from under the parasol and displayed his crop. Every palace slave looked upon that crop with dread—even I, who had never experienced it across my own back. Peki returned to his digging with renewed enthusiasm.

Morgai had given birth to Peki in the Pavilion of Slaves. A free palace washerwoman, Morgai had been sentenced to death for stealing a sweet cake off an untended platter, but the merciful King—Shahryar's father, who had appointed Ali-Haram court poet—commuted her sentence to life enslavement.

"Your ladyship does me great honor with this visit," Bourzou said, returning to our blessed shade. "Not long ago you were one of my slaves. To think, I took care of you, mentored you, and taught you everything you know. Now look how you have risen in the world. What business could you possibly have with your old Master?"

He took pleasure in being disrespectful to me. But I was deeply ashamed of what had brought me, and I wanted to get our business over with as quickly as possible.

"I need you to tell me what this says."

From the sleeve of my gown, I drew a square of felt fabric and handed it to him. Farsi letters I could not read covered the fabric. I had copied them as carefully as I could from Ali-Haram's parchment—the same one he groaned over whenever he thought I wasn't watching. I had not dared bring the parchment itself and risk my husband missing it.

"I think it might be a list of gambling debts." I tried not to cry in my humiliation. "Bourzou, you cannot tell anybody about this meeting. No one. Most especially not Scheherazade or my lord husband. Do you swear?"

He nodded. I watched his lips move silently as he read.

"Hmm—fifty darics to the King's vizier—eighteen to the trader from Nippon—ten to a post herald, two to the King's cupbearer, six to a scribe—" He pursed his lips and gave me a look that might have been pity. "Ali-Haram?"

I didn't answer. But Bourzou was no fool.

"Actually," he said, studying the cloth further, "the worst is this one for four darics."

"Only four?" I said.

"Yes, but owed to the moneylender."

I stared, not understanding. He explained:

"A moneylender charges a fee for his loan. This fee is known as interest. He gives you one daric, and you pay back two. If you do not pay the two, it turns into four. This is how he makes his sinful living."

My worst fears were confirmed. No one would have called my lord husband wealthy, at least by palace standards, and now he was running up a mountain of debts racing asses. And the debts had forced him into dealings with a moneylender. Worst of all, he had tried to keep it all from me.

I couldn't read the amounts and creditors on Ali-Haram's parchment, but his silences, worries, foul moods—what wife couldn't read these?

"Tell me, Bourzou, and if you have ever been honest, be honest now. When I lived in the Pavilion of Slaves, what was my appraisal?"

"What do you mean?"

"I think you know, but I will put it plainly. If someone had wanted to buy me, what price would you have asked?"

"Ariana, you wound me. I would never have advised the King to sell you, not at any price. You were far too valuable."

Yes, Bourzou. I was valuable—especially to you. I ran your secret errands. I covered for your blunders. I gave comfort to the other slaves after they tasted your crop.

"I know there was a number next to my name in your scroll of slave valuations. All I'm asking is what that number was."

He looked at his feet, at the slave holding our umbrella, out at Peki, at the maple saplings and jute sacks—everywhere but at my face. Finally:

"All right, I appraised you at five hundred darics. But that was only a number on a scroll, something to satisfy the palace scribes. I had to—"

"What could you get for me now?"

"But why would—"

He flinched then, as though I had struck him. It was starting to dawn on him.

"Be accurate," I said. "Everything depends on it."

He looked torn.

"I have to—you know—" he mumbled.

"I understand. Do your duty."

He walked several circles around me. He made motions without meeting my eyes: open your mouth, display your teeth; remove your slippers and show me your feet. I burned with a shame I thought I would never know again since the day Ali-Haram paid my head-price.

"As I live, Ariana," Bourzou said at last, "in today's market you would fetch eight hundred, and not a daric less."

The slaves sweated and shoveled in the sun. Bourzou had told Ali-Haram's agent that I was "worth more than all the other slaves put together." A moment's doubts flew at me: did those wretched beings deserve freedom from Bourzou's crop any less than my husband deserved freedom from his debts?

But there was another debt to consider—my own. The one I owed to Ali-Haram.

Still, there was something I had to be sure of first.

"Read off the debts to me, and I'll add them up." Bourzou could read, but sums were not his strong point. "I'll include your customary fee, naturally."

"Again, you wound me. If I understand what you intend, how could I take a fee?"

I didn't believe his protest but chose not to press the point. We went through the numbers on the cloth twice, to make sure my sum was correct.

My plan was to tell Ali-Haram that word had come from Maqazza: my mother had taken terribly ill. I had to go home to take care of her. I had already completed—on my own—several new chapters of the King's story for Scheherazade. Debts would no longer fetter Ali-Haram. By the time he began to suspect I wasn't returning, he would have taken up his writing again.

I don't know if I really believed in my own plan.

"Just find a buyer," I told Bourzou. "As soon as I am gone, give the proceeds to Ali-Haram, less your commission, in a pouch. Mark the pouch 'For your debts, from an unnamed friend.' That, and nothing more."

One day my lord husband would find out what had really happened. By then he might even be able to buy me back. But in the worst case, if I never saw him again, I would still have the memory of the fleeting time I was free, when he and I were together.

"You would do all this for a man who squandered everything he had wagering on ass races?"

"Don't judge him poorly," I said. "I was a slave to the King. Ali-Haram freed me, out of love. Now he is a slave himself, to debt. I am going to free him the only way I know."

The Slavemaster shook his head.

"But such a sacrifice—"

I didn't stay to hear the rest. I would not cry in front of him. I turned on my heel and left him alone with his judgments and the slave who was holding his parasol.

*

"The sorcerer Thukamon intrigues us. We have known ones like him."

A slave had come into the royal bedchamber with a steaming plate of pita with toasted cheese and quince jelly. Scheherazade plumped the King's pillows under his shoulders so he could sit up and attend to his late-night snack.

"They grin and smile and laugh," he went on. "Their happiness seems to derive from the misfortunes of others. What could Thukamon's story be, we wonder? Why is he at my ancestor's court, and yet no one knows where Vahid is?"

Scheherazade drew open the silk curtain, and I looked out the window on a pale crescent moon, queen of her cold realm of stars. The perfume of roses, honeysuckle, and wisteria wafted up from the royal hanging gardens.

"O great and wise King, Thukamon's story is indeed a fascinating one." This time I was prepared for the King's request. "And it indeed involves Vahid, as well as someone else who, in time, will be important to Dilara's story. I shall go back in time and tell you how the Egyptian sorcerer got his grin—and his lamp."

"A story within a story again," the King said.

"A bowl inside a bowl." Scheherazade smiled. "A box inside a chest."

I had decided my own fate. I had arranged the details. If not happy, I was at least at peace.

"O majesty," I began, "you might find it difficult to picture Vahid and Thukamon as young men, but long ago—"

114

*

—long ago (centuries, in fact, for sorcerers are quite long-lived) the two were students together, attending the college of magic in Babylon. They were fast friends and constant companions. In study or leisure time alike, when you saw one, you were sure to see the other. However, an unwelcome guest arrived to pay a visit and cast his long shadow over their bond.

This guest was Jealousy.

Then as today, the land of Lebanon sold its famed cedars all over the world. The Queen of Lebanon, a descendant of the prophet Solomon, used the wealth gained in this trade to obtain a seat for her daughter as the first girl to attend the Babylon college. This girl's name was Zaib.

Naturally, both Vahid and Thukamon fell in love with Zaib.

Of the two, Zaib loved Thukamon best. His conversation, wit, and appearance deeply attracted her. She gave her heart to him. When she explained her decision to Vahid, she happened to mention the one thing that still troubled her about Thukamon. This was his grin.

Whenever he grinned, it unsettled and disturbed her. She could not help imagining ill will and devilment in his expression. But Thukamon was usually serious in those days of study and work. His grins were infrequent, and so she was able to put them out of her mind.

Meanwhile, Vahid remained desperately in love with the Lebanese princess. He concocted a scheme to injure his rival.

One evening, as the two students sat in a roofed courtyard at the college, a storm moved across Babylon. Vahid proposed to Thukamon that they pass the time by telling stories. As the rain drummed on the roof, and thunder rolled all around them, they told each other tale after tale. Thukamon recited chapters of Homer and Gilgamesh from memory, while Vahid related anecdotes of his own childhood.

These anecdotes abounded with scrapes and misadventures. They displayed Vahid in a ridiculous light. The entertained Thukamon laughed and grinned. At the precise moment of one such wide grin, a lightning strike lit up the courtyard. This was what Vahid had waited for. He invoked the Conjuration of Physical Immutability. (By doing so, he broke several rules, since this spell was forbidden to all but the most advanced students, and then only with written authorization.) The Conjuration permanently froze the grin on Thukamon's face.

Zaib tried to ignore this change to her beloved, but, for her, the unchanging grin robbed him of his charm. His face, which before had seemed loving and wise, took on, for her, a malignant cast. The love she had felt for Thukamon drained from her heart, leaving an open wound behind. She tried to remember and reconstruct her love—but of course one cannot dictate to the heart. At length she sent a tear-stained letter to her mother the Queen, asking permission to resign from the college. When permission came by return post, she departed Babylon forever, leaving both rivals behind.

The once inseparable companions became implacable enemies. Gone was their once-famous friendship. Deadly hatred took its place. And thus matters stood for many a year, even long after their days in Babylon—

Still, time is a salve that can treat, if not cure, and sorcerers live far longer than men and women. Eventually the two returned to cordiality. They made the long journey between Baghdad and Alexandria to pay each other visits. They conversed and reminisced and even conducted sorcerous experiments together, as in bygone days. But whenever Thukamon happened to look in a mirror, he would again see the grin frozen on his face, and he would remember his lost love, the Lebanese princess Zaib, and the great wrong done him. He privately vowed revenge on Vahid.

Now, a rumor reached Thukamon of a certain scroll-seller in Athens who was said to have in his possession the original scroll in which Ptolemy proved that the sun and moon revolved about the Earth. Thukamon made the journey to Athens and at length located the scroll-seller. But after examining the manuscript, he judged it a counterfeit. Disappointed, he wandered into the shop of a nearby curio dealer.

Two items in this shop particularly interested Thukamon. One was a rolled-up carpet, red and gold, with emerald tassels. The carpet showed the tell-tale signs of windburn. He guessed it had once been the magic carpet of some sorcerer of antiquity. Could it be restored to airworthiness?

The other item was a brass lamp which the dealer claimed had been owned by Merlin himself. This seemed doubtful in light of the Carthaginian inscriptions on the base, but certain other aspects of the lamp suggested that, in the right hands, it would not only be suitable for performing sorcerous transformations, but perfect for exacting sweet revenge on his rival.

Thukamon could easily afford the posted prices but took pleasure in haggling. When the dealer finally agreed to throw in a pot of invisible lamp oil, the deal was struck—

*

"But we still wonder what became of Vahid," the King said. "Thukamon call him 'indisposed.' We suspect that Thukamon used the lamp to transform Vahid into another creature. Maybe he's one of the eyes or ears. Or perhaps he became that sheep which was wobbling on Thukamon's magic carpet and staring so oddly at Dilara."

Scheherazade did not give me a chance to invent an answer.

"Ariana will relate all these things," she said to the King, "but only in the fullness of the story. And so my lord husband, while in every other matter your will is law, when it comes to this story you must wait."

18. How Omid Got Her Freedom, and Parsi Got His Horns

(O King, last night we left the travelers inside Vahid's chambers in the windcatcher tower, where the sorcerer Thukamon had transformed the sheep Parsi into mouth-watering kebabs, and then turned his attention to Gu Gu—)

The crowded divan flew ever north, following the winding blue ribbon of the Tigris. The tireless eyes and ears kept pace alongside. Woods, crop fields, scattered villages, and the thin lines of ox trails passed far below. Hawks, eagles, and cranes kept wary eyes on the new creature that shared their sky. Dilara's eyes watered in the wind.

By experimentation, she and Gu Gu had worked out rules for steering. A vigorous tap on Parsi's nose caused the divan to climb; two taps, to descend. To change direction required a pull on the appropriate ear.

After two demonstrations, as Thukamon called them, he and Dilara had done some hard bargaining. Now she felt like reminiscing.

"The funniest part of you being a chimpanzee," Dilara said, "was when you jumped about and scratched your ribs and said Gu Gu."

"My career as an ape was short but mortifying," Gu Gu said.

"How did you get Thukamon to transform us back, mistress?" Parsi was once more in his uncooked, fleeced form.

"He may have turned Gu Gu into a chimpanzee, and you into kebabs, but I knew he would not transform me again. Prince Feroze will only return with us if he genuinely believes I am Maria Irena. That is why I told Thukamon if he did not change you two back, I would abandon the mission."

During these negotiations, one of the ears had lighted on the sorcerer's nose and transmitted an urgent vibration. Thukamon had frowned and announced that Dilara was to return with him at once to Baghdad. A matter of great importance had come up. A delay in the mission was unavoidable.

Dilara's heart had fallen. Every day apart from Feroze, whom she still loved blindly and hopelessly, was torment. She proposed going ahead on her own: after all (she suggested to Thukamon), how hard could it be to follow the Tigris to Nineveh and find the Frankish delegation?

Out of the question, the sorcerer answered. Dilara clearly required supervision. She made a counter-proposal. If he ordered the eyes and ears to go with her, they could report her every move to him. Of course, she would need the chimpanzee and kebab platter as engineer and pilot, respectively. Eventually, agreement was reached, and the sorcerer grudgingly restored her companions.

But then the most unexpected part of the transaction had taken place.

"I have something to add to the duties of your mission. You are to give this to the Franks." Thukamon handed her the brass lamp. "I wish them to convey it to Charles Magnus himself, with my compliments. Tell the interpreter—no, sun sickness took your voice. And Gu Gu can only say Gu Gu. Parsi, it falls to you to bleat the following: the King of the Franks should rub the lamp twice back to front, and once down each side, while saying—" He pronounced the syllables. "His court will then witness a truly memorable sight."

"How will you do transformations without your lamp?" Dilara had asked.

"Do not concern yourself with that. I have other mediums in my possession. This lamp's primary purpose has always been to play a tr—

that is, to be my personal gift to Charles Magnus. Remember: give my message to the Franks as precisely as I gave it to you. I have spoken."

And with that Thukamon had returned to the balcony and stepped onto the hovering carpet where the yellow-fleeced sheep still wobbled. The carpet had raced away—

Now Dilara studied herself in the lamp's shiny brass surface: the strange blue eyes, the pale skin, the yellow roses that streamed behind her. She sternly reminded herself that she was only borrowing the Princess's form. She was a Persian, not a Frank, and not a drop of royal blood flowed in her veins. She had no right to Feroze's love.

But how her heart leaped at the prospect of being with him again—

*

Gu Gu pulled Dilara's arm excitedly.

"Look below, Mistress!" he cried. "Carts, camels, wagons—we have caught up with the Franks already. Let us land at once. The end of your mission is imminent."

Dilara was dubious.

"Thukamon said we would find them further north, in Nineveh. But very well. Put down behind that line of trees that overlooks the river. Best to keep the flying divan out of sight for now."

Gu Gu double-tapped Parsi's nose, which had begun to swell from the demands of navigation. The ground rose up. The divan came to rest on a low mound that was covered with pink and yellow wildflowers.

"You stay here," Gu Gu said to Parsi. "The Franks have surely never seen a talking sheep. They would ask questions." But the instruction was unnecessary; Parsi had already disembarked and was helping himself to a snack of wildflowers.

"What about the lamp?" Dilara asked.

Thukamon's lamp lay on the divan, glittering in the afternoon light. From a sleeve of his tunic, Gu Gu produced the oblong of goose-bone and placed it next to the lamp, saying:

"O most virtuous Locque, I beg you to let no one run off with our magic lamp."

"Or the flying divan." Dilara did not want to overlook anything.

"I trust only the friends of Parsi," Locque said in Vahid's booming voice. Tumblers clunked into place. "I will prevent others from committing the sin of theft so that they may have a place in Paradise."

Dilara started to put on her veil and headscarf, but Gu Gu said, "Maria Irena is an unbeliever. She would not wear those."

"But I will bring them just in case."

The two made their way toward the wagons. (The eyes and ears held a conference, which resulted in the ears following after Dilara and Gu Gu, and the eyes staying at the divan.)

Alongside the wagons, a girl was lurching forward with a small child clinging to her back. The child squealed with delight. Dilara thought the lurching girl looked oddly familiar. A woman, possibly the child's mother, watched anxiously from nearby.

"Faster! Faster!" the child shouted. Hearing this, Dilara put on her veil and headscarf.

"The child is speaking our tongue, Gu Gu," she said. "This is not the Frankish delegation. It is an ordinary Persian caravan."

When the ride ended, the woman tossed a coin to the girl, who accepted it mutely.

"What!" the woman said. "You cannot even say a polite thank-you?"

A tall hawk-faced boy in a red skull cap came up at once. He took the coin from the girl, who stood with eyes downcast.

"A thousand pardons for this one's behavior," he said. "She is under a curse because of her many sins. She cannot speak, but only bray like an ass."

Everything became clear. The boy in the skull cap was none other than her almost-betrothed Naseem. And the girl with him was—herself. That is, she was Omid, transformed into a perfect copy of Dilara. Dilara reminded herself that she was Maria Irena now, and Naseem knew her only in her disguise of Khashar.

The woman took the child's hand and left in a huff. Omid gave an anxious bray, for which Naseem boxed her ears.

"I am Maria," Dilara said politely. "And this is Gu Gu."

Naseem introduced himself. Then:

"This is my bride Dilara. We were joined in holy union this very morning. When the Matchmaker first introduced us, Dilara was standoffish. She did not say a word. In fact, she left home once the Matchmaker took her leave. But this was doubtless only to think things over. Returning, she covered me in kisses. This persuaded me of her love, although she still said nothing. We went to a licensed wise woman, who wed us. But after the rites, when I took Dilara to my bed of straw, she began to bray like an ass."

Omid gave Dilara a bleak, imploring look.

"I took her back to see the wise woman, who said my bride had come under a powerful spell, which could be reversed only by the sorcerer who cast it. But who knows who the sorcerer was? When I ask Dilara, she only brays."

"Why did you join the caravan?"

"We are going to Nineveh. The wise woman said the waters there work miracles, if one's faith is strong enough."

"Let us pray to Heaven for strong faith," Dilara said with emotion.

"Well, I am her lord now. If she does not regain her speech, it is my right to sell her into slavery at the Nineveh auctions."

Omid's shoulders slumped. She stared forlornly at the ground. The caravan continued its slow progress. Carts clattered, oxen lowed, camels snorted.

Dilara considered informing Naseem that Omid was enslaved already, in the service of the sorcerer Thukamon. But Naseem might ask questions she was not prepared to answer.

"O traveler Naseem, why does your wife carry children on her back?"

"To pay our passage in the caravan, of course. Children need entertainment after long hours of travel."

"Gu Gu!" Gu Gu tugged on Dilara's sleeve. She leaned down and let him whisper to her. The ears circled low, trying to hear. "Let me use the lamp. I will pour the invisible oil on her and restore her to her original form, which would be better than the state she is in now."

"But only Thukamon can reverse the spell, unless food is involved."

"Or so he said." Gu Gu gave her a knowing look. "Besides, this Naseem does not know about the sorcerer's code of ethics."

"Do you remember what sounds to make?"

"According to my scroll of basic wizardry, the sounds serve a purely theatrical purpose."

Dilara could not help remembering guiltily the part she herself had played in poor Omid becoming Naseem's wife.

"O Naseem," she said, "a certain magic relic has come into my possession. It might be used to restore your bride's voice."

"Fine, take her and try. But be warned, I cannot pay. And bring her back soon. I promised her as a footstool during dinner to a pilgrim who suffers from gout."

Dilara, Gu Gu, and Omid left the caravan and climbed back up the wooded hill. Omid wept and brayed, while Dilara responded with comforting words.

When the three reached the shadows behind the line of trees, they found Parsi missing. Dilara looked beyond the hill, where a narrow trail ran down to a glen dense with green and blue grasses. A flock of sheep grazed under the watch of a snoring shepherd who lay propped against a low tree, crook still in hand.

Dilara said: "Could our noble pilot be over there?"

"Who can tell? One brown fleece looks like another. Perhaps he found new wildflowers to eat."

"Or he wanted the companionship of his own kind. We should look for him."

"First I plan to transform Omid. O Locque, who, if instructed to secure life, would keep death itself at bay, I wish to use the lamp to conduct an experiment."

"He who experiments with eggs may have to pick up eggshells."

With this proverb, Locque released the lamp. Omid knelt before Gu Gu and placed her hands over her heart in prayerful supplication. Her face shone with anticipation. Gu Gu rubbed the lamp several times and then tilted it over Omid's head.

"Be careful, Gu Gu!" Dilara said. "You are not fully trained in these arts. You do not know what might—"

A crack sounded, like the snap of a whip. There was a whiff of sulfur. Omid ascended, her face contorted in terror. She grew long and narrow. She was a hovering, trembling reed. With a whoosh, she disappeared into the lamp spout.

Dilara and Gu Gu stared at the lamp, dumbfounded. The eyes and ears blinked and twitched, respectively.

"Hello! How did you get in?" A muffled voice issued from the lamp spout. "Kindly move your elbow, madam; space is at a premium here. Gu Gu, is this your doing? Your tutors will not be pleased."

Gu Gu rubbed his chin thoughtfully.

"Thukamon said to rub once front to back and twice up each side—right?"

A new voice joined the conversation in the lamp.

"You must be that Persian sorcerer who keeps losing bets to Thukamon."

"I am Vahid, madam."

"Omid, Gu Gu really did give you your voice back!" Dilara cried. "And master, is that truly you in there? But how did you end up inside the lamp? You must be very cramped. Did Thukamon take away more of your height?"

"No, I am my usual size, as is, it appears, my new companion. (Please move your knee a little, my dear.) These are close quarters, I admit, but it is all in the spirit of inquiry. When we have the opportunity, I shall explain fully."

Omid's voice came from the lamp: "Sir sorcerer, I am new to the race of Men and should not judge. But you have, as my dear Papa used to say, a face only a mother could love. However, I am not in a position to be choosy. Besides, I have a hunch you are wealthy."

At this point, a familiar odor made Dilara look up. A sheep climbed onto the divan.

"Why, Parsi!" she said. "Look at you, your horns are coming in!"

The horns were striped black-and-white. They curled extravagantly up and back and forward again, ending in sharp points. (A jagged, oozing wound also ran from ear to ear.)

"I found true love today." Parsi's bleats projected new power and strength. "How wonderful she is. How lovely are her eyes and fleece. She is the sheep of my dreams. O mistress, love is greater than any magic. I no longer wish to return to the form of a mere man."

Vahid had a muffled and triumphant remark to make.

"Now you see my decisions are for the best, Parsi. I ensheeped you for your own good."

19. Parsi's Mortal Enemy

Scheherazade straightened the muslin coverlet across King Shahryar's belly and legs.

"After hearing your story last night," the King said, "we have begun to feel sympathy for Thukamon. We have something in common with him—namely, betrayal in love. No greater pain exists."

He fixed his gaze meaningfully on Scheherazade.

"A man with a loose tongue accused me," she murmured. "But while I live out the days Heaven has allotted me, may you suffer betrayal no more."

The look that passed between them then was, for me, as unreadable as a scroll of Dilara's story copied out in Ali-Haram's hand. Then the King said:

"Now we should like to know more about Vahid. You told us about his time at the college in Babylon, and his rivalry with Thukamon. How did he come to be the court sorcerer for our revered ancestor, King Alcimedes?"

"O great and wise King," I said, "Vahid's story is indeed surprising and worthy of telling. During his first years at the college he received the highest of marks. He was an excellent student and showed immense potential. His professors were all certain he would go far."

I was making up this tale as I went along—it would be my last such invention. Bourzou had found a buyer. The deal was all but complete. Ali-Haram would have cash to pay off his debts. He would return to writing the story of Dilara for Scheherazade to tell the King. That was my plan. A happy conclusion for everyone, except me—but best not to dwell on that.

"As you remember, Princess Zaib left the college and returned to Lebanon. Vahid was heartbroken. He could no longer concentrate. He blamed all his unhappiness on his rival Thukamon. His work turned poor. His marks fell. (There was also the matter of punishment for casting the forbidden Conjuration of Physical Immutability.) A tribunal of professors dismissed him from the college.

"Without a diploma, he could not apprentice with any member of the Sorcerers Guild. He had to take work as a common laborer. He shoveled night soil on the fields, carried litters for the rich, swept streets behind carriage horses. But he saved all he earned, and in time was able to set up his own laboratorium. He could not use any of the spells and enchantments he had learned at the college, and so he began to craft his own.

"One day a mysterious lady, cloaked and veiled, found her way to his laboratorium.

"'Sir,' the lady explained, 'my husband is a Prince from the land of Arabia. We are both the children of rulers, and we wedded for political purposes. For bravery in battle and handsomeness, none surpasses my husband. He is a scholar. He composes and recites poetry. His wealth is vast; he owns many palaces and white Arabian stallions.'

"'Count yourself fortunate, then,' said Vahid. 'Why have you come to me?'

"'For this reason: despite his wealth, I live a life of misery. The Prince wastes no opportunity to criticize me, belittle my family, or question my ability to produce an heir. This he does from morning to night, both with friends and in private. I wish to commission a custom spell. The spell I have in mind would transform, not the prince, but the things he says to me. Every cruel word would become kind, and every ill word good, whether he intends it or not.'

"'An interesting challenge,' Vahid said. 'But you should know: I have no official credentials. The Sorcerers Guild has many respectable members you could have consulted.'

"'But none of them gave Thukamon the grin he will wear forever.'

"And so saying, the lady removed her veil. Vahid saw that his mysterious new client was none other than the Lebanese princess, Zaib.

"He accepted her commission. After some calculations, he hit upon a concoction of goat weed, spearmint, and golden root. He instructed Zaib to sprinkle the concoction on her husband's lips while he slept. Due to a bungled sub-charm, the spell failed-or succeeded in an unforeseen way: the Prince's words were transformed not from cruel to kind, but to something else entirely: winged beings. Every time Zaib's husband undertook to utter a critical or wicked word, an Angel issued from his mouth instead. Indeed, so many cruel things did he have stored up to say, that his jaws grew weary, and the Angels grew to a multitude. Upon emerging, they winged their way toward Baghdad. (That is why, even today, our city is known as the Abode of Peace.) As for the Prince, he produced so many Angels that he ascended to Heaven himself. Thus was Zaib left husbandless and satisfied.

"When a position opened for a sorcerer in the court of your ancestor Alcimedes, Zaib sent the King a letter, written in perfect Persian, recommending Vahid. The King, who was desirous of acquiring goodwill in respect of potential trade agreements for the famed cedars of Lebanon, accepted the recommendation. And that is how Vahid, without diploma or credentials, came to his post.

"Many years passed. One day, a letter arrived for Vahid from distant Alexandria. The letter was from his college rival Thukamon, who by now was a consulting sorcerer for the Egyptian government. Thukamon proposed a truce. 'After all,' he wrote, 'we have much in common. Were we not both spurned by the cold-hearted Zaib?'

"And so Thukamon arrived in Baghdad on his flying carpet. Vahid threw a banquet in his honor. The two talked deep into the night. They retold their college adventures and philosophized about love and sorcery. To all appearances, they resumed their former comradeship. But, as I have related, Thukamon never let go of his secret desire to take revenge for the spell that had left him with the permanent grin.

"Now, Vahid had a weakness for wagering, and was unskilled at it. For example, once he challenged Thukamon to a magic carpet race to the moon. He lost the race and forfeited his carpet as Thukamon's prize. Vahid was unable to return to Earth for years, until a comet was procured to pick him up, for which he had to pay a hefty fee.

"Then there was the time Thukamon and Vahid discussed the proposition that a man cannot eat an entire cake. The proof, authored by the renowned Greek wizard Zeno, ran thus: one first must eat half the cake, then half of the remaining part, and so forth. The cake can never be consumed, for half of the previous portion always remains. Thukamon announced he had discovered a method of outwitting this theorem. Vahid challenged his friend to a wager on this point. The palace kitchen brought a delicious almond and honey cake, and of course Thukamon polished off the whole thing, leaving not a crumb. Having lost the wager, Vahid was transformed to a left sandal, which Thukamon wore for the following year."

The King observed: "And we remember the time Vahid wagered that he could ride a sunbeam. That did not turn out well for him either. We wonder what bet he lost that caused him to end up inside the lamp?"

"Majesty, it was not exactly a lost wager—not yet anyway. But here again, the time has not come to relate these details, and I must beg your patience."

From beyond the window came the sweet chirrups of a nightingale.

"Poor Vahid," said King Shahryar. "He suffered from a disease that still cripples men in our modern age."

Your own court poet is one of those, I thought. And the disease cripples not only men, but also the women who love them.

*

(O King, my story left off with Vahid and Omid confined together inside the brass lamp, and Parsi bleating about his newfound love—)

The sound of rapid footfall drew Dilara's attention toward the line of woods. A tall boy with a red skullcap was approaching.

"—at once!" Naseem's anger raced ahead of him. "A pony has turned its ankle and needs to be carried. The caravan master paid a deposit of a half-daric, and—"

Dilara tapped Parsi's nose—the divan ascended. (The ever-vigilant eyes and ears followed.) Naseem looked up in stupefaction. Parsi, anticipating another tap, buried his nose in the velvet cushions. The divan hovered.

"No more of your tricks!" Naseem leaped but could not reach. "Hand over my bride."

"O Naseem," Dilara said, "look for yourself. Clearly, she is not sitting on the divan."

"What have you done with her?"

"She has found a place where you can neither box her ears nor force her to bear ponies on her back."

Dilara briefly reflected, however, that confinement in the brass lamp with Vahid might be an equally disagreeable state of existence.

"I curse you, with your wealth and fancy flying divan!" Naseem shook his fist. "You travel the countryside without a care, while I, who have nothing and still must pay my passage to the caravan master, am denied my only means of earning——"

The enterprising Gu Gu reached into the food bag for a handful of dried leeks, which he sprinkled on Parsi's snout. Parsi jerked up his head and sneezed. Gu Gu took the opportunity to apply a quick tap. The divan rose swiftly.

The woods and Naseem were soon far below.

*

The Tigris, in its indecision, meandered from a northerly to westerly course and back again. Dilara tugged on Parsi's ear as necessary to keep the Angel of Rivers in sight below.

"I find their behavior shameful," she said. Gu Gu had been educating her with tales of the Greek deities. "Hera threw her own son off a mountaintop because he was ugly. Zeus ate his wife because he thought her child would murder him. I find such gods unworthy of worship."

"According to my tutors," Gu Gu answered, "Allah and the Greek gods both edify us, if by different means. Allah sets out clearly what we may and may not do, while Hera, Zeus, and the others teach the valuable lesson that power corrupts all, even the mightiest."

"I would say Zeus is not a god at all, but an imposter."

"Perhaps the Greeks themselves would agree," Gu Gu said. "In our age, they have turned to new gods. Like Charles Magnus and the Franks, they are Christians now. They worship a certain Jesus."

"Who is this Jesus, Gu Gu?"

"Regrettably, this is a unit my tutors have not yet come to. But now—look at that pod of pelicans, Dilara. Their formation reminds me of the Spartans who fought against Darius in our ancient wars. Let us change course and get a closer look——"

But Parsi unexpectedly snorted and shook his head. His new horns were prominent and fearsome.

"Hands off my ear!" he bleated. The surprised Gu Gu let go. "I have an announcement to make. Henceforth there will be no more nose-tapping. No more ear-pulling. I am the pilot, and we go where I say. I will take you to Nineveh, after which I shall return here, to rejoin my beloved."

"O Parsi!" Dilara cried in admiration. "You have truly become a new sheep."

"Love has transformed me. Power and strength are coursing through my blood. However—" His head drooped; he fell silent.

"However—?" Dilara prompted.

"It is no matter. Sometimes the lover must fight for his love. As it is in the world of men, so it is in the world of sheep. I shall win her or die."

"Tell us everything that has happened to you," Dilara begged. "Leave nothing out."

And so Parsi told his story: after finishing off the wildflowers next to the divan, he had caught sight of the flock down the hill. To pass the time while Dilara and Gu Gu investigated the caravan, he had wandered in that direction. The sheep proved friendly and welcoming, and their shepherd was napping. The flock showed him where to find the best-tasting grasses. Then a certain lady sheep approached—

"Her name was, well, I cannot pronounce it in the human tongue. You say it this way—"

He made a sound that was part baa and part wind moving through the grass.

Baa-Wind had gazed at him with her large sheep eyes. Her fleece was black and soft, her nose warm. Parsi told her his story of enslavement and ensheepment. It was love at first bleat. Then—

A sudden shocking impact. A roaring pain in his hindquarters. He collapsed on his front knees. He twisted around to see. Behind him was an enormous ram. The ram's eyes blazed with deadly menace. The curling horns ended in tips like sword-points. Around the neck was a tin bell, which marked the ram as the bellwether of the flock. The ram's name was—here, Parsi made another sound, part bellow and part rumble.

Bellow-Rumble had informed Parsi that Baa-Wind was his, and his alone. He warned Parsi to keep his mangy fleece away from her, or he would be sorry. The other sheep gathered round, bleating "Fight! Fight!"

One of the sheep edged close to Parsi and gave him encouragement, of a sort.

"Bellow-Rumble is the meanest and strongest of our whole flock. We have been waiting a long time for someone to take him down a peg."

The shepherd dozed through it all. The flock cleared a space for the showdown. Bellow-Rumble and Parsi circled. Bellow-Rumble let loose a terrible roar and charged, head down.

"He got me just below the eyes," Parsi said. "He raked me ear to ear with a horn-point. When I came to, the other sheep were gone, save for Baa-Wind, who stood over me, nudging my nose and licking my wound."

"'Bellow-Rumble is my mate,' she told me. 'But he treats me cruelly. The others fear him. Only you can free me from my unhappiness.'"

Parsi had struggled to his wobbly hooves. He was ready to take on his enemy again. But Bellow-Rumble had left with the others.

"Baa-Wind bleated, 'Our shepherd woke up and moved the flock to another field. I doubled back to find you. Bellow-Rumble said that you are to meet him here in seven days. You will fight him then, to the death. After you defeat him, I will be yours. We will live happily together, ram and wife forever.'

"And that, Mistress, is why I must return here."

"I never imagined life in the world of sheep could be so dangerous," said the astonished Dilara. "But O Parsi, O Gu Gu! Look ahead, to the north—"

A city loomed on the horizon. With its walls of bleached stone, its battlements and towers covered in ivy, its spires that sparkled in the afternoon light, the city could only be ancient Nineveh.

But even as the flying divan neared the walls, dark clouds began to fill the sky. Lightning flashed; thunder rolled. The first raindrops pelted the travelers. The divan whirled and lurched. It rose and plummeted with each wet gust.

Gu Gu and Dilara tried desperately to navigate through the wind and rain. Parsi even let the two pull his ears and vigorously tap his nose. But the storm was too fierce. The divan spun out of control.

The eyes and ears disappeared into the mouth of the gale. Parsi sprawled on his knees, eyes tightly shut. Gu Gu clung to Dilara. Dilara clung to the divan arms and prayed that they were not flung out into the void—

20. *The Sorrow Seller*

The storm spent its fury at last, as all storms must. The wind rested, getting its breath back. The sky wrung out its last few raindrops and invited the sun back to its accustomed place. But by the time the drenched travelers regained control of the flying divan, the walls of Nineveh had vanished. The Tigris was gone from sight as well. A changed landscape passed below: rolling grassland, stands of acacia, fields of rock and brush. A rainbow spanned the landscape and set it aglow.

A cluster of colorful mismatched dwellings and rectangular grain fields came into view. A low, rambling stone wall separated town and fields. A market bustled at the center of town.

"Let us set down here," Dilara said. "We can ask the townspeople in which direction Nineveh lies."

"And get supper at the market," Gu Gu said. He and Dilara had emptied the food bag of its last dried carp, dried date, and dried leek.

"With what money?" Dilara asked.

Gu Gu scratched his chin in thought, and then addressed Locque.

"O virtuous and secure one, permit me to take the lamp, in order to earn supper by performing little magics for the people."

"May Heaven provide, if magic fails," Locque remarked as the tumblers fell.

"I will remain behind," Parsi announced. "I need to practice my martial horn and shoulder maneuvers."

The sun redoubled its brilliance after the storm. The rainbow retreated, and steam rose from the dripping stones of the wall. In the market, merchants under striped awnings called out deals and discounts. The air smelled of cinnamon and frying-oil. All was noise and motion and money. Shoppers elbowed, jostled, argued. This was the town of Qa-ari.

No one noticed or spoke to Dilara and Gu Gu. They were alone in the crowd. Curiously, several men in the crowd limped on bandaged feet.

A three-man procession passed briskly. Two of these, wearing the red armbands of town bailiffs, held the third firmly arm-in-arm between them. Following the procession closely was a veiled woman who loudly berated the man in the middle, accusing him of offenses against women in general and herself specifically. The bailiffs took their captive to a low platform. Shoppers and merchants alike left their stands and circled the platform.

"What is happening, Gu Gu?"

"Local justice appears imminent. Let us move closer and take moral instruction."

A man with a blue sash over his embroidered robe mounted the platform. Dilara guessed this was the town Headman. He addressed the crowd through cupped hands.

"People of Qa-ari! We have apprehended yet another man bringing sorrow to his wife. Let us please Heaven by serving out justice. The bailiffs will now collect a donation of a quarter-daric from each merchant and shopper to pay for the punishment of the wrongdoer."

The crowd groaned. The bailiffs circulated. Hands reached sullenly into purses and money boxes. A figure in a black robe and hood stepped onto the platform. He swished a rod through the air as though testing it. The bailiffs secured the bringer of sorrow with his legs raised and sandals removed.

Suddenly—crack, flash, sulfur—the culprit burst free of his bonds. He rose, hovered, spun, thinned to a reed, and—whoosh—disappeared into the spout of the lamp in Gu Gu's arms. "Oooh!—" the watching crowd cried. The robed and hooded figure slashed his rod through empty air and addressed the Heavens with his bitter complaints.

Gu Gu said to Dilara: "A curious effect. I must have been rubbing the brass absently."

The Headman wore a thoughtful expression. Then he stepped to the front of the platform and raised his arms to regain the crowd's attention.

"People of Qa-ari!" He pointed at Gu Gu. "A child has come unto us bearing a magical lamp, into which a criminal has descended. What could this child be but a mighty sorcerer, sent by Heaven to spare us the continual expense of punishing cheaters. I call upon all merchants to show the magician our appreciation. Let us ply him with gifts, in hope he will choose to abide here in Qa-ari. O young sorcerer, you could do worse for a home. And by using your lamp to imprison men who bring sorrow to their wives, you will free us from our unending payments to the Bastinadists' Guild."

The bastinadist and bailiffs gave each other unhappy looks and scowled at the Headman. But the crowd approvingly cheered and stamped its feet.

Presently Dilara and Gu Gu found themselves seated on a stone bench near the platform, platters propped on their knees. The platters were heaped with steaming sausages in grape leaves, saffron rice with barberries, spiced meat topped with lemon and onions, lotus loaves, and yoghurt cake. At their feet were sacks full of other gifts: new tunics, sandals, veils, headscarves, skullcaps, chewing mints, velvet patches for the divan cushions, strips of birch bark for tooth-cleaning, and so on, all contributed by the grateful merchants of Qa-ari.

While Dilara and Gu Gu ate, voices issued from the brass lamp.

"Hey, move over there, and make some room!" "Move yourself. This lady and I were doing quite well in our confinement until you showed up." "Newcomer, I am quite overtaken by your handsomeness!" "Then climb over this old man so you can be closer. I will show you the talents for which I barely escaped the bastinado."

Dilara spoke into the lamp spout.

"O newcomer, fate has thrown us all together on a great adventure. I beg you to tell us your story and leave out nothing."

"Gladly, Mistress," came the answering voice. "I am Tayab. All my woes I owe to Qa-ari's new sorrow seller. Now, you might think it impossible that one could turn a profit selling sorrow. But hear my story, and you will understand.

"The sorrow seller only recently arrived here in Qa-ari. Our council of elders enacted a new law, under which the town has undertaken to punish unfaithful husbands. Coincidentally, the sorrow seller is an expert in detecting lapses in marital fidelity, once an aggrieved wife has agreed to pay the fee. There is no trial, nor may contrary evidence introduced. The town pays the Bastinadists' Guild out of donations, which are mandatory.

"Like many others, I labor every day in the grain fields outside the town walls. During today's afternoon dinner break, I headed to the market. There I noticed my wife Wazi conferring with the sorrow seller. They both turned to look at me. Their lips were pursed, their brows narrowed.

"I guessed what was up. But the town bailiffs closed in before I could run. They forcibly escorted me to the stall of the sorrow seller. Wazi watched closely as the sorrow seller scanned me head to toe. She sniffed my skin, examined my nails, traced the lines on my hands."

"Wait," Dilara said. "Did you say 'she?'" Tayab did not seem to notice the interruption.

"'The signs are indisputable,' the sorrow seller told Wazi. 'This man is cheating on you. In fact, he plans to see another woman this very night, and she is only the latest of many.'

"With that, Wazi tore her clothes and began wailing to the sky. The sorrow seller said, 'I have sold you sorrow, as promised. My fee is one daric, which I accept in installments.'"

"It was as though the sorrow seller had seen into my heart. I had indeed made plans to see the other woman, and true, she was the latest of many. But my intent today—may Heaven strike me down if it is not so—had been to inform her we must meet no more, at least as long as the new merchant was selling sorrow. My feet are quite tender. I need them intact so that I may toil in the fields. True, this lamp is cramped, but by summoning me here, the young magician has given me a reprieve."

"O Tayab," Dilara asked, "did this new merchant happen to have a pink top knot?"

"Why, yes, now that you mention it."

"And was there anything else unusual about her?"

"I recall now her skin was blue, which, come to think of it, is somewhat unusual."

Dilara rose.

"It is time I had a little talk with the sorrow seller of Qa-ari," she said.

"I will accompany you," Gu Gu said.

Idrosun's stall was at the far end of the market, squeezed between the stands of a mercer and a glover. Town bailiffs with their red arm bands leaned idly against the poles that held up the awning.

"Greetings once more, Idrosun," Dilara said. "This is my friend Gu Gu. He is teaching me about navigation and Greek gods."

"Greetings to you both," Idrosun said. "O my heart, how different you look. It is as though you come from some distant northern land, where the lack of sun leaves the skin the color of milk, and no flowers will grow in the frozen soil, so the women must grow them on their own heads. Still, I recognize your essence."

"It is Heaven's will that our paths keep crossing."

"How true, how true. And to think, I had hoped we would make life's journey together as ex-Djinn and wife, but then the inconsiderate sorcerer Vahid took my love and would not give it back."

No reply to this declaration issued from the lamp under Gu Gu's arm.

"Is it true you are selling sorrow now?"

"My heart, you forbade me to sell happiness. Now I cannot sell sorrow either?"

"What made you think that man, Tayab, was cheating on his wife?"

"Every man cheats on his wife," Idrosun said sadly, "or thinks about doing so. I found this out from centuries of granting wishes. By confirming the fears of Tayab's wife Wazi, I enabled her to experience the pleasure of seeing her worst expectations met."

"While you gained a profit. O Idrosun, how have you learned so much about human emotions?"

"Sorrow is the only emotion I truly understand. This is because I am in love with Vahid, who claims to be married to someone called 'My Work,' and alone among men, would never cheat."

Again, no comment came from the lamp.

The bastindadist arrived in his black robe and hood, rod hanging from his belt.

"Here is your share." He handed Idrosun a jingling bag. "Today's take is regrettably smaller than usual. This child sorcerer took one from us with heels unstriped."

"Gu Gu," the child sorcerer commented with a shrug.

The bailiffs also received clinking bags.

"The arrangement is clear to me." Dilara gave Idrosun a stern look. "You provide customers to the Bastinadists' Guild, which pays a cut to you and the others who are in on the scheme. But it is the people who must pay. O Idrosun, if only you still lived in the Ever Dark Wood, where the sins of the world would not have stained you."

A single tear fell upon the trembling blue chin.

"O Dilara, I left the Ever Dark Wood because of my love for you."

Crack, flash, sulfur, whoosh—Tayab stood in their midst, dazed, wobbly, blinking. The startled bailiffs kept enough wits about them to seize the wrongdoer by the arms. They dragged him back toward the platform. Dilara looked at Gu Gu.

"I have not yet achieved total command over how to hold the lamp," Gu Gu said, upon reflection.

"You have not shown me all of your talents yet, handsome Tayab!" Omid called from the lamp. "Do return to me after your bastinado."

The bastinadist gazed speculatively at Gu Gu.

"To prove the Guild's good will, we will punish this sinner at no cost to Qa-ari. But let us work out a mutually satisfactory arrangement for the future, O great sorcerer. In this business, there is profit enough for all."

"Gu Gu," was the great sorcerer's enigmatic response.

Idrosun twisted her top knot in her hands.

"I have lived for centuries, and yet I am but a child in this world," she said mournfully. "How can I ever learn all its evils? Only the heart of Vahid is perfect and true, and it is a heart denied to me."

For the third time, the lamp had nothing to say.

*

I have saved up all my tears through this terrible day. When Yenibi departs with her candle and leaves me alone in the dark—I'll shed them then.

A dingy closet serves for my sleeping quarters. Aprons, tunics, and mantles hang from iron pegs. My bed is a grain sack which Yenibi stuffed with straw and rags.

Yenibi is sitting cross-legged in the corner, an inkhorn and unrolled scroll in her lap. Fancy golden tassels hang from the scroll rod. She is taking down my every word. I told her I am not worth the ink. She said she is doing it out of habit. The twin brothers Gasparo and Kamran are my new owners, and Yenibi is their amanuensis. She follows them all day and writes everything they say. They dictate letters to her. She signs for deliveries. She records every aspect of the family business. And this morning she went to the royal palace to fetch the new slave.

Yenibi, a free woman, starts her work before sunup and continues late into the night. I, the new slave, have nothing to do. We agreed to be friends so we can share our loneliness.

Yenibi said Gasparo and Kamran purchased me because they need a slave for appearances. None of their neighbors or business associates own slaves. My presence will signal the twins' wealth and status when they host events.

One of these events, Yenibi told me, is the Storytellers Club. This group meets every week. I find this thrilling news. How I look forward to hearing tales told by others. I wonder if these stories will have sorcerers and Djinns. Will there be magic carpets and flying divans? Will characters suffer the torment of blind and hopeless love?

What would the men in the Storytellers Club think about a tale in which a character is enslaved by the Persians, and her son is taken away from her moments after he is born? What would they think if this slave invents stories to tell the King, is bought and freed by the man who loves her, and sells herself back into slavery in order to free him from debt?

I long to be the one who tells this very story to the Storytellers Club.

But I am a slave now. And a slave does not have the luxury of longing.

*

It seems as though an age has already passed. Was it only last night that I met Bourzou in the courtyard behind the Pavilion of Slaves? Ali-Haram had not awakened; I had not slept. It was the lightless time after moonset. Even the owls and nightingales had retired. The only noise was Bourzou looping the iron chains around my wrists and ankles, and keying the locks in place.

There was a creak of wagon wheels. A swinging lantern light approached. Oxen snorted. A figure climbed down from the wagon and moved in shadow toward us.

"This is Yenibi," Bourzou said. "She will take you to your new home. May Heaven protect you from harm."

A cloth bag passed from Yenibi to Bourzou. He placed the bag briefly in my palm so I could feel the weight of coins.

"Do my new owners know—?" I whispered.

"Of your past, nothing. Only that you come highly recommended. And child—" Bourzou hadn't called me that in many years. He seemed to search for words. Then: "Well, I'll see that Ali-Haram has the money today."

Would my husband start writing again once his debts were paid? Everything depended on it. Nevertheless, I had prepared several more chapters on my own, and I had taught them all to Scheherazade.

(But the Queen Consort did not know my plan. In fact, she had questioned why she had to learn so much at once. I mumbled something about the King sending Ali-Haram out on some new mission, and thus our need to get ahead in producing chapters. She raised a brow at this but chose not to question me further.)

Yenibi took the chain-handle. The iron links clanked as she led me toward the waiting wagon.

21. Lessons in Jealousy

(O lord husband—Scheherazade began the night's story, in my imagination—we left the travelers in the town of Qa-ari, where they found Idrosun selling sorrow in the local market. Meanwhile Gu Gu accidentally performed a feat of magic which resulted in an alarming loss of revenue for the Bastinadists' Guild.)

The merchants, shoppers, and townspeople of Qa-ari followed Gu Gu, the acclaimed child sorcerer, and Dilara out past the town walls. The parade made its way up a path of beaten earth lined with ferns, bread palms, and fragrant, white-flowering jasmine. Tayab sat on the shoulders of the satisfied Wazi, his feet wrapped in jute strips soaked in chamomile and blood.

The sorrow seller had joined the parade as well; she sniffed the air as though hunting prey.

Up ahead was the warlike figure of Parsi. He sprang repeatedly against some invisible foe, muzzle and horns lowered, front hooves tucked beneath him. The parade reached its end, and the Qa-arians watched in respectful silence as Dilara and Gu Gu took their places on the divan. Parsi, having finished his martial training, jumped up lightly and laid his noble head upon Dilara's knee. She scratched behind his new horns. The brass lamp rested in Gu Gu's lap. Idrosun crept ever closer, still sniffing.

The Headman was standing for reelection—the time had come for a speech. He addressed the travelers but declaimed loudly for all the voters to hear.

"O mighty sorcerer Gu Gu, I beg you not to leave us in the thrall of the Bastinadists Guild. Stay, and you will lack for nothing. In fact, as Headman I have entreated our council of elders to rename our town as

Gu Gu-ari, and they have so proclaimed!"

Polite stamping of feet from the assembled voters.

Idrosun suddenly leaped, issuing a terrifying howl. From experience Dilara recognized this howl as the love cry of the Lesser Tree Djinn. In a bound, Idrosun reached the divan and seized the lamp from Gu Gu's hands. She put the spout to her eye.

"Aha!" she cried. "There you are! I followed your scent, beloved. I see you have gotten yourself trapped in this lamp. I told you and told you about gambling with Thukamon. Well, tell your friend to move over. I am coming in. Gu Gu, work your magic—but wait. How strange I suddenly feel. What is happening to me?"

She dropped to her knees and clutched her pink braid.

"O Idrosun!" Dilara said anxiously. "What is wrong?"

"After all this time, here I am so close to Vahid, and yet for some reason I feel nothing. My heart is dead as a stone to him."

"The Spell of Blind and Hopeless love has finally worn off," Dilara said.

"My heart feels empty, and yet it is free of a great weight of longing. I no longer love Vahid. But—that means—"

Idrosun's eyes glowed. She rose and took Dilara's face in her hands. Startled, Dilara watched the blue face draw closer, closer, until the lips landed wetly on her own. A sigh of pleasure rose from the watching crowd.

It was Dilara's first kiss. The Dream Interpreter had given her dark warnings about kisses. She tried to imagine the lips as those of Prince Feroze.

"Voters of Gu Gu-ari," the Headman called out, improvising, "in my next term I call for more kissing and fewer bastinadoes!"

Idrosun had a speech of her own to make. She put a hand on her heart.

"O Dilara, formerly known as Khashar, the cruel chain of love that bound me to Vahid has snapped. I am free to love you at last. Where you lead, I will follow, even to the ends of the earth, for my heart is true."

More foot-stamping followed, especially from the men—the prospect of the sorrow seller leaving town did not displease them.

"We should reconsider," Gu Gu said to Dilara. His face was

unusually sullen. "Who will sell sorrow in Gu Gu-ari? Not to mention that the bastinadist's income will suffer as well."

"I renounce the sale of sorrow and happiness alike," Idrosun said solemnly. "My Dilara has taught me that human emotions should be neither bought nor sold."

Gu Gu had more objections.

"The divan is crowded already. A being of Idrosun's size would find it quite uncomfortable."

"I will follow on the ground," Idrosun announced. "It is all the same to me. As a bonus, I will bear on my back all the provisions given by the good people of Gu Gu-ari."

"Vahid has been with us since our journey began," Gu Gu said. (Why did he look so resentful?) "He should have a vote too."

A voice issued from the lamp.

"I magnanimously and of my own free will hereby renounce in perpetuity all romantic claims to Djinns, current or former. In this matter, let her follow her heart."

Dilara asked the Headman the way to Nineveh, but he had never heard of such a place, nor had any others in the crowd. Thukamon's eyes and ears knew the way, but the storm had swallowed them up. The most advisable course was to fly west in search of the blue ribbon of the Tigris.

The divan ascended. The waving townspeople diminished to a multi-colored patch on the earth, and then were gone from sight.

"Look at Idrosun," Dilara said to Gu Gu. "She is a blue speck, running to follow our drifting shadow. What a true, devoted friend."

Gu Gu's face darkened.

*

"O Master," Dilara addressed the lamp, "you said you owed your confinement in the lamp to the spirit of inquiry. What did that mean? Tell us your story now. Leave out nothing."

The landscape rolled past beneath—woods and thickets, valleys and hills, lakes and creeks, plains and plateaus—and not a glimpse of the Angel of Rivers.

"It all began," Vahid answered, "when Thukamon and I were debating a most interesting theoretical topic, namely, the most secure and humane means to imprison a man. I might have consumed more than one moon aura fizz. Anyway, I argued for planting the victim in soil. With watering and sunlight, his feet would turn to roots, his arms to branches. He would become at once man and plant, fixed in place. What could be more secure?

"What is humane? Consider. Being rooted, a prisoner would be as comfortable as any tree or shrub. He would even have the freedom to grow upward, if not laterally.

"Thukamon for his part proposed confining the victim in as small a space as possible—a lamp, for example. Such punishment would be humane, he argued, in that it would save the victim from any painful illusions of one day gaining freedom. As an added benefit, it would free up dungeon space for other deserving criminals.

"We agreed on a wager. We would serve ten years each in both prisons. After forty years, the superior method would doubtless be clear. He extended me the courtesy of going first."

Dilara could see that Thukamon had withheld certain aspects of his plan from Vahid.

"Master, I believe you should know all. Thukamon ordered me to deliver the lamp to the Frankish delegation. It is to be his personal gift to Charles Magnus. He said when the counterspell is applied, the Frankish court will witness a memorable magic."

"A magic, you say? Hmm—tell me this counterspell."

She recited it.

"I recognize the incantation. Thukamon's plan is clear. The so-called memorable magic is to be my emergence from the lamp in the form of a macaque. An elaborate prank, an act of revenge. I should have guessed. Thukamon has held a grudge for centuries because of a certain incident in our college days which—but never mind all that. Well, to be a macaque will be a novel experience, and I have never seen Europe—"

"Master, I do not wish to be a party to pranks or revenge. I will not deliver you up to the Franks." Dilara felt a glow of inner purpose and determination. "I will fetch Prince Feroze as agreed, thus preserving the alliance and world peace. Thukamon will have to be satisfied with that. Also, I know you have your Code of Ethics, but Gu Gu has been practicing—maybe he can extract you from the lamp."

"I would advise against it. The spell is inherently unstable. Witness what happened to that bringer of sorrows, Tayab. Besides, Omid and I are making this lamp a home. I have made improvements—a garden, a bath, a ledge to keep our feet above the invisible oil. Of course, space is limited, and so the improvements are only conjurings—"

The next morning, Parsi announced a change in the divan's heading.

"We will no longer try to reach Nineveh." Like Dilara, he was showing his resolve. He was truly a new sheep. "The time has come for me to return to the valley where my Baa-Wind lives. Bellow-Rumble and I will conduct our sacred final combat. Only one of us will leave the battlefield on four hooves."

"How will you find the valley?" Dilara asked.

"My pure heart will lead me. Besides, Baa-Wind's love calls me across the leagues."

"How will Gu Gu and I fly the divan when you are gone?"

The flying divan banked, turned, and soared toward the setting sun.

"Mistress, I have learned that suffering must precede nobility. You must purify your hearts. I have bleated."

Far below, tirelessly keeping pace with the flying divan, the blue speck ran on, league after league.

*

The following day, the travelers put the divan to earth. They took lunch in the soft grass beneath an acacia tree.

While bees droned above the dense yellow acacia blossoms, Dilara munched pears and almond crumble cake (both gifts of the grateful merchants of Gu Gu-ari). When a delegation of flies came to investigate her snack, Idrosun whirled her long pink braid sling-like and drove them off. Gu Gu, not to be outdone, traced the bees back to their hive and, fashioning a spout from a hollow grass stem, brought Dilara a bowl of fresh, warm honey.

Dilara watched as the two glared at each other and competed for her favor.

She pondered a memory from a summer past—

A new boy had turned up in the Ragged Quarter. He gave his name as Metipo; his age was ten years and three. He had joined Ghazi, Naseem, Khashar, and all the others in their games and adventures through the hot Baghdad afternoons.

Dilara had her suspicions of this Metipo, who like herself (and unlike the other skullcap-wearing boys), wore a turban of wound cotton cloth. But she said nothing and only watched.

One day the children were playing Bare-the-Hair. In this contest, pairs of combatants got within a square scratched in the dust, and tried to snatch off each other's head covering. The loser had to get on all fours and carry the winner on his back for the rest of the day.

Bare-the-Hair was a dangerous game for Dilara. Girls were not allowed—by the boys or the girls' own parents—to play in the streets of the Ragged Quarter. None of the boys suspected Dilara was a girl. She disguised herself by smearing dirt on her face, pitching her voice, stuffing her hair inside the green turban, and taking the boy's name Khashar. She was quick on her feet. No one had ever caught her out in her disguise.

Metipo had stepped into the square with Naseem. They circled. Metipo made a lunge. Naseem dodged, barely keeping his skullcap. Naseem made his own grab, but Metipo danced away with turban intact. The boys outside the circle shouted and cheered and laid wagers with money they did not have.

Naseem went limp. He grimaced—he had hurt his knee. But no, it was a ruse. Metipo chose the moment to make another move—Naseem's foot flew out to hook his opponent's leg. Metipo landed in the dust. The turban flew off—Naseem seized it—Metipo's long black hair tumbled down unbound.

The boys stared, thunderstruck. The truth dawned on them: a girl had snuck into their private world. Naseem broke the stunned silence.

"Coat her face in dust and give her rocks to swallow. This is the penalty for girls who sin by passing as boys."

"How about a good bastinado!" another boy had cried. He was learning the trade from his uncle, a member of the Guild.

Ghazi chose this moment to contest his ally and comrade for leadership. He stepped forward and held up a hand.

"Wait. What about the rest of you?" He had gazed at each face in its turn; no one answered. He looked at Dilara. "What do you think we should do—Khashar?"

Dilara's heart pounded. Why had Ghazi picked her out to answer? Did he suspect her own secret? Her world teetered on its edge. She chose her words carefully.

"What has Metipo done wrong?" she began. The boys stared in puzzlement at this question. Naseem scowled. Ghazi looked thoughtful. "If I were a girl, I would think it unfair to live in the shadows and waste my childhood years weaving. I would want to play and run and shout like the boys. That is all Metipo wants. I say, let her stay and be one of us—I, Khashar, have spoken."

This speech carried the day. The afternoon adventurers of the Ragged Quarter fully admitted Metipo into their band.

No other girls came along, nor did Dilara change her own disguise. Metipo was a girl among boys. And inevitably, all the boys fell in love with her—even Naseem. Each of these loves had the painful intensity of first infatuation. Challenges, issued and accepted, took the place of the usual games and adventures. Metipo presided, queen-like, over the fighting. Dilara found shadows to slip into.

The fighting went on. Soon all the rivals had fallen, save for Ghazi and Naseem.

Until now, the companionship between the two had been unbreakable. True, they were seeming opposites—Naseem surly and mean-spirited, Ghazi good-natured and guileless—and yet they had always been the staunchest of friends.

"We will fight for her," Naseem had said to Ghazi in front of the entire group. His voice was formal and deadly. "There will be no rules, and no quarter given. To the victor goes Metipo."

"So be it," Ghazi agreed.

They circled, faces set with fury and hatred. Before the first blow could land, a shriek cut through the air. Metipo rushed between the combatants. She threw herself at Ghazi's feet.

"I love Naseem!" she cried, sobbing. "O Ghazi, I beg you. Do not hurt a hair on his head."

Her declaration came too late. The fight could not be stopped. An epic battle ensued. It lasted through the long hot afternoon. Metipo suffered, covering her eyes, and peeking between her fingers at the combat. With each blow Ghazi landed, she cried out in pain and anguish. When a bloody cut opened over Naseem's eye, a similar wound appeared on Metipo.

When night fell, Ghazi nor Naseem alike limped home battered and scarred. Their battle had no winner. Metipo did not appear the next day, nor the day following. Never again was she seen in the Ragged Quarter.

It was as though she had only come to stir up hearts and test friendships.

In the fullness of time, the boys patched up their friendships. They restored their alliances. The games and adventures of the long Baghdad afternoons gradually returned to normal. Even Naseem and Ghazi forgot the fury and resentment that had driven them to blows.

But Dilara would never forget the strained and sullen faces, the set lips, the deadly rages.

Parsi and Bellow-Rumble. Naseem and Ghazi. And now Gu Gu and Idrosun.

Gu Gu was not old enough to know his own heart. But it was clear to Dilara. He had fallen in love with her.

The boy had drunk from the bitter cup of jealousy.

*

There was a hard uprush of air. A narrow valley, lush with clover and blue and green grass, rose between stands of wood. Wild climbing roses covered the bottom halves of the trees. It was a solid white hedge bounding the valley. A shepherd (awake this time) leaned on his crook, back turned to the descending divan.

"We have arrived, Mistress," Parsi announced. "The time has come. I shall win Baa-Wind, or die in the trying."

The flock of sheep lifted heads as one. Parsi leaped down as the divan neared the ground; he made his way toward the flock, head raised proudly. The shepherd turned. A turkey feather waggled behind his ear. He stared, wide-eyed. He threw down his crook.

"My Princess!" He ran toward her. "I have died and rejoined you in Paradise. O my love, never again will we be apart!"

Feroze's arms were warm, his kisses sweet. Dilara felt faint; her heart raced. The happiness of love caused the roses to rise and hover. Their perfume wafted through the warm air. She forgot about brave Parsi.

And, for a sweet moment, she forgot she was not Princess Maria Irena.

22. Partings and Reunions

Even after Ali-Haram bought and freed me, it had taken time to adjust to my new legal state. Out of habit I would address palace officials as Master, to their amusement. I had to remind myself not to lower my eyes around the court ladies. At night I dreamed I was back in the Pavilion of Slaves, assigned impossible and endless tasks by Bourzou.

But now that I had sold away my freedom, it did not take me long at all to adjust back to slave life.

The Storytellers Club met earlier this evening. The Storytellers wear brocaded tunics, silk trousers, and boots of fine leather. They have gold rings on their fingers and wear gems on chains around their necks. They are men of wealth. One talked about living on a houseboat that lay at anchor in the Euphrates River. Another had bought a vacated palace from the King himself.

My masters, the twins Gasparo and Kamran, presided over the Club. I was invisible to them. Yenibi gave me my assignments—scrub the floor before and after, cook and serve the food, put feather pillows under the men's heads when they fell unconscious.

No one tells stories at the Storytellers Club. The Club is a guise. The reason the men gather is to take Tears of the Poppy, which they prepare in tinctures to place under the tongue. After taking the Tears, they dance and sing. They chatter crazed nonsense. Eventually they fall asleep, mouths and eyes wide open.

I served one man and, forgetting myself, did not lower my gaze. He gave me an angry slap across the ear. I went reeling, stunned. He demanded that the twins punish me. Gasparo, his eyes glazed, told Yenibi to deal with me. She took me back to my sleeping closet and took a rod—loudly—to a cape that hung from a peg. Then she artfully striped the back of my legs with lip paint. She took me back to the Club to show off her handiwork, but the Storytellers had already forgotten the incident. They were lost to the world.

O Ali-Haram! Did you use my head-price to pay your debts? Are you writing again? I could bear this nightmare if I only knew—

*

(O lord husband—Scheherazade was no doubt beginning, back at the palace—recall that the sorrow seller Idrosun has left Gu Gu-ari to join the travelers, the acclaimed boy wizard Gu Gu has fallen in love with

146

Dilara, and Parsi has returned to the valley for his final combat with Bellow-Rumble—)

The Prince smelled of sweat and sheep. He took Dilara in his arms and spun her around—this confused the swarm of butterflies trying to light on the swinging rose petals. Dilara's happiness was complete.

"Now I understand what happened," Feroze said. "I perished and rejoined you in Paradise. And look! There is the Djinn who disrupted our wedding. Well, in my joy I forgive her. But how did I die, I wonder? I remember nothing—"

"O Prince, listen to me." Dilara tried to interrupt. "You are still dwelling in the land of the living."

Feroze was in a transport. He could not stop talking.

"You see, I set out with the Frankish delegation, to offer your father my own head in exchange for your dear departed body, but a terrible storm came up. It washed out the road to Nineveh. I got separated from the group. Lost, I wandered into this valley. I met a shepherd who said his flock had dismissed him from his post, on the charge of sleeping on duty. Hearing this, I felt at once a great calling. I understood that my destiny all along had been to lead not men, but sheep. Sheep are a noble race, free from our base passions. The shepherd handed over his crook and showed me the way to this valley. Of course, I did not yet realize that I had died. What will happen to my father's alliance with Charles Magnus, without my head to atone? Well, worldly affairs are of no concern to you and me, for now we are in Paradise, where—"

Even with the one she loved beside her at last, in her heart Dilara knew that Feroze deserved the truth.

"O Prince, listen to me speak. My words are not in the Frankish tongue, but the Persian. The Princess that you see is only my outer form, which the sorcerer Thukamon gave to me. He sent me on a mission to bring you back to Baghdad. In short, I am not Maria Irena."

Feroze took a step back and studied her. His brow wrinkled with concentration.

"Could it be true? You resemble my bride in every aspect, but somehow the blind and hopeless love I had for her is gone from my heart. But if this is life, and you are not Maria Irena, then—who are you?"

"I am Dilara. Do you not remember me from your wedding day?"

"Of course, I remember Dilara. But if you are truly Dilara, then you know there is no Dilara. That is, Dilara is a disguise worn by Khashar, my devoted viz—but wait! Who is that sitting on the divan? Can it be—?"

"Gu Gu," Gu Gu growled, his jaw set, his brows lowered.

"Ha ha ha, I see you have not changed!"

"You know each other?" Dilara was astonished.

"Do I know him? Does the sun go around the Earth? O, I know him—well enough to tell you what a disappointment he has been to his poor parents."

"Gu Gu!" Gu Gu folded his arms and looked away.

"My lord Prince," Dilara begged, "do not mock the boy. He is a brilliant scholar who has taken a vow to speak to none but me."

"Brilliant scholar? That is a good one. Tell it to his tutors. He has learned two words in his entire life, and they are both Gu. Why, I remember when he—"

Feroze broke off as Parsi drew near. Another sheep was at Parsi's shoulder. The fleece was black save for a white diamond on the head. Dilara's blood ran cold. Could this be the dreaded Bellow-Rumble! With her head swimming from the nearness of Feroze, she had quite forgotten Parsi's imminent battle. Soon one of the enemies would lie dying, and nothing could stop this.

But the newcomer was not Bellow-Rumble.

"O mistress," Parsi bleated, "let me introduce you to my beloved, Baa-Wind."

Baa-Wind! Joy poured into Dilara's heart to meet Parsi's beloved at last.

"Parsi has told me much about you," Baa-Wind bleated. Something in the bleats struck Dilara as strangely familiar. "Welcome to Zozor, which is what we sheep call this valley."

"O Parsi," Dilara said. "I am fearful about your upcoming combat with Bellow-Rumble—"

"My love would have given me the strength to triumph," Parsi said. "But there will be no combat now."

"I will explain to her, beloved." A stray wind lifted Baa-Wind's black fleece. "After the first combat, Bellow-Rumble and I left the flock together. We roamed the land, waiting out the seven days until the appointed second combat. But then, while on our travels, we met a passing ram. Bellow-Rumble quarreled with him, and they fought. Bellow-Rumble killed him."

Parsi took up the story.

"Tracker rams, who enforce our laws, intercepted them. The trackers took their statements and weighed the evidence. They found Bellow-Rumble guilty of killing outside of courtship. This is a great crime in the world of sheep, and for this reason Bellow-Rumble paid the price."

Dilara remembered Feroze characterizing sheep as a race without the base passions of men.

"I returned to Zozor, alone," Baa-Wind continued. "I rejoined my flock. Then Feroze arrived to take up the crook. And to complete my happiness, Parsi returned to me. But child, do you not recognize me? Although, true enough, I barely know myself after all these aeons—"

It was suddenly clear. Dilara threw her arms round the fleecy neck.

"O demi-goddess Abi! Can it truly be you? Are you still trying to remember your true form?"

"So far, I have ruled out owl, tree frog, bear, vole, raven, walking stick, scorpion, and now sheep—well, what does it matter? Now that I am with Parsi, I know the meaning of love. I am content to finish my days in this form." Baa-Wind noticed Idrosun. "And could that be the Djinn of the Ever Dark Wood! What are you doing out of your tree, dear?"

Idrosun twisted her long pink braid through her fingers.

"Love drew me away, demi-goddess."

Idrosun went on to tell Baa-Wind her adventures in the world beyond the Ever Dark Wood. Dilara pulled Gu Gu aside.

"I first met the demi-goddess when I was a little girl. She foresaw that her descendant would enable a kindness for someone I love, in his hour of need."

"And I suppose this someone you love is Idrosun." Gu Gu scowled.

Well, of course he had fallen in love with her. How much unhappiness love could cause—

"I love Feroze," she said with feeling, "and that is only on account of Vahid's spell."

(Although there was, in fact, a certain other one in her heart—but best not to let herself think about him. After all, he did not even know she existed—)

"But Mistress," Idrosun was saying to Baa-Wind, "you too have traveled far. How do you come to be here in Zozor, and not in the Ever Dark Wood?"

"I am not as far from my home as you may think. Listen to my story, and you will understand.

"Certain courtiers hatched a plan to build a great highway joining Baghdad and Nineveh. The courtiers stood to gain great wealth from this project. But the Ever Dark Wood lay along the planned path of the highway. I lifted the Curtain of Blessed Invisibility, so the courtiers would see the challenge facing them and so change their route.

"But in their arrogance, they grew more determined than ever. Axes and picks and hammers began to ring along the edges of my Wood. Work gangs arrived with carts full of paving stones. Only one course of action remained open to me.

"The lovely woods that border this valley are like walls of white, from the wild roses that climb up the trees. High in one of these trees, on a broad limb, is an abandoned eagle's nest. I cast a Spell of Compression over the Ever Dark Wood, grew an egg about the Wood, and left the egg in the nest. The trees, the brooks, all the life that crawls or runs or flies or springs up from roots, even the glowing mushrooms, will go on undisturbed within the egg, until the day the Spell of Compression is removed. Only then will the Wood resume its place in the world."

Parsi came to stand beside Baa-Wind. He addressed the gathering:

"The time has come for goodbyes. Flock, we enjoin you to obey your shepherd Feroze in all things. Travelers, from now on you must journey afoot. I will no longer be your pilot. My love and I are leaving Zozor. We will live out our days together journeying through the wide world. Henceforth, we will no longer speak the words of men and women. We will use only the sacred tongue of sheep. I have bleated."

And with that, Parsi and Baa-Wind moved through the flock, which respectfully parted for them. When the two reached the edge of the valley, they turned back and called out their final farewells—wild animal sounds, emptied of human words.

*

Dilara, Gu Gu, and Feroze took their places on the pilotless divan (which was now only useful for sitting) and produced the evening meal from what remained of the bounty provided by grateful Gu Gu-ari. The opening course was saffron-rice-barberry cake. Feroze's flock lazily munched lush clover nearby.

(Inside the lamp Vahid and Omid dined on roast octopus and guava fruit topped with star dust. The conjured feast was regrettably less than filling.)

Dilara begged Feroze for news from home. But the Prince had nothing to tell of events in the Ragged Quarter. For general news he had but a single item:

"The day we learned of Maria Irena's death from sun sickness, a kitchen slave claimed to have entered Thukamon's laboratorium and seen the ghost of the Princess shackled there. Naturally, the slave was soundly beaten for his lies. As if anyone in our modern age believes in ghosts. But the slave later returned to the laboratorium, and this time said the shackled ghost-figure had changed to a sheep with blue eyes and yellow fleece. All this proved most aggrieving and hurtful to the Franks, who were still mourning their dead Princess. Naturally, the slave was beaten anew."

Dilara thought: a yellow-fleeced sheep? She had seen an animal of that very description wobbling on Thukamon's magic carpet—

"O Prince," Idrosun said, while slices of fresh honeycomb were passed around, "did you know Dilara can ride sunbeams? Well, I can, too."

Gu Gu would not be outdone. When Feroze briefly left the divan to attend to his flock, Gu Gu (ever faithful to his speech-vows) took the opportunity to boast:

"Did you know this tasty honeycomb comes from Gu Gu-ari? The natives named the town after me."

Feroze returned to the divan. Dilara's fingers trembled from his closeness, and her heart pounded from the intensity of love.

"O Prince," she said, "you spoke of the boy Khashar. Tell me more about him."

"Ah, Khashar! My devoted and clever one," Feroze said with a sigh. "Wise, daring, brave. And I should add, a master of disguise. One day he will return to me, and I will train him to be my shepherd-vizier. We will multiply my flock until it is the pride of all Persia. But enough about him. Gu Gu, explain to me how you came into possession of Thukamon's brass lamp."

"Gu Gu," was the stubborn answer.

Dilara related Thukamon's deceitful attempt to have the lamp, with Vahid inside, sent to the court of Charles Magnus.

"Wait. Father's sorcerer is living in the lamp?" Feroze was confused.

"I am indeed, O Prince," came a familiar voice from the lamp spout. "You see, my wife and I have—"

Now Dilara was the confused one. She interrupted.

"O Master Vahid, something fooled my ears. Did you say your wife?"

"Yes, word reached us concerning the annulment of her earlier union. By ancient law, we jumped over a broom together three times, saying 'I wed thee, I wed thee, I wed thee.' The broom and jumping were perforce conjurings, naturally. But I am somewhat sure of the legality. Dear Omid, tell Dilara how happy we are."

"True, he is a few centuries older than I," Omid said, "but what does that matter? He is quite handy with magic. I convinced him to use his powers to transform his face into that of Tayab, the handsome Gu Gu-arian who is no longer in the lamp with us."

"By the way," Vahid added, "I have been in communication through the aether with Thukamon."

"I hope you did not tell him our whereabouts—?" Dilara said with unease.

"Gu Gu!" Gu Gu pointed toward the horizon, where a black dot was crossing the bloated, lowering sun. The dot grew steadily larger, and the sunlight transformed the black to gold and red.

"Failing to do so would have been rude," Vahid said. "He requested the pleasure of a visit. Besides, he and I have certain negotiations to pursue."

A few moments later, the magic carpet hovered above the company. The emerald-colored tassels fluttered in the breeze. The eyes and ears, bloodshot and chapped, respectively, from the storm, made wobbly circles around the grinning sorcerer's serpent headdress. Next to Thukamon on the carpet was the sheep with yellow fleece.

"Stay," he told the sheep sharply. "I have business to conduct."

The light shifted, and Dilara saw the sheep's blue eyes. She had an instant of understanding.

"O Thukamon," she said, drawing a deep breath for courage, "it was you who turned the Princess into a sheep. Now I beg you to reverse the transformation."

Of course, once he did so, there would be two of her. Both would have the face, the form, the hair—but only one the essence. Feroze would have his Princess once more, and Dilara would lose Feroze forever. But the true Maria Irena must return to the court of Charles Magnus. Only this would prevent war.

"I must decline, on the grounds of inconvenience." Thukamon slapped his passenger on the rump, and she jumped down from the carpet. "But from the goodness of my heart, I will let her to graze here on the grasses of Zozor while I conduct my business with Vahid. But then we are off to Constantinople, where I anticipate a handsome profit from her."

The yellow-fleeced sheep trotted straight for the shepherd. She nudged his knee; she fixed her luminous blue eyes on him.

He stared back at her, scratching his head in puzzlement.

23. How Thukamon Lost His Grin

Tears of the Poppy were shed in profusion tonight. Men lay everywhere in their stupors—on mats, on divans, on the floor. The reek was suffocating.

Sometime during the night, back in my sleep quarters, I woke to the clanking of keys. It was Yenibi. She brought in a straw mat, which she laid next to my grain sack. Giggling, she chained our ankles together and laid the key on my belly. We lay together in the dark.

I do not love Yenibi the way I love Ali-Haram. I wouldn't sell myself into slavery for her. But we meet each other's needs, which come from loneliness. The heat of my body comforts her in the night, and she pulls me back from the edge of despair.

"The twins thought they took every precaution," she said later. "But the Holy Ones may have learned what really takes place at the Storytellers Club. We expect a raid—from the Sentinels of the Muhtasib."

My insides went cold.

"O Yenibi, why do the men have to take Tears of the Poppy? If the Sentinels find them out, Gasparo and Kamran will lose everything."

"Without the Tears, the twins would be as poor as you and I. The Tears are the source of all their wealth. The house, the gardens, the pavilions, even you—everything they have, they bought with the darics men pay to take the Tears and lose their minds."

"Is it true the Sentinels are empowered to investigate, judge, and punish, all at once—?"

She nodded gravely.

"In the time of our grandparents, the Muhtasib enforced rules of weights and measures in markets. Today many crimes come under its reach. It is as the defender of public morals."

An idea seized me.

"Why not hire a real storyteller, Yenibi? When the Sentinels get here, they would see a true Storytellers Club, if only for the night."

"An interesting plan." She considered. "The men will not be happy to trade their Tears for stories."

"But if it's that, or years in a dungeon—?"

"Yes. I think the twins will welcome the plan. But why pay a professional? You already have experience. And the twins are always averse to spending darics if they don't have to."

"Surely the men would find it demeaning to listen to a lowly slave, no matter her experience or skills."

"Hmm—do you know anyone else in the storytelling trade?"

"Only one," I answered. "And she is the greatest of us all. But she thinks I am off in distant Maqazza, attending to my ill mother. I may as well be on the moon."

*

(O Majesty—Scheherazade would have begun—my story left off with Parsi and Baa-Wind leaving the valley of Zozor, and Thukamon arriving on his magic carpet.)

"Let us get to business straightaway," the grinning Thukamon said to Dilara. "You did not deliver the lamp to the Frankish delegation. This forces me to take on that most essential task myself. Hand the lamp over if you please."

"Tell him that the lamp is not, strictly speaking, in our custody." Gu Gu, addressing Dilara, remained technically faithful to his vow of infant-talk. "He will have to go through Locque."

"One who does ill with his toys will have them taken away," Locque observed darkly.

Thukamon grinned.

"This Locque looks like something a certain rival of mine would create in a vat. Well, we can get back to the business of the lamp later." He addressed Dilara again. "At any rate, your failure makes our agreement void. Naturally, your parents will not receive the promised eyes."

Dilara's heart filled with resentment and disappointment. She knew a vast sense of injustice. And yet she felt something else—a sweet flood of relief. Her mission had ended. The fate of nations no longer depended on her.

"In that case, return me to my true form," she said. "And tell me the way to Baghdad. I will go back on foot, and trouble you no more."

"We will journey together, my love!" Idrosun cried happily.

A silvery plume issued from the lamp spout. At first the plume hung suspended. Then it began to spin. It clumped, growing chin, lips, nose. The eyes had no pupils, the head no hair.

This disembodied head was Vahid's familiar, Vahidium.

"Thukamon, it was my Master who devised the original plan to bring Feroze back to Baghdad." Vahidium's voice came through unmoving lips, although it boomed and carried like that of the sorcerer himself. The grazing sheep curiously lifted their heads and looked toward the sound. "And you will recall that it was Vahid who informed you how to find Dilara, so the plan could be carried out."

"Your observations, which I do not contest, lack relevance." Thukamon adjusted his serpent headdress.

The familiar went on: "Do they? While you spoke your lofty words about the fate of nations, your true purpose was to play an elaborate and malicious joke on my Master. Well, before we go any farther, will you be so good as to reverse the spell so he may leave the lamp?"

"And deprive Charles Magnus of the opportunity to see a capering Vahid-macaque? Besides, voiding the terms of a wager is poor practice. I stipulate, however, that this 'malicious joke,' as you term it, will serve as retributive payment in full for the Conjuration of Physical Immutability he inflicted on my face."

"My Master wishes to return to that matter later. But first, why did you falsely announce that the Princess had died of sun sickness? And why transform her into a sheep?"

"Because only alive, but out of sight and believed dead, could she serve my purpose."

"What was that purpose?"

"To smuggle her to Constantinople. The Roman emperor plans to use her as a hostage in negotiations with Charles Magnus, his sworn enemy. For this I stand to earn a considerable sum. In fact, now that the Princess is with lamb, I plan to renegotiate my agreement with the emperor. The lamb will have a claim to the Frankish throne, thereby increasing the hostage value of the Princess."

"A clever calculation on your part," Vahidium granted. "But why did you let Dilara and the boy undertake the mission on their own?"

"One of my ears had brought me urgent news. A second accidental witness to the shackling of the Princess had turned up—a palace cook. I had to return to Baghdad and bribe the cook for his silence. If there was suspicion that Maria Irena was, in fact, alive, I would be in a most difficult position. Time was critical. I had no choice but to trust the girl. I intended to catch up with her in Nineveh, but the storm intervened. It took me many days of searching to find the flying divan."

"Back to the girl: was it not her mission to find the Prince? Well, here he is. Regardless of the fate of my Master, surely some reward is due the girl for this, in the interest of fairness."

Dilara made out Vahid's muffled aside coming from the lamp.

"Dearest, go to my laboratorium. Crush spearmint, goat weed, and golden root together, in the ratio four to one to three."

"Yes, lord husband. May I suggest lavender, for the odor?"

"Excellent idea."

Vahidium was saying: "—back to her true form, and give her parents four new eyes."

"One eye, to be shared," Thukamon countered. The bargaining was on. "True, the girl found the Prince, but she did not bring him to me. And that is not even to mention the whole business with the lamp."

"Very well. Her true form, three eyes to be shared between them, and my master will grant your heart's desire."

"My heart's desire? What knowledge could Vahid have of my heart?"

"What was that girl's name? The Lebanese beauty? Ah yes, Zaib. Why did she leave you back in Babylon? Could it have been something to do with that Conjuration you mentioned—?"

Above the frozen grin, Thukamon's eyes narrowed.

"Come to think of it," Vahidium continued, "after Zaib's husband underwent the transformation of his speech, he ascended directly to Heaven, leaving our world. That means Zaib is free to wed again. My Master, having cast the Conjuration upon you, hereby offers to reverse it."

"An empty offer," Thukamon said. "The Conjuration has no known reversal."

"True, you will not find one in the Guild scrollarium. The reversal is my Master's original creation, for which he claims all proprietary interests. In the interests of full disclosure, the reversal may share certain characteristics with the spell used on Zaib's former husband. You suspect a trick? Very well, if Vahid does not remove your grin permanently, you may chain him in the sphere of Venus for two full aeons."

"The sphere of Saturn, and three aeons."

The first shy stars appeared. Darkness settled over Zozor. Nightjars and tree frogs filled the valley with their calls. The moon rose over the far line of trees. At last, the sorcerer and familiar came to an agreement. Thukamon plucked two of the eyes (one for each parent) from their wobbly orbitd and put them into a small cloth sack, which he gave to Dilara. Gu Gu un-Locqued the lamp and handed it over to Thukamon.

"And how are these eyes to be installed?" Vahidium asked.

"Why, I shall do it myself, the very next time I visit the Ragged Quarter." And so saying, Thukamon tilted the lamp over Dilara's head and poured.

She squeezed her eyes shut. The cold penetrated her bones. The world took on a different smell—the perfume of roses vanished. Her facial planes shifted; she felt her belly shrink.

Gu Gu gaped at her.

"Your eyes and hair are dark—" he whispered. "I forgot you were a Persian."

"The reversal has been prepared," Vahidium announced. He

vanished into the lamp, and now a second plume appeared. This plume bore the strong scent of lavender. It assumed the form of lips, which attached themselves to Thukamon's face. The sorcerer's mouth began to work, as though chewing something too large for it.

Vahid spoke up from the lamp.

"For the benefit of a monograph I hope to write, would you be so good as to describe your sensations?"

But Thukamon was unable to speak. He opened his mouth, wider, wider. His jaws clenched, unclenched, and then came unhinged, like those of a serpent. A light glowed between his lips. The light grew; it took on arms, head, legs, wings. A little being of light formed. The being clasped its hands as though in prayer. It lifted luminous eyes toward Heaven.

Another being of light followed, and another. Over and over, they exited Thukamon's mouth. They drifted across the valley, forming a starry ring that lined the horizons. Protrusions appeared on the sorcerer's own back. The protrusions grew, becoming wings. Thukamon, having authored so many celestial beings, was turning into an Angel himself. The grin finally vanished, replaced by an aura. The aura absorbed his mouth and eyes and shimmered along his legs, arms, and wings.

Thukamon ascended. He merged with the light and vanished to human sight.

The eyes and ears tried to follow their Master, but when the air thinned, they plunged back earthward. (Where they landed is unknown to this day.)

Omid said: "O husband, Thukamon is no longer the greatest sorcerer of our age. For this reason, he is not bound by the code of ethics. Will he free us from the lamp now?"

"It is quite doubtful," Vahid answered. "Angels dwell in Paradise. What do they care for the affairs of this world? Do not despair, my dear. I have many plans for conjured improvements in our home. A pavilion here, a greenhouse there, a bustling market where you can shop–"

"O Master," Dilara observed admiringly, "truly you rid Thukamon of his grin."

Vahid said: "For the true peace that Angels experience, no facial expression exists."

*

"And now, Prince Feroze, it is time for you to return to Baghdad," Vahid said. "No more of this sheep-herding nonsense. You are the heir. You must consult with your father and tell him all that has happened. You must forcefully convey how Thukamon betrayed him, and how he must take steps to save the alliance with Charles Magnus. There is no time to lose."

"I am blindly and hopelessly drawn to this sheep," Feroze said, with feeling. "At the same time, I am strangely detecting the nearby essence of Princess Maria Irena."

Understanding, lit by Angel-light, crept slowly across his face.

In time the edges of the world returned to darkness. The Angels produced by Thukamon had followed their Master to Paradise.

"If only we could find Parsi again, with his pure and noble heart," Dilara said, "and convince him to pilot the flying divan."

The head of the yellow-fleeced sheep lay tenderly across Feroze's knee. Dilara felt the familiar stab of jealousy—her breath and belly and hair were her own once more, but the reversal of her transformation held no power against that single smear of ointment, after which had come that accidental glance in the wedding mirror.

"Hmm—Thukamon, who can get around with his wings now, will have no use for a magic carpet," Vahid observed. "I am sure he will not mind if we use it to return to the palace."

The Prince thumped his crook on the ground.

"My loyalty is to Maria Irena. If I cannot have my love and helpmate with me in her Frankish form, then I shall remain with her here, in Zozor. My beloved is part of my flock, and to serve and lead my flock is my destiny."

Vahid tried to reason with the Prince.

"You are the firstborn son of King Alcimedes. Your loyalties properly lie with your father and your Kingdom."

This did now sway Feroze.

"The Princess's unborn is the lamb of my loins. The valley of Zozor is my Kingdom now. The crook is my scepter, and these sheep are my people. Fate has drawn me here to lead and defend them, and to live out my days with them." After a pause he added softly, "Besides, there is another heir."

After a long silence, Vahid said:

"Yes—Faridun."

"Who is Faridun?" Idrosun wondered aloud.

"I heard you speak today, brother," Feroze said, "when you thought I was not listening. It is clear to me you are not the fool you have wanted us to believe all these years."

"Gu Gu," Gu Gu said.

"Well, Prince Faridun, what of it?" Vahid said. "Feroze is abdicating. This makes you the heir. Will you renounce your principles of speech, and reconcile with him before we depart?"

Gu Gu looked at Dilara (who stared back in wide-eyed astonishment), at Idrosun, at the lamp, at the dark line of trees—everywhere but at Feroze.

"Faridun, my brother, your destiny is to rule Persia." Feroze said softly. "I beg forgiveness for the times I mocked you."

Weeping, the brothers embraced. Then Gu Gu pulled free. His face shone in the moonlight.

"Feroze has his beloved beside him," he said. "If I am to ascend to the throne, I must have my love with me as well. Vahid, I order you to engrave a tablet with Dilara's name and mine. Let the tablet be sealed and filed in the archives of the Holy Ones. As soon as I come of age, she and I will be joined in holy union."

Idrosun's brows narrowed.

"Not while I have anything to say about it!" she growled.

She set her long pink braid into a whirl, ever faster. The new heir to the Persian throne retreated, too slowly. The braid-sling caught him across the temple.

He fell to the dewy grass, in love and unconscious.

*

And there he lay, lord husband. (So Scheherazade would have continued, while King Shahryar sprawled abed as usual, eyes closed, fully awake.) When first light spilled across Zozor, Feroze said his goodbyes and took Maria Irena and the rest of his flock to the far end of the valley, where the dew lay lightest on the wildflowers. Vahid sent the remorseful Idrosun to collect wild blueberries and saffron crocus, from which to make a poultice for Gu Gu's aching head.

Vahid then gave the new heir his first political lessons:

"It is not possible for you to choose your own bride. She must serve political purposes."

"But if I were to wed Dilara," Gu Gu rebutted, "it would signal to the population of the Ragged Quarter that the future King is a man of the people. They would know that he would always have their interests in his heart."

Vahid said: "The good will of one Charles Magnus is worth that of a thousand Ragged Quarters. Regrettably, this is the nature of our world."

Gu Gu grunted stubbornly. In his agitation, he pushed the poultice away.

"Above all," the sorcerer continued, "your love for Dilara cannot be, for this simple rule: you may only wed one of royal blood. She is a commoner."

Gu Gu rolled over in the damp grass and gazed unhappily at the lamp. But finally he rose to his feet. He squared his shoulders. Something had changed in him. Dilara sensed his new assurance and vision. She also sensed a new, unbridgeable distance between them.

The Prince took the brass lamp under his arm, mounted Thukamon's magic carpet, and left for Baghdad. He said no goodbyes, nor did he look back. Within moments, the carpet was no larger to the eye than a distant eagle. Then it was gone, and Dilara and Idrosun stood alone in the valley of Zozor. And thus, O majesty, I bring this part of the story to an end.

*

"Your story has pleased us," Shahryar might have said at this point. "Still, we have one observation to make. We must fault Our ancestor, King Alcimedes, for letting his sons become estranged. Royal blood must rise above pride and petty rivalries. The fates of so many are in our hands. It is to the boys' credit that they understood this in the end."

"The King's wisdom is boundless," Scheherazade would have murmured.

"But, wife, what of the eyes Thukamon promised to install for the Cobbler and Dream Interpreter? Surely no Angel would willingly leave Heaven to visit the Ragged Quarter."

"In the end, Dilara's parents were brought to the royal palace, where Vahidium himself installed the eyes, one to each, under Vahid's supervision from the lamp. Unfortunately, one of the subspells was bungled, and until the end of their lives, whenever the moon was new and Venus reversed procession, the Cobbler and Dream Interpreter saw night without its darkness, animals without their fur, and people without their hatreds."

"But what did the two say when people asked them about their missing daughter Dilara?"

"That her husband Naseem had taken her to Nineveh for the waters, and that they would return to the Ragged Quarter when her curse of braying was finally lifted."

"And what of Dilara and Idrosun? Did they stay in the valley with Feroze and his flock?"

At this point Scheherazade might have yawned. Or she might have poured the King more Water of Angels. Or she might have only gazed through the arched window at the setting moon.

"O my lord husband, it is late in the night, and even the eyelids of a great King must grow heavy. Soon enough you will hear the next amazing adventure of Dilara and Idrosun, and other wondrous stories as well—"

24. A Certain Dwelling, Not Far from the Palace

"We are in for a very long day tomorrow."

Yenibi's fingertips brushed mine in the darkness. I rolled onto my side, facing her.

"Yes, the Storytellers Club meets in the evening. I must clean before and after, and there's all the cooking—"

"You'll be doing a lot more than that, Ariana. Gasparo and Kamran expect a raid from the Muhtasib. We need to find a spot in the garden to bury the Tears of the Poppy, along with the bowls, pestles, droppers and all the rest."

"What if the Sentinels question us?"

"We are women. It would never occur to them."

"You found a storyteller?"

The twins had put Yenibi's plan in place. For a single evening, the Storytellers Club would pretend to be a Storytellers Club.

"I can tell you it's someone with experience and talent," she said. "Although the storyteller inexplicably refused to take a fee."

We slept then, and awakened before daybreak. After unfastening my chains, she plopped cross-legged onto my grain-sack bedding, holding the pen and inkhorn she carried everywhere, along with the scroll with the golden tassels.

"Let's continue. You told me why you sold yourself back into slavery. But I don't understand why Ali-Haram would not let you be with your son." She scratched away with her pen.

"Now you're my amanuensis as well as the twins?"

"I'm writing your life."

"A waste of good ink. But anyway, as for my husband, he had made a bargain with the child's foster mother. He promised to pay for all of Emre's needs, and she agreed to take the boy into her home, on the condition that Emre never meet his true mother."

"Poor Ariana," she murmured. "Such a hard condition."

"Not that hard, I suppose, when I lived in the Pavilion of Slaves. But when Ali-Haram freed and married me, I let myself hope. What little money I had, I used on foolish schemes to see the boy, even while my husband kept reducing my household allowance to pay off his gambling debts."

Yenibi blew on the unrolled parchment.

"What a disease gambling is," she said. "If only Ali-Haram had only suffered from leprosy, or consumption—"

*

I was spooning stuffed peppers onto a platter when Yenibi came into the kitchen.

"Gasparo told me to fetch more Water of Angels," she said.

"After all his complaining about how much that Turkish trader at the palace was charging for frozen chunks of water." I handed her a slicing knife. "Cut up a cucumber for the pitcher before you take it in, will you?"

She used the knife inexpertly, tongue between her lips in concentration. A fist pounded on the house's oak door—a jolt went through me—but no, no, it was only Yenibi's knife chopping against the marble block. My dread had me on edge.

"O Yenibi," I said, "if the Sentinels come and arrest the twins, what will happen to me? I could be sold off at auction. All my plans would come to nothing. I'd never see my husband or son again—"

"The Sentinels are already here. They have not arrested anyone. I don't know if they appreciate the storytelling, but it didn't take them long to finish off the rosewater sorbet you set out and ask for more."

A burst of laughter came through the wall which the Club chambers shared with the kitchen. I sent a silent prayer of thanks to Heaven.

"Let me come and hear the storyteller," I begged.

"Bring another tray of sorbet. Then you may stay and listen."

The men were in their usual places—divans, sitting rugs, wicker stools. The two Sentinels leaned against the wall in their black robes and hoods. Their scimitars hung from their kaftans in curved leather scabbards. The twins sat cross-legged on tasseled velvet cushions. The men were rapt. I set my tray on a table.

The storyteller stood before the group in a plain green tunic, baggy green trousers, headscarf and veil of plain white cloth, and wooden sandals. She wore no jewelry. Her head bent over an unrolled scroll. I could not see her eyes.

She was reading aloud—

> "'—the people will rise up. They will demand that Father step down in my favor. My first act of office will be to order the beheading of the sorcerer Vahid. In fact, you will have several beheadings to carry out, because—'"

I recognized the voice before the words. I forgot my duties, I forgot my place, I forgot everything. A happiness filled me that I thought I would never know again. When the storyteller looked up and realized who was rushing toward her, she dropped her scroll; it rolled along the floor, unwinding to its full length. She spread her arms wide to welcome me.

In their shock, the men sucked in their breath; they grumbled, shouted, cursed. Who was this slave to enter their Storytellers Club? How dared she interrupt their entertainment?

In our happiness the storyteller and I ignored them.

O you men who put aside the Tears of the Poppy for a single night, this story that has held you spellbound, made you laugh, roused your hearts, led you to cheer and stamp your feet—the insolent slave you see before you is the very one who created this story.

And the one who has been reading it to you is the greatest storyteller history has ever known: the incomparable Scheherazade.

*

Back in the kitchen, after the reading, Scheherazade and I wept and laughed and talked all at once. She set a cloth bag on the counter. The bag clinked.

"This is for Gasparo and Kamran," she said. "It is more than what they paid for you. They will profit handsomely."

I didn't understand. Enslavement had dulled my wits.

"I won't let you use your money to buy me back," I said. "It has to be money that my husband has earned."

"But it is, Ariana." She handed me her scroll, all rolled up again. I felt ashamed for her to see the calluses and scrapes on my fingers. "Don't you see? This is the story you and he wrote, the tale of Dilara and Idrosun and Feroze and all the others. Your husband is paying copyists now. Day and night they bend over their work to prepare scrolls for sale. He has subscriptions in hand for future stories. He even had a few copies inked on Paper made from flax—he sells those at a premium price."

I started to understand, a little. The scroll, the story, the money— but there was one question I had to have answered above all.

"Ali-Haram—did he—"

All that mattered was whether my husband had used my slave price—that bag of coins Yenibi had brought the day I left the palace—to pay his gambling debts. But a fresh welling of tears stung my eyes, and I broke off, unable to speak.

Scheherazade did not have to hear my question to know what I needed to know.

"O Ariana, how else could I have brought the money to buy you back from Gasparo and Kamran? Listen, I wanted Ali-Haram to be the one to tell you, but I am weak. I can't keep the secret any longer. He never wagered on ass races to buy wine. He wanted to buy something, but not for himself.

"You see, he'd found a certain house, not far from the palace. It had windows that looked out on a garden, and a real door made of wood. This house was to be a new dwelling place for Merdad's foster mother. In exchange, she agreed to let your son stay with you in the palace for two months every year until he is grown. It was to be a surprise, Ali-Haram's

165

special gift for you."

I told myself to breathe, breathe.

"And as for this bag of darics—" She shook it, letting the coins clink. "You have another, just as heavy, waiting for you at home. You won't be baking your own bread anymore. You'll be able to pay for Emre to have an education, if you want. He'll have tutors."

"Tutors!" How difficult it all was to take in. "Imagine it—my son, learning to read."

"And he won't be reading just anything." She showed me a second scroll—I recognized the tassels on the rod. "He is going to read the life of his mother. It is a farewell gift for you, from Yenibi."

Ali-Haram once told me that if one is not used to happiness, it can be impossible to bear.

And surely no wife, no mother, no slave, no woman has ever been as happy as I was, in that moment—

SCROLL THREE:

LOVE AND EYESIGHT

25. The Four Daughters

King Shahryar, bathed, massaged, oiled, scented with musk and jasmine and cloves, sat on the bed. Bibeb stood in the corner, slowly moving the palm leaf fan. The King pulled the embroidered blanket over himself before slipping the silk robe off his shoulders—a courtesy to me. If Bibeb had been the only other one in the bedchamber, he wouldn't have bothered.

The slave Bibeb was clumsy and slight; she gripped the handle of the fan with both hands, awkwardly bracing the weight against her hip. I wondered how she had drawn this duty. Bourzou was doubtless punishing her for something. A breeze entered through the open window.

"Do you need the fan tonight, Majesty? I am a little cool."

He waved dismissively.

"We really do not care one way or the other. Suit yourself."

"Bibeb, you're dismissed," I said sharply. "Stand the fan in that corner."

She gave me a grateful look and hurried out.

"Where is our wife tonight?" the King asked.

"In her chambers, Highness. She was ill this morning, and didn't want to risk passing it on to you. She sent word for me to attend you. I will be your storyteller tonight."

"Do you really know all of Scheherazade's story by heart?"

"As if I'd written it myself, Majesty."

"You are a marvel of our age. Here you are, an uneducated ex-slave. You cannot read or write. And yet somehow, you have committed our wife's entire story to memory."

I thought: would I still be such a marvel in your eyes if you knew that the creator of the story was not your wife, but the ex-slave herself? Or would you be furious at the whole deception that we have practiced on you?

Although in truth I am no longer the story's sole creator. Ali-Haram is free from his gambling debts, which in turn has freed the two of us from our cloud of misunderstanding. (And another form of freedom—my legal tablet, safely back on its brass pedestal in the great room of our chambers. The seal tells the world that Ali-Haram's wife has regained her freedom.) Every day the two of us sit in the palace gardens, with scroll, pens, inkhorn, and a pitcher of the Water of Angels. We tell our story into being, arguing and laughing. It is all my joy.

"Tonight, Majesty, I am going to start a brand-new adventure for you. It takes place many years before the story of Dilara and Idrosun and Feroze. And yet you have already met certain of its characters. I have not called them by their true names before, so at first you may not recognize them."

"Before you start—?"

He gestured with his crystal goblet, which I dutifully filled with the Water of Angels.

*

Once there was a woman who had four daughters. This woman's name was Homa.

Homa and her husband dwelled in a mansion in Baghdad, with a fine view of the domes and spires of the royal palace. Expensive tapestries hung on the walls. There were woven carpets in every chamber. The children had tutors. Behind the house stood a stable, in which were kept two fine riding horses.

Homa's husband was a high-ranking royal official. He managed the sowing and reaping in the southeast grain field. He made important decisions, handled a great deal of money, and (some said) even attended luncheons with the King. But then there came an accusation: gleaning privileges had been sold to an unlicensed trader. Homa's husband had kept the proceeds for himself. A search turned up the funds, buried in a cloth bag in the garden beneath the orchids.

Because of his position, the husband was granted the courtesy of a trial. The trial was not lengthy, and a scimitar made quick work of his head. With her husband gone, along with his ill-gotten income, Homa could no longer afford the house with the stables and view of the palace. She and her four daughters moved to the Ragged Quarter.

Now, in our Persian tongue the Homa is an invisible, mythic bird which is forever in flight, and never alights on the earth. But despite her name, Homa possessed no magical talents. However, each of her daughters did, after a fashion. Homa put much thought into how she might make a living from her daughters' skills.

I will not burden you, O King, with the names of the four daughters, save the youngest, when I get to her. One, the eldest, showed promise in the art of second sight. She foretold events with accuracy. For instance, she correctly prophesied a three-day rain that left a plague of serpents in the streets, the appearance of a giant wart on the moneylender's chin, and the lightning-strike that left a wise woman's sister mute and utterly hairless.

Unfortunately, it is difficult to earn steady income from predictions. Everyone knows the future will be bad. Who pays good money to hear bad news?

Two, the next daughter, had a most unusual skill. She could break the hold of love on a heart. Surely, thought Homa, this magic would attract mothers whose daughters had fallen in love with unsuitable boys.

When a mother brought her daughter in for a session, Two would instruct the daughter to close her eyes and picture in her mind the boy she loved. While this went ahead, Mother Homa poured a sackful of rose hips on the girl. (For an added fee, Forget-Me-Not petals could be used.) The rose hips, or flower petals, would then be gathered up and set afire. Two would sprinkle sage on the flame while the girl and her mama chanted the boy's name. This potent magic unfailingly turned the girl's passion to vapor.

The human heart, however, is nothing if not resilient and stubborn. And thus the abiding problem with this spell: the girl would fall in love all over again, the very next day, typically with the same boy. The mother would come storming back to Homa, demanding a refund. In short, Two's spells lacked permanence, and thus proved unprofitable.

So much for the talents of One and Two.

On the other hand, what type of magic would seem to offer the prospect of profit like the talent of bringing misfortune to another? Who has never longed in his secret heart to injure an enemy? Here lay the special talent of Three. Even One and Two had learned early on not to annoy their little sister, whose retaliation was often quite imaginative.

As a professional, her first customer was a baker who paid a half-daric for his business rival to step in dung, before witnesses. Mother

Homa found an ideal heap in a public place, and Three unerringly guided the rival's footsteps toward it—but at the very moment the rival arrived the spell overbalanced, and the dung underwent a transformation to sugar and honey. (Spells of misfortune are, by their very nature, highly unstable.) The sweet smell of the rival's sandals drew customers from all over the Ragged Quarter. People queued up to follow him to his bakery, and he recorded large profits that day.

The man who had commissioned the spell complained widely about Three's incompetence. The bad publicity made it necessary for Homa to offer the girl's services at reduced rates.

The discount attracted a few new customers. One of these was a woman bitterly disappointed in love. Mother Homa recommended a spell to turn the man who had spurned her into a leper. The woman made a deposit and commissioned the spell. Three carved a figurine from white willow; this represented the man. She coated the figurine with henbane and oil of verbena. Meanwhile the client recited the man's name backwards.

The man developed a few promising sores on his arms. But the instability of the spell had its way: instead of becoming leprous, the formerly bald spurner of women instead developed a lush growth of hair. Thus he soon found himself with many new female admirers to turn his back on.

So much for the magical career of Three.

That left the youngest daughter. This girl's name was Afsoon, which in our Persian tongue means spell or charm. And indeed, Afsoon showed great promise as a medium. Moreover, while her older sisters frittered away their nights with unprofitable sleep, Afsoon studied diligently to improve her art. She conducted endless experiments and pored over a certain scholarly scroll titled "The Unpredictability of the Dead: A Compendium of Case Studies, Annotated."

It was this very unpredictability, the mage Soqob argued in this scroll, that made summoning spirits the single most challenging field in the entire realm of magic. The unknown (to us) nature of the afterworlds causes one's personality, in death, to undergo unexpected changes. And if the dead are unpredictable, then so too must be the outcomes of seances.

Now it happened that Bahar, the mother of Baghdad's leading bloodletter, passed from our world of sorrow under mysterious circumstances. The lady's health had previously been excellent. Bahar had worked tirelessly to collect debts from patients who did not pay up, and thus was essential to her son's business.

After the Holy Ones read the services for the dead, and the body waas delivered to the family tomb, the mourners decided to investigate the death of their beloved Bahar. They paid a visit to Mother Homa to request a seance.

Homa quoted a fee of five darics. The mourners were shocked; to raise such an amount would require a visit to the moneylender, that sinful usurer. Homa shrewdly reminded them that if a crime had indeed been committed, they could bring a legal action, evidence produced in a seance being admissible in such cases. The aggrieved could well enjoy a tidy return. Homa kept a handy list of practicing legalists she personally recommended. Of course, money could hardly compensate for the death of poor Bahar. But think of the satisfaction in knowing justice was served.

The mourners found this line of reasoning persuasive. With gleaming eyes, they paid the deposit. Mother Homa sent out One, Two, and Three (who were temporarily without clients of their own) with the deposit to buy the necessary supplies: frankincense, silver candles, sandalwood oil, tourmaline chips, and so forth—

*

"Ah, think of it, Ariana," the King interrupted with a sigh of pleasure. "Four daughters! Each one must have brought Mother Homa great happiness. It is truly written that children are trusts placed in us by Heaven. Perhaps one day Heaven will bless Scheherazade with such a trust."

That made me recall the dreadful-smelling ointment the royal physician had given Scheherazade to help her conceive. The King had fallen quiet. The silence lasted so long I thought he had finally drifted off to sleep. The night breeze through the window was thick with the scent of honeysuckle. I rose to tiptoe from the chamber—

"Heaven blessed you with a son, Ariana," the King said. I sat back on my stool; of course he was not asleep.

In keeping with Ali-Haram's agreement with the foster mother, my son had moved into our chambers for his first two-month stay. Things were awkward and uncomfortable. The boy found himself living with people he did not know, in surroundings of unaccustomed luxury. He was uncooperative with his tutor. We argued over his name; why was I calling him Emre when his name was Merdad?

"His first days with us haven't been that smooth," I said. "He mopes—"

"You uprooted him. He misses his friends and playmates back in the Ragged Quarter."

"Ali-Haram put his work aside this morning and took the boy to shoot." With a mother's pride, I added: "He brought down a grackle from a tree branch on his second try, using only a child's bow."

"He shows talent in other areas too. Only this afternoon, it seems, the son of one of our scribes, a few years older than your Merdad, challenged him to a fight with sword sticks, in front of the other boys. Merdad beat him soundly. The news did our heart good. The scribe's son is a bully and a braggart. Ariana, we believe we have produced the answer to Merdad's loneliness.

"You see, we have decided to organize a Children's Battery. One of our own officers will oversee this company. The boys will receive training in the sword, the javelin, and principles of siegecraft. They will march alongside our army and see other lands. We have decided to give your Merdad a place in this Battery."

I managed a weak smile, but the King's words filled me with dread. Emre, son of Emre, in the Persian army! His father had died on a battlefield. I didn't want the boy to be a soldier; I wanted him to learn to read and write. I wanted him to be a scholar like his stepfather, Ali-Haram.

What would my lord husband have to say about this Children's Battery? What about Emre's foster mother? And what about Emre himself—what did the boy want?

And what did any of that matter if the King of Persia willed otherwise?

26. Who Murdered Bahur?

(O Majesty, last night my—that is, Scheherazade's story left off with Mother Homa accepting a commission in which her youngest daughter Afsoon would, in the interest of justice and profit, summon the spirit of Bahur, the bloodletter's mother, from the afterworlds, for questioning.)

The young man Qazem joined the queue to enter the fishmonger's shop. Mother Homa stood at the entrance way, keeping a close eye while One, Two, and Three sold tickets. In keeping with the solemn occasion, Homa and her daughters were in gowns, veils, and headscarves of somber black. For his part, Qazem wore his usual threadbare gray robe, frayed belt of braided hemp, and patched wool slippers. Fixed to his skullcap were the kitten and thunderbolt pins that marked him as Apprentice to the mage Soqob, Class Aleph, Fourth Level.

"Ah, the Apprentice," Mother Homa said to him, checking her parchment. "Qazem, is it? No ticket needed for this one, girls. He's on our guest list."

"I look forward to the summoning." Qazem bowed.

"I hope we can count on you to send a good report to your Soqob—?" Mother Homa said.

"I am here strictly as an observer." This was not entirely true.

"By the way, these are my daughters. They are all talented in various aspects of magic and, I might add, unwed, although I assure you it is not for lack of offers. Girls, show Qazem downstairs."

At this point, Qazem's insides judged that a protest was in order.

"Goodness, Apprentice!" Mother Homa said with a smile. "Is that your belly growling?"

"My apologies," he said. "I have not had lunch yet."

In fact, he had missed breakfast too. Such was the life of one in service to Soqob. The mage's philosophy was to keep stipends low; by such means, he reasoned, his Apprentices would be more likely to succeed once they became practitioners. This is because they would have learned to understand poverty, which would be the lot of most of their clients.

"In that case, you must join the mourners themselves at their table," Homa said brightly. "And do include the food in your report to your esteemed Master."

Qazem bowed again and followed the three daughters down the uneven stone steps to the basement. This chamber lay in the dim light which came from a long quarter-window high in the wall, just above ground level. Candles on a low oval table guttered and flared.

The floor was hard packed earth, strewn with straw. Ticketed guests stood against the bare walls. Rugs ringed the table. The deceased was a woman, and for this reason there was no portrait of her, only a drawing in ink of a black rose.

A fourth girl entered the chamber. She carried a tray with flatbreads, bowls of soup, and tureens of walnut chicken stew. The pleasing smells of turmeric and cinnamon filled the air. Along with the black gown and veil, the girl wore an extravagant silver headdress with jade beads. The beads swayed and clicked with each movement.

Qazem took no more notice of the first three sisters.

"My daughter Afsoon," Mother Homa whispered to him. (She had rejoined the milling crowd in the basement.) "She will be the summoner today. That name is A, F, S—"

Sandals shuffled on the stone steps. The mourners, who had draped black mourning-stoles over their brightly colored tunics and gowns, made their appearances. They took their places on the rugs and at once dug into the feast. Qazem found himself kneeling on a rug next to Afsoon. He dipped a hunk of flatbread into his soup.

"Mama said Soqob himself sent you—?" Afsoon's veil concealed her lips, but Qazem saw the smile lines that creased the edges of her flashing eyes. Dark curls escaped from the silver headdress.

"Your work summoning spirits has attracted his attention," Qazem said. The mourners ate with noisy enthusiasm and paid no attention to this dialogue.

"Soqob is an inspiration to me. I have studied his 'Unpredictability' scroll over and over."

"It is one of his best sellers."

Qazem did not tell her that his master was known more for scholarly manuscripts than actual magic. The real reason Soqob had sent him to the seance was to discover if the girl had anything new to offer that Soqob could make use of in future profitable scrolls. Qazem had attended amateur seances before; the summoner typically turned out to be a skillful fraud, whose "spirit" was nothing more than a voice echoing from behind a curtain.

Afsoon rose from her rug and cleared the table, while One, Two, and Three brought out slices of almond-yoghurt cake. From the talk of the mourners, it became clear to Qazem that suspicion for Bahur's death centered on three individuals.

The first of these was a certain minstrel, who had long kept up regular bloodlettings for his dancing monkey. Despite this healthy regimen, the monkey had mysteriously expired at the mere age of ninety-nine years. Bahur had refused to refund the minstrel's fee. So the minstrel had motive.

Next was a poisoner who bought let blood for her own shadowy purposes. When costs forced Bahur to raise prices, the poisoner protested that this would put her out of business. The two had exchanged angry words. Thus the poisoner also had motive, and needless to add, means.

Qazem learned the identity of the third suspect when the bloodletter's wife, choking back sobs, rose and left the table briefly.

"Look at Esme, pretending to suffer," one mourner said.

"She and her mother-in-law quarreled constantly, you know," another said.

"Bahur always said Esme did not feed her husband properly. She complained his clothes did not stay clean and mended."

"Who would want to be rid of a mother-in-law more than a daughter-in-law?"

"Say, where is the bloodletter, anyway?"

"He said his grief was so great he could not bear to attend."

Afsoon's sisters cleared away the dessert dishes and stacked them in a corner. Mother Homa extinguished all the candles, save for the one next to the picture of the black rose. Afsoon's eyes began to glow (doubtless through some trick of firelight and shadow). She dropped a pinch of dried lavender on the flame; there was a burst of burnt fragrance. At her directions, the guests laid their hands on the table, palms down. She began to intone a string of words that seemed at first not to be words.

It took Qazem a moment to recognize the ancient tongue of the Medes. He realized that the girl was reciting, from memory, the summoning spell contained in the appendix of 'Unpredictability.' The basement ceiling rumbled; a fall of pebbles clattered down the stone steps. The candle flame bent low. The odor of earth filled the chamber. The astonished Qazem felt a chill; this Afsoon was no fraud.

"O thou who hath journeyed from the spirit world to be with us today, be welcome." Afsoon spoke in High Persian. "I, Afsoon, adjure thee to answer questions. Art thou the bloodletter's mother, called Bahur?"

"I am Bahur." Afsoon answered herself in a different voice—flat and lower-pitched. The mourners gasped; the ticketholders stamped their feet in appreciation.

Returning to her rug, the bloodletter's wife wiped her eyes and leaned forward.

"O Bahur, it is Esme, wife of your beloved son. Tell us who killed you, dear mama."

The whites of Afsoon's eyes were alive with light.

"Only yes-no questions may be directed to the spirit," Mother Homa gently reminded Esme.

"One of your son's patients brought you a cake the day you died." Esme rephrased. "Was the cake poisoned?"

"No," the flat voice answered.

More questions. Did the minstrel do it? Was it that accursed monkey? No, and no. What about your son's wife? (This, after Esme left the table sobbing again.) Each no grew less toneless; the spirit's voice rose and showed emotion.

"Enough!" The spirit could endure no more. "Your questions are exasperating. You called me out of Paradise for this? A few hours ago, handsome Persian warriors were feeding me fruit and almonds dipped in chocolate. Believe me, I told the other spirits everything, including how my daughter-in-law gave away my silver before I was even cold. Ungrateful children! You best believe I can see everything from up there."

Qazem was astonished at this display. It was unseemly for spirits to engage in outbursts. Soqob would be most interested in this field example of spirit unpredictability.

"And do not think I missed what my nieces said either. I saw their bitterness when I did not leave them my jewelry or lace. And where is that no-good son of mine, anyway? All those years I worked my fingers to the bone for him, and he—"

Bahur had a multitude of other complaints. Her so-called loved ones had skimped on dirt to toss on her corpse. ("I saw who did not throw the full three handfuls.") They had not observed all the formalities. ("My nephew failed to recite a prayer when the halva was served, can you believe the nerve? The other spirits are still laughing at me.") And how dared anyone accuse the poor poisoner? ("All right, maybe we had words at times, but she was the truest friend a woman ever had—")

With each grievance, Bahur's ire grew. The stack of dirty plates in the corner began to shake. A plate rose from the stack. It hovered, and then went hurtling across the room. The plate shattered against a wall; shards flew. The mourners ducked and scrambled to their feet. The ticket holders, appreciating the show, stamped their feet again. Afsoon staggered; Qazem leapt up and put arms under hers as she slumped. Blood spotted her veil. A shard had cut her eye. One, Two, and Three cowered against a wall.

"O thou spirit—" Afsoon's voice trembled. "I conjure thee—do not yet depart this world—" But the odor of earth was gone.

"We will never forget this humiliation!" Bahur's daughter-in-law Esme shouted from the top of the stone steps. "We are going to tell everyone how your bungling magic has nearly destroyed our family. Naturally, there is no question of paying your fee."

Qazem held Afsoon. Her scent and closeness made him dizzy. She wept and bled on him.

Several days passed. Qazem resumed his studies, and—

*

"Wait, 'several days passed?'" The King rolled onto his side and gave me a stern look. "Aren't you going to tell us who really murdered Bahur?"

Ali-Haram and I had not been careless this time. We had worked out the answer already; I needed no invention. I knew that a matter of justice, even in a made-up story, would fire the royal blood. The King would take pleasure in guessing where guilt lay in the affair.

"Ah, Majesty," I said, "let us take a moment to examine each suspect. Was it the poisoner? Investigators questioned the women who prepared the body. Each swore there had been no rash, no bluing of the lips, no burns about the nose."

"Hmm—yes, and we recall the spirit called the poisoner her truest friend," the King said. "Well then, what about the daughter-in-law Esme? There was no love lost between her and the deceased."

"But didn't Esme leave the table several times so the other mourners wouldn't have to see her weeping?"

"True, true. But there is also the bloodletter himself. We find his behavior quite suspicious. The ungrateful wretch did not attend the summoning of his own mother's spirit."

"But to look too closely into the bloodletter's role in the affair might have threatened the family's income. He was the main breadwinner. You see, Majesty, in the end it was easiest to blame the minstrel—even though he had showed up at the graveside, monkey-less, and had sung without charge."

"We suspected the minstrel all along. He only sang to deflect attention from his guilt. Very well, we are satisfied."

The King sank back into his blankets. The blessed sound of snoring soon filled the bedchamber.

27. Summoning, Sacrifice, and Assassination

(O King, last night I told you how Qazem, on instructions of his Master Soqob, came to the fishmonger's basement to observe Afsoon's spirit-summoning, and how this ended in blood and disaster.)

Qazem could not afford parchment on the meager stipend Soqob paid, so he wrote his letter on the back of an assigned worksheet of spells.

> Mother Homa, I beg you to let me to call on your daughter Afsoon at a time of your choosing, in order that I may show her and your family all due honor and respect.

Homa responded right away:

> Well, why waste time? Come this evening. A client recently paid with a honeycomb and a bag of pistachios, and so I thought I might whip up a cake. Unfortunately, Afsoon's father has departed this life, but my other daughters will be there to help me chaperone. Have I mentioned they too are unwed?

When Qazem arrived, the three sisters escorted him through the dwelling and into the courtyard where Mother Homa waited. He took note of the snacks and kneeling rugs and snacks laid out in the striped shadows of a date palm.

Homa rose to welcome her guest, saying: "Have you turned in your report to Soqoh yet? I hope you were able to overlook the minor disturbances that took place during the summoning."

"To summon spirits is one thing," Qazem answered. "To control them is another. Many a mage has devoted a career to mastering this difficult skill."

Afsoon, in white tunic, blue silk trousers, and white slippers, walked unsteadily toward the palm with the sisters. Her headscarf was tied across her head, under her chin, and over her left eye. Purple orchids and red blood stains covered the scarf.

Mother Homa led a round of small talk concerning Baghdad's recent hot spell, a certain street musician creating a nuisance on the next block, and whether falling stars augured changes in the world. No one mentioned Afsoon's eye. One by one, Homa and her daughters found excuses to leave the courtyard.

Finally, Afsoon and Qazem were alone.

"I am ashamed for you to see me this way," Afsoon said, her head bowed. "I beg your forgiveness."

"But your eye—"

"What is an eye? I have another. Let us discuss other things. I bungled the summoning of mama Bahur. I wish you had not witnessed my failure. I am trying very hard."

Hearing this, Qazem's heart filled. He wanted to place his hand over hers. He wanted to comfort her. He wanted to untie the scarf and kiss the ruined eye. All these desires made heat rise to his face.

"No aspect of magic is more challenging than summoning spirits," he said, mastering himself. "The truth is you showed remarkable promise. And that is what I told my master. Based on my report, he has offered you an Apprenticeship. I urge you to accept."

He heard her sharp intake of breath, and the sigh that followed. She did not answer. Qazem understood—she was the only one in the family bringing in steady income. Mother Homa would hardly give that up so her daughter could take the vow of poverty that was required of a mage's Apprentice.

"Anyway, you must not lose heart," Qazem went on. "Wishing to master your craft is to your credit. You know, in our business we are bound by something called the Principle of Giving Up and Acquiring. The idea is that to gain our mage powers we must be willing to—"

He broke off. Why had he brought up this subject? He found it unsettling and uncomfortable to consider. His Master had been pressing him for a decision, and so far, he had answered evasively.

"Willing to give up something?" She guessed what Qazem meant right away. "Yes, I understand. Of course, it would have to be something of immense value. What about you? You will soon have your own career in magic. What have you decided to give up?"

Historically, mages often renounced their desire for the opposite sex. The spell was simple to apply. But this option did not appeal to Qazem— especially with Afsoon so enchantingly close.

"Well, there was Fildonez, from the thirteenth sub-epoch, who gave up his power of speech." Rather than reflect on his own self-doubts, Qazem gave a history lesson. "Muteness was not much of an obstacle to his career. He gave instructions to his Apprentices with hand signals, who then spoke for him to clients.

"Then there was Tyesh, who renounced dreaming. The sacrifice gained him great powers, but without dreams, he went mad, and—"

And so forth. Qazem's own Master, Soqob, had sacrificed his sense of smell. Such a loss was at most an inconvenience in the laboratory, where potions and vapors sometimes emitted telling odors. Qazem wondered (not for the first time) if the narrowness of Soqob's sacrifice might explain his limited career achievements.

For as long as he could remember, Qazem had wanted to be a mage. When he was a child, tales of the ancient sorcerers had fired his mind. He had longed to hurl thunderbolts, conjure fire, transform dogs into dragons. But now, as his Apprenticeship neared an end, his Giving Up decision loomed. It was time to choose his personal sacrifice. How high should he aim? Did he truly aspire to greatness in his profession—or would he be content to spend a mediocre career reading palms or casting spells to treat sore throats?

"Speaking, smelling, dreaming—" Afsoon whispered. "Yes, I too am prepared to give up something to gain something. I have already lost one eye. Does a summoner need to view the spirits she summons? O Qazem, I say this now before you: what was done to one eye can be done to the other. I will renounce seeing."

The declaration struck Qazem speechless. To sacrifice her eyesight! Afsoon's drive to master her craft was far stronger than his. He felt ashamed before her. No sorcerer in history had ever gone so far. What could he do to impress her? How could he ever win her admiration?

In his transport, he heard himself declare with feeling:

"Then I too renounce seeing!"

*

"The Lesser Tree Djinn will typically seek out the hollow of an oak tree for a dwelling place. As a rule, the older the tree, the better."

Qazem spoke the lines aloud. Did they match his Master's style? Did they pique the interest but still strike a scholarly note? A family of toads crouched on a stone bench in the fern glade and listened, clearly unimpressed.

Qazem tried again: "Unfortunately, as the race of men has taken to gathering acorns in ever-greater quantities for use in tanning and dyeing, there are fewer oaks than in past millennia. This in turn has reduced the potential living space for Djinns—"

Soqob did not ordinarily allow Apprentices in his private garden. But he had given Qazem an important assignment: to draft a preface for his upcoming scroll ("The Lesser Tree Djinn: A Case Study in Imminent Extinction"). The assignment entitled Qazem to stroll the paths and trails of Soqob's garden as needed for inspiration. But today it was hard to concentrate.

In his mind's eye Qazem kept picturing Afsoon's blood-stained scarf. She had lost an eye, and now proposed to sacrifice the other, all to the pursuit of a career in magic. And he had rashly declared that he would join her in giving up sight.

Love had left him unable to think clearly. He was confused and assailed by doubts.

"I am pleased to see you applying yourself to your assignment, Apprentice." Before him stood a peafowl of purest white, its tail feathers spread wide. On each feather was a single golden eyespot. This peafowl was Soqob, his master. (Soqob believed himself the target of certain aggrieved ex-colleagues, and thus always traveled in disguise.) Qazem had to listen carefully to the peafowl's honks to make out the mage's words.

"But my history of the Djinns can wait. I have other work for you. It seems there has been an assassination."

"An assassination, Master?"

"Yesterday, the ambassador from the Kush kingdom, one Arkiman, arrived here in Baghdad, with his delegation. Arkiman's mission was to negotiate a trade agreement with the King. Kush has gold, spices, leopard furs, and other desirable items to sell. The King gave a feast in Arkiman's honor last night. The ambassador's body was found this morning in his bedchamber. His throat had been cut."

"That is shocking news, Master. What will happen to the negotiations?"

Soqob folded and re-spread his tail feathers: a peafowl's shrug.

"That aspect of the case is unimportant. Affairs of state are hardly our concern. But now a crime has been committed on Persian soil. Justice must be served. The King's investigator wishes to question the deceased. He has requested a summoning of Arkiman's spirit from the afterworlds. Of course I could do this myself with minimal effort, but I am feeling the pressing call of my many research projects. That girl you went to observe—do you think she would take the job?"

"I am certain she would be pleased to conduct such a summoning, Master." Mother Homa would be glad for the fee, and Afsoon for the chance to redeem herself.

"One thing worries me. My auguries suggest the possibility of a tagalong spirit—"

Soqob had written a scroll about tagalongs: "A Theoretical Framework for Post-Life Transport of Mages Between the Worlds, with Anecdotal Evidence." Departed mages could return from the afterworlds by attaching themselves to properly summoned mortal spirits.

"But Master, in your scroll you proved that tagalongs pose no danger to the spirit being summoned."

"It is not Arkiman I am concerned about. Now, pluck one of my feathers. Any of them will do for—ouch! Easy there. Pin it to your tunic. If a tagalong materializes, send the eye to report to me."

"Yes, Master. But how will I know if a tagalong is present?"

"Listen for a different cadence of voice from the medium, hostile language, threats, allusions to money owed, that sort of thing. Best to be careful. You never know; the tagalong might be a mage who had, let us say, some minor differences with me while alive."

*

"This story raises an interesting question," the King said, interrupting.

"Majesty?"

"Your Qazem said that to achieve greatness, one must give up something of personal value. We agree with this principle. Such a sacrifice would prove one's worthiness. We find ourselves pondering what we might give up, to be a great and worthy King. You mentioned mages who renounced their desire for the opposite sex. Of course, we could not do that. Our first duty to the Kingdom is to produce an heir, after all."

I refreshed his goblet with the Water of Angels. He abruptly moved to a different subject:

"Our new Children's Battery conducted drills today. The staff officers wanted to see how the boys rode, but every horse had already been requisitioned. So the boys were put on asses, which I hear can be tricky to ride. Your Merdad again showed his skills. He reversed, post trotted, and even cantered. And he continues to display natural leadership among the boys. My officers have even recommended him for a commission in the Battery."

I felt the blood drain from my face.

"Your Majesty does my son great honor," I managed.

Honor him, O King, but please do not send him off to war.

But wasn't it partly my own fault? I had been telling Merdad (I had finally agreed to call him by the name his foster mother gave him) bedtime stories about his father fighting in the Maqazzan rebellion. Losing myself in the tales, I would describe the brave rebels on their black horses and brown camels, the flash of their swords in the sunlight, their war cries striking terror into the hearts of the Persians. Merdad's eyes would shine. I had stirred his blood.

Such is the power of storytelling. I could tell in his imagination he was taking to the battlefield and covering himself with glory. But on the battlefield, glory rides in harness with death.

"Perhaps what we should sacrifice is our nightly story." The King had returned to the Principle of Giving Up and Acquiring. "We have been thinking about going out into the field, and commanding troops the way we once did. When did we last sleep under the stars? This palace living makes a man soft. Reports have reached us about new rebel movements in Maqazza. We are of a mind to ride out and put the rebels down, once and for all."

I thought: O King, if you are away in Maqazza, then at night I can be here, with my husband. Wonderful!

But in the next breath he said:

"Perhaps we'll take the Children's Battery with us. It might be good for them to see their King and his troops in action."

Only a mother can know the terror that froze my blood in that moment.

O Merdad, who am I, in your eyes? Someone unexpectedly thrusted into your life, a woman of the court, a lady in silks and satins. You are a poor boy from the Ragged Quarter; I am a wealthy woman in the royal palace. You have always been free; I've spent most of my life enslaved. I told you those bedtime stories so you would understand what we have in common: we are Maqazzans, not Persians. We are a subject people, but our history is proud.

An act of love created you, during a night of terror. I remember lying alone after Emre left my tent. I remember the groans of the dying drifting in from the killing fields.

O Heaven, please do not let that night be what guides Merdad's destiny in this life.

28. *The Eyes of Mages and Peafowl*

(O Majesty, last night I related the assassination of Arkiman, the Kushite ambassador. I told how Afsoon was engaged to summon his spirit for questioning by the King's investigator.)

Afsoon's sisters stood at the door of the fishmonger's shop with their palms held out—admission tickets were a quarter-daric each.

"What?" Qazem protested. "Even a poor Apprentice has to pay?"

"We have a right to make a living," One said with a sniff.

"Have you seen the price of candles lately?" Two asked.

Three observed: "You cannot be all that poor if you can afford to go about wearing a peacock feather."

Qazem sighed and handed over the quarter-daric, which he had earned the day before by mending a sandal strap.

(Qazem had secretly taken on a second Master. This was Noki, who was teaching him the art of footwear repair. Soqob forbade double Apprenticeships, as they did not advance the principle of student poverty. Unfortunately, Noki's health was failing, and Qazem worried about the day when sandal repair would no longer provide a source of income.)

"And do not think about sneaking food," One added sternly. "A meal ticket will cost you another quarter-daric."

"Now, girls. This is the great mage's favorite Apprentice." Mother Homa had overheard. "If not for him, your sister would not have this profitable commission."

She slipped a meal ticket into Qazem's hand and pulled him inside.

"Do not be alarmed when you see Afsoon," she said while they made their way down the stone steps to the basement. "It was her decision. If it leads to her professional advancement, that will mean more clients, and more income."

Qazem started to ask Mother Homa what she meant by this, but she had already disappeared into the milling crowd of ticket holders. The King's investigator knelt on a rug at the oval table in the center of the basement; behind him stood a Sentinel of the Muhtasib. The Sentinel wore an ankle-length kaftan with wide sleeves and satin brocade. Strapped across his back was a scimitar in a curved leather scabbard. His face lay hidden in the shadow of his gray hood.

The Kush delegation gathered across the table from the investigator, eyes narrowed, faces brooding and dark.

Clink-clink on a goblet. The crowd fell silent. Mother Homa stood next to the investigator.

"The wondrous summoner Afsoon will make her appearance momentarily," she announced. The candlelight cast shifting stripes of light and dark across her face. "But first, a representative of the distinguished Kushite delegation has asked to make an opening statement."

Qazem felt the heat and press of bodies. The eye on the peafowl feather vibrated; its view of the table was blocked. Qazem murmured polite apologies and moved through the crowd. He came to a far corner, where an alcove-like space lay behind a curtain of thin wool cloth.

Two figures in white robes rose from their rugs. The first produced sounds like whistles and wind. The second translated the speech to a heavily accented Persian.

"Arkiman, a man faithful and righteous in all matters, was born to his devoted parents one blessed morning in the year—"

Qazem felt a touch at his elbow. He turned; slender, trembling fingers held the curtain aside for him. He stepped into the alcove, which reeked of fish. Knives and heaps of scales and fish bones lay on a wooden slab. Dust swam in the light streaming from a window near the ceiling.

He stared in horror at the headscarf with the orchids and blood stains. He wanted to ask why she had it tied across both eyes—but in his sinking heart he already knew. Afsoon braced one hand against the wall and the other on the slab.

He whispered: "How did you know it was me in front of the curtain?"

"I sensed you. I smelled you. I felt your presence. I will never need eyes to know you are near. You and I have made our sacrifices. Now we will become masters of our magecraft. What is there for eyes to see? Your heart lies open before me, and mine before you."

She reached with uncertain hands and, groping, found his face; he squeezed his eyes shut before she could touch them. Blood roared in his ears. She believed he had blinded himself. Had he not renounced his own sight before her?

"—and while sleeping in a foreign land, was most foully murdered—"

On the other side of the curtain, the whistles and wind and interpreter's words went on. The crowd muttered impatiently. Mother Homa finally interrupted.

"I am sure we are all grateful for that moving testimonial. And now, the moment for which we have all waited. I, her honored mother, ask you to make welcome—the wondrous summoner Afsoon!"

One pulled aside the curtain. Two and Three took their sister's arms, leading her away from Qazem and through the parting crowd, from which issued a round of expectant foot-stamping.

A call for silence, the picture of the ambassador arranged just so on the table, the candle flame spitting and sparkling with fragrant lavender, the hands of the Kushites presented on the table, palms-up—Afsoon began the summoning. The floor rumbled and rolled as she spoke. The flames bent. The Sentinel gripped the hilt of his scimitar. Odors filled the basement—the smells of roots and earth and death.

Afsoon reached behind her head; the scarf with the orchids and blood stains slipped to the floor. As one, the ticket holders sucked in their breath: Afsoon's eyes were lifeless pools of red.

"O traveler from the world of spirits," she cried, "art thou Arkiman, ambassador from the kingdom of Kush?"

Whistles and wind followed from Afsoon's own lips. The interpreter rendered these sounds as: "I am Arkiman, of Kush."

"O Arkiman, the King's investigator will now put questions to thee, and I, Afsoon, require thee to answer."

"I will answer."

The investigator unrolled a scroll and dipped a pen in his inkhorn.

"Explain, Ambassador," he began, "why you came from Kush to Baghdad—" Mother Homa leaned down to whisper in his ear. "Ah, right. Yes or no only. Ambassador, did you travel from Kush to negotiate a trade agreement with the King of Persia?"

"Yes."

More questions. Yes, no, yes, no. Finally, an impatient Kush delegate spoke up, with some heat. The interpreter translated:

"Just ask him if the assassin was a Persian."

The investigator nodded and said: "Excellency Arkiman, forgive if this is painful to remember, but were you able to see who—"

The candle flames began to twist about each other, tangled strings of red and yellow. A chill wind arose. Qazem's teeth chattered. The wind lifted Afsoon's veil. Sparks streamed from her mouth and converged on the candle. Something was taking shape in the knot of flames—small at first but growing, a pale narrow face, a wispy beard the color of clouds, a turban covered with comets.

"I am Myobec." The new voice did not come from Afsoon, but from the wraith itself. This was the tagalong Soqob had feared. "And I will ask the questions here."

Who was this Myobec? What was happening? Was this part of the show? The hushed ticket holders leaned forward. The annoyed peafowl eye vibrated as bodies edged in front of Qazem. He moved closer to see.

"I have come for the mage Soqob." The voice was high and strident. "Bring him here at once. He owes me three hundred darics. Thought he freed of me when I died, did he? True, no one needs money in the afterworlds, but a debt is a debt, and a mage's word is supposed to be his bond. I will take what the defaulter owes by a series of retributions. Wait—you there—yes, you. I have guessed from that feather-eye pinned to your tunic that you are Soqob's Apprentice—"

Everyone but the blind medium turned to stare at Qazem. Afsoon swayed; her sisters braced her on her feet. Qazem felt himself held fast by Myobec's hard gaze. But then the crowd surged. Bodies pushed between him and the wraith. The hold broke. Remembering his master's instructions, he unpinned the feather and flung it into the air.

"Wind, that eye is Soqob's spy!" Myobec cried. "Bring it to me at once."

The obedient wind reached, but the feather fluttered free. The wind darted and swirled. It began to circle the basement. Ever faster it moved. A vortex took shape, sweeping up dust, straw, headscarves, skullcaps, and the picture of Arkiman. The panicked ticket holders stumbled and shrieked.

"O little eye, come to Myobec." The wraith cooed. "Let me see you up close. You deserve a better master than Soqob. I could use a good spy like you. Hop onto my vortex, yes, just so. Come over here and we will talk terms."

The feather fluttered past Qazem's nose—he seized it and flung it upward, toward the quarter-window by the ceiling—

"Are you trying to ruin my surprise, Apprentice?" the annoyed Myobec said. "If you send the eye back to Soqob, he will know I am coming."

"Sentinel of the Muhtasib!" The King's investigator had regained his feet. The vortex tore the scroll out of his hands. "Do your duty; cut down this abomination."

The Sentinel drew his scimitar and moved forward. The vortex seized the weapon from him. The curved blade rose high. It spun and danced on the wind, a deadly weathervane in a storm. The sisters jumped clear. The blind summoner swayed alone.

O Afsoon, by not blinding myself I betrayed you. And by letting you believe I had done so, I lied to you. With these thoughts, Qazem launched himself onto the table; it rocked unbalanced under him. The scimitar wheeled; the hilt eluded his reach.

"Beloved!" Afsoon cried out. "Do not come closer!"

The vortex made her lose her footing. She staggered in the direction of the blade. Leaping down, Qazem threw himself to the floor, between her and the spinning scimitar. A terrible slicing pain across his face—

He fell heavily.

When he was conscious again, the wind and the din were gone. He tasted blood. His face lay on the cool dirt. Something dug into his shoulder. He fumbled with his free hand and felt the scimitar hilt.

"You saved me." Afsoon whispered somewhere above him. "But how did you know where the sword was? O beloved, your magic is so powerful—it was as though you could see—"

With immense efforr he turned his head toward the voice, trying desperately to find her, and seeing only darkness.

*

When the King left for Maqazza, everything changed. My nights became my own. Every morning Scheherazade and I would breakfast together, while the slave Bibeb made music for us, striking the keys of the dulcet-mer with little ebony hammers. The ambassador from Ceylon had brought the dulcet-mer as a gift for the court. Outside the window, buntings and robins would chirp along.

One morning our silver breakfast tray arrived with peach quarters and dipping bowls of cinnamon and honey.

"What happened to the usual minced lamb?"

Scheherazade made a face.

"All I want now are sweets. I started losing my meals."

"You're still sick?" She did not seem to understand my question. I added: "Your illness."

"Goodness, Ariana. How foolish you can be sometimes. I was never ill. That was a fiction, created for Shahryar. I didn't want him to know until I was sure. Now he can have a happy surprise when he comes home off campaign." She yanked aside her blanket and bolted from the bed. She barely reached the brass pot in time. Afterward, wiping her lips with a napkin: "Little Shahryar is settling himself in."

I finally understood. When we finished crying and laughing, she said:

"Ariana, you are a mother already. Promise to be with me every step of the way, and always tell me what to expect."

"Little Shahryar?" I said, teasing. "What if it's a girl, and the King doesn't get an heir?"

"Not a chance. In my family firstborns are always boys. But if not, well, then I will love her and name her Ariana. You know the saying—a baby girl brings light into the world."

What lovely days those were.

Until the post herald visited, and everything changed—

29. Journey to Maqazza

"Commander!" I leaned out the window and called. "Would you attend me, please?"

He trotted back at once—I was still pinning my veil in place when he pulled alongside my jouncing litter.

"Mistress?"

"Where are we, Commander?"

He shrugged and waved vaguely toward the brush and ravines and rock shelves that stretched away forever. A hawk circled slowly. I didn't care where we were. I wanted the sound of a human voice. I would have preferred to ride on my own, but the King's instructions had been quite clear: a royal litter would take me to Maqazza, as befitted my status as a lady of the court. Luxury and dreadful solitude.

"The same place we were a half hour ago, Mistress. Riding through this forsaken land where no civilized man would live of his own accord. Still, I expect to be in Maqazza by eveningfall." The Commander slapped the back of his neck. "These mosquitoes—will there be anything more, Mistress?"

I was concerned for the slaves but knew better than to ask after them. I knew all eight well—Peki was one of them. They had borne the litter for hours along the beaten earth trail, barefoot, sweating, silent. The Commander didn't allow them to speak, much less sing their usual work songs.

"No, Commander. In fact, I plan to tell his Majesty what excellent care you have provided me." A gentle reminder that he had charge of a cargo precious to his master. He saluted and rode forward.

I laid back on my velvet cushions and thought about what had happened during my final days in Baghdad. I had time to remember every detail—

*

Ali-Haram had been teaching me my letters. I could write ب and خ, and was working on س when a post herald arrived at the door of our chambers. A gift and message had come from the King. The gift was a duvet made from native Maqazzan silk and embroidered with spirals and squares. I stared at the parchment without comprehension. When the post herald left, I gave it to Ali-Haram, who read it to me:

> To Ariana, wife of our court poet Ali-Haram, mother of our Children's Battery lieutenant Merdad, and loyal subject of Shahryar, King of the Age and defender of the faith:

> We hereby summon you to attend us immediately, at our field headquarters. The bearer of this message will arrange your transport. To this order we affix our seal.

"Why do I have to make this long trip?" I complained. "I have a sealed tablet of freedom, and yet I am still his slave. Whatever he bids, I have to do. He's away on campaign—what does he need me for?"

"To tell him his nightly story, of course." Ali-Haram laid the summons parchment atop the scroll that held our latest chapter. "The question is why he asked for you, and not Scheherazade."

"The Royal Physician has confined the Queen Consort to her quarters." Ever alert to palace intrigues, Ali-Haram raised an eyebrow. I had sworn to keep Scheherazade's secret, so I only added (truthfully): "Whatever she has is expected to pass. But I still do not understand. The King said that by sacrificing his story he might become a more worthy king. He talked about leaving his soft palace life behind."

"He may trade his soft life for the battlefield, but his story has become like breathing and eating for him. In our way, we do a service for Persia. When we tell this story to the King, he can ponder questions of justice, sacrifice, and virtue."

I found this suggestion maddening. So we were not only the King's storytellers, but his teachers as well? Did that make us responsible for his wisdom and actions?

Questions of justice, sacrifice, and virtue, Ali-Haram had said. What about the question of slavery?

I imagined telling the King a new story, about a girl who is born a slave. The girl runs away and has a brief taste of freedom, but when her lover is killed, she is enslaved again. A poet frees her. She makes a living as a storyteller. By her own will, she suffers enslavement once more, but her freedom is repurchased from the profits of her own storytelling.

What would Shahryar think of a story like that? He had always been free. For him—and doubtless every free Persian—slavery was simply a station in life to which some unfortunates were born, or reduced. One did not question it. One could not alter it.

The King had the wealth to free ten thousand slaves, but not the imagination.

But Ali-Haram, you had the imagination! May Heaven protect you always, even when you madden me.

*

We stopped. I craned my neck out the window of the litter—my throat went dry with a memory of terror.

A rope bridge loomed ahead. It swayed high above a gorge. I had crossed that very bridge all those years ago, in the terrible hours after Emre was killed in battle. Life was already quickening within me then, although I didn't know it yet. I was a camp follower, one of dozens of women taken prisoner. We were bound for Baghdad and slavery.

The gorge had been so far below we could barely hear the crash of water. The foam towered in clouds. The Persians had strung us together with hemp lines. The bridge planks creaked and moved sickeningly beneath our every step. The lines burned our skin when they pulled taut. I remembered squeezing my eyes closed and praying Heaven to go ahead and take me, as it had already taken Emre—

Now I could hear the Commander and his officers outside the litter, conferring on how to make the crossing. I could hear orders called out. The litter descended and touched ground. Don't think about the gorge, I told myself. Don't think about the rope bridge. Remember those last days in Baghdad instead.

Merdad had not been there for me to mother; the Children's Battery had marched away to some sort of training exercise outside the city.

Scheherazade and I had our breakfasts every day. Sometimes we would walk and talk for hours in the garden. In the evenings Ali-Haram and I unhurriedly created our chapters, after which I lay in his warm arms, gloriously freed from spending the night telling the King his story—

*

"But who assassinated Arkiman?"

It was our last night together. We lay in bed, under the King's gift, the duvet of Maqazzan silk. That night-journeyer, the moon, reached our open window. The silver light out-dazzled even my husband's dozen expensive burning candles.

"What does it matter?" Ali-Haram dipped his pen in the inkhorn—in his usual haste to get his next thought written down, he was careless. I caught the tipping horn before it could spill onto the duvet. "The important question is—"

"The King will want to know. That's why it matters. When justice isn't served, it reflects poorly on the King, who in the story is Shahryar's ancestor. Trust me, his Majesty will question me closely on this point until he's satisfied."

The scroll spilled away untidily to the floor. My husband did his best writing in bed, but ink dries at its own pace. He yawned.

"All right, all right. Who are our suspects?"

"We have none. I propose first, a Persian courtier who has financial reasons to oppose the trade agreement; second, a Kushite with a personal motive for murder; and third—"

I imagined aloud for a while. A snort, a wheeze, a rumble answered me—in short, Ali-Haram was snoring. So much for justice. The moon moved past the window. I rose and pinched out all the candles save the one on the nightstand.

Ali-Haram did not like to wake in the dark. Still, despite all the scrolls we had sold, my frugal habits were dying hard.

I came back to bed. I pulled the duvet over me and moved close to my husband's side.

*

"Mistress?" A rap on the side of the litter. I pulled aside the curtain and showed my face at the window. The mounted Commander bowed his head briefly. "We are ready to cross the gorge. Will you do me the honor of riding behind me? We put leather blinders on the horses."

He was polite, phrasing his order as a question. I answered in kind.

"Thank you, Commander. To tell the truth, it will feel good to get out and stretch my legs."

I stepped out of the litter. Slabs of black rock rose on either side of the packed-earth trail. The soldiers were fixing cloth sacks to long poles. The sacks held our food and other supplies. Pairs of slaves lifted the poles and made their way down roughly carved rock steps to the foot of the bridge, where they laid down the burdens and then hurriedly clambered back up the steps. The broad bloodied shoulders and welted backs of the slaves shone in the late afternoon light.

"I'll have to leave the slaves behind with the litter," the Commander told me in disgust. A wind moved across the gorge and set the bridge asway. "You can beat them all you like, and they still won't cross the bridge."

"Aren't you worried they'll escape while we're in the Maqazzan camp?"

"They're too useless to run away. What is the point of having slaves at all, I will never know."

"My feelings exactly, Commander."

A soldier got on all fours beside the Commander's mare, making a step for me so I could mount.

"I suggest using your scarf to cover your eyes," the Commander said, once he had me settled. "It'll make the crossing easier."

I thought about my Afsoon, who covered her eyes not to keep from seeing, but to keep others from seeing her.

"An excellent idea, Commander," I answered. "I'll do just that."

But I crossed the gorge with eyes wide, staring down at the foam and distant roaring water, gripping the back of his uniform tunic in terror.

*

With the gorge behind us, we picked our way up a long straight slope. The hooves of the Commander's horse kicked up a steady fall of rubble and rock. Ahead, a cloud of dust rose. The cloud gradually drew near. Beneath the dust was a long queue of prisoners, roped together, trudging toward the gorge. The prisoners—Maqazzans, by their garb— did not look up as they passed. Nor had I when we made the same terrifying journey those years ago.

We had understood that enslavement would be our lot as soon as we reached Baghdad. Our lives would no longer be ours. We would wash the clothes of our new owners, scrub their floors, cook their food. And even if Heaven miraculously willed freedom to one of us, she would remain ever a slave to the whim of the King—I have been proof enough of that.

I am a woman with a foot in two worlds—the free and the slave— and a home in neither. Likewise, I am both Persian and Maqazzan. I know peace in my Persian home with my Persian husband—yet how it fires my blood to imagine my people rising against their masters.

"These Maqazzan slaves will see to your needs."

The Commander's words brought me out of my thoughts. Two figures prostrated themselves in the dust, a man and a woman. Behind them, a tent. Yellow flags fluttered atop the pole hub.

"This will be your private quarters," he continued. "You'll be safe here. All the fighting has been a good half-league away. Refresh yourself, take your evening meal. Come nightfall, I'll return for you, so you can attend the King in his field headquarters. He's waiting for your valuable intelligence information."

"Intelligence?" I was confused. "I think there's some mistake—"

"No, I distinctly heard him say you would tell him who assassinated the Kushite ambassador."

*

"O Majesty," I began, "when we last left the story, Myobec, a rival mage to whom Soqob owed money, had returned from the afterworlds as a tagalong with the spirit of Arkiman."

"Ah, right. And we recall also that Soqob sent Qazem to the summoning with a peafowl feather, to watch out for just such an event."

Two Persian soldiers were busy settling the King onto a pile of blankets that served as his field bedding. They pulled an embroidered duvet of Maqazzan silk over him—it was identical to the one the post herald had brought me. A draft under the tent flap set the candles to guttering. Smoking incense filled the tent with the smells of burnt amber and mint. When the soldiers left the tent, I said:

"Soqob was wily. Everything that had happened was part of a trap he was laying for his rival." I had created the side story on that last night in Baghdad, while Ali-Haram snored. "You see, O King, the mage had sent an eagle, one of his familiars, to fly through the Kushite ambassador's open window and steal his soul (for reasons I will soon make clear). The eagle ripped open poor Arkiman's throat to deceive the King's investigator as to the true nature of the crime.

"In short, the investigator had no chance of succeeding. He was looking for a man who had committed a murder—but the murderer was no man. And of course, Soqob, the mastermind of the crime, could count on silence from his own familiar."

"We suspected Soqob all along." Shahryar expressed his satisfaction. "Justice failed the ambassador. Still, our ancestor Alcimedes made an effort, with all good faith. We praise him for that. We fault him only for sullying his hands with magic and its practitioners to begin with. This is a hard lesson every ruler must learn."

30. Debt and Retribution

"I endured my first retribution today." Soqob slumped on the divan in his laboratorium, coughing and wheezing. His face was drawn, his eyes rheumy. "Most unpleasant. Myobec transformed me to a stone and tossed me into the Tigris. I sank to the bottom and eroded to dust over the course of ten million years. Of course, all that time was only a morning for you. Well, my debt is down to two hundred ninety darics. Here, put these scrolls in the chest. They are scholarly projects I hope to work on during my next retribution. That is a long and nasty scar across your face, my boy. Through the feather-eye I saw you put yourself between the girl and the scimitar. You should be more careful; you could have been blinded."

"One eye still sees. I thought I was blind until Mother Homa scraped away the caked blood." Qazem propped open the trunk lid and laid the scrolls neatly atop a stack of undertunics. He thoughtfully added an inkhorn and a clutch of pens. "The other eye, I fear, is destroyed."

"You think you have problems," Soqob said. "I have to spend an aeon on the icy sphere of Saturn as it makes its way around the Earth, and Myobec values the whole retribution at only five darics. Magery can be a trying profession, my boy. It calls for much forbearance."

From their various cages, Soqob's eagle, peafowl, and other familiars watched the packing with disinterest. A single candle flickered on the worktable. Qazem had requested the audience so he might deliver certain news he knew his master would not like hearing, but he was not sure how to broach the subject. Instead, he asked:

"How did you ever incur such a debt, Master?"

The flame from the candle lengthened. It twisted and tangled itself. A bright red face appeared in the fire: Myobec.

"I could not help but overhear," the wraith said. "I will answer your question by posing another. Why did Soqob take my name off our scroll? I co-authored the 'Unpredictability' scroll, you know."

"If you will remember," Soqob said, "we had differences of opinion regarding the manuscript, and for this reason dissolved our partnership."

"I wrote half of it. You agreed to pay me for that portion."

"Sales were slim. I could barely afford to pay the copyists. I had to visit the moneylender. Naturally, interest accrued."

"Consider yourself fortunate. Had I accused you of stealing my work, the guild would have de-maged you."

"But Master," Qazem asked, "why give Myobec the opportunity to return from the afterworlds?"

"I never intended to," Soqog said sadly. "When the eagle returned to my laboratorium on the night of Arkiman's death, I planned to apply certain oils to the Kushite's soul. The oils would have prevented any mage-spirit from adhering to it as a tagalong through the ether."

"A predictable trick," Myobec said triumphantly. "Knowing you would try it, I took counter-steps. Then, once I was back in the world of the living, I needed only to follow the vibrations of the eye to find you and begin your retributions, in which I am taking immense satisfaction."

"If the Sentinel's scimitar had simply disposed of the amateur spirit summoner, all would have been well. Her passage from this world would have yanked you away with her. But no. Qazem had to step in and save her, which shocked her out of her trance."

"And cut me off from the afterworlds, I should add. I am here to stay, Soqob—although I have to say, I find this wraith-form most inconvenient. While you are away, I plan to go through your scrollarium and research methods of re-corporealizing. But enough of that. Hurry now, the sphere of Saturn will not hold its favorable position forever. An aeon is nothing. You can be back by breakfast."

"I have pressing business to discuss with my Apprentice," Soqob said. "Grant us a few moments to confer."

"Very well, but none of your tricks."

The flame hissed and lowered.

Soqob said: "Qazem, the summoning gift of this Afsoon is most impressive. And she will only grow in skill, especially considering the personal sacrifice she chose. But I fear this will enable more dead mages to slip back from the afterworlds as tagalongs. Some of them may claim that I owe them money. In short, we must strip the girl must of her powers."

Qazem was shocked.

"But summoning is everything for her, master! It is her life. And without the income, her family would be destitute. You must find some other way to—"

Soqob waved away Qazem's objections.

"Larger matters are at stake here, my boy. Besides, her family will be stronger for having lived through a little suffering and sorrow. Then they will have a greater appreciation for true happiness, should it come. But let me turn to another topic, one that may hold great profit for you. Qazem, you are the least incompetent of all my Apprentices, and that is a compliment I do not hand out lightly. If I should not return from Myobec's retributions, I want you to take over my practice. My scrolls, familiars, laboratorium, all will be yours. With a little reorganization, it might even turn a profit again."

Qazem swallowed hard. No more delay: he had to give Soqob the unwelcome news.

"Master, it is with great shame and sadness that I must tell you something. I have misled you. I broke your rules. I have taken a second Apprenticeship—"

Soqob shrugged.

"Yes, yes, my familiars reported it to me. You are a little rebellious; that is not all bad. It shows you have spirit. I forgive and pardon you."

"But there is more. My other master, Noki—may Heaven preserve his soul—has left our world of sorrow. He has willed me his business. I have decided to leave magery for the art of sandal repair."

"Is it the Giving Up that has you so worried? True, your girlfriend blinded herself, but surely, we can find something for you that is less inconvenient—"

"I plan to blind myself as well, master. One of my eyes has already been ruined; the other is going to join it. Not to advance my career, but because only thus will I be worthy to bind my life to Afsoon's."

"Love has addled you, my boy," Soqob said. "You are not thinking clearly. How will you repair sandals without your sight?"

"Noki trained me with tools and leather strips in my hands, and a scarf over my eyes. It is the fingers that see."

Soqob sighed.

"You are already blind, Qazem—your heart has made you so."

The candle-flame grew. Myobec reappeared.

"Are you done packing yet?" the wraith said. "Better bring a mantle; I understand it gets chilly on Saturn. Soqob, my old enemy, I foresee a day when our world will revolve about the sun, not the other way around. Then Saturn will be many more spheres away, and that much colder. Count yourself fortunate. Apprentice, I suggest you remove yourself from the laboratorium now, or you may accidentally end up where your Master is heading."

"Wait until this time tomorrow," Soqob whispered to Qazem. "Do nothing rash. While I am away, I will ponder matters and devise a solution by which everyone will be satisfied."

Qazem secured the last lock on the chest.

"Goodbye, Master," he said.

*

The striped shadows of the date palm crept across the courtyard flagstones. Qazem and Afsoon knelt on their rugs. A knife with a bone handle, wrapped in a white cloth, lay between them.

"I did not blind myself," Qazem said.

"I was wrong to expect that you would," Afsoon answered.

"By not telling you, I lied."

"You gave your eye to save my life. It was your Giving Up."

Mother Homa came to the courtyard; on her tray were grape leaves stuffed with almond cake. Other inhabitants of the courtyard assumed positions to snatch crumbs: flies steadily circled, crows queued on a roof edge, a monkey inched head-first down the date palm. Homa served out the dessert and sighed happily.

"What a lovely picture the two of you make together. Qazem, I should be honored if you made me an offer for—well, you know."

Qazem felt heat rise to his face; Mother Homa was referring to Afsoon's bride-price. The monkey chose the moment of distraction to spring. Landing, it seized a fistful of cake and dashed away with a shriek. Homa answered the thief with a shriek of her own, scattering the crows. While she gathered up the remains of the dessert, she added:

"And if you get the opportunity, talk to your Soqob. He might have salaried positions suitable for Afsoon's sisters—?"

After Homa left the courtyard, Qazem slipped the knife from its cloth. He tested the blade against his thumb. He gazed at Afsoon, at her uncovered, sightless eyes. He was certain of his course. Yes, he and she would walk through their dark world together. They would make their way by the senses left to them, and by their love for each other.

He gazed on the world for the last time, fixing it in his memory: the cracked and weed-grown flagstones, the date palms, the brilliant sun, the lovely and blind Afsoon. He lifted the knife to the light. The point glinted. His heart pounded; his fingers tightened on the bone handle.

"Ah, there you are. I found you at last. And, it appears, just in time."

Qazem's knife paused at this honking. The white peafowl moved closer, head bobbing. The tail feathers fanned with their golden eyespots.

"I had thirty thousand years to think it over," Soqob continued. "And I have a solution. The girl still has to give up her summoning powers, naturally, but what if I give her a minor, alternative talent as compensation? Would you like to interpret sheep entrails, my dear? It is steady work, although you may want to lay in a supply of wormwood for the odor. As for you, ex-Apprentice Qazem, I give you my blessing to continue in the heel-repair business."

"O beloved, who is this?" Afsoon whispered. "Can it be the great Soqob? I have studied all your scrolls, Master. The ones I could afford, that is."

Qazem put down the knife. His thoughts pivoted from sacrifice to bargaining.

"Afsoon gave up her sight so she could master her magecraft. Now you are going to take away that craft. We cannot stop you. But it is only right that you restore her seeing."

"The girl's eyes have been ruined," Soqob honked. "I am merely a great mage. You must not expect the impossible."

"Here is something that is not impossible: take two eyes from your tail feathers and install them in place of her sightless ones."

"Regrettably, Myobec has already taken a lien on those eyes for my debt. His ungenerous valuation was six to the daric."

"Then take my remaining eye and give it to Afsoon. I know you can do this. You wrote a scroll on the very subject."

"O Qazem!" Afsoon cried, "Then you would be the blind one! I cannot accept such a gift. Although perhaps—"

She paused. Qazem and the peafowl glanced at each other uncertainly.

"Master Soqob, I cannot allow my beloved to give me his eye. But— could we not share?"

"Sadly, my dear," Soqob answered, "an eye is indivisible."

"I do not propose to share his eye, but his sight itself. The seeing of one working eye would be shared out to the four we have between us."

"Hmm. The idea is not without merit—" (Qazem smiled at Afsoon's cleverness. Soqob's first published scroll had been "The Spell of Functional Sense-Sharing: a Proposed Protocol") "Of course, the spell itself is quite difficult—"

Afsoon smiled.

"True. Only the very greatest of mages would dare to undertake it," she suggested.

"If the spell is successful, you would sell more scrolls," Qazem added.

A dragonfly hovered near the date palm. A flash of gold—the beak struck. The peafowl raised his head and swallowed.

"Very well. But I must tell you something, my girl. I have done further research since I wrote that scroll. I discovered that the Spell of Functional Sense-Sharing will require one further sacrifice of you. And it is a sacrifice so hard that you may well prefer remaining blind."

31. Inviolable Rules of Magic

How weary I was, from the long day of travel and the long night of storytelling. King Shahryar lay on his field bedding, hands behind his head. The moon was down. Even the owls and bats had retired for the night.

The King had an observation to offer.

"True, Soqob is undergoing his retributions, although Myobec imposed those not for the crime of murder, but for unpaid debts. Still, suffering is suffering. We take this lesson: Heaven sends justice in many forms."

I yawned and waited for the King to dismiss me. But his Majesty had more on his mind.

"Our scouts found the hideout of a rebel band two leagues from here. The hideout is a deep cave in the hills east of the road. We have put together this battle plan: two regiments dispatched to the hideout, from opposite directions. They attack at first light. There is a pass below the cave that the rebels could try to use for an escape route, so a company of javelins will wait for them at the bottom. Our officers have praised this plan. Yet knowing that Persian soldiers may fall is a terrible weight on our heart. All our men are like sons to us."

"After any battle, mothers and fathers on both sides weep for their dead sons." I spoke my pious words while selfishly feeling relief that Merdad was at his field exercises instead of preparing to fight in a real battle at sunup.

"—so go on with your story," King Shahryar was saying, "if only for another hour. Distract us from our worries."

*

O Majesty, the sacrifice that Soqob's spell would require from Afsoon arose from one of the inviolable rules of magic. When one loses or forgoes a talent, that one must also lose all memory of the time when she used the talent.

In short, Afsoon would not only lose her power to summon spirits, but she would remember nothing of doing magic, meeting Qazem, losing her sight, or Qazem saving her life. All these memories would disappear forever.

"The sacrifice is unfair," Qazem complained. Soqob, in his peafowl form, pecked a clump of pistachio cake the careless monkey had dropped from the tree. "It is too great a price to ask her to pay."

Afsoon said calmly: "O beloved, there is no price I would not pay to see you once more."

But if she lost all her memories of how they fell in love, how could he bear to remember them alone?

"O Soqob," he said, "I am no longer your Apprentice. I am Master of Noki's business now. I am going to earn my bread from footwear-repairing, not spellcasting. I do not need the magecraft you taught me. And I do not want to remember anything my beloved does not remember. If you must drain away Afsoon's powers and memories—then I request you to do the same for me."

"Qazem, no!" Afsoon cried. "I am certain of your love. I do not need more proofs."

They argued, as those in love will do. But finally, all parties reached agreement. They made their slow way back to Soqob's laboratorium. The one-eyed Qazem carefully guided the sightless Afsoon by the elbow, while the mage bobbed his beak and fanned his tail feathers.

The peafowl entered his cage, and a few moments later a bent and wheezing Soqob came back out. He rummaged through his shelves for the scrolls needed for the Spell of Functional Sense-Sharing, while he sorrowfully told his guests the details of Myobec's next retribution.

"He is sending me to solve a famous problem of ancient history. Do you know the story of the knot of Gordias?"

"It was an intricate knotted rope located in Phrygia," Afsoon said. "According to an oracle, whoever unknotted it would conquer all of Asia.

Some say Alexander Magnus used his own hands to untangle it. Others say he sliced it in two with his sword."

"How are you going to determine the truth?" Qazem asked.

"Myobec plans to transform me in time as well as substance. I am returning to the time of Alexander, as the knot itself."

Soqob began to prepare the tincture.

"O great Master," Afsoon said, "what is the alternate talent you are giving me? Am I really going to learn how to tell the future from sheep entrails?"

"My dear, you will see past, present, and future alike. You will look directly into hearts. But you will have to figure this out on your own, for regrettably, you will have no memory of these words I am saying."

Like the summoning spell, the lines of the sharing spell were in the ancient tongue of the Medes. Afsoon politely corrected the mage's pronunciation as the spell proceeded. Then, while the lovers held hands very tightly, Soqob poured the tinctures into their eyes.

Qazem and Afsoon began to sneeze—this was the manifestation of their powers of magecraft departing. Next, they wept uncontrollably—their tears were memories leaving.

*

O great Majesty, the story of Qazem and Afsoon now ends. You can well imagine how confused the two were as they left the mage's laboratorium. Qazem had no idea where he was, or why he was there, or who the bent and wheezing man was, or who the girl beside him was.

Qazem could not stop blinking. Why was his vision so hazy? Objects looked indistinct and blurred. Lights glared and ran together. He sneaked a glance at the girl—and found her staring back at him. She gasped with each step, as though every sight on the street amazed her. Her eyes had pools of red where the whites should have been. A gash crossed her face, from temple to nose to temple.

Qazem felt powerfully drawn to her, in a way he did not understand.

From here, the story of Qazem and Afsoon is a familiar one: two people meet, come to know each other, and in the fullness of time, fall in love.

But there is a part of the story I have not told you yet. You see, Qazem was his parents' only child. His mother had died when he was very young, and his father had spent most of his time away from home. Qazem's childhood was cheerless and solitary. How often he had wished for a brother or sister to care for, and to keep him company.

Now on his wedding night, Qazem experienced a vivid and extraordinary dream. In this dream he was a child once more, and his father unexpectedly brought him a baby sister to dandle upon his knee. As the baby cooed and mewled, Qazem's heart glowed with joy. All his loneliness flew away. His happy tears fell on the infant's head.

But then, in the dream, his father left, and Afsoon arrived. She took the child and unexpectedly threw her into the sky. Qazem looked up, up, into the dazzling blue, and there, above the highest cloud, the baby girl lay, belly down, atop a sunbeam.

When Qazem woke, a long time passed before he realized it had been only a dream, so vivid and powerful had it been. He excitedly related the dream to his bride.

"I understand what this dream means," she said without hesitation. "The baby girl stands for the child that you will father. Throwing the girl into the sky is my bringing her into the world. The sunbeam stands for a great adventure our daughter will have in her life."

"I wish with all my heart that this will be so," Qazem said.

"I have never been so certain of anything."

This is when Afsoon first realized she had somehow come to own the power of interpreting dreams. Of course, she did not remember the bent and wheezing man's promise to give her a new, alternate talent. (But Majesty, you and I remember!)

But now for the most wonderful part of this whole story—

While Soqob was pouring his tinctures into the eyes of Qazem and Afsoon, he experienced a moment of pity for the two young lovers. This was a most unfamiliar feeling for him, and at first, he was ashamed of himself for having emotions. But then he thought—what harm could a small kindness do?

He searched his laboratorium shelves for a certain powder. He spoke a phrase and introduced a pinch of the powder into each tincture.

And so it was, as the years passed, that from time to time Afsoon would wake with the morning light and, turning to her husband, say:

"I had the strangest dream. I dreamed that you and I met each other for the first time in the basement of a fishmonger's shop, and I lost my sight and won your heart, and then you saved me from a whirling scimitar."

"What could such a dream mean?" the Cobbler would ask sleepily. For he himself had awakened from the very same dream.

But the Dream Interpreter would shake her head and say: "It is one dream I do not know the meaning of. But O husband—what wonderful happiness it brought me!"

SCROLL FOUR:

THE EPIDEMIC OF LOVE

32. *How Blue Was Our World*

Many leagues east of Baghdad lay the remote village of Viroo.

The good people of Viroo had never heard of Baghdad. They were unaware that they were part of the kingdom of Persia. The King's census takers, tax collectors, scribes, road builders, and military engineers (all of whom, to be fair, already had an extensive empire to deal with) had never gotten around to visiting. One found Viroo on no official maps.

The travelers Sheydah and Zajeel arrived in Viroo weary, hungry, and footsore. The Viroosh, a kindly folk, did not turn the two away. It was obvious to them that the blue-skinned Zajeel was a Djinn, and they learned (after only a little prying) that Sheydah came from a distant and mysterious land known as the Ragged Quarter.

Yar and Caspara, a childless couple, took Sheydah in and put her to work tending their orchard. Zajeel received a cozy cave to sleep in, along with the job of entertaining children at name-day parties, which he did by relating tales set in a place called the Blue Land.

*

"Aha!" said the King. "Your stories, with their twists and turns, have fooled us before, but not this time. We are onto you. This Sheydah, of course, is Dilara, who for some reason has taken a new name. As for Zajeel, he is the Djinn Idrosun, disguised in male dress."

I tried to hide my smile.

"Your Majesty is most perceptive. But I assure you, Zajeel is a Djinn in his own right. As the story opens, he doesn't even know Idrosun. And as for Sheydah, she isn't Dilara, although she is someone you've met before in this tale, going by a different name."

Shahryar harrumphed and frowned.

"Are you ever going to tell us what happened to Dilara and Idrosun after they left the flying divan behind?"

"Patience, O King. I will reveal all in time. Remember that a story is a flower, which buds and blossoms in its own time."

"Very well with your flower, but at least explain why Sheydah and Zajeel would travel such a distance to this remote Viroo."

"I will do so now, Majesty. To begin with, picture a girl journeying on foot. Baghdad lies far behind her. Her head sags and her eyes droop from lack of sleep. She longs to lie down in the warm sun and rest but does not dare. The trail winds through a wood—"

*

The trail wound through a wood. The canopy grew dense, the light gloomy. The way was steep. The girl moved steadily upward. She tried to move in silence, ducking under branches, stepping over brush and rubble. The trail bent back tightly upon itself. She came upon a small mountain pool, and gratefully knelt to drink. I will rest, she thought, only for a moment—

A sound—crunching brush—woke her. Her throat seized. How long had she slept? Could he have already caught up with her? Barely breathing, she rolled onto her belly and peered over the edge. A thick stand of ferns hid her face.

Directly below her was a man in a gray hooded kaftan and leather boots. He had an unsheathed scimitar strapped to his back. He was so near on the switchback she could have almost touched his hood. It did not occur to him to glance up.

She watched while he settled his bedroll and gathered brush and sticks for a fire. After dinner of jerky and an apple (her mouth watered), he produced a rope and practiced tying nooses. It was clear he was bedding down for the night. She got very slowly and quietly to her feet and returned to the trail on tiptoe. Two more switchbacks brought her directly above the man again. He had stretched out in front of his fire.

The girl's name was Sheydah. She was fleeing justice.

The Sentinel of the Muhtasib was in pursuit.

*

The stars appeared abruptly, as though candles beyond number had been lit all at once in the sky—this was because the roof of the canopy had ended. Despite the starlight, on the earth the dark was impenetrable. The trail, emerging from the forest, began a long invisible descent.

Sheydah's feet and back ached. She had walked through the night.

In time the stars receded, and the first glimmers of day shone through the mists on the ground. The Sentinel would have arisen by now, she guessed.

Some time after sunup the trail crossed a gully, and in the gully lay something blue—the sort of blue one usually found only in peafowl and bluebirds. A row of grackles perched along the something. Sheydah crept closer to look.

Could it be true? O wondrous fortune!

She pinned her veil back in place and adjusted her headscarf. She eased herself down into the gully. The snoring creature wore a torn blue vest and ragged blue trousers. Beetles nested in the pink top knot that sprouted from an otherwise hairless blue head. The bare feet were padded, clawed, and furred.

She took hold of a toe and gave it a tug. The creature lurched to its feet, blinking against the light. The grackles rose and scattered.

"I, Sheydah, a traveler from the Ragged Quarter, have found you, O Djinn." She spoke in the ritual form remembered from children's tales. "By right you must grant me a wish."

The Djinn brushed twigs and leaves from trousers.

"Ah, if only I could." He yawned hugely. "Regrettably, I am not much of a Djinn. I lost my assigned tree and thus have no powers. I cannot grant wishes to you or anyone. Let us sit along the edge of this gully—did you happen to bring any snacks?—and I, Zajeel, will tell you my sad story."

Sheydah's heart fell. There would be no magical deliverance for her.

"I am fleeing Baghdad," she said, "and a Sentinel is on my trail. I do not dare stop. But if you walk with me, I will listen to your tale."

And so the two took to the narrow trail together, faces turned to the sun. The brilliant light was burning off the morning mists.

"I was raised in the Blue Land, as are all my kind." Zajeel hurried to keep up with Sheydah's quick pace. "What happy memories! How we ran and played as Djinnlets. How blue was our world. I remember the sea horses and schools of carp and dolphins that flew through the very air. We studied and practiced for our careers in wish-granting. The trick, you see, lies in distinguishing the levels of the heart. I am sorry to say, however, that I have never granted a wish, from the bottom of the heart or any other place.

"After completing my studies in the Blue Land—I do not mind telling you I earned the highest marks in my class—a prestigious placement came my way. This was a certain famed walnut tree, in Madagascar, said to be a half-aeon in age. It had grown to such a height it scraped the bottoms of the clouds. It was so wide it had scores of excellent hollows for me to choose among. But the day before I was to arrive and take possession, a great storm arose. The ancient tree toppled. Tremors were felt as far away as Arabia.

"That was centuries ago. I applied for a new placement, of course, but my only offer has been a cave outside Nineveh—and I ask you, is a Lesser Tree Djinn to dwell in some hole of stone, like the lowly Spotted Cave Djinn? No, I deserve a suitable tree, and that is why I travel the world in search of the Blue Land, so that I might make my case to the Ancient Blue Ones in person. But enough about me. What about you, my new friend Sheydah? How does a girl such as yourself come to be traveling alone through the wilds of Persia?"

The sun lit up crystals in the outcrops of rock along the trail, which fell in narrow, rutted steps. The dark outline of a new wood appeared ahead.

"My story too is unhappy," Sheydah answered, "but quick to tell. A crime was committed. I was accused of the crime. Now I am on the run."

"What was this crime?" Zajeel asked.

"An act so terrible that I cannot even bring myself to describe it. But even worse than the crime was the betrayal by a friend."

"And where are you heading now?"

"Away from the Sentinel," Sheydah said simply and hopelessly.

"Then let us travel together." Zajeel's voice took on a new resolve. "I have lain in gullies long enough. Two are safer together than alone. To the east is a certain village I have heard of. It is so remote it has never heard of Persia or the Muhtasib."

*

In most places, the arrival of a newcomer with blue skin and pink top knot might have caused a sensation. But not in Viroo. Nor did the Viroosh seem all that surprised to discover that Zajeel—who with his blue skin and pink top knot was obviously a Djinn—did not grant wishes.

For all the village's remoteness, it nonetheless hosted a bustling monthly affair known grandly as the Eminent Viroovian Exchange. Traders and customers came from all over. The Exchange was known as a place to shop for bargains, and Viroo as a place to enjoy a holiday off the beaten path. The Persian empire had yet to put in place all its taxes, fees, and regulations. This is why prices at the Exchange were reasonable, and profits steady.

As it happened, Exchange Day came the day after Sheydah and Zajeel arrived in Viroo.

Yar and Caspara, regular vendors at the Exchange, brought along their new boarder and assigned her a few minor tasks. These included: unloading and stacking goods, fixing the awning to the orchard stand, feeding and watering the elderly oxen Honey and Woodbine, washing out the oxcart, hanging up bags of fly repellent (a paste of basil, soda, and vinegar), and taking a turn through the crowd to offer free samples (apples roasted with rosemary and sprinkled with cinnamon). When Sheydah completed all this, Caspara advanced her half of a quarter-daric against future earnings and gave her the rest of the day off.

Vendors from every stand called out their discounts and bargains. Customers queued and milled. One could buy (or barter for) hen eggs, daffodil bulbs, prayer rugs, bolts of silk in every color, grilled chickpea cakes, fried peach pies, scented candles (wax or tallow), under-tunics (linen, muslin, or wool), board games, platters and bowls fired from white river clay and colorfully enameled, tooth-cleaning linen strips (coated with crushed pepper and mint), hobnails and sandal straps, skullcaps and turbans, and purses made of oxhide. There were tattoo artists, face-painters, hair-braiders, nail polishers, muscle manipulators, and neck re-aligners. Stilt walkers, knife jugglers, storytellers, harpers, minstrels, and figures capering about in painted masks provided general entertainment.

(One vendor even traded in kittens, although in truth he was paying his customers, rather than the other way around.)

Sheydah noticed a queue that was longer than all the others. At the head of this queue was not the usual awning stretched across wooden poles, but a small blue tent.

"What is being sold over there?" Sheydah said, through her veil, to a vendor at a nearby stand. "There are no smells, or stacks of goods."

"What that vendor sells has no smell." The neighbor spoke in a confiding tone. "She has no inventory, and yet her supply is unlimited. Nothing in Viroo rivals her product in popularity. It costs more than anyone can afford, but those who buy it anyway are highly satisfied. They say it would be a bargain at twice the price."

Listening to this riddle, Sheydah reached into a fold of her tunic and gave her half of a quarter-daric a possessive squeeze.

"Tell me more about this mysterious product."

"I have to get back to work now." The neighbor pulled her headscarf lower against the rising sun. "Visit her tent yourself and find out. If I sell enough today, I might just do the same."

Sheydah watched customer after customer leave the blue tent aglow with happiness. She took her place at the tail of the queue, and finally it was her turn. She pulled aside the tent-flap and, to her amazement, found herself facing another creature with blue skin and a long braid that fell from a pink top knot.

"Welcome, customer." The blue vendor bowed. "Let us sit on this rug and discuss business. As you have doubtless guessed, I am a Djinn. For technical reasons, I no longer grant wishes as such. Nevertheless, for a price I will fill your heart with joy. My product carries a lifetime guarantee, as long as you believe. You are in great luck. For the next hour only, I have a special price for first time customers, which is—" (Here the vendor gave Sheydah a careful gaze, as though taking the measure of her means.) "—a mere half of a quarter-daric."

"But what exactly are you sell—"

At this point the tent flap opened. A girl stormed in. She wore a blue tunic, yellow silk trousers, a blue headscarf covered with silver stars, and bast sandals. Hands on hips, she addressed the Djinn sternly.

"O Idrosun, what am I going to do with you? First it was Happiness, and then Sorrow, and now I hear you are selling True Love?"

Sheydah found the newcomer strangely familiar. Where had she seen her before?

"But Dilara, my beloved, look at our earnings!" The Djinn Idrosun lifted a sack of jingling coins. "Soon we will have a travel stake. We will be able to buy boots, supplies, and camels. We will not have to stay here in Viroo any longer. We can explore the wide world and forge our destiny together."

Dilara (so it became clear as Sheydah listened to their talk) was employed by the village sorceress, working for room and board. Dilara disliked her work, which was weaving. Specifically, she wove spells. She had spent the entire previous day attaching spider silk tassels to the squares of cloth. Her thumbs ached.

The sorceress usually kept Dilara chained to her work bench, but this morning had forgotten to secure the locking spell. Dilara had sneaked out while the sorceress took her nap.

Dilara and Idrosun ignored Sheydah while they argued. Their talk touched on: a sorcerer who had become an Angel, a man who bought two years (less one day) of happiness, and a boy who had become heir to the throne of Persia without speaking a word. Sheydah's head spun.

"In short," Dilara said, "you came by your earnings dishonestly. True Love is not a commodity to be bought and sold."

"O Dilara, as I roam this world, I have learned that people believe in what they pay for. The more I charge, the more I sell. The more I sell, the more people fall in True Love. The result is more joy in Viroovian hearts, not to mention profit for us."

"We will continue this discussion later. I must get back to my worktable before the sorceress awakens."

Opening the tent flap to leave, Dilara gave Sheydah (still in veil and headscarf) a sidelong glance, seeming to notice her for the first time. There was puzzlement in Dilara's gaze, as though she found the customer as oddly familiar as the customer found her.

And in that moment, as the two locked eyes, something shifted in Sheydah's heart. Her breath quickened. She felt warmth in her face. Her world turned upside down. She had never known such a feeling.

When Dilara was gone, Sheydah said in a voice filled with emotion: "Half a quarter-daric, you said?"

The product (Idrosun explained, after Sheydah handed over the payment), consisted of a few carefully selected phrases, which if spoken properly and with genuine feeling, would melt and transform the heart of the one listening. The listener could not help falling in True Love with the one speaking the expensive words.

For practice, Idrosun made Sheydah repeat the words of True Love several times but put hands over her own blue ears to keep from falling under their dangerous power.

33. Freedom From Love

The Commander let me ride back to my tent on a pony of my own, although he joined us, saddle horn to saddle horn, by a hemp line. It was as well: I nodded off as we rode, shook myself awake, drifted off again. Steep hills loomed along the roadside. When the moon fell behind the hills, the world was so dark I could not see the pony's hooves beneath me. We stopped shortly after first light.

My Maqazzan slaves were Wa-atuq and Wafa. Wa-atuq wore a ragged brown hooded robe, Wafa a threadbare gray shift. After the Commander took his leave, I stepped down onto the back of the kneeling Wa-atuq. When I reached the ground, he scrambled up and slid his bony shoulder under mine before I collapsed. We wobbled toward my tent.

"Shall I have Wafa make breakfast, Lady?" Wa-atuq's words were a jumble of Persian and Maqazzan. "She has wild turkey eggs this morning."

All I wanted was to sleep.

"Could I eat later?" I ventured. They stared blankly at the strange Persian lady who did not know how to give orders to slaves. Slave, free, slave, free—I always had to remember which world I lived in. I tried again: "Have Wafa take me to a place to bathe this afternoon. I will take supper afterward."

Sounds drifted down from the hills. Distant war cries, the clanging of blades—I realized dully that this was the battle the King had planned and told me was coming.

"Yes, Lady." Wa-atuq opened the tent flap for me. "As for bathing, we know a mountain lake. A bit of a climb to reach, but the water is not that cold this time of year. Wafa can show you how to brace yourself under the falls and—"

I heard no more, but fell into my rude bedding, asleep at once.

*

"In sleep the soul departs the body and is united with Allah. Waking, the soul and body rejoin. Thus Heaven reminds us of our mortality."

These were the words Ali-Haram recited each morning when we rose. And so his blessed dream-form said again, as sleep left me in the warm Maqazzan afternoon.

I stuck my head out the tent flap and called for Wafa to take me to that promised bathing spot. When we returned, I was refreshed and hungry. Wa-atuq, still in the brown hooded robe, bowed and asked if I was ready to dine.

"Wa-atuq, I—"

"Lady?"

But what was I going to say? I wanted to know if he had completed his day's labors. I wanted to ask how the Commander treated him, if he had found time to take his own bath in the falls, if he had taken his supper yet. But these were not proper questions for me to ask. Why should a Persian lady need to know anything about the life of an enslaved Maqazzan? I was free, and he was not. We stood next to each other, worlds apart. He carefully did not meet my eyes.

"Never mind. Please bring food now. Will you ask Wafa to keep me company?"

He frowned. Another error.

"She has many other duties to attend to. You'll be served in your tent, Lady."

What use to resist?

The tent was cool and dark. The only sound was the growling of my belly. Wafa brought in an embroidered eating-rug; she moved my bedding to a corner of the tent to make room. The brown hooded figure entered and set out my meal: flatbread with persimmon jelly, fried mushrooms, and something inside a seared palm leaf that smelled delectable. I peeled the leaf back and peeked inside.

"Wa-atuq!" I cried. "What joy—you brought me a lamb shoulder."

"Field rations. I packed them myself—Mama."

He pulled back the hood. I was too stunned to speak.

"I talked Wa-atuq into letting me bring your supper," Merdad said. "He let me wear his robe so I could surprise you."

I couldn't hold back a surge of anger.

"I thought you were safe! You were supposed to be at your field exercises—"

"But I am, Mama. We are holding our exercises here, in Maqazza. Look at the medal I won."

The silver disk bore the engraving of a mounted Persian warrior, sword in his raised hand. Merdad's eyes shone as he told his story. The fighting had begun at sunup, while I was sleeping off my own exhaustion. The Persian attack had put the rebels to flight from their cave stronghold, while more regulars blocked the pass below. The Children's Battery was posted with these regulars. Merdad commanded a company of bows—four other boys.

Some of the King's staff officers considered the bow a weapon for peasants and outlaws. The Commander had set up Merdad's single company (of children) as an experiment.

"The rebels came rushing and screaming down the slope," Merdad recounted. "One headed straight toward me with a hand-axe. I had my bow nocked. He was so close I could smell his hot breath. But then—"

He stopped. I felt my heart pounding. I wanted to throw my arms around him. I wanted to kiss him, to prove to myself that he was alive, that he really was there with me. The miracle of my child.

He plopped beside me on the eating-rug. He tore a hunk of flatbread and used it to scoop mushrooms.

"I have to go back soon; let's eat." His battle-story was over. "This isn't how your palace cooks do it, Mama. You dig a hole two feet down and build a fire in it. When it burns out, you wrap the meat in leaves and lay the leaves on the embers. Then you cover everything with dirt. It cooks for the fiull day."

"It tastes wonderful, Merdad."

"We're moving to a new position tonight. The Commander said every boy had to write to his mother first."

That made my blood run cold. What could such an order mean, but that some boys were not expected to return home alive?

"One boy made fun of me for not knowing my letters. I gave him a bloody nose. The Commander said I could visit you while the others did their writing."

His lip curled in triumph—how he looked like his father in that moment.

Merdad ate and talked rapidly. As the huge meal disappeared, he told me about training and making camp and using a bow. Finally, he returned to the battle—

"As we waited for the fight, all those stories you told me about Papa went through my mind. How brave he was. How he had given his life for Maqazza's freedom. When that rebel came at me with his axe, for a moment he could have been Papa himself. I had my bow drawn, and I let fly, over his head. I missed him on purpose. But one of the other boys in my company brought him down. Do you want that last flatbread?"

O Merdad! My heart tells me I'm a slave pretending to be free, and yours says you're a Maqazzan pretending to be a Persian. Who are we, really? A great betrayer, the heart.

Or maybe it is our truest part.

Away in the distance, a blood-chilling sound—a wolf's howl? No, a horn, summoning the Persian troops. Merdad kissed me on the head and slipped out of the tent.

*

(O Majesty, I have related how Sheydah became a fugitive from justice, with a Sentinel of the Muhtasib in pursuit. And I related how she fell into the company of the Djinn Zajeel, and so came to the remote village of Viroo.)

Zajeel's cave lay in the red stone hills beyond the village. It was not the easiest place to reach. First one crossed a trackless wildflower meadow, through a droning cloud of bumblebees. Then, past the meadow, a swift, shallow creek, forded across slick creek-rocks—a misstep had sent Sheydah tumbling into the chilly water. Her silk trousers were still annoyingly damp. After this, a narrow goat path up the hills—pebbles kicked up beneath her heels and settled inside her bast sandals. At the end of the goal trail, one had to count boulders: one, two—Zajeel's assigned cave lay behind number five.

This cave was domed and shallow, with an opening in the shape of a quarter circle. Abundant ferns and tamarisk rose on the stepped earth above the cave. Zajeel lay on a rock shelf toward the back of the cave, atop a heap of sleeping hides. The usual line of grackles perched on his blue legs. His snores were answered by snore-echoes off the cave walls.

Sheydah poked the Djinn's feet. The snores broke off. The grackles scattered and re-settled on the boulder outside the cafe.

"You turned down a cave in Nineveh," Sheydah said, smiling, "and look at you now."

"It is a temporary home. Once I know you are safe, I will resume my travels. One day I will find the Blue Land. Did Yar and Gaspara excuse you from your duties?"

221

"This morning, I picked beetles off the peaches, brushed wasps off the figs, and carried water to the almond trees, one by one. Hot and sweaty work, but the afternoon hours are mine, to do as I will."

She handed him a fresh pear from the orchard; he stuffed it into his mouth, stem, core, and all. She went on:

"I figured out why the Viroosh were not surprised when you showed up. There is another Djinn in the village, and she can't grant wishes either."

"Yes, her name is Idrosun." He sat up and stretched. "She lives in the next cave over. We may be the last two of our kind in the world. I am in love with her. I want to wed her and take her to the Blue Land, where we will raise a family of Djinnlets. Unfortunately, she loves another."

"I too have fallen in love," Sheydah said. "It took a single look. Now I must find the courage to get her alone and say the words of True Love, which I bought from Idrosun with all the money I had."

Sheydah had already spent several days in uncourageous misery, as is a lover's right.

"So you are in love. What is the name of this lucky girl?"

"The one who fills my dreams, who rouses my heart, who resides in my very soul—is Dilara."

"Dilara! Why, she is Idrosun's closest companion. They came to Viroo together, as you and I did. In fact, I understand Idrosun is in love with her. Worse luck for you, Dilara is blindly and hopelessly in love with some shepherd named Feroze. Well, you are not likely to talk to her anyway, for the sorceress who employs her rarely lets her leave her worktable."

"If only you could grant wishes," Sheydah said. "O Zajeel, what am I going to do?"

The Djinn propped his chin in his hand. He was a picture of concentration, if not wish-granting.

"First," he said, upon consideration, "you must get her to notice you. Find a way to be alone with her. That way you can take your veil off and she can see your face. Come to think of it, I have never seen you unveiled myself. Well, we are alone now. Why not show me what you look like, Sheydah?"

"That—would not be proper."

But Sheydah was not considering the issue of propriety. She was remembering the Sentinel of the Muhtasib. Her insides went cold at the thought. Zajeel shrugged.

"Did you bring me any hazelnuts, O veiled one?" He sighed with the pleasure of anticipation. "Ah, what happy times dear Idrosun and I will enjoy together in the Blue Land. I will dandle our Djinnlets on my knee. And I will get a new tree assignment at last. My love and I will share the tree and grant wishes to passers-by. Say, this True Love you bought—I wonder if it works on the one who sells it?"

"It is so powerful she covered her own ears."

A crunch of gravel outside the cave, a soft slide of rocks—a moment later, the figure of Dilara herself passed the cave entrance, deep in thought. She did not look their way. Sheydah's heart skipped.

"She must have come to visit Idrosun," Zajeel said. He held his ear at an awkward angle to the cave wall.

"Zajeel!" Sheydah scolded. "It is impolite to overhear." But she placed her head beside his.

"—know there is another Djinn in Viroo?" The voice came muffled through the rock.

"Yes, his name is Zajeel. I am afraid he has fallen in love with me. But do not be concerned with that, beloved. My heart is yours always."

There was more talk then. But it was low and muted by the thickness of rock; they could not make out the words.

Dilara gave a sudden cry.

"O Idrosun—how odd I suddenly feel. What is happening to me! Am I dying? But no, I feel wonderfully alive. Strange! My mind is so clear. I feel released. My heart has been fluttering and racing for so long, and now it is steady and sure—"

"Aha! This is a feeling I know quite well. The spell cast by the sorcerer Vahid has finally let go of its hold on you. You are free at last to love who you will."

"That ridiculous feather Feroze always wears—how did I ever adore it so? How could I have loved him the way I did? O Idrosun, I am free! No more longing, no more hopeless sighing—"

The voices on the other side of the stone grew faint once more.

"The way is clear, Sheydah," Zajeel said. "Run, fly to this girl. There is no time to lose. Speak the words of True Love to her. This is your chance for happiness. For me, the way is less clear. My beloved is your rival. But I will win her in the end—you will see."

Zajeel gave Sheydah an encouraging push, but she stopped short of the cave entrance.

She had spent her fortune on True Love, after all—not Bravery.

34. The Holy Broom of Dissolution

Nights were cooler in Maqazza than Baghdad. The wind swooped down the steep hills and set the flags on the King's tent snapping. I wrapped myself in a woolen blanket and tried to rub heat into my arms; Shahryar burrowed into his field bedding.

"Your story shows the many twists and turns of love," Shahryar said. "But it also teaches about belief. Idrosun can't grant wishes the way she used to. And she is no sorceress. But she sells True Love, which is as powerful as Vahid's Spell of Blind and Hopeless Love. Her customers believe it works, and therefore it does."

And I thought: we all have the things we need to believe. I had to convince myself that Ali-Haram would continue to write, that he wouldn't go back to gambling or drinking, that he would still love me when I wasn't at his side. Otherwise, how could I have ever found the strength to sell myself back into slavery?

Now if only I could make myself believe that no rebel arrow or blade would find Merdad in the upcoming battle. If my belief was strong enough, would it make it so?

The King went on:

"We understand your son's company performed bravely today. How proud you must be. Ah, when we were his age! What a warrior we were, in our time. A good battle rouses a man's blood. Unfortunately, our officers will not allow us to join the fighting against the rebels."

"They fear for your safety, O King," I said. "If you were to fall in battle, who would lead them?"

"You're right, of course. What a cruel fate a King faces. He gives the command for his men to fight, but then must watch them march off to glory while he stays behind."

I did not answer. His self-pity struck me as unbearable.

"But as we have pondered such things," he went on, "we have produced an idea for making Scheherezade's story even better. Now she has her sorcerers, flying divans, talking animals, all that sort of thing. But what about combat? That's what her story is missing. Armed men standing shoulder to shoulder, javelins held aloft, swords drawn, ready to shed blood for their King. What a fine story that sort of thing would make."

We (Ali-Haram and I, not Scheherezade) had created the story of Dilara and Idrosun as a diversion, a harmless way for Shahryar to escape the awful realities of Kingship—war among them. But like Merdad, the King had a child's view of fighting. For him, it was all glory, strategy, bravery. His officers blocked him from the battlefield. He could only taste combat in his nightly story.

Well, I was the one telling this story. I had experience with the truths of war and wanted nothing more to do with them.

I said evasively: "O Majesty, I don't think Her Highness knows anything about war and bloodshed."

"Exactly. That's why we have a plan for her to learn. You see, our scouts have reported new rebel battalions—they pop up like mushrooms after rain—circling behind the pass. The Maqazzans think they can outflank us. But to do so, they will have to cross a lake and a falls. Our battle plan for tomorrow night is based on this. We have been informed there will be a full moon. The Commander knows a ridge top with an excellent view of the falls. You will join us there."

I felt the blood drain from my face. He noticed and laughed.

"There's nothing to fear. You and I will be high above the action. What danger could there be?"

He thought I was frightened for myself!

"We'll observe and evaluate our troops," he went on. "Meanwhile, you can learn about fighting. When you get back to Baghdad, you'll share everything with Scheherazade, so she can add them to our story."

"We obey, Majesty." I thought about the boys writing their letters home. I could barely get my words out. "During this battle—where will—the Children's Battery—be?"

"Such things are petty details. Our officers take care of all the deployments. No, I want you to watch how the moonlight glints off the sword blades. To listen to the war cries from the men when they charge. Things like that."

Was there any way out of this nightmare?

"Majesty, these hills are very steep. I don't want to hold you back as you climb to the ridge top."

"How foolish you are sometimes. We will be carried, of course. Orderly!"

A uniformed aide hurried into the tent and prostrated himself.

"Tell the Commander to fetch Ariana at sundown tomorrow," Shahryar ordered. "And have our litter made ready, with eight strong and trusted slaves to bear it."

The aide climbed to his feet and dashed out of the tent.

"Now divert us for a few hours. Tell us how Sheydah courted and hopefully won Dilara—but why are you squeezing your eyes shut, Ariana? Don't tell us you have forgotten the next chapter—?"

I hadn't forgotten anything. I was picturing a cloud sliding across Shahryar's full moon, and a blackness sliding over the Maqazzan hills: Death, stalking a boy somewhere in those hills.

I opened my eyes. With some effort, I managed to give the King a weak smile.

*

(Last night, O King, I told you how the Spell of Blind and Hopeless Love wore off Dilara at last, and how Zajeel declared his intention to wed Idrosun and raise a Djinn family before their kind vanished from the world forever. But now a month has passed since the last chapter, and the time has come again for the Eminent Viroovian Exchange.)

Sheydah led Woodbine and Honey to a patch of shade behind the orchard stand. The other vendors were already busy setting up their stands, putting awnings into place, laying out goods. Frying oil popped; smoke drifted from cook fires. The first customers were already milling about. Sheydah did not see anyone looking her way. She lifted her veil and ran the back of her hand across her sweating face.

"You are that girl Yar and Caspara took in." The voice came from the next stand, where the vendor sold soap made from sheep fat and wood ash and scented with peppermint and lemon. "Where are they this morning?"

Sheydah hastily lowered her veil back into place.

"They bought a board game here last month. They spend all their time playing it. When I left this morning, they were arguing over how many spaces the Ruk and Queen Consort can move."

"Your grapes and plums look good. And I see you have hazelnuts and walnuts. I will buy some later. Have you memorized all your prices?"

They chatted while Sheydah finished her preparations. The orchard stand was soon ready for business.

"I wish you trader's profit," the soap vendor said. "May you sell all you brought."

"And you as well," Sheydah returned.

The flap of the white tent opened. Idrosun stepped out and waved.

"Greetings, customer and fellow trader," the Djinn called. "Well, are you still satisfied with your purchase? Will you and your beloved be standing before a wedding mirror soon?"

"Now I need to buy bravery," Sheydah said with honesty, "or else I will never be able to say the words of True Love to her."

"Bravery is not something I stock. I do have a new product to feature today, but it would not help in your case. Well, I wish you trader's profit."

Later in the morning came snorts and the creak of harness. Two riders—a man and a boy—approached the orchard stand. The riders wore ordinary tunics and skullcaps, but Sheydah observed the riders' boots of polished leather, and the royal seal stitched into the saddles. (A child from the Ragged Quarter learned to notice such things.)

The two dismounted. The man helped himself to a plum.

"They are a quarter-daric the four," Sheydah said politely.

"For us they are nothing the four," the man said, taking three more plums in hand. The boy shook his head.

"Your behavior is not worthy, Vaktan. Pay the girl."

The man, Vaktan, spat in disgust, but reached into his tunic for a coin, which he flipped in the air. Sheydah caught it neatly and dropped it into the cloth sack at her feet.

"We are strangers in this land, fruit vendor." The boy's voice was high, as a boy's will be, but his words were those of a man. His tone carried a quiet authority that belied his age (which was, Sheydah guessed, five years and four, or so). "Certain rumors have reached us in the capital. They may be nothing; legends grow in the telling. But the rumors speak of an epidemic in this part of the empire."

Sheydah caught her breath. Her aunty had once told her about an epidemic that had coursed through the Ragged Quarter in the old days.

Many people had sickened and died. Aunty had noticed that the disease followed the rats, but the neighborhood wise woman scolded her for superstition. An epidemic, the wise woman said, was Heaven's curse on the people for their evil ways.

"The symptoms are sleeplessness, excitement, and a racing heart," the boy went on. He smiled. "It is, in other words, an epidemic of love."

Two hand-holding customers parted the flap of the white tent and disappeared inside.

"To be sure, Lord," Sheydah said, "Viroo has seen many a wedding in the past month."

Vaktan and the boy exchanged glances.

"Has it now?" Vaktan said. "Do these Viroosh know that, in order to wed, a couple is required to purchase a parchment with the King's seal?"

"What is a King?"

Vaktan spat again and turned away. Several leather saddlebags hung from the saddle of the boy's horse; the boy took one of them in hand and held it to his mouth, as though speaking confidentially to it. Sheydah could not make out his words.

She saw Vaktan then; he was watching her watch the boy. Vaktan grinned and mimicked biting into a plum.

At that moment, the two customers departed the white tent. They cast dark looks at each other, and they no longer held hands. The orchard stand had no customers. Sheydah went to the white tent, scratched the flap, let herself in.

"Officials from Baghdad have come to Viroo," she told Idrosun. "I think they have heard about you selling True Love."

"They will be disappointed," Idrosun said. "I am no longer in the True Love trade. My friend Dilara, whose understanding of business ethics is superior to my own, has taught me that one should never profit from love. Today I am offering a new product by which I hope to right my earlier wrongs. By the way, why wear a veil in his heat? It is only you and I here in this tent."

An invitation to show her face—Sheydah pretended not to hear.

"What is this new product?" she asked.

"Something I learned from a great sorcerer with whom I used to be in love. Well, he used it to join lovers together, but why should it not work in reverse?"

Another scratch on the tent flap—a young couple entered. Sheydah moved aside to watch. The girl and boy touched and kissed each other shamelessly. Idrosun coughed to get their attention.

"Satisfied customers, I see. I trust you two will be standing before the wedding mirror soon—?"

"We are, in fact, greatly dissatisfied," the boy said. "Our unhappiness knows no bounds. But it is not the fault of your product, which worked entirely as advertised. I will share our story. I spoke the words of True Love to this girl, and in no time at all, her heart was mine. But then our parents found out. My family has less money than hers, and so they have forbidden us to love."

The girl added: "But being in True Love, and needing to be together, we secretly wed. We are now husband and wife. You must help us. We need a product that changes the hearts of parents."

"Yours is a sad story," Idrosun said. "I have heard it many times today. I cannot change a parent's heart—who can?—although I do carry a new product which might prove useful. Look behind the tent—" (this last was directed at Sheydah) "—and fetch the Holy Broom of Dissolution. Meanwhile, I will ask these young lovers some important questions."

Sheydah let herself out of the tent. The Holy Broom—a long willow limb with a bundle of straw tied to one end—lay propped against a tent pole.

"—slurps her soup," the boy was saying as Sheydah brought the broom in. "I must admit, this makes me grind my teeth."

"And you, dear?" Idrosun addressed the girl. "What faults does your husband have, no matter how minor?"

"Well, he constantly clears his throat, which anyone would find annoying."

Upon further questioning, each spouse produced more personal shortcomings in the other.

"It appears you are not perfect for each other, after all," Idrosun said. "Like a perfect diamond, love must have no flaws."

Husband and wife eyed each other with distaste. The first cracks had appeared in the glass that is known as True Love.

"Sheydah," Idrosun said, "give me one end of the Holy Broom of Dissolution, while you take the other. Hold it a little off the ground, just so, there. Now, you two turn around. Jump backwards over the Holy Broom three times, and say, 'I divorce thee,' 'I divorce thee,' 'I divorce thee.'" The ex-lovers having completed the rite of annulment, Idrosun held out her palm. "One quarter-daric, please. I am giving you my special youth discount. Tell all your friends."

Sheydah returned to her stand. The trader's profit the other vendors had wished her held true; by closing time the ox cart was empty. Every fruit and nut had been sold. Woodbine and Honey would have an easy time of it on the journey home. Vendors had begun to pack up; Sheydah reached to take down the awning over the orchard stand—and stopped in her tracks.

Standing at the soap vendor's stand was a man in a gray hooded robe, a scimitar strapped behind his back. Blood pounded in Sheydah's ears. She edged backward and crouched as quietly as she could behind the counter of her stand.

"Perhaps you can help me." The Sentinel's words to the soap vendor drifted through the still air. "You see, I am a simple tradesperson, like yourself. You sell cleanliness, and I sell justice. What would the world be without each of these? A customer has commissioned me to search for someone who might have come this way. This someone has committed the foulest of crimes, namely the unlawful taking of another's life."

"We do not have—murderers—in Viroo." The soap vendor's voice trembled.

"No? Then Viroo is unique in the world. Well, you will see me around. If you hear anything, let me know. The Muhtasib will serve justice. You may count on it. I have a perfect record. I bid you a good day."

Sheydah counted out ten slow breaths, ten times, before she raised her head to peek out.

The soap vendor and Sentinel were gone; the field of the Eminent Viroovian Exchange was empty.

Woodbine and Honey were waiting patiently.

35. Fussy Old Men and Poor Choices in Youth

I shivered; my teeth chattered. I pulled my shawl and blanket tighter against the chill.

Our ridge top was a flat half-oval, glowing silver. A swath of stars and a slice of full moon showed above us; twin rock walls led away from the ridge and blocked the rest of the sky. Stretching out below us and into the distance, enclosed by the walls, was a narrow winding ribbon of shadow: the pass.

A cloud of mist rose toward us, coming from the falls Wafa had taken me to. The falls pounded the small mountain lake.

My mule whimpered. The litter ordered by the King had turned out to have a cracked pole; the Commander found mules for us instead. They were sure-footed and slow.

"We positioned our troops above the trail that leads down to the camp. Look—can you make them out from here?" The King talked rapidly in his excitement. "The rebels will pass through the falls, you see. Our men will pick them off as they cross. Now if—"

"Majesty." The Commander appeared on the ridge top. His mule whinnied; ours answered. "I may have gotten you here too early."

"Too early?" The King had a way of breathing in his throat that gave away his annoyance.

"The rebels are moving slower than expected. They are on foot, of course, and the pass is narrow—well, the troops are ready, and still in place. But I don't expect an engagement for a few more hours."

The Commander dismissed himself. The only sounds in the world were the breathing of the mules and the drumming of water. Shahryar said:

"Now we sit in the cold and wait, Ariana."

"Yes, your Majesty." I knew what was coming. I was prepared.

"Go on with your story, then. It'll pass the time."

"Yes, O King. I plan to tell you more about a character you've met already, if briefly. She is about to become important to the tale."

"Another story within a story?"

"Yes. You'll recall that a local sorceress had taken in Dilara—"

*

—and put her to work weaving spells. Now, whenever parents in Viroo told their children "There is no such thing as magic," they cited as evidence the so-called sorceress who lived in a treehouse near the village.

The sorceress worked quite hard to maintain her reputation.

She had engaged a few vendors at the Exchange to sell her spells. These were squares of cloth decorated with cryptic symbols and tassels of spider silk. Everyone knew the spells were worthless, but locals and visitors alike bought them (at six to the daric) for harmless, humorous souvenirs.

The sorceress had chosen the woods outside Viroo as a dwelling place specifically for their remoteness. Let the Viroosh shake their heads and laugh at the pretend-sorceress in her treehouse. It served her purpose for others to think her incompetent and leave her alone.

You see, before the sorceress moved to Viroo, she had worked in Babylon, that queen city of olden times. There she was employed by the Sorcerers Guild—not in a magical line, but as a rug cleaner. She labored on hands and knees, with brushes, rags, and powders. Once the last sorcerer had left for the day, she would summon a concentrated vortex to finish the cleaning and make her way to the Guild scrollarium.

A conjured Hydra with poison-tipped claws and six serpent heads guarded the scrollarium, but the rug cleaner used a simple spell to immobilize the guardian. In fact, she took pleasure in reducing the Hydra to slavish servility and riding its armored back up to the fourth floor, to the Hall of Statues.

Here, representations in bronze, marble, and alabaster of the famed sorcerers of every epoch collected cobwebs and dust. And at the very back of the Hall of Statues was the Alcove of Strictly Forbidden Writings. This is where manuscripts the Guild authorities had adjudged unsuitable or subversive were kept. Only the most senior faculty could request access to these scrolls, and then only for approved scholarly research, under the Guildmaster's direct supervision.

In the very back of the Alcove of Strictly Forbidden Writings were stored the most intolerable, the most dangerous, scrolls of all. Why so intolerable? Because their author was one who did not belong to the Sorcerers Guild. These scrolls were, in short, the work of an unlicensed imposter who, flouting all Guild traditions and proprietary protocols, had dared to invent his own spells.

True, he had talents—no one denied it—but the fact was, the college of magic in Babylon had dismissed him, thus dashing his hopes of gaining admission to the Sorcerers Guild.

Throughout the night the rug cleaner would sit on the floor and sift through the forbidden writings. She would pore over the astonishing inventions. She would take extensive notes, copy important passages, marvel at the originality. (The Hydra counterspell had in fact come from one of these selfsame scrolls.)

By now you may have guessed, O King, that the author of these scrolls was none other than our own Vahid.

Like Vahid, the rug cleaner had left the college of magic without earning a diploma. But also like Vahid, she had natural talents and gifts. She knew magic was in her bones. She refused to abandon her dreams. If Vahid could find an alternate path to success in his chosen profession, then so could she.

She had two great ambitions. The first of these was to archive Vahid's spells. In fact, she planned to collect, organize, and annotate his entire body of work. In time the Guild might lift its ban, and then future generations of sorcerers and scholars would thank her.

But why should the Guild change its decision? Why would it ever lift the ban on the imposter? Ah, this brings us to the sorceress's second ambition—to recruit Vahid as an ally against the Guild itself. Why should they not join forces? Why not combine their skills? They would make a formidable team. The Guild would be no match for their talents and powers. Together they would bring down those arrogant, fussy old men. Together they would take sweet revenge for the centuries of exclusion and scorn they had suffered. And once they toppled the Guild, they would consolidate their power. They would exercise absolute control over the practice of sorcery worldwide—

One day, she felt certain, she would meet Vahid again. She need only be patient. The memories of the girl Dilara would lead her to him, in time. And when that day came, she would reveal to him the improvements and modifications she had devised for his spells. How could he not be impressed with her skill, her talent, her potential—?

*

233

"Aha! We have guessed who this sorceress is," the King said. "She is that Lebanese princess. What was her name? Ah yes, Zaib. We recall that she did not leave the college because of poor marks, but because of the grin Vahid had fixed on the face of Thukamon."

"The King's memory is excellent," I said, smiling.

"We remember too she was married to that prince who spoke to her so cruelly. She commissioned a spell from Vahid, and he transformed the Prince's words into Angels."

"O Majesty, on the day Zaib came to commission that very spell, and she met Vahid after all those years, something shifted in her heart. She fell in love with him. Not because of any spell, nor words of True Love bought in a market, but in the ordinary manner of male and female, which is a mystery none in our mortal world can ever understand. And she remembered well that Vahid had loved her once, back in their college days. Could it be, she wondered, that he loved her still?"

"Poor Zaib. In love with Vahid, the sorcerer of her dreams—and yet for the great distance that separated Baghdad and Viroo, the two of them might as well have lived on different worlds."

"In this, O King, you might be surprised."

Somewhere above the sound of the falls came the screech of an owl and the drawn-out call of a wolf.

I could not stop picturing it: the rebels wading through the knee-deep water, nearing the falls, holding their weapons clear. The roar of water swallowing their war cries, the rocks underfoot slick. One of the rebels slipping, righting himself, the water swirling and pulling. Moonlight revealing him: Merdad, in his Maqazzan blue, bursting free through the tower of mist—the Persians waiting above, letting loose their javelins—

No! I shook my head to drive away the waking nightmare. I pictured it another way—Merdad with the Children's Battery, wearing Persian red. The boys in position on the trail above the oncoming rebels. Merdad drawing his bow. His father plunging through the falls. He and Merdad recognizing each other; their eyes locking. Merdad letting fly, over Emre's head—

"Ariana, have you fallen asleep?"

The King's impatient voice brought me back.

"No, Majesty, I was only—my mind was wandering. I'll continue the story now."

*

One question remains: why had Zaib taken in the girl Dilara as a boarder? The offer certainly did not arise from public spiritedness.

It was custom in Viroo for village authorities to interview all newcomers, and by such means direct them to proper employment and accommodations. In Dilara's interview she mentioned, as a qualification, having once worked for a sorcerer.

"A sorcerer, you say?" Zaib had asked the authorities when she heard about this. "Did the girl perchance mention a name?"

A written account of the interview was found.

"It is a sorcerer said to be employed by the King, in Baghdad. We doubt this story, as we have never heard of a King, or Baghdad. But the girl gave the name Vahid."

Zaib felt a thrill course through her; she replied as casually as she could.

"I have decided to give the girl room, board, and honest work. It is my civic duty."

And so the sorceress had taken Dilara to her treehouse outside the village and assigned her spells to weave. (The spell that chained her to the worktable was a mere security precaution.) The girl weaved ineptly and without enthusiasm, but this did not matter. The spells were a front. They were harmless busywork designed to keep her occupied, while her memories were scanned and studied at Zaib's leisure.

What had Zaib seen during this scan? Rowdy games with boys in the Ragged Quarter of Baghdad—rides on sunbeams—a transformation into a Frankish Princess (with a mane of roses growing from her head)— a Prince who renounced the throne of Persia to take up a shepherd's crook—a journey through the sky on a flying divan. Well, the girl certainly had an active imagination.

And what was that smell? An aroma, an aura of remnant magic. Zaib thought back to the forbidden scrolls; she sniffed again. Why, the girl had recently suffered under the Spell of Blind and Hopeless Love—a particularly inspired Vahidian creation—

It was true, then. Dilara had worked in the employ of the great one.

Still, no matter how the sorceress scanned, she could find nothing in the girl's memories concerning Vahid's present whereabouts.

*

On the day Idrosun began selling annulments at the Exchange (the girl had pleaded to go, but Zaib sternly kept her at her weaving) the sorceress entered her laboratorium and set out a dish of quicksilver. She peered for a long time into the still surface of liquid, waiting for a swirl, a ripple, a dimple—anything. She yawned.

Then she bolted upright.

"Eye-spy, show me that horse up close." She addressed the quicksilver. The eye, stationed on a treetop above the horse, dived obediently. "No, the other one."

The view appeared above the quicksilver. A man atop one horse; a boy dismounted next to the other. Who could these two be? Look at the way the boy carried himself. He had a natural authority about him. Why was he talking to his saddlebag?

And what were the two doing in remote Viroo?

Zaib had found the original design for eye-spies in Appendix Zeta of the fifth forbidden scroll. She had overheard from Guild sorcerers (while on her knees cleaning rugs) that Vahid had lost the eye-spy design to Thukamon after losing a wager, and that Thukamon had since extended the principle to the ear as well. Zaib had thought: why not combine eye and ear into a single familiar? Why not add lips and tongue in the bargain? Why not give it the ability to worm? Really, only the imagination limited the possibilities.

"Eye-spy, I wish to see inside that saddlebag." She tapped her finger on the rim of the dish. The boy had climbed back in his saddle; he and the man were speaking in low voices. The spy inched across the stiff leather, and onto the underside of the flap. Zaib made out a chain, a handle, a spout: a brass lamp. The quicksilver quivered. The view cleared: eyes, nose, lips.

The sorceress felt her heart pound. That dear face!

"—who is that looking at me?" The thickness of quicksilver muffled the words. "Is it you, Thukamon? I thought I sent you packing off to Paradise."

"Vahid!" Zaib cried. She was in a transport of joy. "Have you forgotten your Lebanese princess? How you competed for my hand once—well, I made poor choices in youth. But look at you, cramped inside that silly lamp—"

"One gets used to it, my dear. Besides, I have conjured any number of improvements—garden, orchard, stables. I ride every day. I plan to expand my laboratorium. How is your Arabian prince?"

"He ascended to Heaven. It is the fate of those who love me. But what are you doing in this backwater?"

"I could ask you the same, my dear. But to answer, Viroo is experiencing an epidemic of love. I am investigating possible unauthorized use of my Spell of Blind and Hopeless Love without due compensation."

Wait—was that another nose in the lamp? She made out a second pair of eyes. The face had a female cast. Zaib's brow narrowed. A rival!

"Listen, I have a nice treehouse outside Viroo." The sorceress did not mention that the treehouse was based on another of Vahid's original designs. Best not to quarrel over user fees just yet. "There is plenty of extra room. You can stay as long as you like. You can have a proper laboratorium again. Together we will get to the bottom of this unauthorized use business."

Vahid finally agreed to pay a visit. The female competitor—her name was Omid—expressed several loud complaints, but Vahid made assurances that the visit would be for old time's sake only. Zaib wasted no time. With a snap of her fingers, she unlocked the spell that chained her boarder to the worktable. She immediately set Dilara to work scrubbing floors, dusting shelves, laundering bedclothes. Once all these chores had been completed, the sorceress unceremoniously dismissed Dilara from her employ.

The girl had served her purpose, and could be turned out without further thought.

36. Little Timo, the Matchmaker's Son

Below us, screaming and shouting and the clang of weapons—

The Commander reappeared on the ridge top. Our mules whinnied and struck their hooves nervously on the stone.

"Majesty, you and the woman are to leave at once," he said. "I can no longer guarantee your safety."

The King did not want to understand.

"We were supposed to be safe from the rebels here. You said no \arrow could reach us here."

"The ridge top is safe. The camp isn't. You are to return to Baghdad. We have no time to lose."

He gave the King's mule a swat on the rump. Soon we were picking our way down toward the main trail. The Commander gave his report while we descended. The rebels, playing their game of deception, had sent only a single company through the falls: patriots who chose to give their lives for the cause. Meanwhile, the main body had taken an arduous route, circling around by ways even the goats avoided. The Persians were intent on the trail below—the rebels fell on them from above.

As we neared the falls my heart was in my throat. The mules whimpered, smelling death. We saw the bodies then. A few wore blue; most were in red. Sprawled, bent, crumpled, hacked, spitted on javelins—Death signed his work the same way in every war. The groans of the dying rose above the pounding of water.

I silently thanked Heaven for not seeing children. For not seeing Merdad.

"Sons of Persia." The King's voice broke with emotion. "Sons of our own. We shall stop and attend."

"No, your Majesty. We are not stopping." The Commander was brooking no disobedience from his King. "I've detailed others to do their duty to the fallen."

At the camp, flames leaped from the tents and wicker storage sheds. Men chased down terrified horses. I lost sight of the King: soldiers moved in to ring him and lead him away on his mule. Officers rode up to confer with the Commander. I overheard: "Fire arrows came down like rain." "The rebels must have had excellent intelligence." "How did they guess where we'd set our trap?"

"Round up men at arms for the King's escort," the Commander gave orders rapidly to one of his officers. "I will lead it myself. Requisition a pack mule and two days' supplies. You'll be in charge here till I return. Organize a fire brigade—"

I finally got the Commander's attention.

"Please, where's the Children's Battery?" I tried to keep my voice from trembling.

"The boys? I posted them up in the hills, behind the pass. Once you and the King are gone, and these fires are out, I'll have them ordered back."

Dawn glimmered. Haze and smoke lay over the camp. The light transformed the flames from yellow to red. The cool of the hills had long vanished; my shawl and blanket had fallen off somewhere on the trail. One of the Commander's men helped me down from the mule and led me to a mare waiting beyond the flames. Another man arrived with the travel bag I had brought from Baghdad. He quickly strapped the bag across the back of my new mount. I saw the King, a little ahead.

We moved out quickly. Soon we were on the Baghdad road, riding in formation: two soldiers at point, the Commander and four other men ringing the King and me, two more behind. Horses and men alike smelled of ash and sour sweat.

The brilliant sun rose and took its own assigned position, on our left.

*

"Just think, Majesty, you'll be back home in no time." I forced a gaiety I didn't feel into my voice. I was glad for my veil, despite the heat: dust rose in columns from the stamping hooves and drifted back atop us in the trailing breeze. I watched the Commander raise his uniform tunic to cover his nose and mouth. "Soon you'll be eating meals from the palace cooks and sleeping in your own bed."

"Those dead men—" The King rode with slumped shoulders and bowed head. "They were someone's sons. They were our own sons. Our battle plan—"

More self-pity. Well, it was my job to try to lift his spirits, if only to make him a better traveling companion. I reined my mount closer to his and tried again.

"Soon you'll be reunited with your dear wife." I counted moons—Scheherazade would be showing by now. "Imagine what surprises she might have for you after all this time."

No answer. One of the point riders called to the Commander, who trotted forward, and then back to us.

"Majesty, the gorge is in sight. After we cross the bridge, you can get in the royal litter and be out of this sun."

The King didn't answer him either. I reached under my headscarf to mop away sweat; the silk was drenched. We dismounted at the gorge. The men tied blinds over their mounts' eyes. Even if the beasts could not see the rushing death far below them, they heard and smelled it. They kicked, bucked, whinnied. The Commander ran a line joining the King and me to himself.

Another terrifying crossing. Peki and the other palace slaves were where we had left them, huddled in the meager shade of the litter. A heap of rabbit bones and the charred remains of a cookfire lay nearby. Freedom had been theirs for the taking, here in the wild Maqazzan hills and scrub. But life without masters held no meaning for them. They had waited, with the patience of Angels, next to the litter they had borne from Baghdad.

They returned to servitude without question or protest. They took up their positions at the litter poles. As soon as I had the King seated in the litter, with pillows settled beneath and behind him, we rose and began to move.

The litter jounced along. My mind was racing: was Merdad safe? Had the boys returned to the camp yet? What would happen if the Children's Battery ran into the rebels along the way?

"Why don't I return to the story then?" If I couldn't distract his Majesty from his misfortunes, I could forget my own fears, if only for a while. "Where was I? O yes, I remember: Zaib has invited the sorcerer Vahid to visit her in her treehouse—"

*

The ox cart neared a hedge of pink meadowsweet and wild roses. Woodbine lunged for the roses, which hung irresistibly at head-height. The lunge startled Honey (who, having taken ill, was moving more slowly than usual) and nearly overturned the cart. Sheydah caught the sack of grapes before it landed, but the almonds and pomegranates spilled across the beaten-earth road.

"Wicked ox," she scolded, for form, while she stooped to pick up her goods. "How do you hope to ever enter Paradise?"

In an act of atonement, Woodbine dropped an unchewed rose, which the grateful Honey lapped up from the road.

A sudden chorus of bleats came from a trail that crossed the road ahead. Sheydah glanced up: a figure was heading briskly in her direction. A flock of sheep scattered in his path. An angry shepherd was shaking his crook; the approaching figure paid him no attention. Sheydah saw the kaftan, and the hilt of the scimitar strapped to his back. Her throat went dry—

Willing herself not to run, nor to appear suspicious by moving in haste, she carefully arranged her spilled goods back in the ox cart. The Sentinel drew near. His eyes were hard and lightless as stones. He did not waste time on polite greetings.

"You run the orchard stand next to the soap vendor. I wanted to interview you at the Exchange, but you hid under the counter; perhaps you suddenly took ill. Now at last we are meeting. You see, I am searching for a criminal." From a leather pouch at his belt, he produced the end of a hemp rope. He tied and untied noose knots while he spoke. "Someone was killed. A child, in fact. It happened on the streets of the Ragged Quarter, in Baghdad."

"Baghdad? Where is that?" Sheydah tried to look confused. The ploy did not work as it had with Vaktan.

"I have spoken to some others. They say you are a newcomer to the village. They have heard you talk about the Ragged Quarter, and about a long journey you recently took. Moreover, you look the right age, according to witnesses. I would take you back to Baghdad to face justice, but unfortunately the witnesses all agree the murderer was a boy."

"He who willfully takes a life will spend eternity in hell." Sheydah answered piously, but her voice trembled.

"Yes, yes. Now, the murderer was a certain Ghazi, formerly the best friend of his accuser, Naseem. This Ghazi stole Naseem's dagger—a nice one, I might add, with a fancy hilt. I have examined it myself. Anyway, Ghazi used this same dagger to commit the deed. Several witnesses testify to seeing the dagger in his hand afterwards. And Naseem has testified to making a heroic effort to stop the killing blow. You know this Ghazi, perhaps? It is his trail that has led me here to Viroo."

"May you find the true murderer." Sheydah could not make herself meet the Sentinel's hard gaze.

"I have a perfect record. You may have no doubt of that. Well, I am sure we will talk again."

Later, nearing the dwelling where a customer awaited delivery, Sheydah thought: what value do the lives of the poor have? Who cares if one less rag-wearing child runs through the alleyways of Baghdad? Only a mother, weeping in the darkness. Why had the Sentinels of the Muhtasib gotten involved in the case? Money had moved from purse to fist, of course. The weeping mother was the Matchmaker, who doubtless had a pot buried behind her dwelling, stuffed with grimy coins.

Sheydah remembered it: how Naseem, having returned to the Ragged Quarter after his travels, had told everyone the many wrongs done to him. How a girl was under a spell which caused her to bray like an ass, and how he had been tricked into wedding this girl. How he had to take work like a common laborer so he could search for a cure. How mysterious travelers had taunted him from their fancy flying divan after they took her away from him. The exorbitant fee a Holy One had charged to annul the union. Each retelling of his story included new injustices.

A frequent target of Naseem's abuse was the Matchmaker. Had she not lured him into the union, with her discounts and false guarantees? Had she not concealed the girl's condition from him? An eternal curse on the Matchmaker.

Sheydah had known Naseem for a long time. She knew well the violence he was capable of.

Little Timo, the Matchmaker's son, was a slight and peaceful child. He joined in the Ragged Quarter games whenever his mother was at her work. He revered Naseem and vied daily for the older boy's approval. Whatever the older boy ordered, Little Timo did happily and right away.

For this reason, each new grievance from Naseem about the Matchmaker was like a physical blow to Little Timo. At last, he could take no more.

Where Naseem had gotten the dagger, none knew. He said he had found it on a dead man; perhaps he had stolen it. Often during his rants, he would brandish the dagger and stab the hot, defenseless air. One day he said in a deadly voice—his eyes fixed on Little Timo—that a son should pay for the crimes of a mother.

Something snapped in the Matchmaker's son.

The ferocity of the attack shocked Ghazi, and he was slow to react. Little Timo threw himself at Naseem. The older boy, surprised, went tumbling. Little Timo leaped upon him. Both boys were out of their minds with fury. They regained their feet. Ghazi got between them and tried to take the dagger away—Naseem swung the blade at Ghazi, who evaded the blow. At that instant Little Timo leaped up, like a hummingbird attacking a wolf.

The knife sank. The boy cried out and crumpled. The Ragged Quarter children stared in horror. The dust beneath Little Timo's neck turned to red. Ghazi knelt, placed fingers against the boy's neck, closed the eyelids. He picked up the bloodied dagger, which had fallen. He stared at the blade which had taken a life in the space of a single breath. Naseem turned on his friend.

"Killer! Murderer of children! All of you, look at Ghazi. Look at him holding the weapon that took Timo's life. You were all witnesses."

Ghazi stared at the watching faces. He read the terror in them. There was no doubt; the children would back Naseem's story, out of fear of him.

Ghazi understood that his own life had changed forever. But what would he do now? Where could he go?

That night, he made a bundle with his few possessions, kissed his sleeping mother, and slipped out of the Ragged Quarter. He followed the moon shadows, and before morning he was long gone from Baghdad—

37. Holy Usman and the Blue Land

Sheydah and Zajeel set out food, bowls, cups, rugs, finger-cleaning cloths, and a basket of catnip leaves (to repel mosquitoes) in the shade of a pomegranate tree. The red fruits hanging from the tree looked like children's balloons. Time to harvest soon.

"Yar and Caspara do not mind if we eat lunch in their orchard?" Zajeel asked.

"All they care about is their new game," Sheydah said. "Mostly they argue about moving the pieces. Yar says the horse moves one to the side and four up, Caspara says it is three and then two. Why did you ask me to invite Idrosun to lunch?"

The Djinn's blue cheeks purpled from a blush.

"I have an important question to ask her. Your presence will help me find the bravery I need. All my happiness depends on her answer."

There was something Sheydah was concealing from the world. How hard it was to keep a secret. She must tell someone or go mad.

"O Zajeel, you have been a good companion and true. We have traveled many a league together. But there is something about me you do not know."

"No? Perhaps I can guess? Was it you who committed that crime, after all? If the Sentinel has come this far, could the crime have been murder? Well, it is for Heaven to judge. Let them come for you. You will find me a stout defender of my friends."

"That!" Sheydah cried. "No, I swear I have murdered no one. I am innocent of any crime. You must believe me."

"Then what is your secret?"

"I—I am—"

"Here we are!" A figure appeared at the end of the row of trees, with the sun behind. The figure's top knot tossed with each step, in black outline. A smaller figure trailed the first, causing Sheydah's heart to skip. "I brought Dilara. Is that all right? She is hungry too."

The four seated themselves on the rugs.

"O friend Dilara," Zajeel said with a smile, "we see you so rarely. How did you get the sorceress to give you a break from your spell-weaving?"

"Zaib has dismissed me from her service. I am no longer boarding at her treehouse, and I am not weaving spells for her anymore. But do not be concerned about that. I will find new employment, and for now Idrosun is letting me stay in her cave."

"You may stay with me forever, beloved," Idrosun said. "I have earned enough from True Love and the Holy Broom of Dissolution to support us both. May I have more of this delicious almond cake?"

Sheydah daintily lifted the corner of her veil to nibble cake.

"But why should we eat and talk through veils?" Idrosun added. "After all, we are only Djinns and ladies here."

Idrosun and Dilara uncovered their faces—Sheydah did not. She felt the curious gazes of the others.

"Sheydah is pious and shy." Zajeel excused her.

The four made small talk: did the days seem hotter than in summers past, were peaches best eaten peeled or unpeeled, how would the Viroosh wrestlers do in the upcoming games? Sheydah stole admiring glances at Dilara. Zajeel looked nervous. He stammered and coughed, and even dropped his cake. (A regiment of ants formed up at once.)

When lunch was over, Zajeel climbed to his feet. He cleared his throat and placed a hand over his heart. The others fell respectfully silent, awaiting a speech.

"Until I came to Viroo I despaired of being blessed with descendants." He fixed his gaze intently on Idrosun. "I thought myself the very last of the Lesser Tree Djinns. But now I know there is another like me in the world. O Idrosun, you have given me inspiration and purpose. Help me find the Blue Land. We can start our family there and ensure that our kind does not die out. I humbly ask for your blue hand in holy union. Do you say you will have me, dear Idrosun."

Idrosun watched him in contemplation and amazement. Then she stood and faced her suitor. She put a hand on her own heart.

"O my friend Zajeel, I have not known you for long. Your speech honors and humbles me. You are a worthy Djinn. You deserve the most devoted of wives, and the happiest of families. But you speak of duty, and I have vowed to wed only for love."

Zajeel's head bowed.

"You love another," he said simply.

"I love one who does not love me." Idrosun glanced meaningfully at Dilara. "For years she was bound by the Spell of Blind and Hopeless Love, from which she was only recently freed. Her heart is still confused. But one day I will win her. That is my life's goal, just as yours is to find the Blue Land."

Sheydah wished she could give Zajeel her powerful words of True Love, which she could not say to Dilara for want of bravery. Zajeel had the bravery, but not the words.

"But what of our race, dear one?" Zajeel renewed his argument. "What will become of the Lesser Tree Djinns?"

"O Zajeel, 'who are we as Djinns, really?" She answered with questions of her own. "We cannot grant wishes. What purpose do we even serve?"

"When we find the Blue Land, we will convince the Ancient Blue Ones to assign us a tree, which is all we need. Our powers will be enabled once more. Imagine it—living happily in a wood somewhere, raising up our brood of Djinnlets, granting wishes to passers-by."

"I admire your commitment to this great plan." But more than this Idrosun would not say. Sheydah watched Dilara, who was watching Idrosun.

Sheydah was feverish with yearning. First love! It brought bliss and agony, in equal measure. She must delay no longer. The time had come.

She rose and faced Dilara, hand on her own heart.

"Now it is—is my—turn to—to speak." Her tongue was in knots. She blanked her mind, closed her eyes, drew a deep breath.

And at last, Sheydah uttered the words she had bought with her entire fortune of half of a quarter-daric—

In that moment, as the words entered the orchard, the power of True Love hung over the world. Redwings and bluebirds burst into song. Starlings wheeled and cavorted. A rainbow appeared, spanning the sky. The leaves of the trees quivered. Their hanging fruits grew riper.

But Dilara unexpectedly buried her face in her hands. Idrosun gave Sheydah a look of rebuke and put a comforting arm around Dilara's shoulder. When Dilara's well of tears ran out, she wiped her eyes and faced Sheydah. A fourth hand rested upon a fourth heart.

"O my friend Sheydah, you have only recently arrived here in Viroo. And yet strangely, it seems as though I have known you all my life. Your speech today has moved me. But I must now reveal something to you that no one, not even Idrosun, knows. In fact, it is something which—in a way I do not yet understand—your words have only now made me realize.

"You see, I too love another. I have loved him all my life. He is kind, gentle, and handsome. But he lives far away, in the Ragged Quarter of Baghdad, and does not even know I exist."

Sheydah's heart fell. The words of True Love had failed. At the same time, she felt the painful stab of jealousy. Sheydah knew everyone in the Ragged Quarter—who could this kind and handsome boy be, for Dilara to love him so?

At that moment, a memory came to Sheydah. As memories will, it arose for no seeming reason. She was holding a basket of flowers. All around were other Ragged Quarter children. Prince Feroze's wedding procession was passing. A veiled girl in the procession stopped to speak for some reason, as though she expected the children to know who she was.

That girl had been Dilara. But of course. That was where Sheydah had seen her before. But why had Dilara stopped to speak that day? And how did she come to be in Viroo now, so far from home?

Sheydah realized Zajeel was speaking again. But the talk of love was over. The Djinn had returned to a favorite topic:

*

"Once during my journeys in the mountains of Persia, I met a wandering holy man." Zajeel sat with his back against the pomegranate tree. "His name was Usman, which means servant of God. He wore a robe woven of bark, leaves, and grapevines. His feet had become hooved for ease of travel. Usman had been one of the original Angels at the Creation, but he decided he could do more good by taking on human form and traveling through our world of woe.

"Having been formed from pure light, Usman could kindle a blaze without wood. He cooked up a feast of manna and honey for us. As we sat by our fire, he entertained me with stories about his friends Gabriella and Mikhail, and I told him about my quest to find the Blue Land, where I hoped to get a new tree assignment and find a mate to start a family.

"Holy Usman, in whom resided all knowledge, said we needed only to find a brook or creek or any stream of water. The barest rivulet would do if we followed it long enough. The next day we happened upon a trickle of water which was pooling up from a crack in the stony ground. My journey to the Blue Land began at that moment, and Holy Usman agreed to come with me. How excited I was!

"As we followed the water in its course, the flow gradually widened. A stream bed of polished rocks developed. We followed the water day after day, steadily descending the mountain. In time we reached the meadows and fields of Mother Persia, always following the bank of our stream.

"One day the stream met a mighty river. The river was so wide we could not see the other side. Dolphins leaped; gulls wheeled above. The wind whipped white crests on the surface. We had reached the Tigris, Angel of Rivers. As we made our way downstream, the bank grew wider and muddier. The water became a slow-moving featureless sheet of blue.

"We spent many long days walking. We kept our strength by eating the fish and turtles Heaven sent to the shallows for us to scoop up. One day, without warning, Holy Usman stopped.

"'We are here,' he said simply. He eased down the bank and entered the water.

"'But Master,' I cried, 'we will drown!'

"The water covered his legs, his shoulders, his head. He was lost to my sight. I understood that this was a test of my faith. I murmured a prayer to Heaven and followed him into the river. The water closed over me. I held my breath as long as I could, and then, prepared to die, I inhaled.

"To my astonishment, my chest filled with sweet air. Schools of carp, eels, and seahorses flew past. Holy Usman, walking by my side, explained the illusion: the Blue Land was in fact a vast air bubble lying on the bottom of the Tigris. The sea life swam outside the bubble, and the blue was the water that surrounded us in every direction.

"'Once a primeval river dragon lived here, in the Tigris,' Holy Usman told me. 'The dragon, called Zophanax, was a full league in length. His snaking body followed the bends of the river. Zophanax and I became boon companions. We spent many a pleasant hour discussing philosophy and the future of the world, which was still in its infancy.

"'One day a woman came floating down the river in a hollowed-out log. This was the first woman ever in Persia. Her name was Saramunde, and she had been born in the Garden. She was charting the Euphrates and Tigris and exploring the Garden's other environs. Both Zophanax and I fell in love with her. We competed for her attentions. The world was young then. Its rules were not all settled. A woman could love a man or a dragon, as she wished. Despite all my efforts, Saramunde chose my rival, Zophanax.

"'In my misery and fury, I committed my first sin. I merged with all the light on the earth. This caused Zophanax to thrash about in the total darkness until he came to the sea, where he perished, not being adapted to the salt. Saramunde, unwilling to stay in Persia without her beloved, left to explore other lands. I was alone.

"'As an act of penance, I returned to human form and began to build a great bubble of breath in the Tigris. This took me many aeons. When at last I completed the bubble, I presented it as a gift to the race of Lesser Tree Djinns. It became their Blue Land.'

"Having explained this history to me, Holy Usman led me on a tour. How great was my amazement! Here, Djinnlets scampered and played; there, they sat in groups, listening respectfully to the Ancient Blue Ones, who gave talks on the art of granting wishes and understanding the levels of the heart. Djinn couples walked arm in arm, discussing love and tree assignments. And I could not fail to notice Djinn maidens giving me sidelong glances and smiles as we passed.

"We passed many contented months in the Blue Land. The Ancient Blue Ones honored me with requests to deliver guest lectures, and Holy Usman discoursed learnedly on many topics, producing awe in all who listened.

"One day, without warning, everything changed. The blue air took on a strange, shimmering quality. A hole developed in the skin of the bubble, followed by a tiny stream of water pouring in, as from a fountain. More such holes appeared; the water rose to our ankles, to our knees, to our ribs. The Djinnlets, the Ancient Blue Ones, the couples, the maidens all blurred and then disappeared altogether. Having dwelled so long in the Blue Land, they became one with the water.

"Soon the water was above our heads. Holy Usman floated, inert. I clasped him to me and swam upward until we finally broke the surface. With supreme effort I swam to the bank with him under one arm. We crawled onto the mud, and each spat up great quantities of water.

"An immense sense of loss settled over me. The Blue Land was gone. My life no longer held meaning. But then the most astonishing thing of all happened.

"A dome heaved up out of the river, streaming water on all sides. Waves rolled to shore, covering us again and again with their foam.

"'An island is being born!' I cried.

"'It is no island,' Holy Usman answered.

"An undulating head rose. Scales like armor covered the creature's body and tail, which stretched upstream beyond our sight. Jaws opened wide. A forked tongue darted. With a roar that made us cover our ears, the creature exhaled. Something shot into the sky, rising above the clouds, and soon disappearing from our view.

"Following this exhalation, a violent wind coursed over the land. Holy Usman and I held fast to each other. The creature sank slowly below the surface of the water.

"'The dragon Zophanax, sensing my presence, has returned to life,' Holy Usman told me. 'The air bubble of the Blue Land served as his reviving breath. Then, no longer needing the bubble, he expelled it.'

"'But where will the Blue Land come to rest, Master?' I asked anxiously. 'How will I find it again?'

"'The winds, which follow their own whims, will carry it somewhere. The Blue Land could turn up anywhere in our world, or on one of the crystal spheres to which Heaven has fastened the stars. I fear, Zajeel, that you are indeed the last of your kind.'

"The next day, Heaven recalled Holy Usman. His journey through our world had ended. Wishing me fortune in my search for the Blue Land, he shed his bark and leaves. As the Ancient Blue Ones and their students had merged with the water of the Tigris, Usman merged with the sky.

"But for all his great learning, in his final words my Master was wrong." Zajeel stood and brushed away the crumbs of lunch. "No matter where the Blue Land comes to rest, I am not the last of the Lesser Tree Djinns. The proof of this stands here before me—in the person of my beloved Idrosun."

38. Life With the Rebels

Wild neighing, droning whistles, shouts, cries of pain. The floor of the litter tilted beneath us and dropped away. My travel bag tumbled to the floor. The King fell from his cushions, coming to rest stunned beside me. I crawled to the window and pulled open the shutter.

A band of hooded riders ringed us in the twilight. Their mounts pawed the ground and nickered. Arrows protruded from crumpled bodies—I could see the Commander and poor Peki among them. Groans issued from free and slave alike in the act of dying. A few of the royal escort still lived; these knelt with hands clasped behind their heads. The hooded riders trained their bows on them.

One of the riders dismounted and drew near the litter. He squatted at the window. His face was dark in the shadow of his hood.

"We will permit the King to return to Baghdad." The words were a familiar blend of Maqazzan and Persian: I recognized the voice of Wa-atuq. "You, Lady, are in the hands of the rebels now. We are setting the ransom for your safe return at a chest of gold darics—"

"I'll have all of you hunted down!" Behind me, the King raged. "You'll be put to the sword, and your families—"

Wa-atuq calmly listed the ransom goods. Arrows fletched with turkey feathers. Bone javelin heads. Horses. A chest of gold darics. Withdraw a quarter of all troops from Maqazza. The King had till the next full moon to meet the demands.

I stepped out of the litter as one in a dream. Wa-atuq produced a rope and bound my wrists behind me. While one rebel led away the Persian horses as prizes, another brought up a mule and forced the King, who was still furious and ranting, to mount. The remaining Persian troops and slaves were ordered to their feet and assembled around the King. A slap on the flank sent the mule into motion; the small escort moved to keep up.

Dread seized me. The Maqazzans would have no pity for a Persian lady. What lay in store for me? Would the rebels enslave me, as the Persians had done to Wa-atuq and Wafa and others? Would I ever see Ali-Haram or Merdad again?

Never have I felt more alone and afraid. A glowing half-oval lay ahead: the mouth of a cave. Wa-atuq led me across the uneven ground toward the glow. From the hills came the baying of wild dogs. Night fell quickly. Behind the cave, the moon rose, huge and orange. I thought about Idrosun telling Khashar to wish for a chest of gold darics—I tried to picture all the darics it would take to fill a chest—

"The King won't bother to ransom me," I said to Wa-atuq, in the Maqazzan tongue. "I am no one, only a storyteller. When he is reunited with Scheherazade, he won't have any more need for me."

"In that case, Lady, why should we keep you alive?"

More of the hooded riders crowded near us. Torchlight from within the cave gave them dark outlines but left them faceless.

"There's something you should know," Wa-atuq said. "We defeated the Persians at the falls because your son secured the Persian battle plan for us."

I produced a shaky laugh, with effort.

"How could Merdad have known about that plan? The King only briefed his officers."

"Wasn't your son an officer, in the Children's Battery?"

"He would never betray his King."

"Each officer received a map on parchment. The map showed the assigned positions of the troops. The night before last, when your son went to your tent wearing my robe, he slipped his map into the sleeve. I brought the map back to the rebels."

I didn't know what to believe. I thought again about Merdad firing above the charging rebel's head—

A push from behind; I stumbled toward the cave. The light was patchy, the cave shadowy and smoky. Torches stuck out of gaps in the rock; the smell of burning pine was overwhelming. Water dripped down the stone walls and plopped into earthen pots. The hooded riders milled about. At a sign from Wa-atuq, two of them rose from a natural stone bench, making room for me to sit. My hands were still bound behind me. One rebel—I would learn this was Abbas, the senior rebel officer— stood and signaled silence.

"The name of our prize is Ariana," Abbas said. "We have told the King of Persia the ransom demand. Anyone who would speak, speak now."

"What if the King doesn't pay and comes back with his army?" someone asked.

"We don't yet have the numbers to give open fight," another said.

"We'll have lost nothing," Abbas answered. "We have scouts stationed all along the Baghdad road. They will ride ahead and let us know if they see Persian troops. We'll take our prize, melt back into the hills, and bide our time."

Someone else said: "I say the ransom is too high. This Ariana is only another highborn court lady. King Shahryar hardly lacks for those."

Another rebel, smaller and shorter than the others, spoke up from the back of the cave. For some reason he pulled his hood across his mouth, muffling his voice.

"Don't you know about the scrolls they sell in Baghdad with the story of Dilara and Idrosun? This Ariana wrote them. The King called her to Maqazza so she could tell the story to him. He can't sleep at night without it. If the story ever runs out, the Queen Consort will lose her head."

Abbas weighed in.

"Then let us do as the King. Ariana will remain with us. She can keep her head as long as we get to hear a new story every night."

The rebels stamped their feet to show their approval.

So here, in this cave, in the wild barrens of Maqazza, was where my own story was to end. I could give these men tales for a while, stretching them out, making them last, but eventually, like Scheherazade, I would run out. How would they do it? Would I get an arrow in the belly, like the Commander and Peki? Or would they leave me in the hills for the wild dogs?

A stubborn, bitter resolve took hold of me.

"I'll not be your storyteller," I told the small rider. "Do what you will. But know this. I am Maqazzan like you. I was born a slave to the Persians. Kill me, and you kill one of your own."

Having said my piece, I turned on the stone bench and set my face toward the cave wall.

Wa-atuq said softly: "Do you always speak that way to your own blood?"

The small rider gently turned me by the shoulders. I watched him draw his hood away from his mouth. When he spoke, he did not pitch his voice low.

"Yes, is that how you speak to me—Mama?"

"Merdad!" I stared in utter astonishment.

"Who is this Merdad?" Wa-atuq said. "You don't know your own son?"

"I'm sorry, Mama." My son—Emre to the Maqazzans—rapidly unbound my hands. "The rebels are hard men. You must forgive their little jokes."

*

I lived with the rebels for many days and nights. We rode through the wild hills of Maqazza. We raided, reconnoitered, replenished supplies. When the sun went down the rebels prepared their plain fare— boiled beans, unseasoned flatbreads, venison roasted on spits. These meals were as wonderful as any feasts at court.

I relented from my vow and became the rebels' storyteller. I began at the beginning, with Khashar and Sorayah. Then Prince Feroze's wedding, Vahid turning Thukamon into an Angel, Afsoon and Qazem losing their eyes and gaining their sight. Sheydah and Zajeel arriving in Viroo. The Sentinel's relentless pursuit.

The men could not get enough.

One night, while I was telling about Idrosun becoming a vendor at the Eminent Viroovian Exchange, one of them interrupted.

"What exactly are these words of True Love, Aunty? Not that I need to know for myself—" His comrades hooted. "—but these others may be curious."

People listen to stories for excitement and entertainment. But sometimes they crave more. They are searching for wisdom or insight which I—who can only create and tell the story—am unfit to provide. But that night Heaven moved me to answer this way:

"The words have been lost to the world, as punishment for its evils. But the Angels still remember the words. One day, when men and women prove themselves worthy, the Angels will whisper the words in every ear, and True Love will spread across the world like sunshine."

*

Emre and I spoke one morning at breakfast:

"Mama, when I came to your tent, I couldn't tell you everything yet. You were with the King every night, and so it was safer for you not to know. You see, I asked Wa-atuq if I could surprise you with supper. He looked closely at me, and then his eyes went wide. He called Wafa. She came and put a hand over her mouth. Then she said, "It's him!'"

"They knew you?" I didn't understand.

"They were in the detail to gather up the dead and dying. They had found Wafa's brother at the bottom of the hill, with an arrow in him. Can you believe it, Mama? He was the one I had missed on purpose. Wafa knew what I looked like from her brother's description. The boy in my company who shot him caught him above the heart, and they say he will live, may Heaven be praised."

"Have you truly joined the rebels, then?"

"Why, Mama, you told me yourself how brave Papa and the other rebels were, and Wa-atuq told me how the King treats our people. How he steals land and horses and crops, and lays taxes, and if you can't pay, you're made a slave."

"How did you get out of the camp?"

"The Children's Battery was up in the hills. We missed the action. An officer rode up and ordered us to report to the camp for fire brigade duty. When we got there, I found Wa-atuq. We slipped away in the confusion and rode hard for the rebel cave."

Abbas came up, saying:

"Emre, here is the bone needle you lent me. I thank you." He handed Emre the needle and left us. Emre reached into the leather pouch at his waist. As he put the needle in its cloth wrap, something slipped free—a Paper.

I picked up the Paper. I couldn't read the writing on it, but I didn't need to. I recognized the hand, and the eye drawn at the bottom, at once.

"You still have it!" I was amazed.

"It was the day I saw you in the carriage, remember? The man with you—my stepfather, of course—dropped the Paper out the window for me."

I will remember it always, I said to myself. That was the day Ali-Haram gave me love and freedom.

"But you don't know how to read any more than I do," I said. "How did you find out what the Paper says?"

"A wise woman in the Ragged Quarter read it to me. It was the day I won the ass race, remember? I used my prize of one daric to pay her. That's how I learned about the Primrose, who was a slave, then free, and then a slave again. And there was a poem on the Paper about her, too. But I still didn't understand why the Paper was given to me, or who the Primrose was, until the wise woman got to the very last line—"

He recited the line for me from memory then, and to myself I said the words with him. I had heard them from Ali-Haram himself that day in the carriage, and had sealed them in my memory forever:

"Merdad, son of Emre, today you saw your mother Ariana, the woman whom Ali-Haram loves. May Heaven be praised."

*

Back in the palace, upon leaving the royal bedchamber I'd always caught up on sleep whenever I could—morning, midday, afternoon.

But in the field with the rebels, storytime lasted only until Abbas himself began to yawn. Then it was time for all to bed down or stand a watch, according to the schedule he set.

How wonderful to wrap myself in a bundle of ragged hides, and to lie under the stars, while a pair of nearby rebels stood my guard till dawn. And how wonderful those nights when Heaven, where all our needs are known, blessed me with dreamless sleep.

39. Secrets Revealed

One morning, I awoke to the sounds of a camp in uproar: men shouting, horses whinnying, carts creaking and rattling. I wrapped a sleeping hide around me and crept to the cave mouth to peer out.

Everywhere were oxen, mules, and horses, unnerved at the confusion. The rebels were trying to herd the animals into rude paddocks constructed of stakes and ropes. The animals were not impressed by their new lodgings. The mules backed and bucked; the horses reared and stamped and whinnied.

An unsealed burlap sack lay on the ground by the cave. Inside the sack were leaf-shaped points of iron: javelin heads. I saw Abbas and two other rebels nearby, prying open a wooden chest. They whistled when the lid gave way. They tossed handfuls of darics into the air; the coins glinted in the morning light and clinked upon landing.

A gloomy-faced Persian was holding a parchment and inkpot. He glanced at me, and then looked away. In his shame, he pretended not to know me. It was Bourzou, the palace Slavemaster. Abbas came to sign the parchment.

"Hand over the prize," Bourzou said stiffly (Wa-atuq stood behind Abbas and interpreted), "and we'll be on our way."

It took me a moment to remember who the prize was. The King usually entrusted Ali-Haram with such missions; why send Bourzou this time? But I guessed the answer. Scheherazade would have arranged it behind the scenes. She knew better than to risk my husband's emotions getting the better of him in the exchange.

"So soon? Why the rush?" Abbas grinned. He wanted to savor the moment. He had bluffed the Persians, and triumphed. "Stay and have breakfast. We can cook up some sand vermin and scorpion cake."

"Besides," another rebel said, "you'll make good time back to Baghdad without all those goods to slow you down."

Bourzou had no choice but to stay. And like children at bedtime, the rebels wouldn't let me go until they heard one more chapter of their story—

*

(Rebels of Maqazza, last night I told you how Zajeel asked for Idrosun's hand in holy union. And I know it broke your hearts to learn that Dilara loved a boy in the Ragged Quarter of Baghdad—a boy who, she said, did not even know she existed.)

Sheydah plucked a peach and gave it a critical inspection. The fuzzy skin was deep red, with yellow blushes. An order for fruit from the sorceress waited for filling and delivery: peaches, pomegranates, apricots, quinces, dates, pears, plums, limes. (Zaib was convinced the Sorcerers Guild was plotting to poison her. She would only eat fresh fruit.) The peach order only called for a half-bushel, but one look at the trees told Sheydah they could not wait another day for harvesting. The summer had been extremely hot, and then heavy rains had come for three straight days. Canker, scab, and rot would set in soon. The best fruits would be at the tops of the trees, naturally. She would have to climb; the rough, cracking bark would leave its marks and scratches.

Only the birds could hear her sighs as she unstacked her harvest baskets. She made heaps of old blankets to cushion the fruits when they dropped. The first peach she took for herself, as a fee. She made up a peach-picking song:

> "Fruit will not harvest itself.
> Do not ask Yar or Caspara—
> All they do is argue over castles and Kings.
> I wish somebody would help me.
> How wonderful company would be."

"Greetings, Sheydah." A pink top knot appeared above a grapevine hedge. Sheydah, looking down from the highest branch of the peach tree, hurriedly fastened her veil back into place.

"Idrosun! How odd, I was just now wishing for help."

"I know. I was passing by the orchard when I heard you singing, and I knew right away you were wishing from the bottom of your heart. My powers are returning."

"Zajeel says Djinns cannot grant wishes without a tree to dwell in."

"Heaven is rewarding me," Idrosun answered. "I have stopped trying to profit from happiness or sorrow or love. A Djinn must use her powers only to glorify God. My wise Dilara taught me this."

Idrosun made up her own song while she picked:

> "Having lots of Djinnlets,
> And doing his duty to his race:
> These are the words of someone
> Who is in love with me—
> And so I ask myself:
> Do I love the Djinn Zajeel?
> Tell me, self, how do I feel?"

A cuckoo, seduced by the high, lovely voice, settled on a nearby branch and cuckooed along.

"Our baskets are not filling quickly enough," Sheydah said. "I wish we had more help."

A few moments later Zajeel arrived in the orchard, scratching his head in confusion.

"I was having a nice nap." He took up an empty basket. "Then I woke up with a sudden urge to stand in the hot sun and pick peaches."

Idrosun gave Sheydah a wise look.

Soon the ground was strewn with leaves and bark peelings and pits (these last from peaches taken as fees). When the fruits had all left their homes, Zajeel stood and stretched.

"A fine day's work," he said. "I will return to my nap now."

"No, wait." Idrosun put a hand on his elbow. "I have something to say. Several days ago, we ate lunch here, in the orchard. It was the day you told us the story of Holy Usman and the Blue Land."

"I remember," Zajeel said. "It was also the day I made a certain proposal."

A purple blush rose into Idrosun's cheeks.

"That is what I want to talk about." She took a deep breath and solemnly placed a hand on her heart. "O Zajeel, I told you that day I would only wed for love, but now I know the one I love will never be mine. For she loves another—her mysterious Ragged Quarter boy. And so, I have made my decision. I will love you instead. I will join you in your dream of saving our race of Lesser Tree Djinns. We will raise our Djinnlets and teach them how to grant wishes. Aunty Dilara will teach them how to strive for happiness and true love, without profit."

Zajeel's blue face glowed with emotion.

"Beloved," he said, "you have made me the happiest of Djinns. But you should know we will not easily achieve our dream. We must first find the Blue Land so the Ancient Blue Ones can assign us a tree. Our search may take centuries—"

"We do not need to find the Blue Land. In fact, the tree we need is in a nearby forest, or will be very soon, and I know how to get us there."

"Where is this forest?" Zajeel exclaimed. "What are we waiting for? Let us go straightaway."

"No, there are things to be done first," Idrosun said. "The next time you see me will be the day we wed. I will send word. In the meantime, compose your Name Poem for our rites, in keeping with our customs."

"But why the delay? I do not understand."

"You must trust me now, Zajeel."

*

Sweaty and dirty, her sandals catching on brambles, Sheydah edged down a steep slope behind the orchard. A path led through a thicket to a shallow creek. The creek bed stayed mostly dry in the summer, but recent rains had left water in a small outflow pool. Sheydah laid her veil and headscarf on the ground and lowered her face into the cool water. The dragonflies and frogs shared with her.

"Sheydah! I came looking for Idrosun and saw you leave the orchard, so I came to talk to—O!"

Startled, Sheydah jumped up, head dripping, unveiled. Standing before her was Dilara. Dilara's eyes, above her own veil, were wide in astonishment. She had a small bundle tied with string under her arm; she stooped and laid the bundle beside the pool.

"I can expl—" Sheydah began. But Dilara said:

"No, I understand now. You pretended to be a girl. You covered your hair, wore a veil, pitched your voice. Yet I always had a strange feeling that I knew you from somewhere. But what has taken you so far from the Ragged Quarter? Answer me—Ghazi."

Ghazi (for as you have no doubt guessed by now, O King, Sheydah was he—the disguised Ragged Quarter companion of Naseem and Khashar) was utterly bewildered.

"But how do you know my real name? Before Zajeel and I came to Viroo, you and I had only met once, and then for a passing moment. You were in Prince Feroze's wedding procession, and I was standing with the other children, holding a sack of flower petals. You stopped and spoke as though you knew me and Naseem. You even called us friends and companions."

"O Ghazi! I promise you will understand everything very soon. But first tell me your own story. Leave out nothing."

They sat together at the edge of the pool, trailing their toes in the cool water. Ghazi told Dilara how Naseem had wrongfully accused him of murdering little Timo, the Matchmaker's son. How he had fled Baghdad in the night. How a Sentinel of the Muhtasib had picked up the trail and followed him. How he had ended up in the remote village of Viroo with Zajeel.

"Only my disguise has saved me from the Sentinel thus far. I beg you to keep my secret. You must call me Sheydah when others are nearby to hear. But now tell me: how was your curse finally lifted?"

"Curse?" Dilara looked confused. "What curse?"

"Of course, none of us knew you personally. Girls in the Ragged Quarter are not allowed to play with the boys. All we knew was what Naseem told us. He said he and you had joined in holy union, but then he sought an annulment on the grounds that his bride was under a curse. She could not speak, but only bray like an ass."

Dilara laughed till tears came.

"O Ghazi! I was not Naseem's wife. That was poor Omid."

"But who is Omid?"

"Someone who had only my form, face, and name—no more."

So many things he wanted to ask, but one question loomed above all—and how hard it was to ask it. Had she not already turned him down, even after he had spoken the expensive words of True Love?

But he had to know.

"O Dilara, please tell me. Who is the boy in the Ragged Quarter? The one you realized you loved that day we ate lunch in the orchard? The one who is so kind, gentle, and handsome?"

Dilara's eyes sparkled.

"Close your eyes while I open this bundle. Do not open them till I say, and then you will have your answer."

He stared at her. His insides churned; his throat went dry. He did not understand. But obeying, he closed his eyes. As he waited, he heard: the untying of a string, the rustle of cloth, a scratching in the dirt.

"Now look," she said after a moment. "And tell me who you see."

Ghazi opened his eyes—but where had Dilara gone? Before him stood (quite impossibly!) none other than Khashar—his Ragged Quarter friend. A green turban topped Khashar's head. His face was streaked with dirt. His tunic was ragged and threadbare. But in his hands were a veil and headscarf.

Ghazi stared in confusion.

Then Khashar tossed the turban to the ground. Dark curls tumbled down.

"O Ghazi, do you see now?" Dilara said. Her warm lips met his. "Only the boys could go out and play games in the Ragged Quarter, and so I became Khashar. You were always gentle and kind to me. Then, when you spoke Idrosun's words of True Love to me, I was able at last to admit to myself that I have loved you all along. But I never knew until now you were here in Viroo. You see, it is you I love, Ghazi. You!"

*

The drivers stood next to their oxen and their emptied carts. The sour-faced Bourzou sat his horse and held the lead of my waiting mare. The Maqazzan rebels ringed me, and one by one they drew close to bid me farewell.

When it was Abbas's turn, he said:

"Lady, your Emre trained under me all those years ago. He was a promising young warrior. I wept when we lost him. When Wa-atuq brought your son to me, I saw Emre in his face at once. The eyes, the nose, the chin. I thank you for both of your gifts, Ariana."

"What gifts, Abbas? I came empty-handed, and I am leaving the same."

He smiled, and then I understood: he meant my story and my son.

When Lieutenant Emre approached, a cold dread seized me.

"May Heaven preserve you." My hot tears stung. "Your home is with the rebels now. What if this is the last time we meet in this world?"

"Then we will meet in the next. Please don't worry about me, Mama."

"I love you, Emre. You are my life."

As Bourzou led me and my small escort onto the Baghdad road, one of the rebels called:

"Next time, bring the words of True Love, aunty!"

As we rode, the sun lifted behind the endless hills. The heat rose like dust. Bourzou and the others had nothing to say. It was as if a curse of silence lay across us. I passed the hours telling my mount the next chapter of Dilara's story.

Every time I paused for a breath or thought the mare turned her head and gave me an impatient snort—

40. The Sentinel's Authority

(O my noble mare, how well you bear me. You never veer. You never get distracted. When you saw that scorpion in the road, you didn't bolt but calmly stepped over. Shall we pass the time with a story? I better catch you up first: Idrosun has accepted Zajeel's proposal of holy union. And she informed him, to his amazement, that their dwelling-tree already existed, or would very soon. And Ghazi discovered that Dilara, with whom he was in love, was in fact none other than his Ragged Quarter friend Khashar. And Dilara found out that her friend Sheydah was in fact Ghazi, whom she had secretly loved for so long. Such happiness! But how long could it last?)

"Haw, stand, come up!"

Ghazi and Dilara were urging Woodbine down the trail. Ghazi used every ox call he knew, but Woodbine was without his longtime yoke-mate Honey, who had passed to the next world, as all mortal beings must. Of the pair, Honey was the one who had memorized the commands.

Ghazi wore his Sheydah disguise (since that was how Viroo knew him), and Dilara wore her Khashar disguise (so Zaib would not recognize her). The peaches and other fruits were not the only passengers in the ox cart. Also packed in were scented candles, fresh-cut flowers (with vases of cut glass), a mirror in a wooden frame (with a handle of real bone), flasks of soap scented with almond flowers (from the Exchange soap vendor), a set of bedclothes of Egyptian linen, a bag of turkey feathers (to stuff a pillow for someone's dear head)—and many other goods from merchants who were happy to pay a fee rather than make the delivery themselves.

"Remember the stolen tin pipe Naseem tried to blame on you?" "I remember how you rode past us on your sunbeam." "Remember when Metipo came to the Ragged Quarter?" "She came as a boy and left as a girl." Ghazi and Dilara reminisced, but mostly laughed with the sheer joy of being in love.

From behind came the clop of hooves. The two exchanged quick glances. Ghazi adjusted his veil, and Dilara tucked a curl back under her turban. They gave another round of Haw, Stand, Come Up—poor, confused, lonely Woodbine. Sneaking a glance behind, Ghazi recognized the riders as the boy who talked to his saddlebag, and his man Vaktan. They came alongside.

"Aha, the fruit vendor who never heard of a King," Vaktan said. He narrowed his eyes at Dilara. "I have not seen this one before."

"This is my friend Khashar," Ghazi said. For some reason Dilara was keeping her head down. "He is helping me."

"Whose goods are these?"

"The sorceress. We are making a delivery."

"A coincidence; we are headed there too. I understand she dwells in a treehouse. Have you been there before?"

The boy spoke for the first time:

"You waste time interrogating the wrong person, Vaktan." He made a clicking sound, and his mount set off in a trot; Vaktan followed. The riders soon passed from sight.

"Those are the ones who questioned me at the Exchange," Ghazi said. "I think they are from Baghdad."

"Haw," Dilara said, to Woodbine.

The trail rose steadily until it reached the edge of a dense oak wood. Vaktan and the boy had already arrived; they were sitting their mounts and gazing at the wood. Woodbine pulled up. Among the trees, pillars of light, like trees themselves, rose wherever the canopy was least dense.

"I do not see any treehouse," Vaktan said impatiently.

"You are looking in the wrong place." Dilara pitched her voice Khashar-low. "It is a different kind of treehouse."

Ghazi recognized it then: a dark trunk, bent to one side, leaning around another tree, branches outstretched like arms—a giant, shy forest creature peeking into the open.

"O Zaib, mighty sorceress!" Ghazi called, his voice pitched Sheydah-high. "We have brought your fruit and other goods."

The tree straightened, with loud grinding, crunching, and sucking noises. Then it rose—that is, its roots emerged from the forest floor. The roots were wide, gnarled claw-feet; they branched and re-branched in tangled masses. The tree scurried out of the wood, trotting on its root-toes. Alarmed birds burst squawking out of the foliage, amid a rain of leaves and acorns. In the tree's lower reaches was a dazzling silver orb, brighter even than the pillars of light.

"The service door is in the back," the orb called. The treehouse drew near the visitors. "Who are these others with you?"

"We will ask the questions here," Vaktan said in his imperious way. The boy looked on, saying nothing. "We have come on the King's authority. So you better answer, and no tricks. Are you a member in good standing of the Sorcerers Guild?"

"The Sorcerers Guild?" The orb's voice dripped with loathing. "That incompetent collection of arrogant daric-grubbers? The ones who presume to ban the scrolls of the great Vahid? I would not join their Guild, in any standing."

"But is it true that your occupation involves the casting of spells?"

"Nothing in the King's law prohibits casting by a lay person, as long as the spells themselves are not Guild-licensed."

"Yes, let us discuss these unlicensed spells of yours—"

The root tips descended into the ground again. The tree sank a few feet before fixing its position and height.

"We can unload the goods while they question her," Dilara said to Ghazi. They pulled sacks from the ox cart and circled behind the tree. "Pull that vine up."

A mossy, boy-sized square of bark lifted free. A mouse scurried out; disturbed beetles milled. Ghazi looked dubiously down into the dimness.

"How do we—?"

"Feet first," Dilara said, "then the rest of you. There is a rock seat and a rope to let yourself down. The earth is hollow below."

Legs through, then knees, then elbows—Ghazi eased himself onto the slab, centered the heavy sack on his lap, felt for the rope. The interior of the tree smelled of moisture and earth. As he descended, flashes intruded on the dark: lights from globes fixed in the walls. Fireflies swarmed in each globe. Narrow dark structures descended all around, twisted, jointed, branching, wider above and gradually narrowing below: these were the treehouse's roots.

"There is a storage cabinet at the bottom." Dilara's voice echoed down the shaft. "Stack those goods there while I bring the rest."

The cabinet had marble shelves, brass-handled drawers, and maple uprights carved into ravens. A cone of light issued from another firefly globe. Ghazi pulled goods from his sack: a glass hookah, velvet slippers, pewter goblets, neatly folded silk tunics. Each tunic had an embroidered gilt **V.** He hoisted himself back up for the next sack. When he and Dilara finished the job, the interrogation was still in progress.

"—familiar with the Spell of Blind and Hopeless Love?" Vaktan was asking.

"Of course. I am a leading authority on Vahid's works if I do say so." The orb glowed. "Of course, that particular spell should be considered an early design."

"It is against the King's law to profit from the creative work of others without obtaining permission and paying a fee, Guild or no Guild."

"I do not practice for profits. Persia has bought the prized cedar timbers of Lebanon since the age of King Solomon himself, and from this trade my mother, the Queen of Lebanon, gives me a most generous allowance. This allows me to devote my career to collecting and preserving Vahid's spells. For instance, he designed the Orb of Dazzling Concealment you see before you now. I receive no fee from the Orb; it is only a precaution I take when strangers such as yourselves visit. I am sure he would approve, were he here.

"True, I sometimes permit myself to experiment with small refinements. This treehouse, for example. The original design comes from the zeta supplement to the third forbidden scroll. I articulated the branches, installed joints in the roots, and improved the trunk lowering mechanism. Minor revisions."

"Back to Blind and Hopeless Love, which I mentioned earlier," Vaktan said. "Have you made refinements in this particular spell?"

"I noticed it wears off unpredictably. I have some notes for a potential sub-charm to regulate the duration of effectiveness—"

The boy finally spoke.

"Sorceress, I thank you for your patience with these questions. I have reason to believe that someone here in Viroo has been casting the Spell of Blind and Hopeless Love. The creator of that spell has the right to earn fees for its use. My intent is to ensure no one infringes his rights."

"Young sir, the greatest sorcerer of our time created that spell. And yet the Sorcerers Guild excludes him—and, I might add, myself as well— from its ranks. My fondest wish—all right, I admit it—is to ally with Vahid to bring down the Guild. I assure you my involvement with his work is purely scientific and archival in nature. If anyone in Viroo is casting the Spell of Blind and Hopeless Love—it is not I."

A new and muffled voice, joined the conversation.

"But if not you, Zaib—then who?"

"That dear voice! O my beloved, you have come to me at last!" Rainbows, sun dogs, and silver sparkles appeared above the Orb of Dazzling Concealment. "How many projects and plans I want to share with you. But darling—why are you still hiding in that saddlebag?"

*

"O Woodbine," Ghazi said, "you have only an empty cart to pull, and look at you, you are slower than ever." The trail back to Viroo stretched ahead. He had not yet changed from his Sheydah guise.

"She is still grieving over—" Dilara mouthed *Honey* as she stuffed her turban into her bundle and ran fingers through her uncovered hair. She was Khashar no longer.

A few moments later, the boy, atop his horse but this time unaccompanied by Vaktan, caught up with them on the trail. As he slowed to pass, Ghazi noticed Dilara making an unnecessary adjustment to Woodbine's yoke—an excuse to turn her face away? But the boy dismounted and moved between her and the ox.

"The yellow roses may be gone," he said. "But did you really think I would not remember you?"

To Ghazi's astonishment, Dilara fell to her knees.

"I am ashamed." She bowed her head; she spoke to the ground. "All the time we were together on our travels, I did not know who you were. I never addressed you correctly. I did not showed you the respect you were due."

"Anyone can bow and scrape, but how many are true friends?"

"Kneel, Ghazi," she said. "This is Prince Faridun, heir to the throne of Persia."

"No, on your feet, both of you." He took Dilara's hands and drew her up. "Leave that name and title for others to call me. To you I shall always be Gu Gu."

They began to reminisce.

"Remember when Qa-ari renamed itself after you?" "What a storm we flew through on the flying divan." "I wonder if the Princess's lamb has been born yet."

Ghazi listened, head spinning.

"Where is your man Vaktan?" Dilara asked the Prince.

"Still at the treehouse, with the lamp. Zaib is trying her best to get Vahid to come out; she already made up the guest bed."

"O Prince Fari—Gu Gu—when we delivered the goods, we overheard Vaktan questioning her. I can tell you the epidemic of love is not the doing of the sorceress, but rather Idrosun. You see, she too is here in Viroo. She did not use the Spell of Blind and Hopeless Love. She relied on the belief of her customers."

"Ah, of course. That is why her product is so powerful. I remember when she sold Sorrow to Hezi, which caused Tayab to get his feet striped."

Dilara's eyes twinkled.

"I remember something else—when you ordered Vahid to join us in holy union."

"Well, I loved you. Can you believe Father has betrothed me to one of Maria Irena's half-sisters? He has re-sealed the alliance with Charles Magnus, and thus prevented war. It looks like I will be in for my own dose of Blind and Hopeless Love when I come of age. But Dilara, I can tell you are in love yourself. And unless I am mistaken—" He turned toward Ghazi and smiled. "—it is with this one here, who, like you throughout our travels, is in disguise."

Dilara reached for Ghazi's hand and drew him close.

"How observant you have always been, Gu Gu. Meet my childhood friend and the sun of my life—Ghazi."

"Aha!" The shout came from nearby. "So it as I suspected it all along!"

A figure in a gray hood crashed through the brush. Ghazi saw the arc of rope spinning through the air. He leaped aside—but too late. The rope settled neatly about his neck. He found himself stumbling toward the Prince's rearing horse. Dilara cried out. The startled Woodbine kicked.

"I told you I have a perfect record." The Sentinel pulled back his hood. He wore a look of triumph. "You led me a long chase indeed, but at last you are my prisoner."

The Prince's eyes flashed.

"Sentinel, I am Prince Faridun, son of King Alcimedes of Persia, and sole heir to his throne. These two are under my personal protection. Explain your actions."

The Sentinel dismounted. He ripped away Ghazi's veil and headscarf. Producing a leather thong, he rapidly bound Ghazi's hands.

"Highness, this one has been accused of murder. I have followed his trail all the way from Baghdad. His disguise threw me off at first, but finally the girl spoke his true name. You heard as well. This name, Ghazi, was the one given to me by a witness to the crime."

"He is innocent, Gu Gu!" Dilara cried. "Naseem committed the crime and then accused Ghazi to shift blame from himself."

The Prince looked thoughtful.

"Who originated the formal Writ of Accusation?"

"The witness himself, Naseem."

"Was there a co-signer?"

"The mother of the deceased, a Matchmaker."

"Then it appears you are correct, Sentinel," the Prince said. "In this matter, you have authority."

"O Gu Gu, no!" Dilara's face was stricken.

Prince Faridun produced some coins from a pouch at his waist and put them in the Sentinel's hand.

"This will help provide for the accused on your return journey. I know you will do your duty, but I would have you treat him with all possible kindness and receive a fair trial."

"Highness." The Sentinel bowed. He tightened his prisoner's noose and gave the other end of the rope a few turns about his shoulder. He turned and headed down the trail, back toward Viroo.

Ghazi staggered at the end of the rope, following his captor.

41. A Morally Instructive Story and an Ambitious Poem

"'—following his captor.' Shall we end the chapter there?"

"It's as good a place as any." Ali-Haram rolled onto his side, pulling with him the duvet the King had given me, and poured another goblet of Water of Angels.

"Then I bid you both a good evening," Lorbu rose from his stool. "May Heaven preserve you. You may look for me after breakfast tomorrow." He packed his pens, nibs, ink pots, and blotting sand in a wooden case, bowed, took his leave.

My husband still did his best writing in bed, but no longer put pen to parchment. The idea of hiring a dictation scribe had horrified me at first, but Ali-Haram said the investment would repay us several times over.

Subscriptions continued to increase. We charged a daric for a parchment scroll (two darics for Paper)—after paying for copyists, blank scrolls, ink, nibs, and the services of Lorbu, we earned a quarter-daric for each scroll sold.

A ticket to one of our Readings cost a sixth of a daric. For that the customer got to hear three full chapters. The Reader kept half the gate. I spent several hours each week training new Readers.

"Remember when we were only writing this story to keep Scheherazade's head on her shoulders?" Ali-Haram said.

"And pay your wine seller," I reminded him. "Now we work harder than ever, and the King does not even want his story anymore. Scheherazade said he sleeps apart and doesn't talk to her, or anyone. He took the defeat in Maqazza hard."

"His spirits will lift when the child is born." Ali-Haram plumped his pillow, which was cased in muslin and stuffed with turkey feathers—luxuries once unimaginable.

"The post herald of the King requests admittance!"

The bellow came from the outer hall.

"What now?" Ali-Haram grumbled. "It's late for messages." He climbed out of bed and pushed aside the beaded curtain that separated our bedchamber from the great room.

I could not move. A terrible dread had seized me.

Somehow I already knew what the message would be.

The beads clicked as my husband returned, followed by the post herald, who carried tiny cups of soil and water. The rolled parchment was under his arm. With great ceremony, he set the cups on the carpet—these symbolized land and sea, the King's domains. The herald carefully kept his eyes from meeting mine. He cleared his throat, unrolled the parchment, and read:

> "'To Ariana, Wife of our Esteemed Poet Ali-Haram, Greetings and Salutations from the King of the Age, Beloved of Heaven, Defender of the Faith, Shahryar, First of His Name.'"

The herald's voice was emotionless and flat. He had read similar messages to many mothers.

> "'Be informed that your son Merdad has departed this life in the service of his King. We extend our condolences upon your loss. May it console you that Merdad perished a hero and is today in Paradise.'"

The herald placed a silver disk next to the cups.

"It was found on the body," he said.

I recognized the disk at once: it was Emre's silver medal, with the sword-bearing Persian warrior engraved on it. Grime and blood caked the medal.

I showed the grief which is proper for a Persian mother. I groaned, wept, and tore my garments—it was an act, of course, for the benefit of Ali-Haram and the post herald. Inside, I was a stone. I would save true grief for later; it was not for others to witness. Throughout my display, I thought: when would the body be brought home? Where had it been found? The message said Emre died a hero, which meant he had not been found in Maqazzan blue—but why not?

I went through the bedchamber and doused every candle, save the one Ali-Haram needed for sleep. My husband said something to me; the words did not register. I laid on my side, on the very edge of the bed. I pulled the silk coverlet over my head and stared into the darkness behind my eyes.

*

("But Lord Ali-Haram, where is my Mistress this morning?" "Ariana will not be with us, Lorbu. You are stuck with me today." "I trust she is well?" "A bad night. We'll let her sleep late." "Very good, Lord. My scrolls and pens are ready." "Where did we leave the story yesterday?" "Idrosun is going to wed Zajeel, and the Sentinel has captured Ghazi." "Ah yes, I remember. All right. New chapter. Working title: 'A Morally Instructive Story and an Ambitious Poem.' Begin first scene: 'From the other side of the road—'")

From the other side of the road, Ghazi watched Dilara put the prayer rug into position at the foot of the spreading tree. Above the rug, an ancient mirror was nailed into the trunk of the tree. Many were the happy couples who had viewed each other in the cracked and discolored glass over the years—this tree was the Marrying Walnut of Viroo.

"Where is Sheydah?" Zajeel spoke in a low voice, but the words hung in the warm still air, and Ghazi could hear them clearly. He watched Zajeel shoo flies away from the cake that waited patiently next to the rug.

Dilara did not answer. She sneaked a glance across the road. For a moment, her hopeless eyes met Ghazi's.

"She took a delivery out to the sorceress yesterday," Zajeel went on. "Well, no doubt there were delays. I do hope she makes it back in time. Idrosun sent word that today is the day."

The Sentinel had used some of Prince Faridun's coins to buy an ass. The beast was too small to ride, but it came with a children's saddle, so that the line from the prisoner's noose could be tied securely to the saddle horn. This marked Ghazi before the world as a doomed criminal.

Yet in all Viroo, only Dilara, the Prince, and the Sentinel knew the true identity of this criminal. The Sentinel had exchanged the prisoner's veil, headscarf, tunic, and sandals for a burlap sack with rough-cut holes for the neck and arms, a grimy burlap skullcap, and the murderer's own bare feet.

"Show patience, Zajeel," Dilara said. "The bride is preparing herself. It is her wedding day, and a bride's beauty should shine more brightly than the sun itself."

"How I shall miss Sheydah. She was my best friend in Viroo. But soon I will be with my beloved, and we will be the happiest of Djinns. This tree we are going to dwell in—I wonder where it is, and how she knew it was there?"

The Sentinel stood at Ghazi's shoulder and sighed with pleasure.

"Ah, the happiness of love," he said. "Being together always, preparing for the joys only lovers and parents know. We should stay for the wedding. I know you are anxious to get back to Baghdad and begin your trial, but the rites should not last long. Besides, I would not say no to a piece of wedding cake. Lemon pistachio, or my nose misleads me."

"O Sentinel," Ghazi said in a sudden burst of pleading, "I beg you for my freedom. I did not murder little Timo. But I was a witness. I was there when everything happened. I can tell you every detail. You see, my friend Naseem—"

"Best save all that for the judge," the Sentinel advised. "He will sort it all out. You know, you should be proud. Every criminal I have brought in has been hanged. In years to come, when people speak of you, they will say, 'He was part of the Sentinel's perfect record.'"

A crowd, drawn by the prospect of love and cake, had begun to gather. They buzzed and waited for the bride.

"While we have time, I will tell you about myself," the Sentinel told Ghazi. "I am sure you will find my story morally instructive. You see, I was once like you, a simple boy from the Ragged Quarter, a noisy rough-houser and good-for-nothing. But then love found me. She was the flower seller's daughter. I fell the first time I talked to her. My heart was no longer my own. I asked the flower seller for the girl's hand; I was informed, quite correctly, that I must first get a respectable job.

"As it happened, the Sentinels of the Muhtasib had come to the Ragged Quarter to investigate a crime—a murder, in fact, such as the one you yourself committed. I talked them into letting me tag along. I discovered I had natural skills in the science of investigation; in fact, I was not long in producing proof that the murderer was one of the Sentinels's own. Once he lost his head, the Muhtasib offered me his vacated position.

"Now I specialize in bringing murderers to justice. The flower seller's daughter and I joined in holy union, and she has borne me three fine sons. One day they too will be Sentinels.

"You may wonder, what is the lesson of this story? It is this: had you won the love of a wonderful girl, as I did, you might have avoided your present sorrow."

Ghazi looked across the road and his eyes met Dilara's. Their glances were loving and despairing—

A happy cry went up. The wedding procession had arrived. Children with scrubbed faces and white gowns led the way. The children skipped and scattered rose petals beneath the hooves of Woodbine, whose honor it was to bear the bride on his venerable back. The Prince, carrying a ritual willow branch across his shoulder (to symbolize vitality and birth), led the ox by the reins. The bride waved to the crowd. She was lovely in her blue gown and blue veil, her top knot tied with blue ribbons. Like the bridegroom, she wore a ceremonial gold sash and open-clawed gold slippers.

"She sold True Love to us, and now look at her, caught herself!" This, from a wit in the crowd.

Idrosun stepped down onto the back of the crouching Vaktan. She joined the beaming Zajeel at the Marrying Walnut. Meanwhile, Prince Faridun addressed the crowd. Solemn authority imbued his boyishly high voice:

"I welcome all to the wedding. The royal sorcerer of Persia will conduct today's rites through his legally authorized familiar, Vahidium."

Vaktan held up a polished brass lamp for all to see. The lamp gleamed like a tiny sun in the afternoon light. A silvery plume issued from the spout. The sound of "Ooohh—!" went up from the assembled as the plume spun and became a disembodied head, bald and beardless, with red pupil-less eyes.

"Dearly beloved, friends, and curious bystanders, we are gathered here, in the sight of Heaven, and so forth and so on." Vahidium's voice boomed and carried. "Groom Zajeel, in accordance with the sacred customs of the Lesser Tree Djinns, recite the Name Poem which thou hast composed for this occasion."

Zajeel cleared his throat. Then, from memory:

> "Our first girl Djinnlet will Sheydah be,
> To honor the best of friends to me.
> And then our second, I proclaim,
> Will have Dilara for her name.
> As for the third, well, who ever knew
> He or she would be Gu Gu—"

When the ambitious poem reached an end, the bride and groom knelt on the prayer rug. Vahidium proceeded to offer several learned and pious observations:

"Heaven enjoineth believers to wed. Remember that a full night of prayer from a single person hath less power than two short prayers by a wife or husband.

"A husband and wife are as each other's tunics. As a tunic protecteth and adorneth, so you two are to protect and adorn each other.

"Zajeel, when thou goest to thy bride's bed, two Angels will guard thee."

Vaktan and the Prince each took an end of the willow branch and held it at knee height. The Djinns joined hands. They jumped.

"I wed thee!"

They turned and jumped a second time.

"I wed thee!"

And a third:

"I wed thee!"

"Now look into the mirror," Vahidium directed them, "and see who thou wilt love forever."

The crowd stamped its approval.

"Ah, I do love a wedding." In the shadows next to Ghazi, the Sentinel wiped away a tear.

"Now, bride Idrosun," Vahidium continued, "in keeping with custom, address thy new husband before these witnesses, speaking from the bottom of thy heart."

Idrosun put a hand on her heart and smiled at her new husband.

"To think, once I was a carefree Djinn maiden. Then for many centuries I lived in a wood and granted wishes. But I left that profession and went on to sell emotions at exorbitant prices. Then I met you, who had a plan to preserve our race of Djinns from extinction.

"The day I saw Gu—I mean, Prince Faridun—talking to his saddlebag, I knew the sorcerer Vahid must be here in Viroo. And when the sorceress Zaib wished from the bottom of her heart that Vahid would stay with her in the treehouse—a wish I perceived with my returning powers—I knew where to find him, so I could arrange for him to join Zajeel and me in holy union, and talk to him about a certain other matter, which will soon be clear to my husband.

"O Zajeel, so many adventures. And now look at me: I am your wife. How strange life is. Well, my new husband, let us bid our friends in Viroo farewell, and make our way at once to the land of Zozor, where I have a happy surprise in store for you."

The rites complete, Vahidium spun, lengthened, and plunged back into the lamp spout.

"Zozor?" the Prince said. "That is a place I happen to have visited recently. It is on the way to Baghdad, as I recall. Vaktan, you and I will go with the happy couple. Sentinel, you and your charge will join us. And Dilara, you will come as well."

"How nice to have company as we begin our journey," the Sentinel said, swatting the ass's rump. Beast and prisoner, joined by the length of hemp, lurched forward.

*

The road wound through scrub pine and low brush, eventually narrowing to a trail of beaten earth.

Prince Faridun led the way, leaning over his mount from time to time to converse with his saddlebag. The newlyweds followed, hand in blue hand. Next came the Sentinel. The ass had a habit of tossing its head; each toss drew the rope taut and pulled the prisoner up roughly. Sometimes the procession paused, and Ghazi was able to turn and see Dilara trudging behind him. She gave him brave smiles from a tear-streaked face. Vaktan, bringing up the rear, grinned at Ghazi and mimicked a hand pulling a noose tight.

The Sentinel grew philosophical.

"Consider this rope," he said to his prisoner. "It will lead you all the way to Baghdad. The noose will remain in place during your trial. This will provide the public with a symbol of justice, and as an added benefit, will make things convenient for the executioner. When the formalities have been observed and the official documents signed and sealed, the rope will draw up over the scaffold. Then—well, have you ever pinched out a candle flame? They say it is a lot like that."

42. Vahid's Close Call and the Unique Odor of Magic

"We will make camp here." The young Prince signaled the company to stop. "Vaktan, gather downed limbs and brush for a cookfire."

The ass, needing no more encouragement, sank its hind end to the ground. Ghazi had been staggering numbly for hours at the end of his line. Dilara helped him draw to a halt. Her hands were steadying and sweet. The Sentinel turned to address his prisoner:

"I must say, you have been a model criminal today. I have a reward for you. Before we left Viroo, I used some of Prince Faridun's generosity to buy a jar of salve." (He said all this loudly, so the Prince would not miss it.) "I understand it is a premium blend of olive oil, beeswax, and mashed-up flatbreads. I will have the girl rub some into your neck after we eat. After all, we want you at your best at the scaffold."

The travelers had entered a lush valley enclosed on two sides by walls of green and white. The green was the foliage of thick stands of wood, the white was wild roses training densely up the trees. The lowering sun balanced atop one wall, setting valley and roses aglow.

"We are back in the valley of Zozor," the Prince told the saddlebag.

"I suspected as much," came the muffled reply. "I detect the unique odor of magic."

"You should see the grass. It is the color of sunshine, and elbow-high in places."

"The race of sheep esteems Zozor not only for its grasses, but also the sweet clover and wildflowers. The valley is sacred to them."

Ghazi watched the activity around him: Vaktan and Dilara building the fire, the Sentinel laying out provisions, Prince Faridun supervising all. But where had Zajeel and Idrosun gone?

The last of the sunlight revealed a blue figure clambering along a tree branch. The figure handed something large and speckled to another blue figure waiting below. The Prince took the brass lamp from its saddlebag and gave it to Dilara.

"Take Vahid to Idrosun," he said. "And then bring him back to me."

Much later, as the campfire cracked and flung its embers into the dark, a figure emerged into the circle of light.

"Feroze!" the Prince cried, rising.

"Faridun," the newcomer said. The two embraced. Feroze laid his crook in the grass and rubbed his hands over the flames.

Feroze? Ghazi stared dully. This scruffy shepherd? The King's son and former heir, who had wedded Princess Maria Irena, and on whose head he and Naseem had tossed flower petals? How long ago all that seemed—

"Well, little brother, are you still a leech on the body of the state?"

"Of course," the Prince said. "I am guided by your legacy."

"I remember when you only knew two words, and they were both Gu. What are you doing here?"

"Father sends me on missions to learn about the empire and its peoples. We have lately returned from our investigation of a mysterious epidemic of love, which took us to a place called Viroo. Vaktan, bring a bowl of stew and my own silver spoon for our guest. Feroze, I hardly recognize you without your turkey feather."

"I am a working man now. I have laid aside the things of childhood."

The Sentinel partially loosened Ghazi's noose and handed Dilara the jar of salve. Feroze looked her way, startled.

"You!" he said. "The girl from my wedding. What is your name? Yes, I remember now—Dilara. The girl who claimed to be my devoted vizier and loyal friend Khashar."

Dilara did not answer. She pressed salve into the chafed hollow of Ghazi's throat, rubbing with vigor and tenderness. A pair of four-legged figures—one of them small and wobbly—moved into the firelight. Their fleeces were bright yellow. Their blue eyes glittered.

"And here are Maria Irena and her newborn, Charles Minimus," Feroze said.

"You named him after his grandfather, then." The Prince bowed gravely to the lamb.

"Yes, he is heir to the Frankish throne."

"And soon to be my kins-lamb by marriage. Vahid, the sheep-form of the heir was not directly Thukamon's doing. It will not violate your code of ethics to restore him to human form, and I therefore instruct you to do so."

The sorcerer's voice came from the lamp.

"Reconsider, Highness. How would his mother care for him? For she remains under the spell cast by Thukamon, who dwells in Paradise now."

Maria Irena began a prolonged bleating.

"Could she be trying to tell us something—?" Feroze said.

"Hmm—I studied the language of sheep back in my college days," Vahid said. "The verbs are highly irregular, and there are thirty words for fleece. Let me see—"

The bleating Princess chopped the ground with a hoof, for emphasis.

Vahid interpreted: "Hmm—well, it seems the Roman emperor in Constantinople wants to send his ransom demand to Charles Magnus, but Maria Irena has not been delivered to him as promised. The emperor has sent agents into Persia to look for her. For this reason, it is safer for her to stay in sheep form."

The bleating went on.

Vahid added: "At any rate, she is happy in her new life and wishes to have nothing more to do with human affairs. In fact, ancient sheep legends bleat about a Yellow-Fleeced One who will one day rule over the race and start a dynasty of a thousand generations. The flock believes Maria Irena is that one."

"Say, where are those two Djinns?" Feroze asked.

"They are newlyweds now," the Prince said. "I gave them permission to stay elsewhere in the valley tonight. Let them have their time together."

Feroze pointed his spoon at the lamp.

"Vahid, are you ever coming out of there?"

"And waste all this remodeling? I added a solarium and lily pond today."

"Our sorcerer had a close call," the Prince said. "He was nearly lured into the sin of bigamy. Tell my brother the story, Vahid."

"I obey, Highness. It all stemmed from my long-standing rivalry with the sorcerer Thukamon. You see, when we were students together at the college of magic in Babylon, we both vied for the hand of Zaib, the daughter of the Queen of Lebanon. One night I invoked a certain spell which—but best not to go into all that now.

"Having discovered that Zaib is a professional sorceress in Viroo, I agreed to stay overnight in her treehouse and review her work. My new bride Omid grew quite jealous and suspicious, but I assured her it would be a courtesy visit only, and that I would not leave the lamp. Anticipating an uneventful evening, I sent Vaktan back to Viroo, with instructions to come for me in the morning.

"Zaib's treehouse is based on a magical design of my own creation. In fact, the sorceress has somehow gained access to many of my original spells. She has even revised them in ways I must admit were ingenious. I have received no fees from these uses, however, since she technically has not derived profits from them. (Highness, I recommend legal enactments to close this loophole.) Anyway, that night, while I slept, the sorceress crept into the guest bedchamber. Despite my promises to Omid, Zaib extracted me from the lamp. I awakened with a start.

"'You are violating our code of ethics,' I protested to her. 'Only Thukamon can reverse my lamp confinement, and he is with the Angels now.'

"'No ethics can withstand the power of true love,' Zaib said. 'Besides, neither you nor I belong to the Sorcerers Guild. The code does not apply to us. Now come here. I will convince you with kisses that I am over Thukamon forever.'

"I was extremely displeased," Omid interposed. "I shouted through the spout, 'Do not leave me in here! The sorcerer must not be away from my close supervision.' 'I have loved him for centuries,' she answered in her cold, deadly voice. 'You are a passing fancy. You will spend the rest of your days in that lamp, listening to us living our happy life together.'"

Vahid took up the story:

"Zaib came at me with a daubing stick. A white paste covered the stick. An aroma from the paste—tribulus vine, I would guess—gave away her intent. I realized she was menacing me with one of my own creations: namely, the Spell of Blind and Hopeless Love. And, based on the smell, a most potent batch."

"Your problems are, as usual, of your own making," Feroze noted. "That you were caught by your own spell strikes me as justice served."

"What a chase she put me through." Vahid continued. "Around and around the treehouse, over the grounds, into the woods, all through the long night. My legs were stiff from long confinement in the lamp. At the glow of first light, to my great relief I saw Vaktan returning for me. I circled back to the treehouse, the sorceress in close pursuit. With the last of my strength, I leapt for the lamp spout.

"I thought I had made it back to the freedom of my prison, but once inside I saw the daubing stick probing for me again. She was thrusting it into the spout. In the tight quarters, she got me across the face—"

"'I am going to extract you again,' I heard her say. 'I have my mirror in hand. I will be the first and only person you will see. You will be blindly and hopelessly mine. You will beg to wed me.'

With heat, Omid said: "'This, even though he had already been joined in holy union to someone, namely, myself!'

"My only recourse was to squeeze my eyes shut," Vahid said, "and prepare to spend the rest of my existence unable to see—"

"I broke into the bedchamber at this point." Vaktan joined the narrative. "I wrested the lamp away from the sorceress and got it away to safety."

Feroze laughed with satisfaction.

"And so," he said, "now you are blindly and hopelessly blind."

"On the contrary," the sorcerer answered. "I see quite clearly, especially in the field of romance. You see, my love and I took the opportunity to renew our own vows."

"I rubbed some of the paste off him and applied it to myself," Omid said. "We gazed upon each other in the brass of the lamp, which is quite reflective on the inside. Now our love is complete, mutual, and permanent, or at least while his face stays transformed to that of the handsome Tayab of Gu Gu-ari."

*

Feroze and Faridun gave each other brotherly embraces and expressions of filial love, after which Feroze left with his flock. The hours of night trudged past. The stars wheeled; the fire died away. In dreams, Ghazi crossed Persia at rope's end. The Sentinel's foot woke him.

"Morning has come. Conditions are ideal for travel. Your destination? The scaffold, and justice for little Timo."

The Prince and Vaktan were nearby, adjusting their tack while their mounts snorted. A wet mist cloaked the valley. Dilara sat up and pulled her sleeping hides around her shoulders.

"O Sentinel," she pleaded, "let us wait for the Djinns to return. Will you not let us say proper goodbyes to our friends?"

"Regrettably, I am required to pay the executioner out of my own commission." The Sentinel tested the knot of his prisoner's line around the ass's saddle horn. "The scoundrel will charge me extra if I keep him waiting."

After a cold breakfast, the company set out. The sun peeked over the rose-covered stand of wood, and the mist soon burned off. The valley steadily narrowed. By mid-morning, the wildflowers and lush grasses of Zozor lay behind, and the travelers found themselves back on the trail of beaten earth.

The Prince abruptly pulled up. The line of travelers stumbled to a halt behind him. Ghazi raised his head and saw large, impassive dark eyes and folded wings. The talons curled as though clinging to an invisible limb. Dilara moved toward the motionless owl.

"Abi!" she said softly. "Is it you? Have you found your true form at last?"

"I am Hezi." A girl's voice was clear amid the hoots. "You know Grand-Maman, then?"

"Twice she invited me into the Ever Dark Wood," Dilara said. "Later, as Baa-Wind, she joined my friend Parsi in holy sheep union."

"So you are Dilara and Khashar. I have been expecting you. Well, what are you waiting for? Blink, blink, and blink again. Let the film fall away from your eyes. Your friends may come with you, although the ass and horses must wait behind."

The Sentinel started to voice objections, but the Prince signaled him to silence. Dilara turned to Ghazi. She touched his face and gently pressed his eyelids closed.

When he looked again, the world was dark and cool. He smelled earth and leaves and the hemp rope at his neck and something else that he was learning to recognize—the decayed-fruit odor of magic.

*

The night was very warm. I tossed from one side of the bed to the other. Even in the heat, I missed my husband's warmth. Ali-Haram had left on some mission or other for the King. At least I didn't have to keep a candle burning and could sleep in proper darkness.

281

I turned my pillow over; the muslin casing was soaked from sweat and tears. Grief sat inside me like a weight.

I dreamed—a shadow was leaning over me. I recognized its smell and shape.

"I have died," I tried to say. "You and I are meeting in the next world." As always in dreams, I could not speak my words clearly.

"Hush, mama." A hand clapped over my lips. "Abbas sent me on an important mission."

"How did you get in? Guards are everywhere." I pushed the words through his fingers. I was not dreaming; my visitor was a ghost.

"Most of them are asleep. Besides, what guard knows every shortcut through the palace?"

"A herald brought your medal. But he didn't tell us how it—happened." Words were failing the storyteller. Still, I had to know.

"That? Wa-atuq took me up to the falls before the scribes came to make their count of the dead. We found a Persian soldier with his head gone. I pinned my medal on his uniform. That was my cover, so I could escape to the rebels."

I understood. The cover had not been for him, but for me. The mother of a traitor could not hope to live long. Nor, for that matter, could his stepfather or foster mother.

Moonlight chose that moment to spill through the bedchamber window. The pale light showed the hawk-like eyes, the curled lip. He was no ghost. Emre was alive. A wild idea seized me.

"Take me with you. I can ride. I can take care of myself. The rebels will welcome me back. Together we can convince Abbas. I am a bird in a cage here. I'm Maqazzan in my heart, you know that. I—"

"Your place is here, Mama. Ali-Haram needs you, and the King needs your story."

"The King? No, he's lost interest. These days we write for subscribers without faces."

"Your story is for all the world."

"Perhaps, perhaps. Well, what is this mission Abbas sent you on? I suppose it's dangerous."

"Extremely dangerous. There are sorcerers and Djinns and terrible spells—"

I stared in confusion. His boyish laugh filled the chamber.

"Don't you see, Mama? Abbas sent me to get the next chapter of Dilara's story. He said there was nothing more important."

Relieved and furious, I pushed myself up on my elbow.

"The devil take Abbas, and you tell him I said so." He grinned his father's grin. My fury drained away. "Very well; take that scroll on the shelf behind the bed."

"You have another copy?"

"Lorbu always makes an extra before he sends our work off to the copyists."

The bed shifted as Emre got to his feet. He stuffed the scroll into his pouch.

"The captain of the guard is going to make his rounds soon." The bed creaked and shifted as Emre got to his feet. "I better leave now, while I can. Goodbye, Mama."

The beads of the curtain clicked as he went out.

"May Heaven protect you!" I whispered. The darkness swallowed my words.

43. The Granting of Wishes Unwished

(O reader or listener—be you king, rebel, slave, or one who simply loves a tale of adventure—recall that we left our travelers as they were entering the Ever Dark Wood with Hezi, granddaughter of the demi-goddess Abi.)

The trail wound past beeches, ironwoods, and carpets of giant ferns. Green-glowing mushrooms lit the gloom. The travelers moved in silence, for the Wood absorbed the very sound of their footfall.

They came to a grove of alders. The dark eyespots on the trunks watched closely. Past the grove ranged row upon row of ancient, twisted oaks. Ghazi's neck was raw from the noose.

Roots rose from the earth. They branched, wandered, crossed. Ghazi felt his foot catch and twist. He stumbled. Something hard and unyielding stopped his fall. His knees gave way; he slid down, slowly, slowly. Bark scraped his shoulders through the burlap sack.

The unyielding something behind him was a vast, spreading oak.

"On your feet there," the Sentinel said. "How will little Timo ever get his justice if you keep taking breaks?"

"Welcome O traveler." The familiar voice seemed to drift from a great height. "We are the Djinns of the Wood and will grant you one wish—well, I will anyhow; my husband is still getting the hang of it. As you no doubt remember from tales of childhood, the wish must come from the bottom of your heart."

"Idrosun!" Dilara cried. "I did not think I would see you two again. How pleased I am. I know this tree. It is where you and I first met."

"You were Khashar then." Idrosun said. "How I loved you!"

"We had to do a little housekeeping." Ghazi recognized Zajeel's friendly voice. "The bats and beetles and leaves had taken over since she left."

"So the egg Abi wove around the Ever Dark Wood must have hatched," Dilara said.

Vahid spoke up from the lamp:

"Abi had left the egg for safekeeping in an eagle's nest, high in a tree in Zozor. Last night, following the odor of magic, Hezi and I found the egg. Zajeel and Idrosun climbed up to retrieve it. Hatching the egg was a simple matter of unlocking the Spell of Compression. Hezi has agreed to serve as the Wood's new guardian."

"On a temporary basis," Hezi noted. "A couple of aeons, or so."

"Then fortune has visited Ghazi at last," the Prince said with satisfaction. "He has come across a Djinn—two in fact. They must grant him a wish."

"What! Now see here." The Sentinel had objections. "We should not waste a perfectly good wish on a murderer. What if his wish should involve miscarrying justice, out of selfish regard for his own neck?"

"Sentinel, I give you my personal guarantee." The Prince spoke with his cold authority. "The heir to the throne of Persia will not permit justice to miscarry."

Dilara helped Ghazi shift his weight against the lichens which circled the base of the oak in spongy, stepped rings.

Zajeel said: "Now Sheydah—Ghazi, I mean—you may make the wish that lies at the bottom of your heart."

"But no fair wishing for freedom," the Sentinel said.

Ghazi stared at Dilara. Her smile was weak; her face pale, tight, tear-streaked.

In a few days, he would be back in Baghdad. There would be a short trial, for form. Parchments would be signed and sealed. The Sentinel would collect his fee; the executioner, his commission. Ghazi would mount the gallows. A crowd, curious about the nature of death and justice, would be on hand to watch—the rope would drop—the candle flame of his life would be pinched out—Dilara would be left without him. She would be alone.

From the bottom of his heart, a wish rose. It came of his own accord. It was urgent and powerful and right.

"My wish is for—Dilara—to find—" He could barely hear his own words. An immense exhaustion descended on him.

Dilara was watching him intently. The Prince and Sentinel waited behind her. Ghazi's mind was quite clear, but to speak took the last of his strength.

"—find someone to love—"

"No, Ghazi!" she cried, interrupting. "I love only you. No matter what comes, I will always—"

How difficult it was to make the simplest of words pass his lips. With supreme effort, Ghazi completed his wish.

"—her as much as—as I do."

Dilara's eyes grew large.

"Did you hear that, Sentinel?" the Prince said. "In his moment of trial, your prisoner shows grace and wisdom."

"His heart is not entirely what one expects from a cold-blooded murderer," the Sentinel admitted.

"I regret to say that Ghazi's wish cannot be granted," Zajeel said.

"What? That is not for you to decide." Idrosun spoke with heat. "In the science of wish-granting, you are still in training, and—"

Their voices fell to agitated whispers as they argued. Then:

"I was mistaken." Idrosun's voice was contrite now. "My husband is quite correct. We cannot grant Ghazi's wish."

"I do not understand," the Prince said. "Explain yourselves."

"Explanations can wait," Vahid said from the lamp. "I anticipated this. I will now suggest a novel solution. Djinns, can you grant a wish unwished?"

The Djinns looked at each other, and then back at the lamp.

"The Ancient Blue Ones do not specifically prohibit it," Idrosun said.

Vahid said: "Remember what we found next to the trail last night? Remember how you left it for Dilara and Ghazi as a wedding present?"

"What wedding?" the Sentinel protested. "Murderers do not have time to waste on such trifles."

"A second guarantee, Sentinel," the Prince said. "Your busy schedule will not be impeded by a wedding."

Vahid added: "There is something, without which the gift will be useless—"

More urgent whispers in the tree.

Zajeel said: "We think we understand what you mean by an unwished wish."

"And—there—" Idrosun stamped her foot twice, and then once more. "I have granted it to him."

A new thought came unbidden to Ghazi: specifically, that he must not pass to the next world without forgiving Naseem. Yes, Naseem had a cruel streak. His anger often led him to wickedness. He never forgot a slight, and he regarded every slight as a betrayal. Yet—had his mother not died when he was an infant? Had his father, an infamous burglar, not forced him in childhood to aid and abet various criminal projects? Had Naseem not learned violence early in life?

And what of the Sentinel? True, he was taking Ghazi to the hangman for a crime committed by someone else. But what of his sense of duty, his single-minded devotion to his job? Did such a quality not deserve praise? True, only the rich can obtain fair trials in our evil world; should the Sentinel be blamed for that?

Ghazi next forgave Zaib for making Dilara weave worthless spells. He forgave Vaktan for trying to take fruit from the ox cart without paying. He forgave the Matchmaker who had co-signed the Writ of Accusation against him—the poor mother had surely been out of her mind with grief.

So many to forgive—something in Ghazi's heart had transformed.

The trail widened. Dapples of sunlight hovered above the green glow. The newlywed Djinns and their dwelling-tree lay a distance behind now. The travelers' footfall grew louder. Birdsong came from every direction. Hezi lighted upon a branch and said:

"O Dilara-Khashar, Grand-maman foresaw that I would one day enable a kindness for someone you love, in his hour of need. And now this has come to pass, although strangely, the nature of my kindness lies beyond my own sight. Well, at any rate, here ends the Ever Dark Wood. This is your third time here, and you may enter the Wood no more in this life. With your next blink, the film will return to your eyes—I have hooted."

All around were rocks and scrub. The horses and ass came back up slowly, heads down, reins trailing. The Sentinel adjusted his prisoner's line and noose. Vaktan and the Prince remounted. Ghazi's respite was over. He trudged forward.

Vahid spoke up.

"Sentinel, why not let the girl hold your prisoner's line for a while?"

"That would be against all—"

"Only for a league or two," Vahid continued. "Think of how it would reduce the strain on the poor ass. After all, where could the prisoner go?"

"By the way," the Prince added, "here is a little something for you, to buy more supplies for the trip."

Ghazi heard coins clink. A moment later, he saw the slack rope in Dilara's hands.

"What wish did the Djinns grant you?" she asked Ghazi while they walked.

Ghazi did not understand the question. He was busy extending forgiveness to more people.

"Look, Gu Gu!" Dilara said suddenly. "Could it be?"

Along the edge of the trail stood a piece of furniture. It had a half-back of carved wood, an ornate mother-of-pearl inlay, and velvet cushions.

"Our flying divan." The Prince clapped his hands. "It must be the wedding present Zajeel and Idrosun promised you."

"I keep reminding everyone," the Sentinel said. "No weddings, no presents, no time."

"And here you are, dear Locque." Dilara took a seat, mindless of the stained and weathered state of the cushions. "Ever on duty."

"I vowed to defend the divan forever," Locque answered (its voice Vahid-like and booming), "or until richer prospective owners came along."

"O Gu Gu," Dilara said, "remember the first time we flew through the sky?"

"It took us a while to learn that climbing required a vigorous tap on Parsi's nose."

"And two to descend."

"And a hard pull on the ear to change direction."

"But Gu Gu, what good is the divan as a wedding present? Ghazi and I will never wed. We will never have a home to put the divan in. Besides, only the pure-hearted Parsi can pilot it."

"Prince Faridun," Vahid said after a moment, "Dilara has been a good servant and true. She has faithfully carried out her missions for your father, the King. She has sacrificed much, and never wavered in her devotion. The time has come for our mid-morning halt and rest. I suggest as a small reward and token of your esteem, you order the Sentinel to let Dilara's beloved sit beside her for a moment."

"It is so ordered." The Prince reined his mount to a halt—Vaktan followed suit—and pointed to the line wound about the Sentinel's fist.

"Now I really must protest!" the Sentinel said. "My charge is a known criminal—" More coins clinked. Ghazi found himself on the divan, next to Dilara.

That odor of overripe fruit again—

"There is something I do not understand," the Sentinel said, keeping a suspicious eye on Ghazi. "The wish the murderer made seemed reasonable enough. Why should the girl not have someone else to love her after he leaves this life? Why would the Djinns not grant such a wish?"

Vahid answered:

"It is quite simple, really. Ghazi wished for someone to love Dilara as much as he does. No such person exists in all the world."

"But then Idrosun granted him a wish unwished," the Prince added thoughtfully. "I wonder what it could have been."

Calls came from above—kee-ar, kee-ar. Hawks circled and soared, crossing the face of the clouds.

"Enough lazing about," the Sentinel said. "Time is darics, as they say. Give the line back to me, and we will be on our way."

A look of understanding came over Dilara's face. She put her lips to Ghazi's ear.

"O beloved," she said, "look at those hawks. Look how they fly, going where they will."

What did her words mean? Ghazi looked into the sky without comprehension.

"Up now," the Sentinel ordered. "Enough rest. Hand me that lead."

"O Ghazi," Dilara said urgently, "what if we could follow those hawks?"

"The time may have come for you to take matters into your own hands," the Prince said.

Ghazi was thinking about others to forgive. Why was Dilara showing him the flat of her hand?

Without warning, she struck him on the nose.

The world fell away. The horse and ass grew small, rearing and scattering. The Sentinel dwindled to a tiny figure, shaking his tiny fist and shouting words that were lost in the streaming wind. Dilara gave Ghazi's ear a hard pull. The flying divan banked and raced toward the sun. Below, the soaring nation of hawks crossed the divan's path. In the distance, sky and earth met in a long blue blur.

Ghazi's ears streamed with tears in the chill. His nose and ears hurt. (He forgave Dilara for hitting him.) The earth was dizzyingly far away. With great effort, he spoke.

"Where are—we going?"

"Where! Why, to Babylon, or Nineveh. Or even back to Viroo." Dilara's eyes shone. "We could go to Gu Gu-ari. The town Headman said whenever I come back, I would want for nothing. You see, Idrosun granted you a wish you did not make, which was to have a pure heart. You are now the pilot of the flying divan. We are well clear of the Sentinel now and can descend. Excuse me while I double-tap your nose. O Ghazi, my beloved, you and I are together. And you are free!"

44. Epilogue: Courage for Truth-Telling

"'—are free!'" Scheherazade rolled up the scroll. "And there it ends."

"Gu gu," King Shahryar said.

"Gu gu." The infant on his knee agreed. The King took the child under the ribs and tossed him upward. Shahryar, son of Shahryar, squealed and fell back into his father's hands.

We were sitting on a bench in Eden, the King's newest garden. As in the actual home of the first man and woman, a channel of water crossed each of Eden's equal quarters, running swiftly over a floor of polished stones, blue, yellow, and black. Cherry and orange trees and wisteria-covered trellises clothed us in blessed shade. Clouds of bees and butterflies settled over the chrysanthemums and orchids and tree peonies. Walls of sandstone brick enclosed the garden.

I tried to enjoy the beauty without thinking about the slaves I had watched toil with picks and shovels for months under the Persian sun, digging Eden's channels, carrying bucket after bucket of water.

"O Majesty, did you hear?" Ali-Haram said. "Dilara's story has come to an end."

"Gu gu," the King said.

"He doesn't need a storyteller anymore," Scheherazade said. "His entire world sits on his knee. As for me, my head is safe on my shoulders, for good. A Holy One has issued a ruling, on the King's orders, freeing him from his earlier vows."

"Gu gu." The King rose and left Eden with his heir.

"The King may not need his story, but our paying readers do," Ali-Haram said. "Baghdad scroll sellers want more tales of Dilara and Idrosun. Our subscription list keeps growing. Who are we to disappoint the paying public? Listen, I had an idea for a new adventure. Tell me what you think of it: one day someone comes walking through the Ever Dark Wood and stops at a certain tree. Zajeel and Idrosun come out of their hollow to grant their visitor a wish, and who should they see, to their great surprise, but Holy Usman?"

"Usman? Didn't he become a being of pure light?" I was always concerned about inconsistencies.

"Well, yes, but who are we to speculate on the transformative powers of Angels?" Ali-Haram leaned forward. "The question is, why is he visiting the djinns?"

I happily followed up my husband's idea:

"After leaving our world, Usman had decided to pay a visit to the afterworlds. There he met the spirit of Ptolemy, who in life had proven the existence of the celestial spheres that form our universe. Usman and Ptolemy had decided to tour the spheres together. When they got to Jupiter, they came across a great bubble of air, inside of which were wise and learned creatures made of water. Usman understood at once.

"He had escorted Ptolemy back to the afterworlds and then, again assuming the form of a man, made his way to Zozor and the Ever Dark Wood. At last, he found the Djinns' tree."

Ali-Haram picked up the story.

"Holy Usman says to Zajeel: 'I have news. I have discovered the Blue Land. It settled on the crystal sphere of Jupiter. The Ancient Blue Ones are there.'

"'Ah, I remember the day the river dragon expelled the Blue Land from our world with its exhalation.'" My husband and I settled into the dialogue. I was Zajeel, he was Usman.

"'I will take you there, Zajeel. Come, let us begin at once. I know a private Angel road we can take—'"

"'O Master, Idrosun and I have our own dwelling tree at last. I no longer need to plead with the Ancient Blue Ones for an assignment.'

"'The trip itself will be enlightening. Besides, I might have promised the Ancient Blue Ones you would present guest lectures on practical wish-granting and art of Djinnlet-raising.' At length, it was agreed, and the two set off—"

"Wait, what about Idrosun?" I raised an eyebrow at my husband. "Zajeel goes off to traipse through the crystal spheres, while his bride has to stay at home and mind the children?"

"By no means." Ali-Haram quickly reversed course. "In fact, Zajeel and Usman insist that she come too. As for the Djinnlets, why, by this time they are all grown up. They have received their own tree assignments."

Scheherazade jumped in with an idea of her own:

"And on their way to Jupiter, what should our travelers come across, abandoned by the side of the Angel road, but a certain velvet-cushioned and weather-stained divan?"

After a while Ali-Haram stood and excused himself. He went back into the palace. When he came back, he was holding a scroll I did not recognize.

"I've taken on a new student." He spoke to Scheherazade but kept his smiling gaze on me. I felt myself flush. "Shall I demonstrate her progress for you?"

"Yes, I look forward to it." Scheherazade put her hands in her lap.

"Go ahead, Ariana." He untied the ribbon and handed me the scroll. "Please read for us."

In front of anyone else, I would have been ashamed to show my poor skills. But my husband had been teaching so patiently, and I was anxious to please him and impress Scheherazade. I took a deep breath and focused on the characters— ب and خ and س and all the others I had learned—and how they fit together to make words, and the words to make sentences. I began:

"'A royal proc—procla—' What is this word? Wait, I know, *proclamation.*'" I was proud of myself. "'His Majesty Shahryar, first of his name, King of the Age, defender of the faith, ruler of Persia and all, uh, trib—tributary lands, hereby orders the beheading of the Queen Consort, to take place on this public spot—'"

I stopped, confused. Scheherazade's face was expressionless.

"I remember this from a poster I saw years ago," I said. "It was on my first trip to the Baghdad market. The Slavemaster had to read it to me. But strange—I was telling all this to our scribe Lorbu only a few days ago."

My husband's smile was mysterious and infuriating. I kept reading:

"'The weather-stained poster was fixed to the west gate—people streaming past took no notice—'But Master, I saw Scheherazade before we left the palace'— 'I bet no one met her eyes.'"

It took me a moment to understand.

"Of course. You instructed Lorbu to take down everything I tell him."

"And I also have the scroll Yenibi gave you," he said. "Think of it: the story of Dilara and the story of Ariana, each told in turn. One and the other, woven together. The story and the storyteller. An inner story and an outer story."

"You're going to lose your tunic on this idea," I told him. "Who would pay good darics to read about my life?"

"I would," Scheherazade said. "Enslaved and freed three times. Kidnapped by rebels. Author of Baghdad's top-selling scroll. A life every bit as interesting as my Ali Baba and Sindbad and Aladdin and the rest."

"An ambassador of the Tang came to the King's court," Ali-Haram went on. "He showed us a poem written by his emperor. The poem was not inked on parchment, but cloth. The Tang carve each character of their language onto its own wooden block. Then they put the blocks in order, ink them, and then press the cloth on them."

"Are the Tang emperor's verses worse than yours?" Scheherazade gave me a wink. A pair of wrens alighted on a stone bridge that crossed a water channel.

"There weren't any ink smudges on the cloth," he went on. "And every individual character was identical. Think: if we used wooden blocks to print our story, we could make more copies in less time. We would save on copyists, as well. Why, we could even—"

Ali-Haram was warming to his subject. But a thought alarmed me.

"Husband, if you sell the story of my life, the world will find out that Emre is alive. Everyone will know he was a traitor to Persia. He'd have a price on his head. He would not be safe anywhere in the world."

"The Persians would never catch Emre," Ali-Haram said. "He'd outrun them forever."

"No, she's right," Scheherazade said. "Maybe Emre wouldn't be caught, but Ariana would, and you as well. Come to think of it, what about me? I played my part in all this. I could lose my head, after all. I think that—"

The King returned, infant Shahryar on his hip. We fell silent. He addressed Scheherazade.

"We have done much thinking about your story. You thought we were not listening, but in fact we paid close attention. We are dissatisfied in only one regard: the King of Persia sits on the greatest throne under Heaven. But if he does not see justice done, is he worthy of his title? Prince Faridun, Gu Gu—" (This last, a cooing aside to the mewling heir.) "—is his father's representative in the affair of the epidemic of love. Ghazi makes good his escape on the flying divan, but what about Naseem? Is it not the Prince's responsibility to see justice meted out to the true murderer of little Timo?"

"My lord husband once again shows his wisdom," Scheherazade gave me an imploring glance.

"O Majesty," I said, thinking quickly, "Prince Faridun understands the law. He knows that the Sentinel has authority in the matter of arrests for breaking the King's peace. Only the King himself may intervene. That is why, when the Prince gets back to Baghdad, he writes a proclamation for his father to issue. Heralds descend to the Ragged Quarter and read the proclamation aloud:

"'LET ALL OUR PEOPLE BE
INFORMED AND INSTRUCTED.

'His Majesty Shahryar, first of his name, King of the Age, defender of the faith, ruler of Persia and all tributary lands, hereby proclaims and announces:

'We have closely examined the evidence presented to us in the matter of the murder of Timo, the Matchmaker's son. We are satisfied with the proofs of innocence of our faithful subject Ghazi, and we so adjudge and declare him blameless.

'Ghazi and his beloved Dilara have faced many hardships and displayed great courage, all in the service of their King. We have therefore issued them each an Acknowledgement of Royal Gratitude, inked on a parchment of finest calfskin and affixed with our official seal. Further, we have ordered our scribes to write down their story on a scroll which will be preserved forever in our palace scrollarium.'

"When the children of the Ragged Quarter heard this proclamation, they rediscovered their courage for truth-telling. They came forward and told the Matchmaker the real story of the murder of little Timo. The Sentinel, who had to provide the hangman with a criminal or else face financial losses (and the end of his own perfect record), made the arrest. Naseem, the true murderer, was displayed in a cage in the center of the Ragged Quarter for a day before his trial, and then—"

Scheherazade interrupted before my story turned grim.

"But let us waste no more thought for that sinner. I'll sit with our guests while you take little Shahryar to his nurse."

Neither the King nor his heir returned to Eden. Scheherazade, Ali-Haram, and I argued late into the evening. The moon rose, the nightjars whistled, the tree-frogs croaked. My husband didn't want to give up his prized idea for a scroll with inner and outer stories, and I didn't want to risk our lives against the King's anger.

*

We have been in touch with Yenibi.

First, we sealed a tablet authorizing her as our agent. Then we gave her our single copy of Ali-Haram's new scroll, the one that tells both Dilara's story and my own.

Yenibi's eyes went wide.

We gave her a money bag with enough to pay for copyists or—who knows?— printing. But this will only happen when Scheherazade, Ali-Haram, Emre, and I have all left this life for Paradise, where the cares and troubles of this world will matter to us no more. Yenibi pledged that her descendants would carry out the plan, should she too be gone by then.

And best of all, the proceeds from scroll sales, less Yenibi's commission, will be used to buy the freedom of Persian slaves, chosen by lot.

*

And so, dear readers, who live in a future I will not see, I hope that this scroll has brought you pleasure and instruction, and that it was worth the hard-earned darics you paid for it.

And I pray that murder, wickedness, and enslavement, which so often appear in my story, are unknown in your own age.

S.R. Daugherty
Carrollton GA, USA
2024

ABOUT THE AUTHOR

Hello, I'm Steven. I wrote this book at Gallery Row, a coffee shop in west Georgia, USA. I used Google Docs on an ipad pro. Absolutely no AI was involved in the making of this novel.

I am, among other things, a retired high school mathematics teacher. My late wife taught high school French and Kindergarten. I have a son, three granddaughters, and a daughter-in-law from France.

I have written several copyrighted songs, and I play in a bluegrass band called Highway 5 Overdrive.

I am a runner, gardener, hiker, and gym rat. I have won my age group twice in 5K races. (At my age, the key to winning 5K's is to outlive everyone else in your age group.)

Before getting into the teaching industry, I sold several fantasy and science fiction stories—most of these are collected in my 2022 book *Ballad of the Rails and Other Stories* (available on Amazon; google *balladoftherails*). I have also published non-fiction in *Bluegrass Unlimited* and a few other periodicals.

Let's see. I should list a few of my other interests and emotional investments: Japanese maples, Russian novels, Georgia Bulldogs football, Martin guitars, 16th century choral music, and silent movies. My gin is Bombay Sapphire. I am no cook but have excellent eating skills. I live with two rescue cats, Pheromone and De-Tail.

One final note: if you enjoyed chapters 37 and 44 of this book, then you will be pleased to learn the working title of my next novel—*Holy Usman: His Life and Times (As Told by the Angels and Ex-Wives Who Knew Him Best)*.

AUTHOR'S AFTERWORD

Scheherazade's One Thousand and Second Night is a book about a book—or more accurately, a book about a scroll. This is why it consists of an Outer Story and an Inner Story. Each of these has its own origin (if you will) story.

When my granddaughters Lorelei and Annabelle were little, the three of us took walks after Sunday dinner at Granny's house. On our way out the door one day, Lorelei said: "Paw Paw, let's make up a story. I'll start: a beautiful princess is held in a tower by an evil wizard—now you go."

I improvised a narrative for a while, inventing the characters Khashar and Sorayah and Ghazi and Naseem along the way. I tried to turn the story back over to the girls.

"No, no, you tell it," they said together. Not that they didn't make important contributions—namely pointing out every inconsistency and posing endless questions.

That was the germ of the Inner Story of this book.

The Outer Story began as a question I asked myself during my first-ever reading, all those years ago, of *The 1001 Nights* itself: if Scheherazade's life depended on her telling a story to the King every night (and bearing in mind that she was a collector, not a writer), what would happen if she ran out of material on the one thousand and second night? This led me to the characters of Ariana and Ali-Haram, and along with the Inner Story, to the novel you have just read.

The stories in *The 1001 Nights* date back (at least!) to the eighth century AD. The first English translation dates to 1706. Today, the most readily available version here in the U.S. is that of British explorer Sir Richard Francis Burton, first published in the 1880's.

Parts of *The 1001 Nights* strike the modern reader as racist and misogynist—jarringly, appallingly so. (One can only imagine how readers fourteen centuries from now will view the literature of our own age.) The book doubtless reflects the age it came from. I have chosen to tell my own story in a way that more closely harmonizes with the sensibilities of the twenty-first century reader. Naturally, I have kept many of the physical settings and fantasy elements of the original—after all, these are what fire the imagination after all these centuries.

I have strived for historical accuracy where it seemed appropriate. If any anachronisms slipped through, in dialogue or setting detail—well, my heart was in the right place.

I am grateful to Oz for heroically reading my manuscript—twice. He also motivated me to enlarge the role of Princess Maria Irena. Katie nudged me to think more deeply about the character and motives of Ali-Haram. Noah gave me advice which became my creative mantra: "the inner story should feel like a tale, and the outer story should feel like life." And Russell was indispensable in general.

I dedicate this book to the late Dr Fred Richards, who came every day to the coffee shop where I worked on my novel, before he got sick, and reminded me without fail that he believed in me.

LIST OF CHARACTERS (IN ORDER OF APPEARANCE)

OUTER STORY

Ariana: an enslaved woman.

Ali-Haram: court poet.

Scheherazade: the Queen Consort.

Shahryar: the King of Persia.

Emre: Maqazzan rebel, Ariana's lover.

Emre, son of Emre: Ariana's child.

Merdad: name given to Ariana's son by his wetnurse and foster mother.

Bourzou: palace Slavemaster.

Poet Boy: the Bey of Antioch.

Peki: a palace slave.

Morgai: Peki's mother.

Gasparo and Kamran: twin brothers who purchase Ariana.

Yenibi: amanuensis to Gasparo and Kamran.

Bibeb: a palace slave.

The Commander: the King's first officer in the Maqazzan campaign.

Wa-atuq and Wafa: enslaved Maqazzans.

Abbas: senior Maqazzan rebel officer.

Lorbu: dictation scribe hired by Ali-Haram and Ariana.

INNER STORY

King Alcimedes: King Shahryar's ancestor.

Khashar: a boy of the Ragged Quarter of Baghdad.

The Cobbler & Dream Interpreter: Khashar's parents.

Ghazi & Naseem: Khashar's playmates.

Princess Sorayah: daughter of King Alcimedes.
Vahid: court sorcerer.
Charles Magnus: King of the Franks.
Princess Maria Irena: daughter of Charles Magnus.
Prince Feroze: son of King Alcimedes.
Abi: demi-goddess of the Ever Dark Wood.
Idrosun: Djinn of the Ever Dark Wood.
Ancient Blue Ones: Djinn teachers in the Blue Land
Dilara: a girl of the Ragged Quarter, often disguised as Khashar.
Parsi: Vahid's slave, frequently ensheeped as punishment.
Ko-kab-a: wedding organizer for Feroze and Maria Irena.
The Matchmaker.
Omid: Thukamon's slave, born an ass.
Thukamon: Egyptian sorcerer, Vahid's archrival.
Masoud: customer who purchases happiness from Idrosun.
Gu Gu: companion of Dilara and Parsi on their adventures.
Locque: creature in charge of security for Vahid.
Zaib: daughter of the Queen of Lebanon.
Baa-Wind: the sheep Parsi falls in love with.
Bellow-Rumble: Parsi's enemy and rival for Baa-Wind.
Tayab: a laborer in Qa-ari, whose wife purchases sorrow from Idrosun.
Wazi: Tayab's wife.
Metipo: a newcomer to the Ragged Quarter.
Vahidium: Vahid's familiar.
Faridun: Feroze's younger brother, called Gu Gu.
Homa: mother of Afsoon.
One, Two, and Three: Afsoon's sisters.
Afsoon: a medium; Homa's youngest daughter.
Soqob: a scholar of magic and Qazem's Master.
Bahar: mother of Baghdad's leading bloodletter.
Qazem: Soqob's Apprentice.
Esme: the bloodletter's wife.
Fildonez & Tyesh: famed mages from ages past.
Arkiman: ambassador to Persia from the Kush kingdom.
Noki: a cobbler, Qazem's second Master.
Myobec: a mage, Soqob's deceased rival.

Sheydah: fugitive from the Ragged Quarter.
The Sentinel: pursuer of justice for Little Timo.
Zajeel: Djinn searching for the Blue Land, Sheydah's friend.
Yar and Caspara: childless couple who take in Sheydah in Viroo.
Honey and Woodbine: Yar and Caspara's venerable oxen.
Vaktan: Prince Faridun's aide.
Little Timo: the Matchmaker's son.
Usman: a wandering holy man, one of the Angels at the Creation.
Zophanax: a primeval river dragon.
Saramunde: the first woman in Persia.
Charles Minimus: firstborn lamb of Feroze and Maria Irena.
Hezi: descendant of Abi, successor-guardian of the Ever Dark Wood.